Prai[illegible]
Mary [illegible]

and her bestselling novels . . .

❖ ❖ ❖

"Balogh's epic love story is a winner."
—***Publishers Weekly***

❖ ❖ ❖

"Thoroughly enjoyable . . . An excellent story that moves as swiftly and smoothly as a river."
—**Janelle Taylor**

❖ ❖ ❖

"From her first book, this superb author has established a reputation for unsurpassed originality and excellence."
—***Romantic Times***

❖ ❖ ❖

"A beautiful, moving romance that should be on the top of every reader's list . . . just plain wonderful. No wonder Ms. Balogh is a favorite of readers everywhere!"
—***Affaire de Coeur***

Titles by Mary Balogh

TRULY
HEARTLESS

TIMESWEPT BRIDES
(an anthology, with Constance O'Banyon, Virginia Brown and Elda Minger)

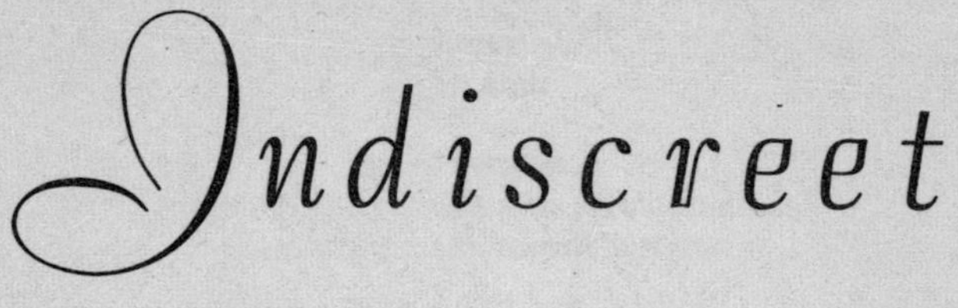

Indiscreet

Mary Balogh

JOVE BOOKS, NEW YORK

INDISCREET

A Jove Book / published by arrangement with
the author

PRINTING HISTORY
Jove edition / January 1997

For information address: The Berkley Publishing Group,
200 Madison Avenue, New York, New York 10016.

The Putnam Berkley World Wide Web site address is
http://www.berkley.com/berkley

ISBN: 0-515-12001-4

A JOVE BOOK®
Jove Books are published by The Berkley Publishing Group,
200 Madison Avenue, New York, New York 10016.
JOVE and the "J" design are trademarks
belonging to Jove Publications, Inc.

PRINTED IN THE UNITED STATES OF AMERICA

10 9 8 7 6 5 4 3 2 1

e village, often
tunate passerby,
of fashionable
own the aisle,
ne padded front
ve without her

One

ONE SURE SIGN of the coming of spring was the return of the Honorable Mr. Claude Adams and his wife to Bodley House, their country home in Derbyshire.

There were other signs, of course. There were snowdrops and primroses and even a few crocuses in the woods and along the hedgerows beside the road, and there were a few shoots of green in otherwise bare gardens. There was a suggestion of green about the branches of trees, though one had to look closely to observe the delicate buds. The air was warmer than it had been and the sun seemed a little brighter. The roads and laneways had dried after the last heavy cover of snow.

Yes, spring was coming. But the surest sign of all, and the one most welcome to many of the inhabitants of the small village of Bodley-on-the-Water, was that the family was returning to the house. Almost invariably they left soon after Christmas, sometimes before, and spent the winter months visiting various friends.

Their absence was a trial to many of the villagers, for whom winter would have been dreary enough anyway. But for those two months they were forced to live without a sight of Mrs. Adams driving through the village, often nodding regally through the window at a fortunate passerby, or of the same Mrs. Adams, a vision of fashionable elegance, entering church and sweeping down the aisle, looking neither to left nor to right, to sit in the padded front pew. The poor and sick and elderly had to live without her personal conveyance of their food baskets—though a footman always carried them from the carriage to the house—and her gracious condescension in inquiring after their health. Those of some social stature had to live without the occasional flattering visit, during which Mrs. Adams would sit inside her carriage, the window down, while the favored recipient of her attention was summoned from the house by a liveried footman in order to stand on the path curtsying or bowing to her and asking how Master William and Miss Juliana did.

Even the children were rarely seen during the winter months, though they were not often taken visiting with their mama and papa. Their nurse was firmly of the belief that winter air was bad for children.

This year Mr. and Mrs. Adams had stayed for the past month at Stratton Park in Kent with no less a personage than Viscount Rawleigh. He was Mr. Adams's elder brother, as everyone knew. The fact was equally well known that his lordship was Mr. Adams's senior by twenty minutes, a singular stroke of good fortune for him since he was now in possession of the title while the younger twin was not. They might have had a viscount and viscountess living at Bodley, some of them often said wistfully during sessions of gossip, if the situation had been reversed. But then perhaps the maternal grandmother would have left the property to the *other* brother and they would still have had a mere mister living there.

Not that they minded the fact that the family had no title.

They had all the other trappings of gentility, and any stranger was soon apprised of the fact that the owner of Bodley was an *Honorable* and the brother of Viscount Rawleigh of Stratton.

The Honorable Mr. Adams and his wife were returning home within the week. One of the footmen at Bodley brought word to the village inn, where he drank his ale nightly, and from the inn the word was spread through the village. They were bringing houseguests with them, the head groom told the blacksmith, and speculation became rife.

Was Viscount Rawleigh to be one of the guests?

Viscount Rawleigh was to be one of the houseguests. Mrs. Croft, the housekeeper at Bodley, brought the news to Mrs. Lovering, the rector's wife. And there were to be several other ladies and gentlemen too as guests. She really had no idea if there were any other titles among them. She would not have known about his lordship except that Mrs. Adams's letter had referred to her brother-in-law, and Mr. Adams had no other brother except the viscount, did he? But one could be certain that any company that included Viscount Rawleigh must be distinguished company.

It was almost worth having been without the family for two dreary months, it was generally agreed. Two years had passed since Mr. and Mrs. Adams had brought home guests with them and it was many years since Viscount Rawleigh had visited his brother in the country.

Anticipation ran high in the village. No one knew the exact hour or day of the arrival, but everyone was on the alert. There was bound to be more than one carriage for the family and visitors and a whole fleet of carriages to bring their belongings and their servants. It was a sight not to be missed. Fortunately there was no way for them to come from Kent except through the village. One just had to hope that they would not arrive after dark. But surely they would not when there were lady travelers and one never knew when highwaymen would be lurking on darkened roads.

Spring was coming at last and with it new life and vigor and splendor—splendor in the woods and hedgerows and splendor of another, even more exciting kind at Bodley.

DESPITE HERSELF, MRS. Catherine Winters, widow, found that she glanced far more often than she normally did through the front windows of her little thatched cottage at the southern end of the village street, and that she listened with heightened senses for the sound of approaching carriages. She loved her back garden more than the front because of the fruit trees with their branches hanging over the lawn and the shade they offered in the summer and because the river flowed and gurgled over mossy stones at the end of the garden. But she found herself more often than not in the front garden these days, watching the crocuses come into bud and a few brave shoots of the daffodil bulbs push through the soil. Though she would have scurried indoors fast enough if she really had heard carriages coming. She did so one morning only to find that it was the Reverend Ebenezer Lovering returning in his one-horse cart from a visit to a nearby farm.

She had mixed feelings about the return of the family to Bodley. The children would be happy. They had been longing for weeks for the return of their mama. She would come laden with gifts when she did come, of course, and spoil them for weeks, so that their classes would be disrupted. But then children needed their mother more than they did lessons of any description. Catherine gave them music lessons at the house twice a week, though neither child had a great deal of aptitude on the pianoforte. Of course, they were young. Juliana was only eight years old, William seven.

Life was marginally more interesting when Mr. Adams and his wife were at home. Occasionally Catherine was invited to the house for dinner or for a card party. She was aware of the fact that it happened only when Mrs. Adams needed to even numbers and was one female short. And she was very aware of the condescension with which she was treated on such occasions. Even so, there was something treacherously pleasant about the opportunity to dress her best—though her self-made clothes must be woefully unfashionable by town standards, she was sure—and to be in company with people who had some conversation.

And Mr. Adams himself was always amiable and courteous. He was an extremely handsome gentleman and had passed on his looks to his children, though Mrs. Adams was rather lovely too. But Catherine had learned to avoid his company at the house. Mrs. Adams's tongue could become decidedly barbed if the two of them fell into conversation together. Foolish woman—as if Catherine's behavior had ever indicated that she was interested in dalliance of any kind.

She was not. She was finished with men. And with love. And with flirtation. They had brought her to where she was now. Not that she was complaining. She had a pleasant enough home in a pleasant enough village and she had learned how to occupy her time usefully so that the days were not unbearably tedious.

She was glad that the family was returning—*partly* glad. But they were bringing houseguests with them—plural. Viscount Rawleigh she did not know. She had never met him and never heard of him before she came to live at Bodley-on-the-Water. But there were to be other guests, doubtless people of *ton*. And there was the chance that she might know one or more of them—or, more to the point, that at least one of them would know her.

It was a remote chance, but it filled her with unease.

She did not want the peace of her life disturbed. It had been too hard won.

They came in the middle of one brisk but sunny afternoon when she was standing at the end of her front path, bidding farewell to Miss Agatha Downes, spinster daughter of a former rector, who had called on her and taken tea with her. It was quite impossible to scurry back inside so that she might cower behind the parlor curtain and observe while remaining unobserved. All she could do was stand there, without even a bonnet to shield her face, and wait to be recognized. She envied Toby, her terrier, who was safe inside the house, barking noisily.

There were three carriages, if one discounted the baggage coaches, which were some distance behind. It was impossible to see who rode in them, though Mrs. Adams leaned forward in her seat in the first of them in order to raise one hand and incline her head to them. Rather like a queen acknowledging her peasant subjects, Catherine thought with the humor that carried her through all her encounters with Mrs. Adams. She nodded her head in reply to the greeting.

There were three gentlemen on horseback. A quick glance assured Catherine that two of them were strangers. And the third was no threat either. She had smiled at Mr. Adams and curtsied to him—something she always avoided doing whenever she could with his wife—before something in his bearing and in the cool, unsmiling, arrogant way he looked back at her alerted her to the fact that he was not Mr. Adams at all.

Of course, Mr. Adams had a twin—Viscount Rawleigh. How humiliating! She could feel the color rising hotly to her cheeks and hoped that he had ridden on far enough not to have noticed. She also hoped it would seem that her curtsy had been in general acknowledgment of the whole group.

"My dear Mrs. Winters," Miss Downes was saying, "how gratifying it is that we happened to be outside and so close to the road when Mr. Adams and his dear wife and their distinguished guests returned home. It was most agreeable of Mrs. Adams to nod to us, I am sure. She might have stayed back in the shadows, as I am certain she was inclined to do after the tedium of a long journey."

"Yes," Catherine agreed, "traveling is indeed a tiresome business, Miss Downes. I am sure they will all be thankful to be at Bodley House in time for tea."

Miss Downes stepped out through the gateway and turned in the direction of home, eager to share what she had just seen with her aged invalid mother. Catherine looked after her down the street and saw in some amusement that everyone seemed to be out of doors. It was as if a great procession had just gone past and everyone was still basking in the glory of having seen it.

She was still feeling mortified. Perhaps Viscount Rawleigh would have realized the mistake she had made in singling him out for her curtsy—and her smile. Perhaps, she thought hopefully, other people in the village had done the same thing. Perhaps some of them did not realize even yet the mistake they had made.

His looks were almost identical to Mr. Adams's, she thought. But if first impressions were anything to judge by—and she judged by them even though she realized that she was perhaps being unfair—he was quite different in character. This man was haughty and lacking in humor. There had been a coldness in his dark eyes. Perhaps it was a difference that twenty fateful minutes had wrought. Lord Rawleigh had all the consequence of a title and a large fortune and a rich and vast property to live up to.

She hoped she would not have the embarrassment of meeting him again. She hoped that his stay at Bodley would be of short duration, though it was altogether probable that he had not even noticed her more particularly than anyone else in his regal progress along the street.

"WELL," EDEN WENDELL, Baron Pelham, said as they progressed along the single street of Bodley-on-the-Water, feeling rather as if they were part of a circus parade, "at least we were wrong about one thing."

His two friends did not ask him what that one thing was since they had talked specifically about it before deciding to rusticate for a while in Derbyshire and during their journey there.

"But only one among the three of us," Mr. Nathaniel Gascoigne said with mock gloom, "unless there are a few dozen others hiding behind the curtains of these cottage windows."

"Ever the dreamer, Nat," Rex Adams, Viscount Rawleigh, said. "At a guess I would say that every villager and his dog is out on the street to gawk at us going by. And by my observations there has been only one looker among them."

Lord Pelham sighed. "And she had eyes for no one but you, Rex, damn your eyes," he said. "My blue eyes have been called irresistible by more than one lady of my acquaintance, but the village looker did not even glance into them. All she saw was you."

"It might have been as well if one lady had not found your eyes so irresistible, Eden," Lord Rawleigh said dryly. "If I had been in town, perhaps she would have looked into mine instead and you would not have been forced to rusticate for a few months, including the whole of the Season."

Lord Pelham winced while Mr. Gascoigne threw back his

head and laughed. "A hit, Ede," he said. "Come, you must admit it."

"She was new to town," Lord Pelham said, scowling, "and had a body to die for. How was I to know that she was married? You two may find the idea of being discovered in bed by a husband and in the act, so to speak, to be uproariously hilarious, but I did not and do not."

"In truth," Mr. Gascoigne said, one hand to his heart, "I feel for you, Ede. The timing was wretched. He might at least have had the decency to wait in the shadows until you were properly—or improperly—finished." He threw back his head and laughed again. Fortunately they were beyond the confines of the village street and in progress up the oak-lined driveway that led to Bodley House.

"Well," his friend said after pursing his lips and deciding against taking up the gauntlet—after all, he had been putting up with this ribbing for several weeks now, "I am not the only one forced to rusticate, Nat. Shall I drop the name Miss Sybil Armstrong onto the breeze?"

"Why not?" Mr. Gascoigne said with a shrug. "You have done so often enough lately, Ede. A Christmas kiss, that was all it was. Beneath the mistletoe. It would have been churlish to have resisted. The chit was standing there deliberately, pretending she had not noticed either it or me. And then brothers and fathers and mothers and cousins and uncles and aunts—"

"We see the picture with painful clarity," the viscount assured him.

"—coming through doorways and walls and ceilings and floors," Mr. Gascoigne said. "All looking at me in expectation of an imminent declaration. I tell you both, it was enough to put the wind up a fellow. Make that a hurricane."

"Yes, we already have on more than one occasion before today," the viscount said. "And so you descended upon me, the two of you, like a pair of frightened rabbits, and I am expected to rusticate with you and miss the Season myself."

"Unfair, Rex," Mr. Gascoigne said. "Did we say anything about you missing the Season and all the young hopefuls and their mamas? Now, did we? Tell him, Ede."

"We offered to keep Stratton warm and lived in while you were gone," Lord Pelham said. "Come, you must admit it, Rex."

The viscount grinned. "It serves you both right," he said, "that my sister-in-law invited us all here and that I decided we would come rather than stay at Stratton and be dull. And it serves you right that the village appears to boast only one looker and that she fancies me."

There was a chorus of protests, but they were incoherent and quickly silenced by their arrival at the house. They dismounted and handed their reins to waiting grooms and proceeded to help the ladies down from the carriages.

She certainly *was* a looker, Viscount Rawleigh thought, though she was no young girl and looked rather too genteel to be a milkmaid or a laundry maid or someone else who might be tumbled for a few coins. She had been standing in the garden of a small but respectable-looking cottage. The odds were high that there was a husband to go along with that cottage and to lay claim to that beauty.

A pity. She was definitely a beauty, with her golden hair and regular features and creamy complexion. And she had a pleasing figure, neither too thin nor too voluptuous. Unlike most men of his acquaintance, he did not favor voluptuous women. Neither was she all crimped and curled and frilled. She allowed her beauty to stand on its own merits, unassisted by art. And her beauty had many merits.

Of course, she was a bold woman. His eyes had found her when she was nodding to Clarissa. He had not failed to notice, then, how her eyes had passed over Eden and Nat before coming to rest on him. She had smiled and curtsied, the baggage, quite pointedly and exclusively for him.

Well, he was not averse to a little discreet dalliance if it should happen by some miracle that there was no husband to find them in compromising circumstances, as poor Eden had been found. Certainly he was not interested in either of the two unattached ladies who were part of Claude's house party, one of them Clarissa's sister. Or in any other matrimonial prospect. If Clarissa only had a brain in her head, she would realize that it was more in her interest to keep him single than to foist her sister on him. Claude was, after all, his heir, and after Claude, Clarissa's own son.

But perhaps she feared that he would allow himself to act on some whim and take on a leg shackle with some other female while she was not present to keep a proprietary eye on him.

She need not entertain any such fear. His one close brush with matrimony had been quite enough to last him a lifetime as well as all the raw and painful emotions that had been part of the experience. Miss Horatia Eckert might go hang for all he cared now, though he had cared a great deal once upon a time. And she had made overtures recently—another reason why he was quite content to come to Bodley with his brother and his friends rather than go to town for the Season. His jaw hardened for a moment.

"Rawleigh." His sister-in-law rested a hand on the sleeve of his greatcoat after he had handed her down from her carriage. She always addressed him by his title, although he had invited her to use his given name. He believed it gave her a greater feeling of consequence to be closely related to a title. "Welcome to Bodley. Do escort Ellen inside. She is very fatigued. She is of such a delicate constitution, you know. Mrs. Croft will be waiting to show you to your rooms."

Clarissa appeared to be of the firm opinion that the more delicate the female, the more attractive she must be as a prospective bride. Certainly she had spent the last couple of weeks, ever since Miss Hudson joined her at Stratton at his suggestion, describing her sister thus to him.

"It will be my pleasure, Clarissa," he said, turning to offer his arm to the younger sister. "Miss Hudson?"

Miss Ellen Hudson was afraid of him, the viscount thought with some irritation. Or in awe of him, which was more or less the same thing and quite as annoying. Yet Clarissa seemed to believe that the two of them would enjoy being irritated and awed together for a lifetime.

Was she married? he wondered, his thoughts straying from the young lady on his arm.

And how soon could he decently find out?

MRS. CLARISSA ADAMS'S cup of joy was running over. There were guests at Bodley for an indeterminate length of time—eleven in all, and there were no fewer than three titles among them, four if she considered her sister-in-law Daphne, whose husband, Sir Clayton Baird, had made her into Lady Baird.

There were Rawleigh and his two friends; his and Claude's sister and her husband; Ellen; Clarissa's dear friend, Hannah Lipton, with Mr. Lipton, their daughter, Miss Veronica Lipton, who was one year longer in the tooth than Ellen and not nearly as pretty or of as delicate a constitution, and their son, Mr. Arthur Lipton and his betrothed, Miss Theresa Hulme. Miss Hulme was only eighteen, a dangerous age, but she was unfortunately quite insipid with her pale auburn hair and pale green eyes. But then she was safely betrothed to the younger Mr. Lipton, and one did not wish to be unkind.

There was only one fact to mar Mrs. Adams's joy. They

were an uneven number. All her hints to Mr. Gascoigne, Rawleigh's *untitled* friend had gone for naught and he had accepted the invitation she had felt compelled to extend to him as well as to Baron Pelham. And her attempt to persuade a young widowed friend to be taken up in their carriage as they returned to Bodley had failed when an answer to her letter had brought the news that the friend was newly betrothed and was to be married within the month.

And so Mrs. Adams felt all the embarrassment of being a hostess who had so mismanaged matters that she had an uneven number of ladies and gentlemen. It was most mortifying. She racked her brains for some suitable female not too far distant from Bodley to be summoned as a houseguest for a few weeks, but there was no one. And so she had to fall back upon the expedient of issuing frequent invitations to some unattached local female who could not reasonably be asked to stay. There was no point in considering with any care who that might be. There was really only one possibility.

Mrs. Catherine Winters.

Mrs. Adams did not like Mrs. Winters. She put on too many airs, considering the fact that she lived in genteel poverty in a small cottage and had a wardrobe of extremely limited size. And no one seemed to know quite where she had come from five years ago or who her husband had been. Or her father, for that matter. But she assumed an air of quiet refinement and her conversation was equally refined and sensible.

It annoyed Mrs. Adams that everyone should assume the woman was a lady merely because she behaved like one. And it irritated her to have to invite Mrs. Winters to dine or to make up a table of cards occasionally when she was the children's music teacher. Not that she would accept any remuneration for that task, it was true, but even so it was lowering to have to consort socially with someone who was almost, if not quite, a servant.

If Mrs. Winters did not dress so unfashionably and style her hair so plainly, she might almost be called handsome. Not as handsome as Ellen, of course. But there were those airs she put on. And Rawleigh's mind must not be distracted from Ellen. He had shown some well-bred interest in the girl during the last two weeks, she was sure.

Interestingly enough, she was never too worried about Claude's eyes straying. Claude was devoted to her. She had had some misgivings about marrying such a handsome and charming young man nine years before, being a girl with some sense as well as a measure of vanity. She did not believe she was the type to smile and affect ignorance while her husband took his pleasure with whores and mistresses. And yet it was such an advantageous match for her—he was after all heir to a viscount. And she liked his looks. And so she had decided to marry him and to hold him too. She had deliberately become both his wife and his mistress, encouraging him to do with her in the privacy of her bedchamber what would have caused most wives of tender sensibilities to die of shock. And she had shocked herself—she liked what he did.

No, Mrs. Adams was not afraid of losing her husband to the likes of Mrs. Winters, even though she did not encourage the woman to get too close. But she would have liked a female who was somewhat—plainer to invite to make up numbers with her guests.

Unfortunately there was no one else.

"I shall send for Mrs. Winters to come to dinner tonight," she told Mr. Adams the morning after their return home. "She will be grateful enough to elevate herself in society for an evening, I daresay. And she can be depended upon not to disgrace the company."

"Ah, Mrs. Winters," her husband said with a warm smile. "She is always agreeable company, my love. Did I keep you awake too late last night after such a long journey? My apologies."

He knew that none were necessary. She crossed his study to his side of the desk and bent her head for his kiss.

"I shall seat her beside Mr. Gascoigne," she said. "They can entertain each other. I do think it provoking of him not to have returned to London after imposing on Rawleigh's hospitality for all of three weeks."

"I think it's a splendid idea to seat them together, my love," he said. There was amusement in his smile. "But I think you waste your efforts trying to pair Ellen with Rex. He is not to be had, or so he says. I begin to believe that he is serious. He was badly hurt by Miss Eckert, I am afraid."

"No man is to be had," she said scornfully, "until he is made to see that a certain lady was made for him. The first one was simply not the right one."

"Ah." He smiled again. "Is that what you made me see, Clarissa? That you were made for me? How perceptive you were."

"Ellen and Rawleigh were made for each other," she said, refusing to have her attention diverted.

"We shall see," he said, laughing.

Two

"IT IS EXTREMELY obliging of Mr. and Mrs. Adams to invite Mrs. Lovering and me to dine at Bodley," the Reverend Ebenezer Lovering said as he handed Catherine down from his cart and turned back to lend assistance to his wife. "And they have done you a singular honor to include you, Mrs. Winters. Especially when they have Viscount Rawleigh as a houseguest."

"Yes, indeed," Catherine murmured. She lifted her hands to smooth over her hair and check that the evening breeze had not ruined her coiffure, simple as it was. She tried to ignore the thumping of her heart. She had decided a hundred times not to accept the invitation, but she had accepted anyway. There was really no point in staying away. She could not hide until all the guests had returned to their various homes. They might be here for several weeks.

She had dressed with some care, wearing a gown of green silk that she knew looked well with her hair. And she had dressed her hair less severely than usual, allowing tendrils to curl at her temples and along her neck. And yet she knew as soon as she had handed her cloak to a footman and had been shown into the drawing room by the butler that she looked woefully plain and unfashionable. Of course, it befitted a poor neighbor who had been honored with an invitation only because for some reason there was one more gentleman than lady, to look slightly shabby, she supposed with a flashing of the old humor. But in truth she could feel little amusement.

"Ah, Mrs. Winters," Mrs. Adams said, sweeping toward her, all flounces and sparkling jewelry and nodding plumes, "how good of you to come." Her eyes swept over her guest and registered clear satisfaction that she was not likely to outshine any other lady present. She turned to greet the rector and his wife.

"Mrs. Winters, how kind of you." Mr. Adams was smiling warmly at her. It was definitely Mr. Adams, she thought before allowing herself to smile back. He was wearing his habitual good-humored expression. Besides, he had called her by name. "Allow me to present you to some of our guests."

She did not have the courage to let her eyes sweep the room. It seemed very full of people. But she looked at each separate person as she was introduced and felt relief each time. None of these people was familiar, except for Miss Ellen Hudson, Mrs. Adams's sister, who had been a guest at Bodley several times over the past five years. She was looking very pretty and grown up and was dressed in what Catherine guessed was the first stare of fashion. She was a younger version of Mrs. Adams, with her rich brown hair and green eyes.

Everyone greeted her politely. She saw admiration in the blue eyes of Lord Pelham, who took her hand and bowed over it, and in the lazy gray eyes of Mr. Gascoigne. Both were handsome young men. It did feel good to be admired, she admitted to herself, although she would never again court admiration or be beguiled by it.

At last there were only two people left to whom she had not been presented. But she had been aware of them—or of one of them at least—with an inward squirming of discomfort since she entered the room. But it had to be faced. Perhaps he had not even noticed her with any particularity yesterday or, if he had, perhaps he would not recognize her now. Or perhaps he realized she had mistaken him for his brother.

"May I present my sister, Daphne, Lady Baird?" Mr. Adams said. "Mrs. Winters, Daph."

Lady Baird was as fair as her brothers were dark. But she was as amiable as Mr. Adams and greeted Catherine with a smile and a few courteous words.

"And my brother, Viscount Rawleigh," Mr. Adams said. "As you can see, Mrs. Winters, we are identical twins. The fact has caused other people embarrassment and us amusement all our lives, has it not, Rex?"

"And they have been known shamelessly and deliberately to exploit the likeness, Mrs. Winters," Lady Baird said. "I could tell you stories to fill the evening and still have enough left for tomorrow."

Lord Rawleigh had made Catherine a stiff bow. "Not now, Daphne," he said. "Maybe some other time. Your servant, Mrs. Winters."

Yes, they were identical, Catherine thought. Both were tall and handsome with dark hair and darker eyes. But they were different. Although she had made that initial mistake in the village, she did not believe she would do so again. They were apparently of the same build and yet it seemed to her that the viscount was more athletic and stronger than Mr. Adams. And his hair was longer—surely unfashionably long. And his face was quite different. Oh, the features were indistinguishable from those of his brother, but whereas Mr.

Adams had an open, amiable countenance, Lord Rawleigh's was arrogant, hooded, cynical.

She liked Mr. Adams. She disliked this man—an opinion that might well be colored by the fact that she had embarrassed herself before his eyes, she was ready to admit to herself.

"*Mister* Winters?" Lady Baird said, looking about the room with brightly curious eyes.

"Is deceased, Daph," Mr. Adams said quickly. "Mrs. Winters is a widow. We are delighted that she chose Bodley-on-the-Water in which to make her home. She reads to the elderly and teaches the children and keeps the church supplied with flowers from her garden during the summer. She teaches Julie and Will to play the pianoforte, though they are displaying all the symptoms of tone deafness that afflict their father, I am afraid."

"Mrs. Winters is what one would call a treasure, then," Viscount Rawleigh said, his eyes looking her up and down and undoubtedly coming to the same conclusion that Mrs. Adams had appeared to come to earlier. Well, it did not matter, Catherine thought, swallowing her mortification. She had not dressed to impress his almighty lordship. If he saw her as a woman of moderate means, living far from any center of fashion, then he was right. That was exactly what she was.

"Beyond all doubt," Mr. Adams said with a smile. "But we are embarrassing you, Mrs. Winters. Tell me how my children have progressed in the past two months. The truth, now." He chuckled.

Catherine was annoyed to realize that she really had blushed. But it was not so much with pleasure or embarrassment at the compliment as with anger that it had not been meant as such. There had been a certain boredom in the viscount's voice. What he had really been saying was that she was a dull woman. Well, she was that too.

"They have both been practicing daily, sir," she said. "And both are developing a competence at their scales and the simple exercises I have set them."

Mr. Adams laughed again. "Ah, the consummate diplomat," he said. "But I suppose that with Julie at least we must persevere. The thought of a young lady growing up without that particular accomplishment is enough to give one the shudders. At least she shows some promise with her brush and watercolors."

"I do not play the pianoforte with any degree of competence either," Lady Baird said, "and I have not been a social pariah since my come-out. Indeed, I believe I did very well for myself in snaring Clayton as a husband, even setting aside the fact that we were head over ears for each other. All one does during a party when asked to play a piece, Mrs. Winters, is smile dazzlingly, hold up both hands, and say something like, 'Look, ten thumbs,' and everyone laughs as if one is a great wit. I assure you it works."

"Perhaps Mrs. Winters should teach your children diplomacy rather than music, then, Claude," Lord Rawleigh said.

"It must indeed be tedious to teach children who are not interested," Lady Baird said with some sympathy.

"Not so, ma'am," Catherine said. "And it is not interest they lack, but—"

"—talent," Mr. Adams supplied when she stopped abruptly. He chuckled again. "Never fear, Mrs. Winters. I love them none the less for their lack of musical aptitude."

"Ah, dinner," Lady Baird said, looking across the room to see the butler speaking with Mrs. Adams. "Good. I am famished."

"Excuse me," Mr. Adams said, "I must lead in Mrs. Lipton."

"Where is Clayton?" Lady Baird looked about her.

Catherine quelled an inner surging of panic. Oh, no, this was too embarrassing. But she was saved, as she might have known she would be, by the arrival of Mrs. Adams, who of course had everything organized.

"Rawleigh," she said, taking his arm, "you will, of course, wish to lead Ellen in." She looked with almost comic condescension at Catherine. "I have asked the Reverend Lovering to lead you in, Mrs. Winters. I thought you would be more comfortable with someone you know."

"Of course," Catherine murmured, amusement replacing the panic. "Thank you, ma'am."

The rector was already bowing at her elbow and assuring her that he would consider it a singular honor to be allowed to take her in to dinner and seat her beside him.

"Mrs. Adams knows," he said while that lady could still hear him, "that a man of my calling favors a table companion of good sense."

Which was wonderful praise indeed, Catherine thought, laying her arm along his, and would undoubtedly confirm Viscount Rawleigh in his opinion of her as a dull woman. Not that she gave the snap of two fingers for his opinion.

She settled philosophically into what was bound to be a dull hour. Mr. Nathaniel Gascoigne sat to her left and appeared to be a pleasant gentleman as well as a handsome one. But she had little opportunity to converse with him. The Reverend Lovering monopolized her attention as he always did when seated beside her, a common occurrence when they were both guests at Bodley. He assured her throughout the meal that they must both feel humble gratitude for the honor bestowed on them by their invitations to be in such illustrious company. And he assured her too of the superior quality of every dish set before them.

Catherine lent him half an ear and enjoyed observing the

company. Mr. Adams at the head of the table was the genial host. Mrs. Adams at the foot was the regal hostess. It always intrigued Catherine that they were apparently quite contented with each other when they were so very different in character. They were, of course, both beautiful people. She noted that Ellen Hudson, seated beside the viscount, made a few nervous attempts to engage his attention. Yet when he gave it, she became mute and noticeably uncomfortable. He would turn his attention back to the conversation of Mrs. Lipton on his other side. Mrs. Adams was noticeably annoyed. Catherine guessed that Mrs. Lipton would be seated far from the viscount in future. She noticed that Lady Baird and Mr. Gascoigne flirted with each other in what was very obviously a harmless manner. She noticed that Miss Theresa Hulme exchanged several longing glances with Mr. Arthur Lipton, her fiancé, who was too far from her at table to be engaged in conversation. She appeared to have little conversation and was soon largely ignored by the gentlemen to her left and right, poor girl. Lord Pelham was deep in conversation with Miss Veronica Lipton throughout dinner.

Catherine enjoyed being an observer rather than a player, though it had not always been so. Being an observer lent amusement to life and saved one much heartache. It was far more pleasant, she had discovered gradually over the years, to guard one's emotions, to keep oneself at one remove from life, so to speak. Not that she did not involve herself in a number of busy activities, and not that she did not have friends. But they were safe activities, safe friends.

She found her eyes caught by Lord Rawleigh's at a moment when half her mind was listening to the Reverend Lovering's eulogy on the roast beef, just consumed, and the other half was woolgathering. She smiled into the familiar face a split second before she remembered that it was not familiar at all. He was a stranger. And she had done it again soon after assuring herself that it could never happen again. Her eyes slid awkwardly away from his and her fork clattered rather noisily on her plate.

But what was wrong with smiling at him when their eyes met by chance across the table? They had, after all, been presented to each other and had conversed in a group together for a few minutes before dinner. There was no reason at all why she should have looked away in confusion. Doing so had made her appear guilty, almost as if she had been stealing admiring glances at him and had been caught in the act. She frowned in chagrin and looked determinedly back at him.

Viscount Rawleigh was still observing her. He raised one dark and haughty eyebrow before she jerked her eyes away again.

And now she had made matters worse. How gauche she was! Merely because he was a handsome man and she felt the pull of his attractiveness as any normal woman would?

She smiled at the Reverend Lovering, and thus encouraged, he launched into praises of the superior discernment Mr. Adams had shown in the choice of chef.

SHE WAS A widow. Interesting. Widows were always many times more desirable than any other type of female. With unmarried ladies one had to tread carefully—very carefully, as Nat had recently discovered to his cost. If one was a man of fortune and some social standing, one was seen as a matrimonial prize, to be netted at all costs by interested relatives, even if not by the young lady herself. Besides, unmarried ladies were quite unbeddable unless one was prepared to pay the ultimate price.

He was not. Only that once. Never again.

And married ladies were dangerous, as Eden had found within the past few months. One could lose one's life in face of an irate husband's bullet or have to live with the guilt of having killed a man one had wronged. Even if the husband was too cowardly to issue a challenge, as appeared to have been the case with the man Eden had cuckolded, there was always the censure of the *ton* to be borne. That meant absenting oneself from London, and even perhaps from Brighton and Bath for a year or so.

Females who were not ladies were generally a bore. They were necessary for the slaking of one's appetites, of course, and they were often marvelously skilled between the sheets. But they were too easily had and they generally had nothing at all to offer except their bodies. They were a bore. It was several years since he had employed a regular mistress. He preferred casual encounters if the choice must be made. But they posed their own danger. He had brought his body more or less safely through six years of fighting in the Peninsula as well as through Waterloo. He had no wish to surrender it to a sexual disease.

No, widows were perfect in every way. He had twice had affairs with a widow. There had been no complications with either. He had left each when he tired of her. Neither had put up any fuss. Both had moved on to the next lover. He remembered them with some fondness.

Mrs. Winters was a widow. And an extraordinarily lovely one. Oh, not in any very obvious way, perhaps. Ellen Hudson was dressed far more richly and fashionably. Her hair was styled far more intricately. She was younger. But it was in the very absence of such lures that Mrs. Winters's beauty shone. In her rather plain and definitely unfashionable green gown, the woman became apparent. The eye did not linger on the appearance of the dress but penetrated beyond to the rather tall, slender, but shapely form within. It was an eminently beddable body. And the simplicity of her hairstyle, smooth over the crown of her head and over her ears, caught in a knot behind, with only a few loose curls to relieve the severity, drew attention, not to itself, but to the rich golden sheen of the hair. And the hair was not fussy enough to draw attention from her face, regular-featured, hazel-eyed, intelligent. Beautiful.

She was a widow. He silently blessed the late Mr. Winters for having the courtesy to die young.

The stay in the country promised to be tedious. Oh, it was good to be back in what had been his grandparents' house. It revived many pleasant childhood memories. And it would be good to spend a few weeks with Claude. They shared the unusual closeness of identical twins and yet their lives had taken quite separate paths since Claude had married at the age of twenty. They no longer saw a great deal of each other. He could not ask, either, for more congenial company than that of two of his three closest friends. They had been close since they were cavalry officers together in the Peninsula. They had been dubbed there by one wag of a fellow officer the Four Horsemen of the Apocalypse, he, Eden, Nat, and Kenneth Woodfall, Earl of Haverford, because it had seemed that they were always in the thick of action.

But the stay was going to be tedious. He could not like Clarissa, though to give her her due, she seemed to be keeping Claude happy enough. It was very obvious to him, though, that she had set herself a mission to be accomplished during the next few weeks. She wanted him for her sister. And so there was all the tedium to be faced of being polite to the girl while giving no false impression that he was courting her. He knew he would be up against Clarissa's determined maneuvering.

Sometimes he cursed himself for a fool for feeling such an obligation to Eden and Nat. Did he have to feel obliged to rusticate with them just because they had no choice but to do so? Could he not leave them to keep each other company? But he knew that they would have done as much for him. Besides, Horatia would probably be in town for the Season. He would be as happy to avoid seeing her.

And so he was stuck here for a few weeks at the very least. He needed more diversion than a brother and two close friends could provide. He needed female diversion.

And Mrs. Winters was a widow.

And available.

She had signaled as much more than once. Quite unmistakably. Her behavior was entirely well-bred throughout the evening. She appeared quiet yet charming, just as a woman of her apparent position and means would be expected to behave. She neither pushed herself forward nor hung back with false modesty. In the drawing room after dinner she conversed with Clayton and Daphne and Mr. Lipton and appeared to be doing so with some sense, if their interested expressions when she was talking were any indication. After Miss Hudson, Miss Lipton, and Miss Hulme had favored the company with pianoforte recitals and songs, she was invited by Claude to play for them and did so without fuss. She played well but did not linger after the one piece as Miss Lipton had done. When Mrs. Lovering rose to leave, Mrs. Winters joined her without hesitation, bade Claude and Clarissa a courteous good night, and nodded politely at the company in general. She waited quietly for the pompous ass of a rector to pile effusive thanks on his hosts, to commend them on their distinguished guests, and to praise the meal they had all enjoyed. Almost ten minutes passed before the three of them finally took their leave, Claude with them to hand the ladies into the rector's conveyance and to see them on their way.

Oh, but she had signaled her availability. There had been the smile and the feigned confusion and the lowered lashes at dinner—beautiful long lashes and they were too, several shades darker than her hair. And there had been the several covert glances in the drawing room, most notably the one she had given him after she had finished playing the pianoforte and was smiling at the smattering of applause. She had looked directly to where he was standing, propped against the mantel, a glass in one hand, and she had blushed. He had not been applauding, but he had raised his glass one inch and had lifted one eyebrow.

Yes, she was definitely available. As he stretched out in bed later that night, having dismissed his valet and extinguished the candles, his loins ached in pleasurable anticipation.

He wondered if the late Mr. Winters had been a good teacher of bedroom skills. But no matter. He would just as soon teach her himself.

Three

SHE HAD JUST walked back the three miles from the small cottage elderly Mr. Clarkwell occupied with his son and daughter-in-law. She had been reading to him as she tried to do at least once a week. He could no longer get about without the aid of two canes, and sitting indoors or even in the doorway all day made him peevish, his daughter-in-law claimed.

Catherine scratched an ecstatic Toby's stomach, first with the toe of her shoe and then with her hand.

"Foolish dog," she said, catching him by the jaw and shaking his head from side to side. "Anyone would think I had been gone for a month." She laughed at his furiously wagging tail.

It was a chilly day despite the sunshine. She poked at the embers of the fire in the kitchen grate and succeeded in coaxing it back to life. She put on more wood and then filled the kettle and set it to boil for tea.

It always felt good to come back home and close the door behind her and know that she did not have to go anywhere for the rest of the day. She thought about last evening and smiled to herself. Such evenings were pleasant and she had found the company congenial despite several moments of embarrassment. But she did not crave them as a general way of life.

Not any longer.

But it seemed the rest of the day was not to be all her own after all. There was a sharp rap on the door. She hurried to answer it, sighing inwardly while Toby went wild with barking. It was a groom from Bodley.

"Mrs. Adams is coming to call on you, ma'am," he said.

Mrs. Adams never called upon those she considered beneath her socially. What she did do was summon a person to the garden gate, regardless of the weather or of what that person might have been busy at inside the house. And there she would speak for a few minutes until she chose to signal her coachman to drive on.

Catherine sighed again and closed the door on an indignant Toby before walking down the path to the gate. It was not the carriage approaching this time, though, she saw immediately, but a group of riders—Mr. and Mrs. Adams, Miss Hudson, Miss Lipton, Lady Baird, Lord Pelham, Mr. Arthur Lipton, and Viscount Rawleigh. They all stopped and there was a chorus of greetings.

"How do you do, Mrs. Winters?" Mr. Adams said with a cheerful grin. "Clarissa decided that she must call you outside in case you missed and failed to admire such a splendid cavalcade of horses and their riders passing by."

Mrs. Adams ignored him. She inclined her head regally. It was a head covered by a very fetching blue riding hat with a feather that curled attractively beneath her chin. She wore a matching blue riding habit. It was new, Catherine believed. And expensive.

"Good day, Mrs. Winters," she said. "I trust you did not take a chill from riding home in the vicar's dogcart last evening? It is a pity you do not keep a carriage, but I do not suppose you would have much need for one."

"Indeed not, ma'am," Catherine agreed, entertaining herself with a mental image of a carriage house in her back garden—twice as large as her cottage. "And it was a very pleasant evening for a drive, provided one was dressed appropriately."

"What a delightful cottage," Lady Baird said. "It is in a quite idyllic setting, is it not, Eden?"

"There are many people in London," Lord Pelham said, his blue eyes twinkling down at Catherine, "who would kill to have property on the river, as you have, Mrs. Winters."

"Then I must be thankful I do not live near London, my lord," she said.

"I do not believe such a small property would be of interest to anyone in town, Pelham," Mrs. Adams said. "Though it must be admitted that the river makes a pleasing setting for the village. And the stone bridge is very picturesque. Did you notice it when we arrived two days ago?"

"We will ride on and pay homage to it," Mr. Adams said, "and allow Mrs. Winters to return to the warmth of her cottage. You are shivering, ma'am."

Catherine smiled at him, and generally at all of them as they bade her farewell and proceeded down the street toward the triple-arched stone bridge at the end of it. Yes, she had shivered. And yes, it was chilly standing outside without her cloak and bonnet.

But it was not the cold that had been her chief discomfort. It was *him*. Perhaps it was nothing at all. Perhaps she was being girlishly silly over a handsome man. She would be very annoyed with herself if that were really the case. She had thought herself past all that. She was five-and-twenty years old and she was living quietly in the country for the rest of her life. She had resigned herself to that, adjusted her life accordingly. And she was happy. No, contented. Happiness involved emotion, and if one was happy, then one could also be unhappy. She wanted nothing more to do with either. She was content to be content.

Or perhaps she was not just being silly. Perhaps there really was something. Certainly he had spent a great deal of last evening looking at her, even though he had made no attempt to converse with her or to join any of the groups of which she was a part—except before dinner, when he had had no choice. It surely could not be coincidence that every time she had glanced at him he had been gazing back. She had felt his eyes even when she was not looking at him. And whenever she had looked, it had been unwillingly to try to prove to herself that she was imagining things.

The same thing had happened today. He had not spoken a word to her but had hung back behind the rest of the group. While they were all glancing about them at her cottage and garden, at the village, and at her, his own eyes had not faltered. She had felt them even though she had not once glanced at him.

And that was ridiculous, she told herself. letting herself back into the house and suffering the excited assault of Toby, who had been denied the pleasure of barking at strangers. She had looked quite easily at all the others, including the other three gentlemen, and had felt no awkwardness or embarrassment at all even though Mr. Adams and Lord Pelham were equally handsome as Viscount Rawleigh and Mr. Lipton too was a good-looking gentleman. Why should she feel embarrassment? They had called on her. She had not presumed to invite them.

Why had she found it impossible to turn either her head or her eyes in the direction of the viscount? And how could she know that he had looked steadily at her with those hooded dark eyes of his since she had not looked to see? And how would he construe the fact that she had not returned his look at least once—coolly and courteously?

She felt like a girl from the schoolroom again, struck dumb and brainless by the mere sight of a handsome male face.

No one had mentioned last evening how long the guests were to remain at Bodley. Perhaps they were there for only a few days. Or for a week or two at the longest. Surely it would not be much longer than that. There was still some time before the Season started in London, but young blades would want to be there before all the balls and routs and such began in earnest. Viscount Rawleigh, Lord Pelham, and Mr. Gascoigne definitely qualified as young blades. Though not so very young either. They must all be close to thirty. The viscount was Mr. Adam's twin, and Mr. Adams had been married long enough to have produced an eight-year-old daughter.

She tried desperately to stop thinking about the houseguests at Bodley and about one of them in particular. She did not want to do so. She liked her new life and she liked herself as she was. She made her tea, poured it after it had steeped for a suitable time, and sat down with one of Daniel Defoe's books, lent her by the rector. Perhaps she could lose herself in an account of the plague year.

She eventually succeeded in doing so. Toby stretched out on the rug at her feet and sighed noisily in deep contentment.

SHE REALLY WAS beautiful. She was one of the rare women who would look so even dressed in a sack. Or in nothing at all. Oh, yes, definitely that. He had sat his horse outside her cottage unclothing her with his eyes while she exchanged small talk with everyone else. And his mental exercise had revealed long limbs, a flat stomach that did not need the aid of corsets, firm, uptilted, rose-peaked breasts, creamy skin. And with his eyes he had let down her hair from its plain and sensible knot and watched it cascade in a golden mane down her back to her waist. It would wave enticingly—he remembered the tendrils that had been allowed to remain loose the evening before.

He had not failed to notice that she did not once look directly at him. Neither had he failed to sense that she was more fully aware of him than of any of the others, at whom she looked and with whom she conversed quite easily. There had been an invisible thread drawn tautly between them and he had pulled on it only very gently. He had no wish to be teased again by Eden. He had no wish for anyone else to notice, especially Claude, between whose mind and his own there was a strange bond.

He was glad that she was discreet. If she were not, of course, he would not pursue his interest in her. He certainly would not take her up on the invitation she had so covertly extended the evening before.

But take her up on it he would. And without delay. His stay would probably be no more than a few weeks long, and he had the feeling that there was enough about Mrs. Winters to hold his interest for a number of weeks.

There were no guests in the evening even though Clarissa appeared to find the uneven numbers an embarrassment. There were enough people interested in cards to make up the tables. He was free.

"I shall step out for some fresh air," he announced languidly, hoping that no one else would discover any burning desire to keep him company. Ellen Hudson, fortunately, was one of the cardplayers.

"It is dusk," Clarissa said, clearly annoyed that he had avoided partnering her sister. "You may get lost, Rawleigh."

Claude chuckled. "Rex and I enjoyed many a clandestine nocturnal adventure here when we were boys, my love," he said. "We will send out a search party if you are not home by midnight, Rex."

"I shall use a ball of string if it will make you easier in your mind, Clarissa," his lordship said, his voice bored.

He was on his way a few minutes later, blessedly alone. And he blessed too his familiarity with the estate, though he had not visited it for years. One did not easily forget boyish haunts. Even in the gathering dusk he knew unerringly the route across the lawn and among the trees and through the postern door in the wall about the park that brought him out onto the road a short distance beyond the far end of the village—Mrs. Winters's end. He did not wish to tempt fate by striding through the village on his way to her cottage.

It was almost dark by the time he stepped through the postern door onto the road. The curtains were drawn across the windows at the front of the cottage, he could see. There was light behind one of them. She was at home, then. He must hope that she was there alone. He must have some sort of excuse to present if she was not.

He opened the gate and closed it carefully behind him. A glance along the street showed it to be deserted. He felt unaccountably nervous now that the time had come. He had never done such a thing in the country before. Certainly never at Stratton. And he had never stayed long enough anywhere else even to consider the desirability of doing so. It was the sort of thing one associated with the anonymity of a large place, like London.

Claude would not be pleased if he got wind of it.

Eden and Nat would be amused and would never let him hear the end of it.

He must make sure that no one got wind of it.

He knocked on the door.

He thought he was going to have to knock again, even though he could hear a dog barking with some enthusiasm inside, but he heard the key turning in the lock just as he was raising his arm, and the door opened a short way. She looked at him in some surprise. She was wearing a lace-trimmed cap, which made her look charmingly pretty instead of matronly. She wore the same high-necked, long-sleeved wool dress she had worn earlier in the day. He wondered if she realized that it emphasized her slimness and clung enticingly to her curves.

"My lord!" she said.

He could hardly hear her above the barking of the dog. He wondered for the first time how it was she could tell the difference between him and Claude. Most people could not, at least on early acquaintance.

"Mrs. Winters?" He removed his hat. "Good evening. May I step inside?"

She looked beyond his shoulder as if she expected to see someone else with him. Some seconds passed before she opened the door wider and stepped to one side so that he could move past her. A small brown-and-white terrier stepped into the breach and announced its intention of guarding its territory.

"I do not bite," he told the dog in languid tones. "I hope you will return the favor, sir."

"Toby," she said, "do be quiet."

But her words were not needed. The dog had turned over onto its back and was thumping its tail on the floor and waving its paws in the air. He tickled it with the toe of his boot and the animal turned right side up and trotted away, apparently satisfied.

He was in a narrow passageway. It seemed like a miniature house. He almost felt as if he should duck his head to avoid hitting it on the ceiling.

She closed the door and stood facing it for longer than seemed strictly necessary. Then she turned to him and looked into his face. They were a very clear hazel, her eyes, with long brown lashes.

"There is no fire in the parlor," she said. "I was not expecting callers. I was in the kitchen."

There was an enticing smell of baking coming from the kitchen, and sure enough he could see as he entered it a tray of small cakes resting on a cloth on the table. It was a cozy room. It looked lived in. The rocker to one side of the fire had a brightly embroidered cushion on the seat. There was a lit lamp on the table beside it and a book opened facedown. The dog was lying on the chair.

He turned to look at Mrs. Winters. She was pale. Even her lips seemed to have lost color.

"Will you have a seat, my lord?" she asked suddenly, her hand indicating rather jerkily the chair at the other side of the fire.

"Thank you." He crossed the room to it and seated himself as she did likewise on the rocker. The terrier had jumped down at her approach. She was graceful, he thought. Her back did not touch the chair, though there was nothing stiff about her posture. Then she jumped to her feet again.

"May I offer you a cup of tea?" she asked. "I am afraid I have nothing stronger."

"Nothing, thank you," he said. Now that he was here with her, he was enjoying the tension between them. And she was quite as aware of it as he. It was a greater tension than he had ever experienced with a woman before.

He watched her school herself to deal with the situation as she sat back down. She rested her hands in her lap, the back of one on the palm of the other, apparently relaxed.

"Did you enjoy your ride this afternoon, my lord?" she

asked politely. "The countryside around here is pretty, is it not, even at this time of year."

"Exceedingly pretty," he said. "One part of it more than any other."

"Oh?" Her mouth remained in the shape of the word. He imagined setting the tip of his tongue to the small opening.

"In the village," he said. "At this end of it. We stopped to view it. Though I suppose it cannot strictly be called countryside."

He watched her become aware of his meaning. She was one of the few women whose blush was becoming, he noticed.

She looked sharply down at her hands. "It must be pleasant for you to see your nephew and niece," she said. "They do not often leave here. I suppose you have not seen a great deal of them."

"Enough to suffice," he said. "I discovered to my cost this morning that children have a tendency to believe that uncles are to be climbed upon."

"And you do not like to be climbed upon?" she asked.

It was just too wicked a question to have been artless, though her blush deepened in the short pause before he replied.

"It depends entirely, Mrs. Winters," he said, "upon who is doing the climbing. I can imagine it being very pleasurable indeed."

She reached out one slippered foot to smooth over the back of the dog, which was stretched out before her. She lowered her eyes to watch what she did. Again it was an artful action. He felt his pulse quicken. But he was enjoying himself. He did not want to hasten matters, he realized, even if a late return to Bodley drew curious questions. He waited for her to renew the conversation.

Her eyes came up at last, hesitated on his chin, and then

met his. "I do not know why you are here, my lord," she said. "It is not quite proper."

Ah. She was not as content as he to let the situation develop at its own pace. She wished to bring him to the point.

"I believe you do know," he said. "And I assure you that no one saw me come here. There will be no gossip."

"Someone who passes the length of the village street rarely goes unseen," she said.

"I came by the postern door," he said. "Perhaps you did not know that Claude and Daphne and I spent a great deal of time here with our grandparents when we were children."

"Yes, of course," she said. "Why are you here now? At my cottage, I mean?"

"I am bored, Mrs. Winters," he said. "It seems likely that I will be at Bodley for several weeks, and while I am very fond of my brother and sister, and came here in company with two of my closest male friends, I lack for congenial female company. I am bored, and my guess is that you are too. You are a widow in a place where there cannot be much in the way of social activity except when Clarissa condescends to invite you to the house. And there must be even less in the way of male company."

Her hands were no longer relaxed. They were clasping each other. "I do not crave social pleasures," she said. "And I have not looked for male company since—since the death of my husband. I am content as I am. I am neither bored nor lonely."

She was going to pretend to indifference. Good. He was enjoying himself. And she was so beautiful to look at from some distance that he was in no hurry to lessen it. He did not want to touch her just yet. Anticipation brought its own pleasure.

"You are a liar, ma'am," he said.

That silenced her for a few moments. Her eyes widened and she stared back at him. "And you are no gentleman, my lord," she said at last.

He looked at her appreciatively, slim and prim and infinitely desirable.

"For the few weeks I am here we might as well alleviate each other's boredom," he said.

"By such visits?" she asked. "They are not proper, my lord. I have no chaperon."

"For which fact we may both say a prayer of thanksgiving tonight," he said. "Yes, by such visits, ma'am. And do we really care about propriety? You are a widow and past the first blush of youth, if I may make so bold as to say so."

"I—" She swallowed. "I do not believe your visiting here would cure our boredom, my lord," she said. "We appear to have very few topics of common interest on which to converse."

She was priceless.

"Then I suppose we would have to entertain each other without words," he said.

"What are you saying?" Her lips had lost their color again. They were lips that needed to be kissed.

"Did you never entertain your husband without words?" he asked her. "Or he you? With a wife of such obvious charms, I cannot imagine that he denied himself one of life's great pleasures."

"You want me to be your whore," she whispered.

"An ugly word," he said. "Whores wander the streets, picking up random customers. I want you to be my mistress, Mrs. Winters."

"There is no difference." She was still whispering.

"On the contrary," he said, "there is a great deal of difference. A man chooses a particular woman to be his mistress. If she is fortunate and is not living in straitened circumstances, a woman chooses the man who is to be her protector. It is not unlike a marriage in some ways."

"In straitened circumstances," she said. "Are you offering to pay me, my lord?"

He had wondered about it. He did not want to offend her, but she might be in need of more money. He was quite prepared to pay her.

"If you wish," he said. "I am sure we can come to an amicable agreement."

"You would pay me," she said, "for lying with you? For going to bed with you? For allowing you access to my body?"

He could not have put it much more erotically himself.

"Yes, ma'am," he said. "I would pay you. Though I would consider it as much my concern to give you pleasure as yours to give it to me."

"Get out," she said so quietly that it took him a moment to realize what she had said.

He raised his eyebrows. "Ma'am?"

"Get out," she said much more distinctly, the flush returning to her face, her nostrils flaring. "Get out and never come back."

The dog was sitting up and growling deep in his throat.

"You have led me to this moment," he said, "only to tell me to get out? Have I misread the signs? There have been too many for me to be mistaken."

She was on her feet. "Get out."

He took his time about getting up. He looked closely at her. She meant what she was saying. There was no chance that she was playing hard to get. He *had* misread the signs. Or if he had not, he had misinterpreted them. She was a virtuous woman—why else would she have taken up residence in such a village? And she was a proud woman—he should never have admitted that he was prepared to pay her. She was attracted to him. Of that there was little doubt. But she had wanted a mild flirtation—something that did not interest him.

But perhaps if he had not rushed into a false interpretation, he might have led her by slow degrees from flirtation to dalliance to an affair. That might have taken weeks, though.

Now it was too late to find out how it might have turned out the other way.

"No," he said as she opened her mouth to speak again, "you do not need to repeat it." He got to his feet. "My heartfelt apologies, ma'am. Your servant." He made her a curt bow before striding out into the passageway, picking up his hat, and letting himself out into the night.

The dog was barking inside the house again.

"TOBY." SHE SANK back into the rocker and made no objection when the dog leapt up onto her lap and proceeded to make himself comfortable. She scratched his ears. "Toby, I have never been so insulted in all my life."

She rested her head against the back of the chair and stared up at the ceiling. She laughed softly. Oh, yes, she had. Was there something about her that invited such insulting behavior?

Was there?

She had looked at him a few times and smiled at him twice when she had mistaken him for Mr. Adams. She had *not* looked at him this afternoon. And for that she had to suffer this? He had thought she would be his mistress? He had thought she would accept payment in return for opening her body to him on a bed?

"I am very angry, Toby," she said. "Very angry indeed."

She continued to scratch the dog's ears and stare upward as she cried, at first silently and then noisily.

What she would not admit even to Toby, of course, was that she had been wretchedly, horrifyingly tempted.

Her body was still aching for his touch.

Four

CATHERINE LAY IN bed the following morning, trying to feel symptoms that might keep her there. But her nasal passages were clear and there was no tickle in her throat; she swallowed twicc and tried to tell herself there was and that it would be wise to stay inside where it was warm rather than venture outside where she might worsen her chill and perhaps even pass it on to the children.

What chill? She felt as healthy as she had ever felt. And from the brightness behind the drawn curtains, it looked like a perfect spring day outside.

No, she could not delay the inevitable. The truth was that it was one of the days for William and Juliana's music lesson and she dreaded going near Bodley House lest she run into *him*. She would die of mortification. The events of last evening seemed even worse this morning than they had appeared at the time. He had visited her alone at her cottage. Her reputation would be severely damaged if anyone had seen him arrive or leave. And he had sat in her kitchen making improper advances and an even more improper proposal.

Oh, how dared he! What had she done to give him the

impression that she would welcome such insolence? She knew the answer, of course. She had twice smiled at him, believing him to be Mr. Adams. But were two smiles irrefutable evidence that she was willing to be his whore?

She had tried so very hard to fit her new identity, to behave as a respectable widow. She had taken up residence in Bodley-on-the-Water and had done her best to be a part of village life. It had not been easy for a stranger to do. She had worked hard at being kind and friendly and neighborly. And she had won respect, she believed, and even affection from some. She had won a measure of peace and contentment.

"Oh, Toby." She turned her head to look at her terrier, who was standing beside her bed. She laughed despite herself. He was always very patient when she was later than usual getting up, standing politely where she could see him, ears cocked and tongue lolling, letting her know by his persistent heavy breathing that he would be most grateful to be let outside within the next half hour or so. "Am I being a dreadful slugabed this morning?" She swung her legs determinedly over the side of the bed and pulled on her warm dressing gown. "Come along then."

He trotted out of the bedchamber ahead of her and bobbed down the steep stairs and along the passageway to the back door.

She spoke to his waving tail. "It is not fair, you know," she said. "And I have not even the glimmering of a headache to keep me home with you. Do you suppose I could pretend to believe that there will be no lessons today, Toby, because the children's mama and papa have so recently returned home?"

Toby did not answer but trotted smartly through the door when she opened it for him.

And then she felt angry. It *was* a beautiful day. The sky

was blue with hardly a cloud visible. She could hear the water gurgling over the stones at the bottom of the garden. There was a freshness in the air that made her shiver for a moment, though she did not close the door. By the afternoon, if there was no drastic change, it would probably be warm. It was the sort of day on which she would normally go for a long walk with Toby.

And she would go too if she still felt like doing so after returning from Bodley House. She would not be able to go out at all if she made illness an excuse for not going this morning.

Why should she not go? Just because she might accidentally run into Viscount Rawleigh? Why should she avoid him? She had done no wrong unless letting him inside her house last evening had been wrong. But his visit had taken her so much by surprise that she had not even thought of refusing his entrance.

She was not going to avoid him. Or hang her head if she saw him again. Or blush or stammer or otherwise give him the satisfaction of knowing that he had discomposed her.

She was still angry—very angry—that the female state made one so weak, gave one such little freedom. She was angry that the world of men had so little use in it for women except in one capacity. She was angry that it was a man's world she lived in. For a few moments, until Toby came trotting back into the house and she closed the door, she felt the old raw and empty feeling of helplessness. But she was not going to feed such negative emotions. She had fought too hard for her peace to have it shattered by a heartless, arrogant rake who believed that because she had smiled at him twice she would smile a third time as he climbed into her bed to take his pleasure of her.

"Toby," she said as she set about building a fire in the kitchen so that she could boil the kettle for her morning tea,

"I should have got myself a female dog. Perhaps a female would not assume that the most comfortable chair in the house must have been designed for her exclusive use. How many times have I told you that you may *not* jump onto my rocker?"

Toby, wriggling into a position of comfort on the embroidered cushion that covered the seat of the rocker, panted at her and thumped his tail, pleased at the attention he was getting. He stayed where he was.

She was going to walk to Bodley House after breakfast to give the children their lessons, just as she always did, she decided. And this afternoon she would take Toby for a long walk. She would behave just as she would if there were no guests at the house. She was *not* going to start hiding or creeping about in fear that she might come face-to-face with him around every corner.

"And that, Toby," she said firmly, brushing coal dust off her hands as the fire caught, "is that."

Toby thumped his tail agreeably.

VISCOUNT RAWLEIGH HAD been out riding with Mr. and Mrs. Adams, Sir Clayton and Lady Baird, Lord Pelham, Miss Veronica Lipton, and Miss Ellen Hudson. They had taken the route north over rolling hills, from which they were able to feast their eyes on several impressive views. It was a glorious day for early spring even if the air was a little nippy.

But the viscount was feeling decidedly out of sorts by the time they rode home. His sister-in-law had maneuvered matters in such a way that he had not only ridden with Miss Hudson most of the way—he had expected that and resigned himself to it—but had also been separated from the rest of the group for much of the distance. He was not sure how she had managed it—Clarissa could be very devious when she set her heart on a certain matter.

Did Clarissa expect him to drop from sight behind some boulder with her sister in order to kiss her soundly and so compromise her that he would be compelled to offer for her and even dash back to London for a special license? He had no intention of being tricked or even nudged in the direction of matrimony, especially with someone as essentially insipid as Ellen Hudson. Not that he disliked the girl or wished her ill, and perhaps it was even ill-natured of him to think of her as insipid. She would doubtless do very well with some gentleman who did not awe her into incoherence. Unfortunately he appeared to have just such an effect on the girl.

He wondered as they at last rode their horses into the stable what Clarissa had in mind for the rest of the morning. A cozy tête-à-tête for him and Miss Hudson in the morning room, while all its other occupants were called upon to run mysterious errands that would take them out of the way? A request that he accompany Miss Hudson into the village to purchase some essential item, like a length of ribbon? He could be quite sure that whatever it was, there would be something.

He drew alongside Daphne and sent her a look that he hoped she would find sufficiently imploring. She obviously did. Her eyes went from him to Miss Hudson and she smiled with understanding and even perhaps sympathy. She winked.

"Rex," she said loudly and brightly, linking her arm through his as soon as they had dismounted, "I promised our nephew and niece that I would look in on their music lesson if I was back in time from our ride. Do come along with me. You are, after all, their only uncle. Not counting Clayton, of course, who is their uncle by marriage. But Clayton is promised to play billiards with Nathaniel."

"Be sure to praise their efforts," Claude said, grinning. "Will was hinting just yesterday that playing that pianoforte is not a manly occupation. Yet Clarissa insists that it is a gentlemanly accomplishment. Encourage him to obey his mama, will you?"

Lord Rawleigh offered his sister his arm and walked determinedly away with her. Not that he was quite sure he had not merely exchanged the frying pan for the fire. It was Mrs. Catherine Winters who taught the children music, was it not? He winced inwardly. He had no burning desire to encounter her again yet. But it seemed he was about to do just that unless the music lessons were already over.

For a short while last evening he had even contemplated having his bags packed and taking his leave this morning. He could return to Stratton for a few weeks and then proceed to London. But life was never that simple. He had accepted his invitation from Clarissa. It would be ill-mannered in the extreme to leave almost before he had arrived, especially as Eden and Nat might well decide to leave with him.

Eden and Nat! They had teased him mercilessly after his return last evening. They had guessed his purpose in deciding to take the evening air, of course. And yet the briefness of his outing had indicated to them that he had met failure. He would be a long time living this ignominy down, he guessed.

And now it seemed he was about to meet her again. So soon. But perhaps it was as well. There could be no avoiding her altogether if he was to spend another few weeks at Bodley. He might as well get this first meeting over with. Convince her by his manner that last evening had been a thoroughly insignificant incident in his life.

He doubted he had slept an hour last night.

"Poor Rex," his sister said, laughing and squeezing his

arm. "I can see that in some ways it must be wretched to have inherited the title and the property and the fortune and to be single and handsome. Not that it would be any easier for you if you looked like the ugliest of bulldogs, I suppose. You are irresistibly marriageable to anyone related to a single female between the ages of sixteen and thirty. But if Clarissa had any sense, she would realize that this is a quite impossible match. Ellen has acquired no real town bronze yet despite a Season last year. Though she is, of course, a sweet girl. And pretty."

"Thank you for rescuing me," he said dryly. "And I daresay Miss Hudson is silently blessing you too. She looks at me as if she expects that at any moment I am going to pick her up with one hand and devour her. What did we do to deserve Clarissa as a sister-in-law, Daphne? I do believe I must have been mad to have accepted her invitation. I knew what was in store for me."

"But it so lovely to be together in one place, the three of us," she said, squeezing his arm again. "It happens so rarely. We all live so far apart. I miss you and Claude despite a happy marriage. Do you still pine for Horatia Eckert?"

"I never did *pine,*" he said, his jaw tightening. "I fell madly in love during the short interval between the Peninsula and Waterloo, got myself betrothed in indecent haste, and might well have lived to regret it. It was as well that she also fell in love—after I had left for Brussels and with someone else."

"With a practiced seducer and fortune hunter," she said. "He is notorious for preying on young, inexperienced girls, especially when they have wealthy papas. He has even ruined a few innocents. Fortunately he has never yet achieved his goal of winning a wealthy bride. It is amazing to me that someone has not put a bullet between his eyes before now. Don't be too harsh on Horatia, Rex. She was very young and very impressionable. And you were gone to war. And nothing came of it after all."

"Perhaps," he said through his teeth, "because the size of her fortune had been greatly exaggerated. I was well out of it, Daphne, and would appreciate not being reminded of it."

"And therein lies a contradiction," she said. "You would not be reluctant to talk of the matter if it had left you as unscarred as you always claim."

"No man likes being reminded of his humiliation at the hands of a woman," he said, wincing inwardly at his memories of the previous evening. "She did break our engagement, Daphne. That made me look somewhat—well, undesirable."

"Undesirable? You?" She laughed again. "Rex. Have you looked at yourself in a glass lately?"

But he was not inclined to continue the conversation. He could hear music coming through the French windows of the music room. The windows had been opened a little to admit the fresh spring air. Someone was playing scales.

The music lesson was still in progress, then. Damn!

"Ah," his sister said, "good. We are not too late."

The occupants of the room were unaware of their presence for all of a minute or two. All three of them had their backs to the windows. Juliana was sitting on a chair writing in what appeared to be a theory book. William was at the pianoforte, playing scales. Mrs. Winters was standing behind him.

His prim, straitlaced widow who was in reality a tease and a hypocrite. He could not remember a time when he had so miscalculated with a woman. He did not feel very kindly disposed toward her.

He had never known a woman who cultivated simplicity to such a degree. Her hair, smooth and shining golden in the light from the windows, was dressed in its usual knot at the back. She was not wearing a cap today, as she had last evening. Her wool dress was as blue as the sky outside and fell straight from its high waistline. It was completely unadorned. The sleeves were long. He would wager that the neckline was high. But the wool clung enticingly to her figure.

It was a dress that suited her—simple and apparently modest and yet designed to tease one's imagination to the woman's body inside it. He wondered how many of the local gentry she had driven to madness in the past few years. His eyes narrowed on her.

He wondered if she ever looked over her shoulder at herself in a looking glass to observe what interesting things wool did for her derriere. Even more interesting things when she leaned forward over Will's shoulder. Both his indignation and his temperature moved up a notch.

"Very nice, William," she said when the scale stumbled to an end. "You are playing far more fluently now. But do try to remember the correct fingering. You will find that the scale will move far more smoothly if you do not run out of fingers at crucial moments."

"Aunt Daphne!" Juliana exclaimed brightly, noticing them at last and bounding to her feet. "Uncle Rex! Have you come to listen to me?"

"Certainly we have," Daphne said. "And to hear Will too. I promised, did I not? And your uncle insisted on accompanying me."

Viscount Rawleigh was unable to join in the conversation for the moment. Will had jumped to his feet too, with all the exuberance of an escaped convict. And Mrs. Winters had looked sharply behind her and met his eyes.

She did not look away again as he expected her to do. Neither did she blush. She kept her eyes steady on his and her chin came up perhaps half an inch. He almost disgraced himself by allowing *his* eyes to waver from *hers,* but he pursed his lips instead and forced himself to look at her with deliberate nonchalance. She was made of stern stuff, it appeared. And he had to confess that she was refreshing after half a morning in Ellen Hudson's company.

The neckline of her dress *was* high. It somehow accentuated the pleasing shape of her bosom. As, of course, it was meant to do. She was obviously a mistress of the art of teasing. He raised one eyebrow.

"Mrs. Winters," Daphne was saying, "how wretchedly ill-mannered of us to walk in on your lesson like this and disrupt it. We intended to creep in and listen undetected, did we not, Rex?"

"Like thieves in the night," he said, and was reminded of how he had approached her cottage via the postern door last evening.

"Children need to be appreciated even at the expense of some lesson time," Mrs. Winters said, smiling. But she had removed her eyes from his to Daphne and could not thus be accused of smiling at him. "I take it you *did* come to appreciate? William has done particularly well with his scales this morning. It is the first time he has consistently played them through without stopping. I am so glad you were here to witness his triumph."

Will's chest swelled with pride.

"I want to play something," Juliana wailed. "I can play Bach, Aunt Daphne. Listen to me."

"I believe," Daphne said, "it is Will's lesson time, Julie."

"William, being the perfect gentleman," Mrs. Winters said, addressing herself to Daphne, "will be quite pleased to relinquish his place at the pianoforte to Juliana, I am sure." She laughed.

And looked quite dazzlingly beautiful. He had not seen or heard her laugh before, the viscount realized. On the few occasions he had seen her, she had appeared as a woman of quiet dignity. A very quiet and subtle tease. He wondered if the laugh was for his benefit, to tie his stomach in knots. If so, she had failed miserably. His stomach felt only the merest flutter. He was still angry with her for making such an ass of him last night and for failing to present him with a face of blushing confusion this morning.

They had to stand and listen to Juliana murder Bach, racing through the passages she knew well, stumbling her way through the more difficult parts. To say that she had no real aptitude for music was to be extraordinarily kind to her.

But Daphne exclaimed with delight when it was over and clapped her hands. And he found himself bowing his head and assuring her that she showed promise. Mrs. Winters, more truthful, praised the child for her effort and for the hard work she had put into learning some of the more difficult parts.

"And those are the parts you should linger over and enjoy," she said with consummate tact. "What a pity to rush them and have them over too soon. The other parts are coming along very nicely too. All that is needed is more time and practice. Even the most experienced concert pianist always needs that."

She was good with children, he conceded. He found himself wondering how long she had been married to the late Mr. Winters. Had it been just a short time or was she barren? But then perhaps the fault had been in Winters, not in her.

"I do apologize for interrupting," Daphne was saying. "But I can see that you would have a hard time forcing them back to work. Shall we take them up to the nursery for you? On such a lovely day you would doubtless appreciate the chance to leave a little early."

Will looked from one to the other of the women with

hope naked in his eyes. A few seconds later, at a nod from his music teacher, he was scampering from the room.

"Thank you," Catherine Winters said. "I always steal half an hour for myself after the children's lessons are over. It was Mr. Adams who suggested it. Today I will be able to take thirty-five minutes."

Juliana took Daphne's hand and pulled on it, anxious to follow her brother before anyone could decide to resume the music lesson after all. Daphne looked inquiringly at her brother.

"I'll follow you in a short while," he said.

She nodded and disappeared with the child. He was left alone with Catherine Winters, who was standing straight-backed and square-chinned close to the pianoforte, glaring at him.

Now, why the devil had he done that? Why had he not seized the chance to escape when it had presented itself on a golden platter?

She was challenging him. That was what she was doing. She was not behaving with the distressed modesty he would have expected from a virtuous woman who had been presented with a very improper proposal in her own home just the evening before. He clasped his hands behind him and strolled toward her.

"Nurseries are not my favorite place," he said. "I do not enjoy being climbed upon, if you will remember. And the rest of the house is not particularly inviting, either. I suppose you noticed that I am expected to pay court to a young lady I have no wish to court. I shall listen to you play, Mrs. Winters. Continue, if you please, just as if I were not here."

He could almost see indignant and even furious words forming in her mind and lining up for escape from her lips. Her lips twitched but did not part. He watched them. Soft, eminently kissable lips, which were going to dry up from lack of use very soon if all she intended to do with gentlemen was turn them away.

But she did not speak. If the sparks that flashed from her eyes were daggers, he would be stretched dead on the floor already, he decided. But they were not and so he was still standing very much alive as she whirled about and sat on the bench of the pianoforte, composed herself, and began to play.

Stern stuff indeed. He had expected at the very least that she would flounce out through the French windows and take herself off home without her usual self-indulgence on the pianoforte. He had even been considering whether he would offer his services as an escort and realizing that doing so would be unwise.

She had played well in Claude's drawing room two evenings ago. Competently and even with some flair. Viscount Rawleigh pursed his lips now as she started to play Mozart, rushed it rather as Juliana had done, stumbled, played a horrid mischord, and stopped.

"No," she muttered, addressing the ivories. "No, you are not going to do this to me. You are not. You were the one *entirely* in the wrong."

The offending keys—or key, since she used the singular form—made no response. He strolled a little closer, staying in her line of vision. He was almost enjoying himself again.

But it seemed that she meant what she had just said. She started again, playing correctly and flawlessly—and after a minute or two with considerable talent and feeling. She closed her eyes and dipped her head forward as if she was lost in the music. And it was no act, he could see.

He could also see why she had not played like this in the drawing room. She would have shown up the other ladies. She would have drawn everyone's attention and silenced all conversation. It would not have been the sociable thing to do to play like this. Or the wise thing—Clarissa, he suspected, would have been annoyed, to say the least.

She kept her eyes closed and her head bowed after she had finished. Who *was* she? he wondered suddenly. She lived in a small country cottage with no instrument, yet she could play like this? What had happened to bring her down in the world? Who had Mr. Winters been? Why had she moved after his death to a strange place to live among strangers? She was something of a mystery.

"You have talent," he said, realizing as he spoke the understatement of his words.

Her head came up and he knew she was back in Claude's music room—with him. "Thank you," she said coolly.

"I wonder," he said as her finger dusted a key that did not need dusting.

He thought she was going to play again without asking the obvious question. Her fingers spread on the keys. But she looked up at him, her expression impassive. Except that she looked slightly square-jawed again. Ah, she was angry. Good.

"You wonder why I refused such a very flattering and advantageous offer as the one you made me last evening?" she said. "I suppose you are not often rejected, are you? You have so many assets both of person and property. Perhaps, my lord, those of us with far fewer assets like to keep those we do have."

"How dull your life must be, Mrs. Winters," he said. He liked to see her angry.

"It is my life," she said. "If I choose to make it dull, then that is my concern. Not that it *is* dull."

"I daresay," he said, "you draw amusement from being a tease." His eyes moved unhurriedly down her figure, outlined quite alluringly against the wool of her dress as she sat on the bench, leaning slightly forward over the keys.

"Do you enjoy issuing invitations with your eyes and with your body and then slamming the door in the face of those gullible enough to accept them?"

Her jaw hardened and her eyes started to shoot sparks again. "I have issued no invitations to you, my lord," she said. "If it is a curtsy and two smiles to which you refer, one when you passed my house on your arrival and one at this house the evening before last at dinner, then perhaps you need to be reminded that you have an identical twin with whom I am familiar."

Damn! He gazed at her for a few moments, arrested. She had mistaken him for *Claude*? It was such a very credible explanation that he could not understand why he had not thought of it for himself.

"You took me for Claude?" he asked.

"Yes." She looked at him in some triumph. "For a moment. Until I remembered that Mr. Adams is a courteous and an amiable gentleman."

His eyebrows shot up. "By Jove, a hit," he said. "You have a barbed tongue, ma'am. It seems I owe you an apology—again."

"Yes, thank you," she said.

At which moment, just when he was thinking of bowing himself out of her presence and licking at this new humiliation, the door opened and Clarissa sailed in.

Five

ALL THAT HAD been able to sustain her was the determination not to show any discomposure. Not to blush. Not to appear embarrassed. Not to lower her eyes before his. Not to allow him the last word.

None of what had happened had been her fault. She had to believe that. She had *not* issued any invitations and he might have guessed that at first she had mistaken him for Mr. Adams. Surely it was not the first time that had happened.

She had been alarmed when she had started to play the pianoforte only to find that her fingers were all thumbs and that her brain was humming with all sorts of thoughts that had nothing to do with music. With an enormous effort of will, she had pulled herself together and played more to her usual standard. Indeed, she had forgotten all else but the music once she had got started.

She had done rather well after that, she believed. Even so, it was an enormous relief when the door opened. Except that it was Mrs. Adams, and she stopped abruptly and looked sharply from one to the other of them. It was obvious she was not at all pleased with what she saw. Catherine realized the impropriety of being alone with Viscount Rawleigh. But again it was *not her fault*.

"Mrs. Winters." The tone was icy, that of mistress to servant. "I believed you were using this time to teach my children music?" Just as if she were being paid a vast fortune to do so, Catherine thought.

"Their lessons are over, ma'am," she said. She would not add more details to try to exonerate herself from whatever crime she was being suspected of. She always treated Mrs. Adams with courteous respect, but she never groveled. She would never be obsequious as the Reverend Lovering was. But then his living depended upon the patronage of Mr. Adams.

"Daphne and I disturbed them before they were quite finished, Clarissa," Lord Rawleigh said, sounding enormously toplofty and bored. "They played their party pieces for us—at least Juliana did. I am not sure William has a party piece yet or ever will have. Daphne took them up to the nursery. I remained to discuss the weather with Mrs. Winters. But it was very wicked of me. I believe Claude has encouraged her to play for a while after she has finished teaching. I have been interfering with that. My apologies, ma'am." He made Catherine an elegant bow.

Catherine could see the steely glint in Mrs. Adams's eyes, though she smiled graciously and linked arms with her brother-in-law.

"I am sure Mrs. Winters is gratified by your attentions, Rawleigh," she said. "Ellen wishes to see the new puppies out in the stable block. Most of the other men are occupied in the billiard room and I do not like her going out alone among the grooms. You will give her your escort?"

"It would be my pleasure, Clarissa," he said, his lips twitching, but whether with amusement or annoyance Catherine could not tell. But she remembered his saying just a short while ago that he was expected to pay court to someone he did not wish to court.

Good. She was glad he was being forced into doing something he did not want to do. Let him enjoy the feeling of being trapped and helpless.

"Good day, Mrs. Winters." Mrs. Adams nodded at her with gracious dismissal.

"We will leave you to your playing, ma'am," Lord Rawleigh said with another bow—and a look that swept her from the crown of her head to the soles of her shoes—before turning to leave the room.

It was impossible to continue playing. Her hands were shaking and her heart was pounding just as if she had been caught in the performance of some dreadful indiscretion. She deeply resented the fact that he had caused that feeling. And that he had caused Mrs. Adams to become suspicious. He could leave within the next few weeks. She had to live on here.

But as she got to her feet and buttoned her cloak and tied the ribbons of her bonnet beneath her chin, she was not feeling altogether upset. At least she had seen him again after last evening. More than that, she had talked with him. It was over now, that first awkward meeting after the embarrassment and humiliation of the night before. From now on it would be easier.

How dull your life must be, Mrs. Winters.

She could hear his voice again, bored, insolent, telling her what her life was like. Just as if he knew. Or thought he knew. He knew nothing about her. And that was the way it would remain.

She hurried through the French windows and was soon striding down the driveway in the direction of the village and home.

How dared he presume to judge her life.

Did he know anything of her life? Anything of the struggles and pain and heartache? The agony? Just so that she could achieve the peace of the life she had now? And the dullness.

It had been a hard-won dullness.

A dullness that was infinitely preferable to what had gone before.

And yet he had spoken it as an accusation. With contempt. *How dull your life must be, Mrs. Winters.*

She turned her mind determinedly to home—her precious little cottage—and to Toby, who would be bursting with energy after his morning alone. She would take him for a long walk this afternoon. Perhaps it was a dull life she led, but it was hers, as she had told him, and she would continue with it.

And she would be thankful that it was only dull.

HE HAD SPENT what remained of the morning ruining Ellen Hudson's enjoyment of the puppies. Not that he had intended any such thing. He had escorted her to the stable block and had hovered in the background while she bent over the puppies, picking them up and cuddling them and cooing over them one by one. But he had felt her self-consciousness, her conviction that he was bored, that he was laughing at her raptures.

They were terrier pups. It was easy to guess where the fierce Toby had come from.

He had no objection to puppies. He could even concede that they were pretty little things with their fat little bodies and stubby legs and little snub noses. He had even been known on occasion to pick up a pup and cradle it on his palm while smoothing a finger between its ears.

But it had irritated him to know that Ellen would have been far happier and more relaxed without his presence but that courtesy kept him hovering so that he might beat off ardent grooms with lascivious intents and give her an arm to lean on during the return journey to the house.

By the time they all sat down for luncheon, he felt that he had suffered enough for one day as a victim of a determined matchmaker. Clarissa was arranging a walk for the afternoon, the weather being too fine to waste. Fortunately—very fortunately—Claude could not participate since there was a distant tenant he felt obliged to call upon.

Viscount Rawleigh decided that he must accompany his brother.

"We see each other so rarely these days," he explained with a smile to a clearly disappointed Clarissa. "But the bond between us continues to be unusually close. It has something to do with the fact that we are twins, you know."

"That was not quite the wise thing to say to Clarissa," his brother said later when they were riding away from the stables, blessedly alone together. "She has always been a little jealous of you, Rex. When you were in Spain and then in Belgium, I worried so much that I sometimes made myself ill. And it always seemed to come on me just at a time we would learn later something unpleasant really had been happening to you. That time you were carried from the field unconscious from loss of blood, for example. I knew it, I swear, a few months before we received any confirmation by letter. Clarissa still swears it was all nonsense."

"There was my sudden attack of anxiety in the Peninsula," the viscount said. "It works both ways, you see. I thought something must have happened to the baby or to Clarissa. It was only a month or so before Juliana was born, was it not?"

"My hunting accident?" his brother said. "Almost to the day. I was still on crutches when she was born."

It felt good to be alone together again. Their business

with the tenant did not take long, but the ride was a lengthy one. They talked about anything and everything as they always had done. Sometimes they were silent together without the necessity of talk. Lord Rawleigh could feel his brother's contentment with being back home. He could feel, without the need of words, that the extended winter visits away from home were a concession to Clarissa but that she by no means ruled the roost. Somehow they had built a relationship of give-and-take, Claude and his wife.

"You are restless," his brother told him when they were riding back to the house. "Anything you wish to talk about?"

"Restless? Me?" the viscount said in some surprise. "I am enjoying the ride. And the visit."

"Are you going to town for the Season?" his brother asked.

Lord Rawleigh shrugged. "Perhaps," he said. "The lure of town in the late spring is always strong. But perhaps not."

"Miss Eckert will be there," Claude told him. It was a statement, not a question.

"What is that to me?" he asked.

"You were very fond of her," his brother said. "You and I believed equally in love and romance, Rex. If you had not bought your commission and gone off fighting for so many years, you would have married as young as I did. You were badly hurt. Not just your pride or even just your heart. Your dreams and ideals were shattered, and for that I am sorry."

The viscount laughed rather harshly. "I grew up, Claude," he said. "I learned that love and romance are for boys and very young men."

"And yet," Claude said, "I am as old as you, Rex, give or take twenty minutes. Is what I still feel for Clarissa not love, then?"

"I am sure it is," the viscount said, chuckling and trying to lighten the tone of the conversation. "I would hate to get into one of our famous quarrels, Claude. We really have outgrown those, I hope."

"Copley would have none of Miss Eckert once she was free to marry him?" Claude said. "It amazes me that someone has not challenged him before now and blown his brains out. I even feared that you might do it."

"I was busy fighting another battle at the time," Lord Rawleigh said. "Besides, I would not have had the right. Horatia released me from my obligation to her. And Copley *has* fought two duels, you know. He maimed both victims."

"Well," his brother said, "I felt and feel sorry for the girl. I also hated her for what she had done to you. And continues to do."

"She wants me back," the viscount said abruptly. "She has had the effrontery to send two discreet messages via her brother. I suppose life is not easy for her under the circumstances, but the last thing I need or want is to have her sniveling all over me in the middle of some *ton* squeeze or other. I could offer her only more humiliation."

"Ah," Claude said sadly. "There is no chance of a reconciliation, then?"

"Good Lord, no," the viscount said.

"I knew it, of course," his brother said. "But I hoped. Oh, not necessarily for a reconciliation. But for some way out of the impasse you are in. I am afraid of one of two things for you."

Lord Rawleigh looked at him with raised eyebrows.

"I am afraid," Claude said, "that you will marry impulsively someone who cannot make you happy. Ellen, for example. She is a sweet girl, Rex. Truly. I have known her since she was a child. But she needs someone less—forbidding than you."

"Thank you," the viscount said.

His brother chuckled. "You are ten chronological years

older than her," he said, "and about thirty years older in experience."

"You need not fear," Lord Rawleigh told him. "I am not about to marry your sister-in-law, impulsively or otherwise. What is your other fear?"

"That you will not marry at all," Claude said. "That you will merely allow your bitterness and cynicism to grow. It would be a shame. You have a great deal to offer by way of love, even if you do not realize it."

The viscount laughed. "We really have moved in opposite directions in the years since your marriage, Claude," he said. "I no longer fit the image you have of me."

"Ah, but I am bound to your soul," his brother said. "I do not need to be with you or living a similar life to yours to know you, Rex."

The conversation was becoming uncomfortably personal. And one-sided, of course. His brother could probe his private life to his heart's content. But he did not have the same freedom. One could not discuss a brother's marriage even if he was an identical twin. The viscount was glad of a diversion.

They were taking a shortcut across a large meadow. So was someone else. At first it seemed that it was only a little dog, which came streaking toward them, barking furiously and seemingly with a death wish, since the two horses were giants in comparison to its size. But the wise dog did not come too close. It danced about at a safe distance, still barking its challenge.

Toby!

Where was she? Lord Rawleigh looked about and saw her approaching from the direction of a stile at the far side of the meadow. She was not hurrying. He guessed that she would have retreated if her dog had not betrayed her presence.

"Ah, Mrs. Winters's dog," Claude said, "with Mrs.

Winters herself not far behind." He smiled and removed his hat and called out a greeting to her as she came closer.

She was dressed in a simple, rather drab gray cloak with a plain blue bonnet to match the blue dress she had worn that morning. She smiled and curtsied to Claude after she had come closer—she seemed to know unerringly which of them was which. Her dog had called off the attack and sat beside her, tongue lolling, ears cocked to give the illusion of intelligent attention. She greeted Claude just as she had greeted *him* on their arrival at Bodley, the viscount thought wryly. With a sweep of the eyes she included him in the greeting.

The viscount remembered, as she and Claude exchanged brief pleasantries and he looked silently on, that she had given him a blistering set-down this morning and that he had been unable to retaliate because Clarissa had interrupted them. She would have been an interesting mistress, he thought with faint regret. All the interest of their relationship would not have been confined to their bed.

And then she was on her way again, her terrier loping off ahead of her. He touched his hat and inclined his head to her.

"A beauty," he said to Claude. "And she has been in residence here for five years, someone was saying? One wonders about the late Mr. Winters. Was he so good that he cannot be replaced? Or was he so bad that he *will* not be replaced?"

"I hope you will exercise the proper care in seeing that she is not compromised," his brother said.

What the devil?

"I suppose Clarissa was convinced that if she had not entered the music room at the precise moment she did," he said irritably, "I would have had Mrs. Winters stretched back over the pianoforte with her skirts hoisted and her body mounted? I concede that the sight would have been a trifle embarrassing for her."

"You need not be vulgar," his twin said.

"Perhaps you should say that to your wife," Lord Rawleigh said.

"Have a care, Rex." It seemed that perhaps one of their quarrels was brewing after all. "It was not wise to be alone with her even in broad daylight. But it is not only to this morning I refer. Did you visit Mrs. Winters last evening?"

Lord Rawleigh shot him a look of pure shock. Denial sprang to his lips. But there was no point in lying to one's twin. His nostrils flared. "How the devil did you know that?" he asked. "Has she lodged a complaint with the lord of the manor?"

"I have eyes in my head," his brother said, "and this link to your mind. Your burning wish to go walking after dark on a chilly evening in early spring did not quite ring true. I'll not have it, Rex."

"You'll— What the devil? *What* will you not have?" His heart was pounding with rage.

"Village life, in case you had forgotten," his brother said calmly—their quarrels had always been made more infuriating by the fact that the rage of one almost invariably aroused the opposite reaction in the other, "is impossible to live quite privately. I will not have her compromised. She is a lady, Rex. A mysterious lady, granted. She arrived here five years ago from goodness knows where and has proceeded to live a quiet and exemplary existence here ever since. No one knows anything of her background or anything of her late husband—including her feelings for him—beyond the fact that he was a Mr. Winters. But everything about her has proclaimed her the lady. I will not have her compromised."

"The devil," the viscount said, his voice trembling with

anger. "At an educated guess, Claude, I would say she has been of age for several years. And therefore free to make her own decisions."

"And at another guess," Claude said, "I would say you were rejected last night, Rex. You returned too early to have been successful. Mrs. Winters *is* a lady. And not at all in desperate circumstances. Her husband must have left her with a competence. And she has not lacked for suitors. It seems to be general knowledge that she has had and rejected at least two quite respectable offers—of *marriage*—since her arrival here."

"If she is such a lady," the viscount said, "and if you are so certain she rejected me, then why the devil are you warning me off, Claude? You want her for yourself?"

"If you want to get down from your horse," his brother said with ominous calm, "I will gladly knock your head from your shoulders here and now, Rex."

"No need," the viscount said curtly. "For that at least I am willing to apologize. It was a stupid thing to say to you of all people. Yes, she rejected me. Out of hand. I even thought her dog was going to attack me, but he seemed to think better of it. So all this lord-of-the-manor stuff was quite unnecessary."

"Except," Claude said, "that I have felt your distraction, Rex. Ever since we returned to Bodley. And there was your unwise presence alone with her in the music room this morning and Clarissa's consequent suspicion. I hope that in your arrogance you have not refused to take no for an answer. I warn you that if you compromise her, you will have made yourself a permanent enemy in me."

"That is supposed to have me trembling in my boots?" Lord Rawleigh asked, looking angrily and haughtily at his brother—at his conscience.

"Yes," Claude said. "Having the other half of yourself as

your enemy will not be comfortable, Rex. Leave her alone. Surely you are not so depraved that celibacy for a few weeks will kill you. You have Eden and Nat and me for company and the ladies for social diversion. And Daphne. It seems wonderful enough to me for the three of us to be together for a few weeks."

"I will behave myself," Lord Rawleigh promised, chuckling despite himself. "But you must admit she is deuced pretty, Claude. Not my type, of course, apart from the physical allure. She is a virtuous woman. I gather she spends her time doing good works—visiting the sick and elderly, teaching the children, and a thousand and one other things, all without asking for any reward. A bloody saint, in other words. Not my type at all."

"Good," his brother said decisively, though he was unable to suppress an answering chuckle. "Now perhaps we should change the subject?"

"She is good with children," the viscount said. "Why the devil did Winters not give her some of her own, do you suppose? Do you think he might have been a doddering old fool? Or an impotent rake? The least a man can do when he takes a woman to wife is give her a child of her own if she dotes on them. If he were alive and in front of me right now, I would be sore put to it not to plant him a facer."

Mr. Adams looked at his twin in some amazement and some alarm. Perhaps he was wise to hold his peace and to change the subject as he had suggested a few moments before. But his brother showed no particular interest in any of the topics that were introduced and soon they lapsed into silence.

She had taken him for Claude, the viscount was thinking. The smiles had been intended for Claude. Knowing that now, he could see that there had been nothing particularly flirtatious about the smiles. He felt a fool. An utter fool.

And quite out of charity with Catherine Winters.

Good Lord, he must be losing his touch. He had suffered nothing but frustration and humiliation at her hands. He had maneuvered a private visit with her last evening, believing that he did so in great secrecy and with admirable discretion. And yet Nat and Eden had been meeting him on his return with ribald comments on the speed with which he had concluded his business. And Claude had known where he went. And this morning Clarissa had drawn her own conclusions from the fact that he had lingered in the music room after Daphne and the children had left it.

And yet he did not even have the satisfaction of having enjoyed some success.

The damned country. One's life was no longer one's own once one ventured beyond the confines of town.

One thing was certain. Mrs. Catherine Winters might rest assured that her virtue was safe from him forever after. He was going to stay as far away from her as possible for the remainder of his stay at Bodley.

Six

THE SUN WAS shining persistently through the curtains onto her bed. It was early, she knew, and chilly beyond the bedcovers. But it was going to be as lovely a day as yesterday had been. And she was clearly going to have no more sleep. She stretched and then dived her arms back beneath the covers. Not that she had slept particularly well at all during the last few nights. She decided to get up and take an early walk with Toby. Some children were coming later in the morning for a reading lesson.

Toby appeared in her bedchamber as she was washing and dressing. He was wagging his tail slowly.

"You may stand there looking eager," she told him. "I am not even going to whisper the W-word until I am opening the door to leave or I will have you prancing all about me so that I cannot move without tripping over you. Give me a moment."

But Toby, it seemed, knew the W-letter quite as well as he knew the *walk* word. His tail became a madly waving pendulum, he whined with excitement, and then he began the anticipated prancing, dancing in circles all about Catherine and taking little rushing steps in the direction of the stairs as if to hurry her along.

She laughed.

A few weeks, she thought as she strode along the village street a short while later and smiled and waved to Mr. Hardwick, the innkeeper, who was personally sweeping the pavement before his doors. The house party could not possibly last beyond a few weeks at the longest, and one of those weeks was just about over. They were bound to return to town for the Season, Viscount Rawleigh and his friends. They were all fashionable gentlemen, after all, and there was not much to keep them here. It was true that Mrs. Adams was trying to push a match between the viscount and Miss Hudson, but there really was not much for the other two gentlemen. There was Miss Lipton, that was all.

No, there was nothing to keep them. She knew the viscount was not interested in Miss Hudson.

If she could hold out for another few weeks—and really she had no choice in the matter, did she?—then everything would return to normal and she would be at peace again. She would not have to fear every time she set foot over her doorstep that she was going to run into him.

"No, not that way, Toby," she called as her dog turned confidently onto the driveway to Bodley. That was the route she usually took, branching off the driveway through the trees before she came in sight of the house. There was no question of trespassing. Mr. Adams liked to have the villagers make free with his park. There was a tacit understanding, of course, that they would not stroll too close to the house and thus encroach upon the privacy of the family. But this morning she strode on along the country lane that was bordered on one side by the moss-covered wall of the park.

She had directed all her energies during the past five

years into making a new and meaningful life for herself. It had not been easy. Her life before had been so different. . . . She had quelled all needs in herself beyond the need to live on. She had not even particularly wanted to do that at the beginning.

Other needs had not been persistent through the five years. She had had company, occupation, a home that she loved. For the past year she had had Toby. She had not been tempted at all by the two offers of marriage she had received, one three years ago, the other just last year, though she had respected both gentlemen and either would have been good to her. She had felt no desire for marriage. No *need* for it.

And yet now, suddenly, she felt needs she had not felt burdened with since she was a girl. Except that they were entirely different, of course. As a girl, she had known nothing about the desires of the flesh. She had felt only the need for romance, for the admiration of a handsome gentleman, for marriage. She had been so innocent. Dangerously innocent.

The cravings she had felt for the last few days alarmed her. They were purely physical. Simply put, they were the cravings for a man. For a man's body touching hers and caressing hers. For a man's body inside hers. For an end to the emptiness and the loneliness.

The new cravings alarmed her because she had no good memories of intimacy. Only the opposite. She would never have expected to want it ever again.

And she was not lonely. Or if she was, then loneliness was the price one paid for independence and self-respect and peace of mind. It was a small price to pay. And it was not loneliness that she felt but aloneness. There was a difference. The aloneness could be alleviated by visits to her numerous friends and neighbors.

But she was afraid that she would not be able to continue to deceive herself. She was afraid that she was about to realize her own loneliness. She was realizing it already.

And all because of one arrogant, insolent man. A man who had sat in her kitchen two evenings ago suggesting that she become his mistress. A man who had tempted her despite her outrage. A man who had almost compromised her yesterday and who, before being taken away by Mrs. Adams, had raked her with his eyes, mentally removing clothes as he did so.

A man she wanted.

The admission horrified her.

And then Toby, who had been loping across a nearby field, exploring, came dashing back toward the lane, barking exuberantly. There were three horsemen approaching from a distance. This early in the morning? Her heart sank. Was there no safe time during which to enjoy a solitary walk?

From a distance, one of the riders might have been Mr. Adams. But she knew it was not he. For one thing, he was riding with Mr. Gascoigne and Lord Pelham. There was no chance of changing direction so that she would not meet them. There was a wall on one side of her, an open field on the other. Besides, just like yesterday, Toby was streaking along the lane to meet them, David facing three Goliaths with foolhardy bravado.

Mr. Gascoigne had to work to control his nervous horse. He grinned while he did so. Lord Pelham swept off his hat and inclined his head to Catherine. Lord Rawleigh stooped down from his saddle and swept up her terrier, who favored him with one more indignant and surprised yip and then settled, panting and cock-eared and floppy-tongued, across the horse in front of the viscount. He had capitulated to the enemy that easily.

"Mrs. Winters," Lord Pelham said, "you complete the

beauty of the morning. I did not know there was a lady alive who rose this early."

"Good morning, my lord," she said, half curtsying to him. He had lovely white teeth, she noticed, and very blue eyes. He was quite as handsome as the viscount and certainly more charming. Why was it that she could look at him and speak with him without feeling even one irregular skip of the heartbeat? "This is the very best part of the day."

"I shall have to trade my horse," Mr. Gascoigne said, chuckling as he swept off his hat and made his bow to her. "I shall never live down the ignominy of having had him take fright at a mere dog. But then if I were a dog and you were my owner, ma'am, I would bark as fiercely in your defense too."

"Good morning, sir," she said, laughing. "I do assure you his bark is altogether worse than his bite." Another handsome gentleman, with laughing eyes and easy charm. No flutters of the heart.

She turned her head before the situation could become awkward—as it had outside her cottage two days ago. "Good morning, my lord," she said to Lord Rawleigh, who was scratching an ecstatic Toby behind the ears. A third handsome gentleman, really no more so than the other two. Her stomach tied itself in knots.

"Ma'am." He held her eyes as he inclined his head.

The situation was awkward after all. She should have been able to smile and walk on. But Toby was still up on the viscount's horse, looking as if he would be happy to stay there for the rest of the morning.

"I suppose," Mr. Gascoigne said, "we cannot pretend that we are going your way, Mrs. Winters?"

She smiled at him.

"We cannot pretend we are going her way, Nat," Lord Pelham said. "Alas. She would acquire stiff neck muscles from looking up at three horsemen while we conversed. And her dog might well frighten your horse into spasms." He chuckled.

Mr. Gascoigne laughed with him. "One of us could offer to let her ride while we walked," he said. "That would be marvelous gallantry."

They were teasing her, quite lightly, quite harmlessly. Viscount Rawleigh merely gazed down at her, his hand absently smoothing over Toby.

"I came out for a walk and exercise, gentlemen," she said. "And so did Toby." She glanced up pointedly at him and noticed how long-fingered and strong and masculine the viscount's hand looked against her dog's back.

He leaned down without a word and set Toby back on the road. Her dog wagged his tail and then trotted on ahead to resume his walk.

"Good day to you, ma'am," Lord Rawleigh said. "We will not keep you." He had not smiled or joined in the teasing.

She walked on, listening to the sound of their horses grow fainter behind her.

Just a few weeks, she thought. That was all. And then life would get back to normal again. Or so she fervently hoped.

But she knew it would not be as easy as that.

"CHARMING," MR. GASCOIGNE said. "Utterly charming. There is something to be said for unfashionable country garb, is there not? And quiet country surroundings?"

"This is not good," Lord Pelham said. "Three of us salivating over the same female. Unfashionable country garb looks charming only on someone who would look lovely even without it, Nat. Especially without it, by God. But this place is alarmingly womanless, Rex—no offense to Claude's sister-in-law."

"I thought that was the idea," the viscount said. "We are all to a certain extent escaping from entanglements with females, are we not? Eden from his married lady, Nat from his unmarried one, me from—well, from a former fiancée. Perhaps it will do us good to be without female companionship for a while. Good for the soul and all that."

"She fancies you, Rex," Lord Pelham said. "She could hardly coax her eyes to turn in your direction, whereas she grinned and chatted with Nat and me as if we were her brothers. Now, that I resent. You did not crack a smile. The question is—do you want her or not? I would hate to see the only looker in this part of the world go to waste because Nat and I are too polite to step in on your territory."

The viscount snorted.

"I believe," Mr. Gascoigne said, "Rex must have had his face slapped the evening before last. Figuratively speaking even if not literally. You *did* pursue her during the evening of the walk, I presume? Were you quite gauche, Rex? Did you offer her carte blanche without even a day or two for maneuvering or courtship? We will have to give you some lessons in seduction, old chap. One does not step up to a virtuous country widow, tap her on the shoulder, and ask her if she would care to slip between the sheets with one. Is that what you did?"

"Go to hell," Lord Rawleigh said.

"That is what he did, Ede," Mr. Gascoigne said.

"It is no wonder he did not smile at her this morning and she could scarce look at him," Lord Pelham said. "And is this our friend, the master seducer of Spanish beauties all those years we were in the Peninsula, Nat? It makes one shudder, does it not, to realize how fast a man can backslide from lack of practice."

"Perhaps," Mr. Gascoigne said, "I will try my hand at her

and see if I have any better results. Hard luck, Rex, old boy, but you seem to have lost your chance."

They were both grinning like hyenas and having a grand old time at his expense, Lord Rawleigh knew. He knew equally that if he wanted the teasing to stop, he must join in and give as good as he was getting. He could not do it. He growled instead.

"Hands off, Nat," he said.

Mr. Gascoigne shot both hands into the air as if someone had just dug a pistol against his spine.

"She is a lady," the viscount said. "She is not someone we take turns at seducing."

"Good Lord," Mr. Gascoigne said, "I do believe he is smitten, Ede."

"I do believe you are right, Nat," Lord Pelham said. "Interesting. Very interesting. And the death knell for your hopes and mine."

Very often the three of them—and Ken too when he was with them—could hold lengthy and intelligent conversations on topics of importance. That was why they were friends. Often too they could exchange light banter and keep one another's spirits up. That ability had been invaluable during the long years they had spent in Portugal and Spain and again in Belgium. They could be serious together and lighthearted together. They could fight wars together and stare death in the face together.

But sometimes, just sometimes, one of them could be out of tune with the others. Sometimes one of them could tell the others to go to hell and mean it.

She was not a topic of light banter.

And yet if he could not pick up the mood of the conversation, they would never leave him alone. Or her.

They had turned onto the driveway on their way back to the stables and the house. Probably there would be a few others up by now and ready for breakfast. Clarissa had planned an excursion for the afternoon to Pinewood Castle five miles distant, weather permitting. Clearly weather was going to permit. He was going to be expected to escort Ellen Hudson. Probably something would have been arranged for this morning also to somehow throw them together.

He drew his horse to a halt suddenly. "You two ride on," he said, making his tone deliberately light. "I would hate to be a distraction to the two of you when you are so deep in mourning."

They both looked at him and at each other in some surprise and the teasing light died from their eyes. One thing they had learned over the years of their friendship was sensitivity to one another's moods. They might not realize immediately that one of the others was not sharing the mood of the group, but as soon as they did, they were immediately sympathetic.

"And you need to be alone," Nat said. "Fair enough, Rex."

"We will see you back at the house," Eden said.

Not a word about believing he was going to ride back to find Catherine Winters. Not a suggestion of a teasing gleam in their eyes. He could not quite understand why he could not himself see the fun of the situation. After all, he had been rejected before. They all had. And they had all usually been able to laugh at their own expense as well as at one another. None of them was infallibly irresistible to the fair sex, after all.

He wheeled his horse without a word and made his way back down the drive. He might have pretended to have an errand in the village, but it was rather early for that. Besides, they would have known that he lied. He turned away from the village when he reached the bottom of the drive and rode back along the lane they had ridden just a few minutes before. He did not hurry. He hoped that enough time had elapsed that she would be gone without a trace. Not that there were many byways along which she might have been lost to sight. And he knew that her dog would have slowed her down since she did not keep him on a leash and he liked to wander and explore as they walked.

He hoped that he would not be able to catch up to her. Even so, he was disappointed when it seemed that she had indeed disappeared from sight. After riding for a few minutes, he could see no sign of her and yet he could see for some distance ahead. He soon realized where she must have gone, though. One of the side gates into the park suddenly came into view. It was closed, but then she would have shut it after her to keep the deer inside. He tried the gate. It opened easily. It was obviously in frequent use. He maneuvered his horse around it and went inside.

There were ancient trees along this border of the park. It had been a favorite childhood playground. Even the smell of it was familiar and the shade and the silence. He dismounted and led his horse by the reins. Perhaps she had not come this way after all. But even if she had not, he would continue on his way and return home by this route. He had always liked trees. For some reason they could always be relied upon to bring a sense of peace.

And then he heard the snapping of twigs and the little brown-and-white terrier came loping along and set its front paws up against his legs. It wagged its tail. He must have made a friend, the viscount thought wryly. It did not even bark.

"Get down, sir," he instructed the dog. "I do not appreciate having paw marks either on my boots or on my pantaloons."

The dog licked at his hand. He had noticed before that the

terrier would never win any prizes for obedience. She had clearly spoiled it.

"Toby, where are you?" he heard her call. "Toby?"

And then, while he was in the process of taking two paws in his hands and setting them on the ground, she came into sight. She stopped and looked at him, and he looked back. This had been foolishness, he thought. Why had he done it? She was a virtuous woman and he wanted nothing to do with virtuous women. Not in a one-on-one situation, anyway.

And what had happened to yesterday afternoon's resolve?

She looked beyond him, as if expecting to see Nat and Eden, and then back. She said nothing.

"I, after all, am on my brother's land," he said. "What is your excuse?"

Her chin came up. "Mr. Adams has opened the park to the people from the village," she said. "But I am on my way back to the gate. It is time we went home."

"Walk back through the trees," he said. "You can get from here all the way to the postern door and avoid the public path and the village. It is a much more pleasant route. I will show you the way."

"I know it, thank you," she said.

He should let it go at that. Walking back through the trees with her, leading his horse and waiting for her dog to explore every tree, would take at least half an hour. Quite alone with her among the trees. Claude would have his head.

He smiled at her. "Then let me accompany you?" he asked. "You are quite safe with me. I do not indulge in seductions this early in the morning."

She blushed and he held her eyes with his, still smiling, pulling gently on that invisible thread between them.

"I can hardly forbid you," she said, "when I am the trespasser and you are the guest."

But she had not said any more about going back through the gate onto the road, he noticed.

They walked side by side, not touching. Yet he felt quite breathlessly aware of her.

"The primroses are all in bloom," he said. "The daffodils will be out soon. Is spring your favorite time of the year, as it is mine?"

"Yes," she said. "New birth. New hope. The promise of summertime ahead. Yes, it is my favorite time of year, even though my garden is not as full of color as it will be later."

New hope. He wondered what her hopes were, what her dreams were. Did she have any of either? Or did she live such a placid and contented existence that she needed nothing else?

"New hope," he said. "What do you hope for? Anything in particular?"

She was gazing ahead, he saw when he glanced down at her. Her eyes looked luminous and he knew the answer to one of his silent questions. There was wistfulness in her gaze, longing.

"Contentment," she said. "Peace."

"And do you have neither that you must hope for them?" he asked.

"I have both" She glanced quickly up at him. "I want to keep them. They are fragile, you know. As fragile as happily-ever-afters. They are no absolute state that one attains and then keeps forever and ever. I wish they were."

He had disturbed her peace. There was no accusation in her voice, but he knew it was so. And happily-ever-afters? Had she discovered with the death of a husband that there was no such thing? As he had discovered it with the fickleness of a betrothed?

"And you?" She looked up at him more steadily. "What are your hopes?"

He shrugged. What did he hope for? What did he dream of? Nothing? It was a disturbing thought but perhaps a true one. Only when one hoped for nothing and dreamed of nothing could one keep control of one's own life. Dreams usually involved other people and other people could never be depended upon not to let one down, not to hurt one.

"I do not dabble in dreams," he said. "I live and enjoy each day as it comes. In dreaming of the future one is wasting the present."

"A common belief." She smiled. "But one impossible to live up to, I believe. I think we all dream. How else can life be made bearable at times?"

"Has life sometimes been unbearable to you, then?" he asked. He wondered if her life really was contented. She had been living here for five years. She had been widowed for at least that long. How old was she? In her mid-twenties at a guess. From the age of twenty or so, then, she had lived alone. Was it really possible that she was contented with such an existence? Of course, it was possible that her marriage had been insupportable to her and the freedom of widowhood seemed a paradise in contrast.

"Life is unbearable to all of us at times," she said. "No one is fortunate enough to escape all of life's darkness, I believe."

They had reached the river, which flowed through the wood and on out of the park to skirt behind the village. It gurgled downhill at this particular point, over stones and under an arched stone bridge with balustrades either side that they had used to balance on as children, arms outstretched.

"If ever you want peace," he said, coming to a stop in the middle of the bridge and resting his arms along the top of the wall, "this is the place. There is nothing as soothing as the sight and sound of flowing water, especially when the light falling on it is filtered through the branches of trees." He let his horse wander to the other side to graze on the grass of the bank.

She stopped beside him and looked down into the water. Her dog ran on ahead.

"I have spent many idle minutes standing just here," she said. Perhaps she did not realize that the tone of wistfulness in her voice said more than her actual words expressed. It told him that she agreed with him and that there had been many occasions when she had needed to seek out peace.

He looked down at her, slim and golden and beautiful beside him. Her fingertips, in kid gloves, were resting on the edge of the balustrade. If only his calculations at the start had been correct, he thought, he would have known her quite intimately by now. He would know what that slender, shapely body felt like beneath his hands and against his own body. He would know how soft and warm and welcoming she was in her depths. He would know if she loved with cool competence or with hot passion. He would know if the first could be converted to the second.

He would wager that it could.

He wondered if once or twice would have satisfied him. Would he be hot for her still, as he was now? Or would he—as he usually was with women—be satisfied once he had known all there was to know? Would he have lost interest and not even have pursued her this morning for this unwise walk through the woods with her?

He could not know. He probably would never know.

He did not realize that he had been standing staring silently down at her until she looked up at him, awareness in her face and in her eyes.

He reached for something to say to her but could think of

nothing. She opened her mouth as if to say something, but closed it again and looked back into the water. He wondered afterward why he did not merely straighten up and suggest that they continue on their way. He wondered why she did not think of the same way of defusing the tension of the moment.

But neither of them thought of it.

He leaned sideways and down, turning his head and finding her mouth with his own. He parted his lips in order to taste her. Her lips trembled quite noticeably before returning the pressure of his. He did not touch her anywhere else. Neither of them turned.

The kiss did not last long, but far longer than it ought to have lasted. He looked back into the water. She presumably did the same thing. He was shaken. He did not know quite where this was headed and he liked to be in control of his affairs. She had refused to be his mistress. And he had been given the firm impression that she had meant it. Kisses for the sake of kisses were pointless especially when they set one on fire. But there was nowhere else for them to lead. He certainly was not interested in any permanent sort of relationship.

"For the sake of my self-esteem," he said, "you must admit that it was not because you did not want to, was it?"

There was a lengthy silence. He did not think she was going to answer. Perhaps she had not understood his question. But she did answer eventually. "No, it was not because of that," she said.

It would have been easier if she had not admitted it. Damnation! What did she want out of life? Only contentment and peace? Not pleasure? Though there was another possibility, of course.

"I suppose," he said, his voice harsher than he had intended it to be, "you want marriage again."

"No," she said quickly. "No, never that. Not again. Why would any woman willingly make herself the property of a man and suffer all the humiliation of submerging her character and her very identity in his? No, I am not trying to tease you into making me an honorable offer, my lord. Or any other type of offer either. I meant my refusal the other evening, and if you believe me to be a tease and take that kiss as evidence, then I apologize. It was not meant to tease. It was not meant to happen at all. I am going home now. Alone, please. I will not get lost, I assure you. Toby!" she yelled.

She hurried across the bridge and onward as soon as her terrier made its appearance from among the trees to pant eagerly at her. He did not try to accompany her. He stayed where he was, his elbows on the balustrade, staring down into the water.

He might have stood there for a long time if the crackling of undergrowth had not brought his head up again. He thought she was returning for something. But it was merely one of Claude's gardeners or gamekeepers, who looked at him a little curiously, pulled on his forelock, and continued on his way.

It was a good thing, Lord Rawleigh thought, that the man had not happened by a few minutes sooner.

Seven

THE VILLAGERS OF Bodley-on-the-Water were finding that their lives had brightened considerably. The weather had been unseasonably sunny and warm for a long stretch of days so that the trees were noticeably green and the early-spring flowers were all in bloom with the promise of more to come as green shoots appeared in the gardens even of those not reputed to be blessed with green thumbs. A few fluffy white lambs were frisking on spindly legs in a few fields alongside their shaggier and yellower mothers.

And of course Mr. and Mrs. Adams were back home with their houseguests, and one or more of them appeared in the village or at least passed through it almost every day. A few of the villagers were even blessed with invitations to the house. The rector and his wife were invited several times, of course. They were both of the gentry class—Mrs. Lovering was second cousin to a baron. Mrs. Winters was invited once. Miss Downes was invited to tea with the ladies one afternoon at the request of Lady Baird, who remembered her from a long time ago. Unfortunately, Mrs. Downes was too frail to leave her home in order to accompany her daughter.

But Miss Downes had reported that Lady Baird was to call one afternoon.

There was to be a dinner and ball at the house one evening. Everyone from miles around with any claim to gentility would be invited to that one, of course. There was to be a proper orchestra instead of just the pianoforte that was played at the occasional village assembly in an upper room at the inn. The greenhouses behind Bodley House were to be ransacked for floral arrangements for the dining room and ballroom.

None of the plans were a secret just as none of the daily activities of the family and guests were. The servants at Bodley were not unusually loose-tongued, but most of them were local people with families either in the village or on the farms about it. And one of the footmen and a few of the gardeners frequented the tavern during their free hours. Mrs. Croft, the housekeeper, was a friend of Mrs. Lovering. News concerning people in whom everyone had an insatiable interest could not be kept entirely under wraps. And nothing was secret, of course.

Unfortunately, the line between news and gossip has ever been a fine one.

Bert Weller, into his fourth mug of ale at the tavern one evening, reported seeing Mrs. Winters walking her dog among the trees inside the walls of Bodley very early that morning. There was nothing so strange about that. Mrs. Winters was ever an early riser. She was often out at the first cockcrow. And she frequently walked in the park, as many of them did. Mr. Adams had informed them they might, though they were not sure that Mrs. Adams approved of their taking such liberties.

The only strange thing—and perhaps it was not strange at all, Bert conceded—was that Viscount Rawleigh had been in the woods too, not very far away, standing on the old bridge, staring down into the water while his horse grazed nearby. Indeed, it had looked for all the world as if Mrs. Winters was coming from the direction of the bridge.

Perhaps they had met and exchanged morning greetings, someone suggested.

Perhaps they had met and exchanged *more* than morning greetings, Percy Lambton suggested, with a leer and a glance all about him for approval.

But he met none. It was one thing to comment on hard fact and even to speculate a little. It was quite another to instigate malicious rumor. His lordship was their Mr. Adams's brother—his *twin* brother—and Mrs. Winters was a respectable citizen of their own village, even if no one knew where she came from or what her life had been like before she came to live at Bodley-on-the-Water.

Perhaps they had met by accident and walked together. They would have been presented to each other at the house when Mrs. Winters was invited there, after all.

They would make rather a handsome couple, someone observed.

Ah, but he was a *viscount,* others remembered. There was too large a social gap even though she was almost without doubt a lady.

"Or a former lady's maid who has learned to ape her betters," Percy Lambton suggested.

The conversation drifted to other matters as Mrs. Hardwick refilled mugs.

But somehow word spread. And it aroused interest in its hearers, though very little malice. It aroused enough interest that they watched with more than usual attention for any sign of an attachment between so great a personage as Viscount Rawleigh and their own Mrs. Winters. There were three incidents before the night of the dinner and ball. Three very minor incidents, it was true, but then to people who lived in such isolation from centers of activity and gossip, even small incidents could assume a significance beyond the facts.

EVERYONE FROM BODLEY House attended church on Sunday morning. Catherine watched in some amusement from her pew as Mrs. Adams, at her regal best, led the procession down the aisle to the padded pew at the front, where she always sat, though not all of them could fit on that favored seat, of course. Most of them had to sit on bare polished wood behind her.

The Reverend and Mrs. Lovering had been invited to the house to dinner again last evening. She, Catherine, had not. It had been a significant omission, considering the fact that Mrs. Adams was one lady short in her guests. Clearly she was punishing Catherine for having had the temerity to be in the music room alone with Viscount Rawleigh. Not that it had been particularly improper, but Mrs. Adams wanted him to have eyes only for her sister for the coming weeks. Any other single women between the ages of eighteen and forty must be seen as a threat.

Juliana sidled into the pew beside Catherine, as she sometimes did, and smiled up at her in conspiratorial fashion. Mrs. Adams did not appear to miss her. She probably assumed that her daughter was with one of the guests. Catherine winked back.

She had had an invitation to the dinner and ball to be held next Friday, but that was hardly surprising either. It was not easy in the country to assemble enough guests to enable one to call a gathering a ball. Every last body was important to the success of the occasion.

She was not sorry to be in Mrs. Adams's bad books. She had been quite happy during the past three days not to set eyes on Viscount Rawleigh. She stole a look at him now, seated on the padded pew beside Miss Hudson and two places from his brother. Goodness, but they looked alike. It seemed amazing that such handsome dark looks could be duplicated.

That kiss! It had been a mere meeting of lips. Nothing else. There had been no more to it than that. But it had left her seared, devastated. It had haunted her for three days and woven itself into all her dreams at night.

It was not so much the fact that he had stolen it as the fact that he had not. She had known it was coming. She would have had to be an imbecile not to know. The air had been charged there on the bridge. She could have broken the tension. She could have said something. She could have moved. She could have continued with her walk. She had done nothing.

It was he who had kissed her. It was he who had moved his mouth to hers—and his lips had been parted. Her own role had been quite passive, though she feared that once his mouth was on hers, she had pushed her lips back against his. She had tried to persuade herself that he was entirely to blame, that it really had been a stolen kiss—after he had assured her that he did not seduce women early in the morning.

But it had not been a stolen kiss. It had been something shared. She was at least equally responsible for it. She had not avoided it because—well, because she had wanted it. She had been curious. Oh, no, that was nonsense. She had been hungry. Simply that.

But how could she cling now to the righteous indignation with which she had greeted his visit to her cottage and his conversation in the music room? She was a hypocrite. But she wanted nothing more to do with him. She had thought herself past all possibility of such foolishness.

Oh, the eternal attraction of the rake, she thought with an

inward sigh, looking down determinedly at her prayer book and bending an ear to the whispered confidences of Juliana. She had ridden up with her uncle Rex yesterday and he had *galloped* his horse when she had begged him to and then her mama had scolded him and told him she had been ready to have the vapors and Papa had laughed and told her that Uncle Rex had been the best horseman in the British cavalry and then Mr. Gascoigne . . .

But then the service began and Juliana had to be shushed—with a smile and a wink.

It had been Catherine's intention to slip out of church just as soon as the service was at an end. She had no wish to come face-to-face with any of the party from Bodley House. But in the event it did not happen that way. Juliana had another story that she was burning to tell. She gave an excited account of the afternoon she had spent at Pinewood Castle, where Lord Pelham had taken her up onto the battlements and she had been frightened and Uncle Rex had taken her down to the dungeon and she had been frightened, though it was not really a dungeon because there was a barred gateway onto the river and Uncle Rex had said that only romantics believed it was a dungeon. In reality it had probably been a storehouse for supplies delivered by water.

By the time the story came to an end everyone was outside and everyone had had a good look at her in passing, since Juliana was seated and prattling beside her. So much for disappearing without being seen, she thought wryly.

Juliana darted out ahead of her and even then Catherine hoped to be able to slip away unnoticed. But it seemed that the whole congregation was gathered on the church path or on the grass at the edges of the churchyard. And the Reverend Lovering, stationed at the top of the steps, kept her hand in his after shaking it and commended her on the arrangements of crocuses and primroses she had set at the altar.

"We must be thankful for the blessing of flowers, even the least splendid blooms of the early spring, with which to adorn our humble church for the eyes of our illustrious guests," he said. "I take it as a decided mark of respect for the cloth, Mrs. Winters, being too humble to believe that there is anything personal in the matter, that all Mr. Adams's guests, including Viscount Rawleigh, have seen fit to worship with us this morning."

"Yes, indeed," Catherine murmured.

But then Lady Baird came to greet her, bringing her husband and Mrs. Lipton with her. And somehow Lord Rawleigh was there too, bowing slightly to her and fixing his eyes on her. She feared—she very much feared—that she was blushing. She tried desperately not to think about their last meeting.

That kiss!

She talked brightly to Lady Baird, Sir Clayton, and Mrs. Lipton. And took her leave of them as soon as she politely could.

"Mrs. Winters," a haughty and rather bored voice said as she turned away, "I shall escort you home, ma'am, if I may."

Almost the full length of the village street. There was the bridge and then Mrs. Downes's house, then the rectory and the church, and then the whole village before the thatched cottage at the opposite end. And the whole village and half the countryside and all the family and guests from Bodley House were still assembled in the churchyard and on the path.

It was nothing very remarkable, of course. They were going to be in full sight of everyone for every step of the way. She had been escorted home from church before now.

If almost any other man had suggested the same thing, she would not have felt the dreadful embarrassment and self-consciousness she felt now. But the one thing she could not do was to follow instinct and assure him that there was no need. That would invite comment.

"Thank you," she said, walking down the path and out onto the street ahead of him. She willed him at least not to offer his arm. He did not. Why on earth was he doing this? Could he not realize that she wanted nothing further to do with him? But why would he realize any such thing? She had permitted him to kiss her during their last encounter. She felt dreadfully mortified, and she felt that every eye of every member of this morning's congregation must be on their backs and that everyone must know that they had met alone in the woods three mornings ago and that he had kissed her.

Pray God, she thought for surely the hundredth time, that Bert Weller had not seen Lord Rawleigh in the woods after he had seen her that morning.

"Mrs. Winters," Lord Rawleigh said now. "I seem to have done you a disservice."

Only one? To which one was he referring, pray?

"You were not at dinner last evening," he said, "or at the informal dance in the drawing room afterward, though Clarissa clearly found the uneven numbers provoking. My guess is that you have fallen from grace and that it is my fault. The music-room incident, you know."

"Nothing happened," she said, "except that I played Mozart rather badly and that you told me you wondered."

"And you administered a magnificent set-down," he said, "to which I was given no time to retaliate. Clarissa was, of course, annoyed to find us together. You are altogether too beautiful for her peace of mind, ma'am."

Foolishly, the compliment pleased her. "She need not

fear," she said. "You are welcome to Miss Hudson or to any other lady of Mrs. Adam's choosing, as far as I am concerned. It really matters not one iota to me."

"And *I* matter not one iota to you," he said with an audible sigh. "How dreadfully lowering you are to a man's self-esteem, Mrs. Winters. Why did you allow me to kiss you?"

"I did not—" she began, and bit the words off short.

"You might well halt mid-sentence," he said, "when you have just come from church. You were about to utter the most atrocious bouncer. My question stands."

"If I did," she said, "I regretted it instantly and have regretted it ever since."

"Yes," he said, "one does feel one's—aloneness at such times, does one not? Have you relived it as often as I have during the past three days—and nights?"

"Not a single time," she said, outraged.

"For which I cannot accuse you of lying, can I?" he said, looking at her sidelong. "I have not relived it a *single* time either, Mrs. Winters. Perhaps a score of times, but that would be a low estimate, I believe. You have not by any chance changed your mind about a certain answer you gave to a certain question?"

They had reached the cottage. She opened the gate, stepped hastily through it, and closed it firmly behind her.

"I most certainly have not, my lord," she said, turning to glare at him. Why must men believe that one kiss denoted one's willingness and even eagerness to surrender all?

"A pity," he said, pursing his lips. "You have whetted my appetite, ma'am, and I hate to have my appetite aroused when there is no feast with which to satisfy it."

She was outraged. What she would really like to do was reach across the gate and slap him hard across the face, she thought. It would be wonderfully satisfying to see the mark of her fingers redden across his handsome cheek. But the thought that someone farther along the street might have vision perfect enough to see it happen denied her this pleasure. Someone might also notice if she wheeled about and stalked off up the path to her door in high dudgeon.

"I am no feast, my lord," she said, "and you will never satisfy your appetite on me. Good day to you." She turned with slow dignity for the benefit of anyone interested in staring down the street at them and made for the door, behind which Toby was having a fit of hysterics.

She made the mistake of glancing back before going inside and thereby marred the effect of her exit line. He was staring after her with pursed lips and what looked suspiciously like amusement in his eyes. He was enjoying this, she thought indignantly. He was entertaining himself at her expense.

After slamming the door behind her, she wished she could go back and do it differently. One slammed doors only when one was angry. She would have preferred to act with icy disdain. The very phrase had a ring to it.

"Oh, Toby," she said, stooping down to rub his stomach and transport him from hysterics to ecstasy, "he is the most horrid man I have ever known. Not only is he a dangerous rake, but he also thinks it amusing to have a victim dangling from his line. I am no victim, Tobe. He will realize that soon enough. He might as well turn his energies toward a more willing woman."

The trouble was that she had glanced at his mouth more than once during their progress along the street. And she had shivered at the memory of how it had felt against hers—warm, moist, lightly enticing. She had wanted to feel it again.

"No," she said firmly, following the dog into the kitchen. "You may not jump onto the rocker."

Toby jumped onto the rocker and proceeded to make himself comfortable.

"Males!" Catherine said with disgust, turning her attention to the fire. "You are all alike. *No* is not in your vocabulary. No means yes to all of you. I do wish—oh, *how* I wish it were possible to live without the whole lot of you."

On behalf of males everywhere, Toby heaved a sigh and gazed at her with contented eyes.

HE WAS NOT at all sure that no meant irrevocably no with Mrs. Catherine Winters. He regretfully suspected that it did, but he was not sure beyond any doubt.

He would be wasting his time to continue pursuing her, he believed. But then he had discovered that there was not anything much more productive with which to occupy his time anyway. He was enjoying quite as much as he had expected being with Claude and Daphne again and of course he always enjoyed the company of his friends. When drawing-room conversation became just too insipid to be borne, they could always go off together, the three of them, and engage in a conversation that required the use of at least a small measure of their intelligence.

But he needed diversion.

It seemed unlikely that Catherine Winters was to be bedded. More was the pity. He very badly wanted to bed her. But even failing that—and he was not quite convinced that it was a hopeless case—there was amusement to be derived from talking with her, goading her, teasing her, outraging her, merely looking at her.

He had to be careful, of course, not to compromise her. Claude was suspicious, Clarissa was suspicious, Nat and Eden were more than suspicious. It would be unfair to try to seek her out alone again and risk being seen—as they almost had been by that gardener. And Clarissa was no longer inviting her to the house.

He had to solve the problem somehow. They had been out for a long morning's ride. He had danced attendance on Miss Hudson as usual, though he had relinquished her to Nat's care for part of the return journey, having noticed that she was far more relaxed in his friend's company than in his own. The weather had become cloudy and chilly. Clarissa had decreed that the afternoon would be spent indoors.

He was offending no one, then, when he suggested a stroll to Daphne and Clayton. The two of them were notorious for their spartan adherence to outdoor activities in all weathers. They brightened visibly. Fortunately no one else did. It was easy enough once they were outside and marching to steer them down across the park toward the postern door, which Daphne had forgotten about and Clayton had never seen, and suggest a walk through the village, up the lane beyond it, and through the gate back into the park that he had entered a few mornings before.

And of course, it was easy once they were through the door to notice that Mrs. Winters's cottage was close by and to suggest that perhaps she would enjoy a walk with them. After all, he pointed out, he was walking alone while Clayton had a lady for his arm.

"Poor Rex," Daphne said, laughing. "You need a wife."

That was the last thing he needed. But his plan worked well. She was at home. This was not one of those afternoons, then, when she was off somewhere doing good works. And Daphne, bless her heart, took upon herself all the burden of persuading her to join them on their walk and spoke as if it had all been her idea.

"Well," Catherine Winters said—she looked quite delicious in one of her plain wool dresses covered with a large white apron, one of her lace caps perched on her golden hair, "I have just finished baking. I hope you will excuse my appearance." Oh, anytime. Anytime at all. "Fresh air would be pleasant. And Toby has not had a walk since early this morning. Would you mind if he came too?"

"What a darling he is," Daphne said, bending to pat him. He had stopped barking in exchange for a stomach rub as soon as they had crossed the threshold.

And so a few minutes later, after she had removed her apron and her cap and donned a cloak and bonnet, his careful plotting had borne fruit and he had her in his company again and on his arm—she could hardly refuse when Daphne was clinging to Clayton's. And they were nodding left and right to villagers and proceeding beyond the village, all chatting together until they were across the bridge and out into countryside and he drew back by imperceptible degrees until they were far enough behind Daphne and Clayton to necessitate a conversation of their own.

"I do apologize if you did not want my company," he said, covering her hand with his own for a moment. "I was dragged kicking and screaming to your door by my sister, who has taken a fancy to you."

She looked skeptically at him.

"It is two days and three hours since I saw you last," he said. "Tell me that you have missed me."

She made a sound that indicated incredulity without the necessity of an intelligible word.

"Yes," he said, "I have missed you too. Is your card full for Friday's ball?"

"Oh," she said indignantly, "*how* you are enjoying yourself."

He found himself grinning at her.

"I want two sets," he said. "The first waltz—I shall bully

Clarissa into including some—and the supper dance. You will reserve them for me?"

"I believe," she said, "that those two dances in particular should be reserved by you for a particular lady."

"Exactly," he said. "That is agreed, then."

"I meant Miss Hudson," she said.

He knew as soon as they followed Daphne and Clayton into the park that she recognized the route they had taken a few mornings before. He deliberately stopped talking so that her attention would not be diverted from the memories—or his.

His sister and brother-in-law had stopped on the bridge.

"Do you remember how we used to balance on the balustrade and walk from one side to the other, Rex?" she called back to him. "It is amazing we did not break our necks."

"Yes," he said. "I have many memories of this bridge, Daphne. Most of them pleasant."

He felt the hand that was resting lightly on his arm stiffen.

"You will come back to the house for tea with us, Mrs. Winters?" Daphne asked with a smile. "I am sure Clarissa would be delighted. She is always lamenting the fact that there is not one more lady."

"No, thank you," Mrs. Winters said hastily. "I have Toby. And I need to be home soon. But thank you."

"It has been pleasant," Daphne said. She laughed. "Rex was the odd man out this afternoon, you see, and was complaining that there was no lady for his arm."

When they came to the main driveway, he was able to put into effect the final part of his plan. They were not far from the village.

"You and Clayton go on to the house, Daphne," he said. "I shall escort Mrs. Winters home."

"Oh," Daphne said, looking from one to the other of

them—he saw light dawn in her eyes. "Yes, if you will excuse us, Mrs. Winters. Thank you so much for giving us your company. And Toby too. He is quite delightful."

"Good afternoon, Mrs. Winters." Clayton tipped his hat to her.

"And I will be very good," the viscount said when they were alone together. "I shall lead you down the garden path, Mrs. Winters, but not to perdition. To the village, in fact. I am afraid to suggest that we slink off in the direction of the postern door. I am afraid that this afternoon I really would get my face slapped. I came close on Sunday, did I not?"

It was very tempting, of course, to take her by the other route and to try to steal another kiss from her among the trees. But plenty of people had seen her walk through the village on his arm. The same people or at least some of them might be on watch for her return. It would not do for those people to see them emerging from the woods and the door.

"Very close," she said. "I still regret that I did not risk being seen to do it."

Several people saw him return her respectably down the drive from Bodley House and along the village street to her gate.

"Alas," he said when she was on one side of it and he was on the other, "you had better not invite me in for tea no matter how strongly you feel inclined to do so. It would not be proper and we have been observed."

She gave him a speaking glance and he let his eyes drop deliberately to her mouth.

"For the same reason," he said, "you had better not offer me a farewell kiss. Another time, perhaps."

"When hell freezes over," she said.

He tutted. "My dear ma'am," he said, "I have come to expect more original pronouncements from you than that. *When hell freezes over.* What a lamentable cliché."

"Good day, my lord," she said coolly, and turned to walk up the path and let herself into her cottage, Toby ahead of her. She did not slam the door this time.

Ah, he thought, if only. He was still not quite convinced that it was out of the question, but even if it was, sparring with her was altogether more pleasurable than dodging a courtship with Ellen Hudson was proving to be.

He was going to have those two dances with her on Friday night too, he thought, even if she believed at the moment that he would not unless hell happened to freeze over in the meanwhile.

Now, why would anyone want to kiss someone else when hell had frozen over? To share body heat? The thought had its appeal.

Eight

SHE HAD BEEN reading to Mr. Clarkwell. Then she had sat and listened to reminiscences of his earlier days that she had heard more than once before.

"You really do not have to humor him," Mrs. Clarkwell had said with some impatience and perhaps a little embarrassment. "He has become a bore in his old age."

"I like to listen," Catherine had said, glad that the words had been spoken out of Mr. Clarkwell's hearing. "He looks so very happy when he talks of the past."

"Yes, I know." His daughter-in-law had rolled her eyes at the ceiling. "And times are not what they used to be. And the Lord only knows what is becoming of this world."

Catherine had taken her leave. Now she was calling upon Mrs. Downes, who had been too poorly to come to church on Sunday. At the same time she could have a good chat with Miss Downes, who was unable to get about as much as she would have liked these days on account of her mother and always welcomed company.

This afternoon she had enough to keep her happy for a whole week to come. Catherine had been there for less than ten minutes—the kettle had not even boiled for tea—when

Lady Baird arrived, accompanied by her brother, Viscount Rawleigh.

Miss Downes was all a-flutter and a-twitter, as she explained to Catherine sotto voce while the latter helped her get the tea.

"What a singular honor, Mrs. Winters," she whispered. "Though it is all on account of dear Mama, of course. I must not become puffed up with my own importance."

Mrs. Downes had plenty to say during tea in her forthright, almost masculine voice. Lady Baird chattered away enough for two persons. Miss Downes fluttered. Lord Rawleigh made himself agreeable. Catherine sat almost mute.

Of course, she realized almost immediately, these four had been acquainted for a long time. When the viscount and his brother and sister had used to visit their grandparents at Bodley House, Mrs. and Miss Downes had lived at the rectory with the Reverend Downes. Apparently Mrs. Downes remembered them fondly as bright, mischievous children, who had liked to make excuses to call at the rectory to sample her currant cakes.

"I would have made some, your ladyship," Miss Downes said, "if I had known you were going to call today. And your lordship too, of course. Not that I am saying your surprise visit is not very welcome, of course. And a great honor, as I was remarking to Mrs. Winters just a few moments ago. But if I had known—"

"You did not, Agatha," Mrs. Downes said firmly. "Lady Baird is ready for more tea."

That put Miss Downes back into a flutter.

Catherine rose before the others. "I must be going home," she said. She smiled at Mrs. Downes. "I shall leave you to enjoy your visitors, ma'am."

"Oh, do wait awhile," Lady Baird said. "We were planning to make two calls in the village, were we not, Rex?

We were to call here first and then on you. It is true we have seen you here, but I must confess that I want an excuse to see the inside of your very charming cottage. May we? Will you wait ten minutes longer?"

For some inexplicable reason Catherine looked at Viscount Rawleigh rather than at Lady Baird. Had this been his idea? He was looking at his sister with raised eyebrows. But he turned to Catherine. He looked amused and perhaps a little—surprised? As if this was the first he had heard of visiting her.

"If you please, ma'am," he said. "I must confess to a similar curiosity to my sister's."

The wretch! Catherine could picture him sitting in her kitchen suggesting that they help alleviate each other's boredom by becoming lover and mistress.

She sat down again.

And so fifteen minutes later the villagers of Bodley-on-the-Water were treated to another view of guests from the house walking the length of the street with Mrs. Winters. Viscount Rawleigh walked with a lady on each arm. And at the end of the street they turned through Mrs. Winters's gate and disappeared inside her house.

"Oh, this darling dog," Lady Baird said as Toby barked and then jumped up to greet her. She pulled gently on his ears. "I am going to steal you when I go home, Toby."

"Will you go into the parlor?" Catherine asked. She felt suffocated with Viscount Rawleigh in the passageway. He was so very large and—male. "I shall set the kettle to boil."

"For more tea?" Lady Baird laughed as Toby licked her hand. "I think not, Mrs. Winters. We will be awash in tea if we drink more, will we not, Rex? This is so very cozy." She glanced into the parlor, though she did not step inside. "I believe I could be happy in a cottage like this—with my dear Clayton, of course."

"With no servants, Daphne?" Lord Rawleigh said dryly. "You would starve in a fortnight."

Lady Baird laughed. "Your cottage backs onto the river, Mrs. Winters," she said. "Mrs. Lovering told us that you have a pretty garden. May we see it?"

It was not very pretty yet, of course. The fruit trees were coming into leaf, it was true, and the grass was a fresher green than it had been even a week or so ago. There were some primroses in clumps down by the river. But the flower beds closer to the house were almost bare and the vegetable patch was entirely so. The rosebushes, which trailed up over the walls on both sides, would be bare of blooms for a few months yet. Even so, it was one of Catherine's favorite places in all the world.

"Ah, yes," Lady Baird said when they had stepped outside. "A little haven of beauty and peace. With meadows and hills across the water. I am going to follow Toby down to the bank. You need not feel obliged to accompany me." She strode off to the bottom of the garden without looking back.

Catherine was left standing on the small terrace outside the back door with Lord Rawleigh. She looked after her departing guest in some dismay—though her back garden was not particularly long.

"I believe," the viscount said, his voice sounding rather bored, "our chaperon is doing what all good chaperons do. She is lending us countenance while at the same time affording us a little time to ourselves."

"Our *chaperon*?" She stiffened. "You have arranged this, my lord? And Lady Baird has consented to be your accomplice? Will she afford us enough time to go *upstairs*?"

"Oh, good Lord, no," he said. "More is the pity. Daphne is all propriety, ma'am. And this is all her idea, I do assure you. She has not consulted me any more than she has consulted you. I believe she has conceived the notion that I have a, ah, *tendre* for you."

And she approved? She was abetting her brother's acquaintance with a woman of unknown background, a woman who lived alone in a small cottage without even a servant?

"And would she be shocked," she asked, "if she knew the real nature of your interest in me, my lord?"

"I might almost say she would have a fit of the vapors," he said, "except that Daphne is made of stern stuff. Rather like you."

"Toby is going to have muddy paws and then cut up nasty when he finds that he has to have them wiped before he can step indoors," she said.

"That terrier," he said, "needs to be taken in hand, ma'am. He is allowed to rule your life. If you are so indulgent with a mere dog, one dreads to think what you might be like with a child."

Fury knifed through her. "How I choose to treat my dog is none of your concern, my lord," she said. "As for the other, how dare you presume to know anything about my maternal instincts. I—"

But he had set his fingertips against her arm and taken one step closer. "That certainly touched a nerve," he said. "My apologies, ma'am. Were you unable to have children?"

Her eyes widened in shock.

"This will not do," he said. "I do wish you had not mistaken me for my twin that first day, Mrs. Winters. Or that your smiles had meant what they seemed to mean. You have a disturbing effect on me."

"I believe it is called—frustration," she said, restraining herself just in time from including the word *sexual*. She was not that ill-bred even with anger as an excuse.

"I daresay you are right." His eyes roamed her face. "Our

chaperon has given us all of—what? Five minutes? She has deemed that quite sufficient."

Lady Baird was strolling back up the lawn. Toby was loping along at her side just as if they were lifelong friends.

"Clarissa has agreed to some waltzes the evening after tomorrow," he said. "I expect to claim the ones I have reserved with you, ma'am. If you are concerned about the progress of my noncourtship, I will explain that I reserved the opening set with Miss Hudson and was maneuvered into reserving the set after supper with her too."

His voice was haughty, commanding. Catherine could not remember ever agreeing to grant him those two sets. The thought of waltzing with him was unbearable. It made her feel as if someone had removed a few essential bones from her legs and as if some giant pump had sucked most of the air from the garden.

"Charming," Lady Baird said as she approached, looking from one to the other of them, though she did not explain what it was she found so charming. "We have taken enough of your time, Mrs. Winters. We must be going, must we not, Rex? I promised Clayton I would be gone for no longer than an hour. You will be at the ball? I so look forward to seeing you there."

Catherine smiled.

She saw them to the front gate and raised a hand in farewell as they walked back along the street. Yes, she looked forward to it too. She ought not to do so. She should have refused her invitation. Even now she should send her excuses. But oh, to dance again. To feel young again. To dance with *him*.

She knew she would not send her excuses.

She stood inside the door a minute later, her back against it, her eyes closed.

One dreads to think what you might be like with a child.

She gave a little moan of distress. She remembered holding a child, a tiny, underdeveloped child. For such a very short time. Ah, so very short. He had survived his birth by a scant three hours, and for the first of those she had been too exhausted to hold him.

She had blamed herself bitterly afterward. It had been all her fault. She had not wanted him at first. She had not nourished him well because she had been unable to find the will or the energy to nourish herself well. And she had cried a great deal. She had felt very sorry for herself in those days. The midwife had told her—too late—that it was important to keep up her spirits. And afterward . . . Perhaps she had wrapped him too warmly or not warmly enough. Perhaps she had held him too tightly or not tightly enough. Perhaps if she had held him for that first hour . . .

He had died.

One dreads to think what you might be like with a child.

She spread her hands over her face and did what she very rarely did these days. She wept.

Toby was nudging her leg with his nose and whining.

MRS. ADAMS HAD expended a great deal of energy on the preparations for the dinner and ball at Bodley House. It was a great deal more difficult to host a ball in the country than in town, she always found. In town one sent invitations to all the *ton* and trusted that enough would attend that the event would be proclaimed a squeeze. And enough people always *did* come. Claude was the brother and heir of Viscount Rawleigh, after all. In the country one sent invitations to almost everyone except the peasantry and hoped that enough would come that the event would not be proclaimed a disaster.

And early spring was not the ideal time to hold a dinner and ball. There were not enough flowers in the gardens and only barely enough in the greenhouses. The head gardner had a long face when ordered to denude them so that the house could blossom for the space of one evening.

But by late afternoon on the Friday, the ballroom and dining room looked festive enough for any *ton* event. The orchestra had arrived and set up their instruments. The extra hands in the kitchen had dinner and supper under control.

All else had to be left to fate. At least it had stopped raining after yesterday's all-day downpour and this morning's dreary drizzle.

Mrs. Adams sat at her dressing table while her maid put the finishing touches to her dress, clasping her diamonds about her neck and at her ears. She looked at her reflection with satisfaction and nodded a dismissal to the girl just as her husband entered the room from the door adjoining his own.

"Ah, beautiful," he said, coming to stand behind her and setting his hands on her bare shoulders. "You grow lovelier with every passing year, Clarissa. Nervous?" He kneaded the tense muscles in her shoulders.

"No," she said decisively. "There are to be forty for dinner. That is definite. As many more have been invited to the ball. Of course they will come. An invitation to Bodley is a coveted thing."

He grinned at her reflection. "That is the spirit," he said. "You look good enough to eat. I suppose I am not allowed a few nibbles yet?" He lowered his head to kiss the back of her neck.

"I wish," she said, "there had been a polite way of not inviting Mrs. Winters."

He lifted his head and looked closely at her reflection. "Mrs. Winters?" he said. "What has she done to offend you, Clarissa? Apart from having been born beautiful, that is."

"She is getting above herself," she said sharply. "She is putting on airs. She is looking too high."

"Doubtless," he said quietly, "you intend to continue."

"Rawleigh is interested in Ellen," she said. "That is plain for all to see. And they are a perfect match. But Mrs. Winters is flirting with him. She had him alone in the music room last week. And when I called yesterday to inquire after Mrs. Downes's health, Miss Downes came out to the carriage and happened to mention that Mrs. Winters was at their house when Daphne and Rawleigh called the day before. And then they escorted her home and *went inside with her*."

"I am sure, my dear," Mr. Adams said, "that with Daphne present all was proper. Indeed, it was probably all her suggestion. Are you imagining something that is just not happening? You know my opinion of the so-called courtship between Rex and Ellen."

"I planned this evening for a purpose," she said. "I thought it would be the perfect occasion for an announcement, Claude. Or at the very least for everyone to see what was in the wind. I will *not* have it ruined."

"Clarissa," he said, a note of firmness in his voice, "Rex is not our puppet. Neither is Ellen. Or Mrs. Winters. I am sure all of them will behave with perfect good breeding tonight. We cannot demand more than that. We cannot orchestrate a courtship for which the participants feel no enthusiasm. And we cannot forbid Rex and Mrs. Winters to look at each other. Or even to dance with each other if they feel so inclined."

She got to her feet and turned to look at him. "I will not have it," she said. "I will not have that woman smiling at him and batting her eyelids at him and distracting him. We do not know who she is, Claude, or what she is. For all we know—"

"We know," he said sternly, "that she has leased a cottage from me in the village and that for the past five years she has conducted herself in exemplary fashion. We know that her every word and action have proclaimed her to be a lady. We also know that she is to be an invited guest in our home this evening. She will be accorded as much courtesy as any other guest, Clarissa."

"Oh," she said, "I hate it when you set your jaw like that and allow your eyes to turn hard. You look more like Rawleigh than ever. Don't, Claude. You know how anxious I am—"

He set his arms about her and drew her against him. "Yes, I know," he said. "You are anxious about tonight and anxious about your sister's future. All will be well with both if you will just relax. Why not enjoy the evening? And save the first waltz for me. I insist. Husband's privilege and all that. I do not care if it is not the fashion for a husband and wife to be seen together when they are hosting an entertainment. You will dance with me."

She sighed. "You are crushing me, Claude," she said. "Oh, I wish I could dance every set with you. You smell good. A new cologne?"

"Purchased with my wife in mind," he said, "and worn with the lecherous hope that there will be enough of the night left when this is all over for me to put it to good use."

"As if you need cologne for that," she said. "Rawleigh has asked Ellen for the first set. That is promising, is it not?"

He chuckled. "It means that neither of them will be wallflowers at the start at least," he said, drawing her arm through his and turning toward the door. "Time to go down to greet our dinner guests, my love."

Mrs. Adams wished again, though silently this time, that Catherine Winters was not one of their number.

. . .

LORD PELHAM AND Mr. Gascoigne were planning to leave next week. They would not wish to outstay their welcome, they had explained. They were not quite sure where they would go or even if they would spend the spring and summer together. Only London seemed off-limits to both of them. They might go down to Dunbarton in Cornwall, the Earl of Haverford's country seat. He had been there since before Christmas and it would be good to see him again.

They were bored at Bodley, Lord Rawleigh knew. He could hardly blame them. Clarissa's guest list could more accurately be called a gathering of friends and relatives than a house party. Certainly there was not much to hold the attention of single and healthy gentlemen. He had fleetingly considered leaving with them. Leaving would be one way of convincing Clarissa that she was backing the wrong horse entirely where her sister was concerned. And he believed that Ellen Hudson herself would be relieved if he took himself off.

But he could not bring himself to leave. Not just yet. Not until he was convinced beyond any reasonable doubt . . .

His pursuit of a handsome widow to fill the temporary position of mistress had been conducted with alarming indiscretion, of course. Daphne was the latest person to have become aware of his interest. Not that she was at all alarmed. Quite the contrary. She heartily approved. She did not know, of course, the nature of his interest, as Catherine Winters herself had put it. Daphne thought he was beginning a courtship of the woman.

"If you wish to come riding with Clayton and me tomorrow," she said to him when they were walking back from Catherine's cottage, "we will take pity on your lone state and call to see if Mrs. Winters will join us, Rex. But she does not have a horse. Hmm. A walk, then. All the better. You can fall a short distance behind us as you did a few afternoons ago, when I first noticed the way you have of looking at her."

But yesterday it had rained, and though Daphne and Clayton had gone trudging off for destinations unknown, he had declined accompanying them. He would probably have done so anyway. Good Lord, he was not going to court a mistress under the indulgent—and uncomprehending—eye of his sister.

But tonight was the night of the ball. He dressed with care, choosing a black coat and knee breeches with white linen and lace. Black was becoming perhaps a little too commonplace in town, it was true, but it was still rarely seen in the country. He placed a diamond pin, his only adornment, in the center of his neckcloth. He scorned dandyism as a rule. Tonight he would have avoided it at all costs. He would not look more gorgeous than his lady.

He was glad of his forethought when he saw her—from a distance across the drawing room before dinner. She was dressed as she had been at dinner when she had been a guest there. She wore her simply styled green dress with only a string of pearls at her throat. There were no plumes or other adornments in her hair.

As on that occasion, she outshone all the other ladies present, including Clarissa, who was sparkling in the diamonds that had been a wedding present from Claude. Catherine was smiling and talking with Mrs. Lipton, an unknown couple, and a man Lord Rawleigh recognized as the tenant he and Claude had called upon a week or so ago. A single man and not a day over thirty-five at the outside. Damn his eyes, which he had better learn to keep to himself if he knew what was good for him.

She caught his eye across the room and half smiled at him. He wondered if she had mistaken him for Claude again. But it was not a bright smile. Perhaps a quarter smile would be a more accurate description. He was going to dance with her tonight, he thought. He hoped she had no plan to avoid the two waltzes he had reserved with her. He was going to steal a kiss tonight too, by hook or by crook. The one on the bridge could hardly be described as a kiss, but it had awoken a hunger in him that had to be satisfied. Even if she was not to be bedded, she was going to be kissed, by God. She was not going to deny him that.

"I have not seen you gaze even at the enemy with such burning zeal, old chap," Lord Pelham said, moving into his line of vision. "She continues obdurate?"

"Perhaps you and Nat will change your plans to leave after tonight," the viscount said, looking about him with his customary mixture of hauteur and boredom. "Clarissa seems to have turned out a number of passably pretty females for the occasion."

"Nat already has his eye on the redhead," Lord Pelham said, nodding his head in the direction of the far corner of the room, where a pretty young girl stood in a group, looking about her with wide and interested eyes. "But he is understandably nervous, Rex. He is trying to ascertain how many parents and cousins and uncles etcetera—you know the old litany—are present and likely to converge on him to demand his intentions if he should happen to so much as smile at the girl."

Viscount Rawleigh chuckled.

Nine

SHE HAD HAD pleasant dinner companions, Mr. Lipton on one side and Sir Clayton Baird on the other. Although Mrs. Adams's greeting had been noticeably cool, everyone else had been courteous and even amiable. She pushed to the back of her mind the knowledge that she looked far plainer than any other lady present. She wore the same green gown she had worn to every evening entertainment for the past two years. And her mother's pearls. She rarely wore those now except on very special occasions.

It did not matter that she was plainly and unfashionably dressed. She had not come in order to be noticed. Merely to enjoy an evening in company. And of course when they adjourned to the ballroom and were joined there by other guests, who had not been invited to dinner, she found that she was no more plainly dressed than several of the wives and daughters of tenant farmers.

She danced the first set of country dances with one of the tenants. She smiled at him and set herself to enjoy the evening. She had always loved a ball with all the rich sounds of an orchestra and all the perfumes of flowers and colognes and all the swirling splendor of colored silks and satins and the glitter of jewels in the candlelight.

She hoped Viscount Rawleigh would change his mind about the two waltzes he had said he would claim. Surely he would. It would be a very public setting in which to single her out for any dance, much less a waltz. And twice? Surely he would not. He had made no move to approach her in the drawing room before dinner. He had been seated almost as far from her at table as he possibly could be. He had not approached her in the ballroom. He was dancing now with Ellen Hudson in a different set from her own.

He had said that he was to dance the opening set with Miss Hudson. What if he meant to keep to his other plan too? Catherine's breath quickened.

There was no mistaking him tonight for his twin. Mr. Adams looked extremely handsome in varying shades of blue. Lord Rawleigh looked suffocatingly elegant and—satanic in black and white.

Mr. Gascoigne asked her for the next set, a quadrille. He set himself to charm her and succeeded. She liked his smiling eyes and handsome figure and wondered again why it was that one man could be quite as handsome as another and far more charming and easy in his manners and yet could stir her to no spark of anything beyond warm liking. Whereas the other . . .

Well, perhaps it was just in her nature to be attracted to the wrong men. The two gentlemen who had offered for her during the past three years had both been perfectly eligible and would have been good to her. But she had never been willing to marry for anything less than love.

Never. That had been half the trouble. . . .

Lord Pelham danced another set of country dances with her.

"After all, Mrs. Winters," he said, bowing to her before

the set began and favoring her with the full force of his very blue eyes, "why should Nat be allowed to get away with being the one to dance with the loveliest girl in the room?"

"Ah," she said, smiling at him, "a flatterer. A man after my own heart, my lord."

He was easy to talk with and laugh with. Not that there was a great deal of time or breath for talk or laughter—it was a vigorous dance.

"I do believe there is to be a waltz next," he said conversationally as he returned her to her place at the end of the set. "I am happy that Mrs. Adams is enlightened enough to bring it to the country. There is no dance for which I prefer taking the floor. Do you know the steps, Mrs. Winters?"

"Oh, yes," she said. "It is a lovely dance. Romantic."

But her heart was pounding and she wished she was carrying a fan. Suddenly the room seemed very hot and airless. Perhaps, she thought in foolish panic, she should hurry away to the ladies' withdrawing room and hide there until the set was in progress. He had danced only with Miss Hudson, Mrs. Adams, and Lady Baird. It would seem very strange for him to dance the first waltz with someone who was not even one of the house party.

But then he probably did not intend to dance it with her at all. Perhaps that was part of her reason for wanting to run away and hide. There would be some humiliation in watching him lead someone else onto the floor.

And then Sir Clayton Baird was at her side and it was too late to run. He talked with her for a minute or two before asking her for the waltz. Oh, dear. But yes, at least this would cover the humiliation. She opened her mouth to reply and half lifted her hand to place in his.

"Sorry, old chap," a bored and haughty voice said from behind her. "I reserved this set well in advance of this evening. Perhaps Mrs. Winters has the next one free for you."

She turned rather sharply and placed her hand in Viscount Rawleigh's outstretched one and allowed him to lead her onto the floor without even a backward glance at Sir Clayton. And she knew without a doubt, even though they were one of the first couples to take the floor and even though most eyes must be upon them—she knew that she was glad. That this was why she had come. That this was what she had waited for all evening.

"You were within a hairbreadth of giving away my waltz to my brother-in-law, Mrs. Winters," he said, his dark eyes holding hers. They were standing facing each other, though not yet touching since the music had not begun. "I would have been very annoyed. You have never seen me annoyed, have you?"

"It would be better if I did not?" she said. "I would be reduced to a mass of quivering jelly? I think not, my lord. I know you were a cavalry officer during the war, but I am not one of your raw recruits."

"I never engaged any of my raw recruits to waltz with me," he said. "I would not so blatantly court scandal."

She laughed despite herself and was rewarded with an answering gleam of amusement in his eyes.

"Ah, this is better," he said. "You laugh all too rarely, Mrs. Winters. I wonder if there was a time when you laughed more freely."

"One would be thought either insane or very immature if one went off into peals of glee at every suggestion of wit, my lord," she said.

"I believe," he said, ignoring her words, "there must have been such a time. Before you came to Bodley-on-the-Water. In God's name, why this place? You must have been little more than a girl then. Let me guess. You had a strong romantic attachment to your husband and swore on his passing never to laugh again."

Oh, dear Lord. Let the music start. She wanted no one playing guessing games with her past.

"Or else," he said, "your marriage was such an unhappy experience that you retreated to a remote corner of the country and still have not learned to laugh freely again."

She had come here tonight to *enjoy* herself. Her lips compressed. "My lord," she said, "you are impertinent."

His eyebrows shot up. "And you, ma'am," he said, "try my patience."

It was not an auspicious manner in which to begin a waltz, the dance she had just called romantic. But the music began at that moment and he moved a little closer to set one hand behind her waist and take her right hand in his. She set her left on his shoulder. He twirled her into the dance.

She had waltzed before. Many times. It had always been her favorite dance. And she had always imagined that it would be wonderful almost beyond bearing to waltz with a man who meant something to her. There was something so suggestive of intimacy and romance in the dance—there, that word again.

It was not romance she felt dancing with Lord Rawleigh. At first it was awareness, so raw and all-encompassing that she thought she might well faint from it. His hand at her waist burned into her. She felt his body heat from crown to soles, although their bodies did not touch. She could smell his cologne and something beyond that. She could smell the very essence of him.

And then she felt exhilaration. He was a superb dancer, twirling her confidently about the ballroom without missing a step and without colliding with any other dancer. She matched her steps to his and felt that she had never come so close to dancing on air before. She had never felt so wonderfully happy.

And finally she felt self-consciousness. She caught Mrs. Adams's eyes fleetingly and unintentionally as that lady danced with her husband. There was a smile on Mrs. Adams's face and steel in her eyes. And fury.

She had been waltzing, Catherine realized, as if no other moment existed beyond this half hour and as if no one else existed but her and the man with whom she danced. She suddenly became aware that they danced in a ballroom filled with other people and that there was indeed time beyond this half hour. A whole leftover lifetime to be lived here among these very people—with the exception of Viscount Rawleigh, who would go away very soon.

She wondered what her face and the motions of her body had revealed during the past fifteen or twenty minutes. And she looked up to see what his face revealed.

He was looking steadily down at her. "God, but I want you, Catherine Winters," he said. The heat of his words was quite at variance with the languor in his eyes.

This was what those people who objected to the waltz meant, she thought. It was a dance that aroused passions that had no business being aroused. And she was to waltz with him again before supper?

"I do believe, my lord," she said, "that you begin to repeat yourself. We have dealt with that matter before now. It is a closed book."

"Is it?" he said, his eyes dropping for a brief moment to her lips. "Is it, Catherine?"

She knew that he was an experienced and masterly seducer. A rake. He was not the first she had met. He knew all the power the sound of her given name on his lips would have over her. And of course he was quite right. She felt touched by tenderness.

Which was quite ridiculous under the circumstances.

Instead of answering, she fixed her eyes on the diamond pin that was winking among the elaborate folds of his neckcloth and danced on.

"I am glad," he said when the music finally drew to an end and he was returning her to her place, "you did not answer my last question, ma'am. I would have hated to be compelled to call you a liar. The supper dance. Do not grant it to anyone else. You would not enjoy having me annoyed with you." He raised her hand to his lips and kissed her fingers before turning to stroll away.

She was going to have to leave before the supper waltz, she decided. She could take no more of this. All the careful work of years was being undone. It might take her five more years to regain the poise and peace she had known just a couple of weeks ago. Perhaps she would never regain them at Bodley-on-the-Water. There would be constant reminders. But she could not leave. The very thought was frightening—starting all over again with strangers. But even if she wanted to try it, she could not. She had to stay here for the rest of her life.

She had come to Bodley House with Reverend and Mrs. Lovering. Perhaps, she thought, they would be ready to leave early, as they sometimes were, though it was unlikely that they would forfeit supper for the sake of an early night. She looked for them without a great deal of hope. But they were nowhere to be found.

She discovered eventually, when she asked the butler, that the rector had been called away to the bedside of Mrs. Lambton, who was very low, and had left to take Mrs. Lovering home before going with Percy, Mrs. Lambton's son, the five miles to their farm. They had left without her, Catherine realized, either because they had forgotten her or, more likely, because it was still early and they had assumed that she would want to stay and would find someone else to give her a ride back to the village at the end of the evening.

Anyone would, of course. Any number of the neighbors would be going through the village on their way home and would be happy enough to set her down at her cottage gate. Mr. Adams would call out a carriage in a moment to take her home. She had no reason to feel stranded. It was not even very far to walk, though it was a cloudy and dark night. Anyway, she did not like to walk alone at night. But she could not possibly ask anyone to drive her home this early unless she could invent some dreadful ailment in a hurry.

She was stuck at the ball until the end, it seemed.

She smiled as Sir Clayton approached to claim his set.

HE BURNED FOR her. He could not remember having been at the mercy of a tease before—if that was what Catherine Winters was. He was more inclined to think that she did not quite know her own mind. But however it was, it was having all the effect she could have desired if she really was teasing.

He had to have her.

He was not at all sure he would be this obsessed if she had become his mistress after that first visit, as he had fully expected she would. He could not believe so. Surely if he had had her then and for the two weeks since then, he would be satisfied. Still desirous of her, perhaps. She was unusually lovely and appeared to have character to go along with the looks. But surely he would not still be as hot for her as he was now.

He even thought briefly of changing his intentions. There was nothing to stop him from offering her marriage if he so chose, he thought. But the idea was not given serious consideration. He did not want to be married. It was true that he had courted and betrothed himself to Horatia with great haste only three years ago, but that very experience had soured him. He had fallen in love with a woman who had soon thrown him over for a rake. He was that poor a judge of female character. There would have been nothing but misery for him if he had married before discovering the weakness of her character or the insincerity of her protestations of love. Before he married, he would have to meet the woman who was as much a part of his soul as he was.

And that, of course, was romantic nonsense.

No, he certainly would not offer marriage to Catherine Winters merely because it seemed there might be no other way of bedding her. Besides, he knew almost nothing about her. It would be sheer madness to marry a virtual stranger, lovely as she was.

But no amount of sensible thinking as he danced and conversed and waited impatiently for the supper set to begin could cool his ardor. He wanted her and by God he would have her if there was a way of doing so short of ravishing her.

It was with considerable annoyance, then—and something deeper than annoyance—that he greeted the fact that she was nowhere to be found as the gentlemen around him were taking their partners for the supper waltz.

"Ellen is free for this set, Rawleigh," Clarissa said archly, coming up from behind him as he looked keenly all about. "Do let me take you to her."

"Pardon me, Clarissa," he said more sharply than he had intended, "but I am engaged to dance with her after supper—for the second time. I have reserved this set with someone else."

"Oh? Who?" Her voice had sharpened too.

He was feeling too annoyed to dissemble. Besides, why should he? When he had found her, he would be waltzing with her for all to see. "Catherine Winters," he said.

"Mrs. Winters?" she said. "Oh. She must be very gratified, Rawleigh. I am sure, at such a mark of attention. And this is the second time you are to dance with her?"

"Excuse me, Clarissa," he said, moving away. She was clearly not in the ballroom. Or on the landing outside. Or in the drawing room, where a few elderly people were playing cards. Where was she hiding? Hiding from him? Had she escaped? Gone home? But he had been present when the Reverend Lovering had been called away. She had not gone with him. She had come with the rector and would have to wait for someone else to take her home at the end of the ball. Unless she had walked. Surely she had not been foolhardy enough to have done that alone. Where was she?

There was only one possibility he could think of. He went to look in the music room.

There was a certain amount of light coming through the French windows, across which the curtains had not been drawn. But apart from that she was in darkness. She sat on the pianoforte bench, facing the keyboard but not playing. The waltz music from the ballroom was loud even down here. She did not look up when he opened the door and stepped inside. He strolled across the room toward her.

"My dance, I believe," he said.

"I never wanted this to happen," she said.

"This?" He felt hope build. She had not wanted it to happen, but it was happening?

She did not answer him for a while. She ran the fingers of her left hand over the keys, though she did not depress them.

"I am five-and-twenty years old," she said. "I have lived here for five years. I have made friends and acquaintances here. I have made a meaningful life here. I have made a home of my cottage. I have a dog to love and be loved by. I have been happy."

"Happy." He would have to quarrel with that word. "Was

your marriage so intolerable that this life—this half-life you have been living—seemed a happy one, Catherine?"

"I have not given you leave to use my name," she said.

"Retaliate by calling me Rex, then," he said. "You want me as much as I want you."

She laughed without humor. "Men and women are so different," she said. "What I want is peace of mind and contentment."

"Dullness," he said.

"If you like." She was not going to argue the point with him even though he stayed silent to give her the chance.

"Were you happy with your husband?" he asked.

Again she was silent for a while. "I do not cultivate either happiness or unhappiness," she said. "The one does not last long enough and the other lasts too long. My marriage is not your concern. *I* am not your concern. I wish you would go back to the ballroom, my lord, and dance with someone else. Any woman there would be glad to dance with you."

"I want to dance with you," he said.

"No."

"Why not?" He gazed down at her. Even the arch of her neck in the faint light from the window was elegant, alluring.

She lifted her shoulders. "I do not like the feeling," she said.

"The feeling of being alive?" he asked. "You are a good dancer. You take the rhythm of the music inside yourself and allow it to move through you."

"I do not like being observed," she said. "It would be remarked upon too particularly if I danced with you for a second time. Your sister-in-law did not like it the first time. I have to live here. For a lifetime. I cannot afford to give rise to even a breath of gossip."

He set one foot on the bench beside her and rested his

forearm on his leg. "You do not have to stay here," he said. "You can come away with me. I will find you a home somewhere where you will not have to worry about anyone's opinion but mine."

She laughed again. "A love nest," she said. "With only one man to please. How very desirable."

"It must have seemed desirable to you once," he said, "when you married. Unless you married for a reason other than love. I somehow cannot imagine your doing so."

"That was a long time ago," she said. "Please don't let anyone find us here together." She drew a deep inward breath. "Please."

"This is my dance," he said. "Come and dance it with me." He stretched out his hand to her and returned his foot to the floor.

"No," she said. "It is too late to join the set now."

"Here," he said. "Dance with me here. The music is loud enough and there is quite sufficient open space and no carpet on the floor."

"Here?" She looked up at him for the first time.

"Come," he said again.

She set her hand slowly in his and got hesitantly to her feet. But when he set his arm about her waist and took her hand in his, she raised her other to his shoulder and they moved to the music, twirling about the darkened room in harmony together. She really was a good dancer. She followed his lead so that he felt no consciousness of drawing her with him and no fear of stepping on her feet.

They danced in silence. At first they danced correctly, the proper distance between them despite the positioning of their hands. But when he looked down at her and a turn brought the light onto her face, he could see that she danced with her eyes closed. He drew her closer until her thighs brushed his as they moved and he could feel the tips of her breasts against his coat. And then he drew her closer still until he turned her hand to hold it palm in against his heart. She leaned her forehead against his shoulder and her hand slid farther about his neck.

The music stopped eventually and they stopped moving.

She was slim and supple and warm against him. She smelled of soap, far more enticing than any of the expensive perfumes with which any of his mistresses had ever doused themselves. He was afraid to move. He hardly dared breathe. If she was in some sort of a trance, he did not want to wake her.

But she lifted her head after a while and looked into his face. He could not see her expression clearly. But her body remained arched warmly into his. He lowered his head and kissed her.

This time her lips were parted too. He moved his tongue along her upper lip from corner to corner and back along the lower lip. She neither withdrew nor responded. She seemed totally relaxed, rather like a woman after love. Except that he had been cheated of the love, he thought ruefully as she drew back her head.

"You do that well," she said. "I suppose you do everything well. Including seduction. No more, though. I am going to go."

Later. There was going to be a later. He would not press the point now. This was enough for now. But when it happened, it would not be seduction. It would be with her full consent. Perhaps she did not even realize it yet.

"Come, then," he said. "We must not wait down here until all the food is gone."

"No," she said. "I did not mean to the supper room. I am going home."

"Who is taking you?" He frowned. "The Reverend Lovering has not returned, has he?"

"I—I have someone," she said. "You see? I brought my cloak down with me."

He did not look, but he gathered that it was lying on a chair.

"You do not lie well," he said. "You were planning to *walk* home alone. Why were you sitting in here, then? Did you not have the courage to do it?"

"There is nothing to it," she said. "There are no wild animals here and no footpads. There is nothing to fear."

But he knew from the tone of her voice that he had guessed correctly. She wanted to walk home but was afraid to do so. And she would consider it too early to ask Claude or anyone else to bring out a carriage to take her. So she had sought refuge in the music room, perhaps hoping to remain here undetected until the end of the ball.

"Wait here," he said. "I shall go up for a cloak and escort you home."

"You will not!" she exclaimed, her voice outraged. "I will go alone."

"Wait here." He set a finger over her lips. "Don't even think of slipping away, Catherine. I will come after you with great noise if you do. I will bring a search party with me to beat the bushes. You will be mortally embarrassed. Wait here until I come."

"No," she said. "No. If we were seen together . . ."

"We will not be." He was at the door already. He turned back to look at her. "Wait here."

"I will come to supper, then," she said. But he was out through the door already. He closed it after him, pretending not to have heard her.

If he had planned it, it could not be more perfect. She had

not planned it. He was certain of that. But he would make her glad of it. He would make her see how perfect it was.

Catherine.

He could not remember being so obsessed with any woman.

Ten

SHE DID NOT know quite how she had got into this. She had tried hard to avoid temptation or the possibility of gossip. Dancing with Viscount Rawleigh and going in to supper with him would have offered the danger of both. And so she had left the ballroom and almost the house. She had taken her cloak and gone to the music room, from which she could slip out into the night without being observed by either footmen or other guests. And then she had stood in the doorway, afraid to leave. It was so very dark outside—and the walk back home was over a mile, much of it among the oak trees of the lower driveway.

Just like a child, she had been afraid of the dark.

And so she had sat on the bench of the pianoforte, trying to get up her courage. Or failing that, she had decided to stay where she was until supper was well over.

It seemed hardly fair that her problems had now been compounded. He was going to be missed. It would take him almost an hour to escort her home and return. She assumed, at least, that he meant to walk with her, not call out a carriage. That would be even worse. He would be missed, and then perhaps someone—Mrs. Adams, certainly—would notice that she was missing too.

She should have said a very firm no to being escorted home. She should have insisted on going back up to the ballroom. Even now, she should slip out alone. He would not find her in the darkness. And she did not believe he would put into effect his threat to make a loud noise in search of her. He would not gather a search party. It had been a foolish threat meant for a gullible female.

Oh dear, Lord, she had not thought she was still gullible to the wiles of men.

But she must be just that. She was still standing undecided in the music room when he returned, looking more satanic than ever with the folds of a dark cloak swinging about him. Without conscious intention, she had put on her own cloak, she realized. She drew the wide hood up over her head and shivered.

"Now," he said briskly, "we may leave."

"This is not right," she said. "It is very improper."

He raised his eyebrows. She wondered if he knew how very arrogant he looked when he did that and decided that he probably did. "Afraid, Mrs. Winters?" he asked.

She was—afraid of him, afraid of the darkness outside, afraid of going back to the ballroom with him. She hated being afraid. She hated feeling weak and vulnerable and under the control of a man. Just like that other time. Except that it was worse this time. This time if she stepped outside with him, she would be doing so voluntarily, knowing exactly what Society could do to her if the truth were ever known.

But what could Society do that it had not already done? Society did not care about her any longer or even know about her. How foolish now to care for her reputation. Except that . . .

"Mrs. Winters?" He was standing at the French windows, one hand on the door handle, the other stretched toward her.

"No," she said, moving toward him. "I am not afraid, my lord."

As soon as she had passed him and stepped onto the terrace and he had closed the door behind him, he set an arm about her waist, encircling her with a fold of his cloak as he did so. He hurried her across the terrace and onto the dark lawn. She drew in a sharp breath. They were not going to walk down the driveway?

"It is a little quicker this way," he said, "and a little more private."

A little more private. The words burned themselves on her mind and she heard her teeth chattering. His arm was warm and firm about her. She could feel his thigh and his hip with her own, firmly muscled, very masculine. Her body was still aching with desire from their waltz and the kiss that had followed it.

A little more private.

Would she be able to resist him? Would she want to? Would she have the willpower? Oh, this was beginning to remind her . . .

It was so very dark. Her eyes had not quite accustomed themselves to the darkness even though she had sat in the darkened music room for half an hour or longer. And yet he was moving with confident strides.

"It is so dark," she said aloud, and heard with dismay the thinness of her voice.

He stopped and turned her against him before kissing her—with wide mouth this time. "You will come to no harm," he said. "I was notorious in the army for my ability to see in the dark. Besides, I came here often as a boy. I would know the way blindfolded."

You will come to no harm. She almost laughed aloud.

It was worse when they got among the trees. She would not have been able to see a hand before her face if she had held one there, she was sure. And the ground was more uneven. But he held her securely to his side and his pace slowed only a little. He really did seem to know just where he was going. And yet she waited for him to stop. She waited for—for ravishment. Though she was not sure it would be that. She was not sure she would have even that much consolation afterward.

"Ah, here we are," he said after what seemed a long age of tense silence—tense on her part anyway. "My sense of direction has not failed me."

And this time she *did* see. A faint gleam of light from among the branches of the trees shone on the latch of the postern door. The road was just the other side of it and her cottage a mere few steps away. He really had brought her straight home, then. Her knees turned weak with relief. And this was even better than having gone down the driveway and through the village. Late as the hour must be, there was a strong chance that they would have been seen in the village.

It was so dreadfully improper to be out alone with him at night like this.

He released his hold on her to open the door and look cautiously out, both ways.

"No one," he said. He reached a hand for hers. She could see almost clearly now that the door was open and the sky was visible beyond it. "Come."

But she held back. "I can go alone from here," she said. "Thank you. It was very kind of you to escort me, my lord."

There was silence for a moment and then a chuckle. "Is that my cue to make you my most elegant bow and to deliver my most polished speech about its having been an honor and a pleasure?" he said. "Come. I will see you home. There may be a score or two of footpads waiting to pounce upon you between here and your cottage. How would I forgive myself if you came to harm?"

He was laughing at her. Half of his face was caught in the dim light of the sky beyond the door. He was so very handsome. She had waltzed with him tonight—twice. Once in the ballroom and once in the music room, when the dance had become not just intimate and romantic, but also lascivious. The music and the rhythm had been a mere excuse for their bodies to touch and to move together. He had kissed her tonight and she had kissed him.

If there had been any doubt in the last couple of weeks, since his first appearance at Bodley, there was none left. All the barriers and masks and armor she had built up about herself in five years had crumbled and disappeared without a trace. She could no longer pretend that she was not a young woman with a young woman's needs and yearnings. And perhaps they did not even disappear with youth. Perhaps it had been foolish to try to persuade herself that she could wait them out.

"Come," he said again, more softly. More irresistibly.

She did not take his hand, but she slipped past him through the doorway and onto the road. She felt for a moment almost as if she had been slapped with reality. He stepped out after her, closed the door, and set his arm and his cloak about her again.

Toby barked when they were coming up the path and when she opened the door. Barking sounded so very loud in the middle of the night. She was so concerned with shushing him that she forgot about turning in the doorway, bidding Lord Rawleigh a firm good night, and closing the door between them.

"Silence, sir," he said in a firm, quiet voice, and Toby fell silent, wagged his tail, and trotted off into the kitchen—doubtless to his comfortable perch on her rocker.

Then the hall was in darkness as the outer door closed. And she was in his arms, his cloak all about her, and being kissed again.

Except that it was not really a kiss. Not by her definition, anyway. His mouth was open and somehow so was hers, and his tongue was plundering deep into her mouth. It was an unbearably intimate kiss. Almost as intimate . . . His hands were beneath her cloak, cupping her breasts, doing something to her nipples that made them tight and hard and sent sensation sizzling through her breasts and down through her womb to her thighs to set them aching and throbbing.

And then his hands were behind her, moving firmly downward, cupping her buttocks, bringing her hard against him, lifting her slightly so that she could feel the hardness of his own need of her.

It must feel thus to drown, she thought—this frantic need to come to the surface, to gulp in air, this opposing instinct to stop fighting, to make it easier upon oneself, to let happen what was going to happen.

"Catherine," he murmured against her lips, his voice low and husky. "So very beautiful."

She could not think. She could not organize her thoughts. His hair was thick and silky between her fingers.

"Take me upstairs," he said against her ear. "This is better done horizontally than vertically."

This. The joining of their bodies. His coming inside hers. For pleasure. Although she had never known pleasure in such a way, she knew that with him she would. Now. Tonight.

She could no longer remember why it was undesirable to be his mistress. She needed a man's body so desperately. *His* man's body. Him. She needed him.

To be his mistress. For how long? A week or two while he

was still at Bodley? He would be tired of her by then. He would not take her away with him as he had suggested sometime recently—she could not remember when. She would be alone again. How would it feel—the aloneness and the emptiness after having been his mistress for a brief time?

Perhaps she would not be quite alone. Perhaps he would leave her with child.

He had been kissing her throat and trailing his mouth up over her chin to her mouth again.

"Come," he said.

"No." Her voice sounded flat, dispassionate. She had not quite realized she was going to speak until she did. But she knew that it had to be said again. "No."

He moved his head back a few inches. She wondered if he could see her. His face was just a shadow.

"You are not going to be difficult, are you?" he asked her.

"Yes." Her voice was a little stronger. "I believe I am. I want you to leave now, please."

"My God." She found that she was pressed against the wall, his hands bracketing her head, braced against it. "Am I a fool? Is my imagination so vivid that I have misread your response? When we first waltzed? In the music room? On the walk home? Here? I cannot have imagined it. You are as much on fire for me as I am for you."

"And therefore," she said, "we go to bed together. It is perfectly logical, is it not?"

"Yes." He sounded baffled and irritated. "Yes, it is. Catherine—"

"I will not be your mistress," she said.

"Why not?" His head moved an inch closer to hers. "Why ever not? Do you believe I will mistreat you? I am accustomed to giving as much pleasure as I receive."

Even then a treacherous desire stabbed through her.

"I will not," she said. "And I do not have to give a reason. I will not. I have told you so before. I tried to avoid you tonight by retiring to the music room. I tried to stop you from bringing me home. I tried to stop you from coming beyond the postern door with me. I have been very clear in my denials."

"As your body has been very clear in its invitations," he said. He was definitely angry now. "You want marriage, is that it, Catherine? You set your favors at the highest price of all. Well, I will pay it. Marry me."

She was shocked into silence for a few moments. "You would marry me," she said, "in order to go to bed with me?"

"Precisely," he said. "If there is no other way. I want you that much. Are you satisfied?"

"Yes, I am satisfied," she said, cold suddenly and as far from feeling desire as she had ever felt. She brushed his arms aside when they reached for her. "I am satisfied that my reason and my common sense have been advising me well for the past two weeks. I am not just a female body, my lord. This is not an empty shell. There is a person inside. A person who dislikes you and resents your arrogant assumption that a few kisses and caresses are sufficient to establish your right to make use of my body for your pleasure. You have done nothing but pursue me since I first mistook you for your brother and smiled at you. Even though I said no quite clearly when you first called on me, you would not believe that any woman could be insane enough to resist you. Well, this woman prefers insanity to becoming your possession."

"Why, you bitch," he said quietly and almost pleasantly. "I do believe you are enjoying yourself. I will give you no further opportunity. You will be plagued with me no longer after tonight, ma'am. I am sure we will be mutually delighted not to set eyes on each other again."

Toby was standing in the passageway, growling. She looked down at him in the shaft of light that came through the door as it opened and then shut again none too gently. She stood where she was for a few minutes, almost as if her weight and spread hands were necessary to hold the wall up. Toby was whining.

"You want to go outside," she said. Her voice sounded quite normal. It seemed strange to perform the familiar and ordinary tasks of letting Toby out through the back door and then going into the kitchen to light the lamp and stoke up the fire in order to boil the kettle for tea. She had to have a cup of tea, late as it was. And she had to sit for a while in the familiar surroundings of her kitchen before going upstairs to bed—where she could have been lying at this very moment with him. . . .

She felt sick. She was not at all sure she was going to be able to drink her tea after all. She felt sick and horribly guilty. He had called her a bitch. No one had ever called her such a dreadfully vulgar name before. That in itself would have caused a feeling of nausea. But worse was the feeling that perhaps he had been justified.

He had once accused her of being a tease. Was she? Had she led him on? She had wanted him so very badly. Had her need shown to the extent that it had become an invitation? She had not tried to avoid any of the three kisses he had given her tonight. Indeed, she had welcomed all three and had participated fully in them.

She had wanted him. Even now her womb throbbed with the leftover need to feel his body inside hers.

It must have been her fault, all that had happened this evening. Just as it had all been her fault that other time. Except that over the years she had regained her self-respect by reasoning it all out and coming to the conclusion that it had not really been her fault. Only a small part of it. Only what might have been called the teasing.

As now. She was a tease, it seemed. Issuing invitations but being unwilling to accept the consequences.

She hated herself—again. How quickly a self-esteem built so painstakingly could disappear.

Toby was scratching on the door. She got up to let him in and noticed that the kettle over the fire was already boiling. She made her tea, stood over the pot while it steeped, and poured a cup while it was still rather too weak for her taste. It did not matter. At least it was hot and wet.

Toby stood before her when she sat down again, his tongue lolling, hope and speculation in his eyes.

"There is no point in my saying no, Tobe," she said to him rather bitterly. "No one ever believes me when I say no anyway."

It was invitation enough. He jumped into her lap and curled into a comfortable ball. He sighed deeply and proceeded to go off to sleep with the aid of a soothing hand smoothing over his back.

She stared upward, rocking slowly in the chair, feeling the kind of deep despair that even a week ago she had remembered with a shudder and tried not to remember at all.

Her tea grew cold on the table beside her and filmed over.

VISCOUNT RAWLEIGH WAS frustrated and angry when he left Catherine's house. He shut the door firmly behind him, disdaining to slam it, and strode across the road toward the postern door, looking neither ahead nor to right nor to left. He pushed the door open, stepped through, and shut that too with a decisive click.

Had he been as alert as he had been when he opened the postern door on his way to the cottage, he would probably have both heard and seen the one-horse cart that was approaching the village from the south, even though it was still some distance away.

Its driver drew the horse to a halt as soon as the cottage door opened.

"Well," Percy Lambton said after the postern door had closed. "Well, bless my soul. That was not a suitable sight for your eyes, I daresay, Reverend."

The Reverend Lovering was frowning. "Who?" he said. "Mr. Adams?"

"Not him," Percy said. "Viscount Rawleigh, Reverend. Coming from Mrs. Winters's cottage at this time of night. And not a light on in the house. Mighty suspicious it looked to me."

"He must have been escorting her home from the ball," the rector said. "Mrs. Lovering and I had to leave early because of your mother's sickness. Very obliging of his lordship, I am sure. But where is his carriage? And why would he escort her alone? It is not at all the thing."

Percy snorted. "This is not for your ears, Reverend," he said, "but it is common knowledge that there have been carryings-on for some time. Clandestine meetings there have been in the park. Ask Bert Weller if you do not believe me. And they have walked together arm in arm through the village brazenlike for all to see. It is pretty clear what has been going on tonight though I am sorry your eyes had to see it."

The Reverend Lovering looked back at the cottage after they had passed it and saw that a light had come on behind the kitchen window. He was frowning and looking stern.

"This is not what we expect from visitors at the house, Percy," he said, "even if they are viscounts. I am sadly disappointed that his lordship would take such license in a respectable neighborhood, as I am sure Mr. Adams and his good lady will be. And it is certainly not what we expect of the respectable citizens of Bodley-on-the-Water. I am deeply disturbed."

"But she is not a true citizen, is she?" Percy said. "She has been here for only a few years. And who is to know where she came from or what sort of life she led before she came here. For all we know she might have been a slut—if you will forgive my use of the word, Reverend."

They had reached the rectory and the Reverend Lovering got down. "Perhaps we have misunderstood, Percy," he said. "I shall call at Bodley House tomorrow and have a word with Viscount Rawleigh and with Mr. Adams. In the meantime it would be as well if you said nothing."

"Me?" Percy asked, amazed. "Mum is the word with me, Reverend. One thing about me, I hate gossip and always know when to keep my mouth shut. A shocking thing, this. I would not sully my lips by talking about it."

The rector nodded. "Your mother will recover, as she usually does," he said. "The next time she believes she is at death's door, it might be as well for you to wait awhile before coming running for me."

"Yes, Reverend," Percy said, turning his cart in the road and setting out on the return journey home.

He glanced at the light in Catherine's kitchen window as he passed and pursed his lips. A whore in Bodley-on-the-Water—he had known it all along, of course. Now everyone else would finally be convinced too. It was a long time since there had been anything local to add such interest to life. He could hardly wait for the morning to come.

INCREDIBLY THE BALL was still in progress when Viscount Rawleigh returned to the house. It seemed to him that hours must have passed since he left. He almost expected to see dawn graying the east. But in reality he guessed he had been gone for less than an hour.

He did not rejoin the festivities. He went up to his room, rang for his valet, and set the man to packing his bags. He scribbled two notes and went personally to Lord Pelham's room and Mr. Gascoigne's to leave them in a prominent place where they would be seen and read without delay. Then he retreated to his room and eventually to bed, though not to sleep.

The bitch, he kept thinking again and again. Almost like a refrain that he had set to repeat itself in his mind in order to block other thoughts.

A person who dislikes you . . .

But she had been happy enough to kiss and cuddle with him.

Well, this woman prefers insanity to becoming your possession.

Devil take it, he had offered her *marriage*. He was the insane one, not she. He had offered her marriage and she had spoken with contempt about becoming his possession. She could have become the Viscountess Rawleigh. But she preferred insanity and her cold virtue.

He hated her.

And he felt suddenly childish. He hated a woman because she had refused to be bedded by him? It had happened before, though not often, it was true. He had always shrugged off rejection. There were endless numbers of women with whom to replace the one who had rejected him, after all.

The same was true now. If he went to London, in no time at all he could have his choice of a casual bedfellow, a more permanent salaried ladybird, or a mistress from among the *ton*. Sex without entanglements.

He really must have been insane to offer marriage in return for sex with Catherine Winters. He would have regretted his decision within a month. The same woman rarely held his interest for longer than that—or even as long.

But how had she had the gall to lead him on as she had only to reject him with such scorn and such righteousness after he had reached a point from which it had been both difficult and physically painful to return?

The b—

But the house had grown quiet at last and his brain had finally stopped whirling between anger and sexual frustration.

She had not wanted to dance that second waltz with him. She had gone to the music room in order to avoid him.

She had not wanted to dance with him there.

She had not wanted him to escort her home.

She had not wanted him to go beyond the postern door with her.

She had said no as soon as he had suggested going upstairs with her.

When he thought about it—he did not *want* to think about it—there had been an almost sickening consistency to her behavior.

She had not wanted him. Oh, physically she had, perhaps. He had little doubt that she was as attracted to him as he was to her. But she had not wanted to surrender her virtue to him. Or her freedom, it seemed.

She had said no. From the beginning she had said no.

It was all his fault, then. If he was feeling frustrated and angry and—oh, yes, and unhappy, it was all his fault for not believing or accepting that one word *no*. She had been right to call him arrogant.

Admitting his own guilt did not make him feel one whit the better. He lay awake still, staring upward, trying to decide if he owed her an apology before leaving tomorrow morning. But he wanted to leave at dawn or as soon after dawn as was possible. He must see Claude first, of course. And he must find out if Nat and Eden were coming with him or if they would wait a day or two longer, as planned.

Besides, he did not believe she would welcome an apology.

And he certainly had no wish to see her again. None.

No, things were better left as they were. He would leave as soon as he could and not come back to Bodley for a long, long time. He would put Mrs. Catherine Winters and this whole nasty episode firmly behind him. Forget the whole thing.

It had been one of the most uncomfortable and shameful episodes of his life.

Devil take it, he thought, trying to impose relaxation on his body and blankness on his mind, he could still feel the leftover ache of wanting her.

Eleven

CLAUDE ADAMS, STANDING beside the bed, leaned over his sleeping wife and kissed her softly on the lips. She mumbled something and sighed.

"I am going out on estate business," he said. "I will be back in time for luncheon and the promised walk with the children and our guests this afternoon."

"Mm," she murmured without opening her eyes.

He hesitated. He was very tempted to leave it at that. When one lived with someone like Clarissa, it was always very tempting to play the coward, to become a husband in retreat, so to speak. But in nine years of marriage it had never been his way. He was not going to change now.

"Rex has just left," he said. "Eden and Nathaniel went with him."

For one moment he thought he was going to be able to escape with the simple announcement. Then her eyes snapped open.

"What?" She frowned—Clarissa frowned all too often these days. "Left for where?"

"For home," he said. "Stratton. I am not sure they were all going there. Eden and Nathaniel talked about going down to

Dunbarton—Haverford's seat. Their friend, the Fourth Horseman of the Apocalypse, you know." He attempted to smile.

She sat up sharply. And, being Clarissa, she jerked the bedclothes up to cover herself even though he had been naked with her beneath those covers little more than an hour ago and had made love to her twice during the short night.

"Gone?" She was almost shrieking. "To *Stratton*? In the middle of a house party? When he is supposed to be courting Ellen?"

"Clarissa," he said, "you know—"

"And after what he *did* to her last night?" she said.

He did not need this after last night, Claude thought with an inward sigh. It had taken a certain amount of sternness on his part—he hated having to play the lord and master with his own wife—to keep her calm during the ball, to prevent her from showing public chagrin at the disappearance of his brother before supper and at his failure to reappear during it. It had taken all his energy to keep her smiling and acting the part of gracious hostess when Rex had failed to return in order to lead Ellen out for the set he had reserved with her after supper. Clarissa had been livid with fury. He had been annoyed too, he had to admit—it was an unpardonable discourtesy—and had promised himself a good talk with his twin this morning. Fortunately Ellen herself had looked almost relieved and had spent most of the set sitting and talking with the son of one of his more prosperous tenants.

What had made matters worse, of course, was that Clarissa had noticed the coinciding absence of Mrs. Winters and had drawn the conclusion that she and Rex were together somewhere. Claude had no opinion on the matter himself and it was really none of his business except that the lady's reputation might suffer if others had drawn the same conclusions as Clarissa. And he had warned Rex. . . .

"Well?" Clarissa said now, a sharp edge to her voice. "Are you going to stand there mute all morning?"

"Rex asked me to convey his apologies to Ellen," he said. "He felt ill and went to bed. He did not want to spoil our evening by telling us and having us worry about him."

He had accepted the lie without question earlier. Rex had known that he did not believe it, but there had been a tacit understanding between them that that was what the ladies would be told. Rex had looked grim and wretched. Obviously something drastic had happened during those hours of the ball when he had been absent—something to make him look like that, something to cause the unexpectedly abrupt departure.

"And he has *gone*?" He could see that Clarissa was only just beginning to digest the implications. "What about Ellen? She has been jilted. She—"

He sat down on the edge of the bed and proceeded to be both soothing and firm with her. It was neither easy nor quickly accomplished. And of course before he could get away to the blessed relief of riding alone across his land, she remembered that he had said Pelham and Gascoigne had gone too. Her house party, all her plans were in ruins.

"And *that woman* is to blame for it all," she said finally, sparks shooting from her eyes. "Claude, if you do not—"

"—throw her out of her cottage and banish her from the village?" he said, his patience beginning to desert him. "I told you last night that Mrs. Winters has done nothing wrong. We have no evidence that Rex was with her last night. He was ill and in his own bed. She was doubtless tired and found her own way home—though I wish she had asked me to call out the carriage and send a maid with her. You cannot turn your spite on her, Clarissa, just because she is a beautiful woman."

They were ill-advised words—words he would not have

used if his temper had not been frayed. But two arguments either side of a very short night's sleep were a little too much. And the sleep had been shortened by the fact that last night's negative emotions had been converted to passion.

Clarissa took exception, of course, to his use of the word *spite*—how could he possibly suggest that she ever acted out of spite? And if he found Mrs. Winters so beautiful, perhaps it was a trial to him to be stuck with such an ugly wife.

He took her none too gently by the shoulders and kissed her hard.

"Enough of this, Clarissa," he said. "This argument is degenerating into sheer stupidity. I have work to accomplish before luncheon. I am leaving now."

And he did so even though she called to him as he opened the door of her bedchamber. That had been an unwise closing speech too, he thought ruefully as he ran down the stairs. But so be it. He had not been feeling so cheerful himself to start with. Heaven knew when he would see Rex next. He always felt for a while whenever they separated that part of himself had been amputated. But he could never explain that to Clarissa. She just would not understand.

MR. ADAMS WAS not at home when the Reverend Lovering called on him later in the morning. But Mrs. Adams consented to see him as soon as she knew who the visitor was. There was a question she wished to ask him.

He hesitated after bowing to her and complimenting her on the fine weather and the daffodils blooming along the edges of the wood and the distinguished guests she and Mr. Adams had invited to grace their home and honor the village of Bodley-on-the-Water. He complimented her on the superior quality of the food at last evening's banquet and the splendor of the ball and apologized for the fact that his pastoral duties had taken him away early. He paid himself the compliment of wondering if his absence had been remarked upon and had perhaps dampened anyone's spirits.

"Sir," Mrs. Adams said abruptly without any of her usual gestures of gracious acceptance for the homage being paid her, "when you conveyed Mrs. Lovering back to the rectory last evening, did you also take Mrs. Winters home?"

That was when the rector hesitated. What he had to say was not for the gentle ears of a lady and certainly not for the delicate sensibilities of such a noble lady as Mrs. Adams. But honesty compelled him to answer the one question at least. After all, if men of the cloth could not be relied upon to speak the truth, then who could? No, he had not conveyed Mrs. Winters home.

"It was *someone else* who did that, ma'am," he added ominously. "Perhaps I should return to discuss the matter with Mr. Adams later. You will wish to be with your dear children, I am sure."

But Mrs. Adams had glimpsed one ray of light in an otherwise bleak morning—the Liptons, perhaps sensing that they were outstaying their welcome, had announced their intention of leaving for home on Monday, the day after tomorrow. Ellen had confided her relief that Rawleigh had gone home without coming to the point with her. She had been dreadfully afraid that he might offer her marriage and that she might find herself awed into accepting. Claude had called her spiteful and ugly and stupid. And Juliana and William were sullen and in disgrace with their nurse after a vicious fight over a single paintbrush, of all things, when there must be a dozen others in the nursery.

Everything was falling apart.

And *that woman* was the cause of it all.

The story she was told, then, by an apologetic and reluctant Reverend Lovering was like a seed falling on fertile soil. She listened to it avidly. She accepted the obvious interpretation uncritically and with considerable malice.

That woman was a whore.

Clarissa Adams was exultant. And furious. And filled with righteous indignation.

She rang for tea and invited the rector to take a seat. They talked for half an hour before he took his leave, bowing and apologizing and complimenting her on her fortitude and wisdom.

No, it was not necessary for him to return to speak with Mr. Adams, she told him. She would handle the matter herself—as he must handle his responsibility as rector and spiritual leader of the community.

She waited for a few moments after the Reverend Lovering had bowed himself from the room before leaving it herself and making straight for the staircase. She instructed a footman, without even looking at him, to send her maid up to her immediately and to have the carriage before the doors in half an hour's time.

CATHERINE FORCED HERSELF out of bed at her usual hour, though she had hardly slept and though a massive inertia urged her to stay lying there, doing nothing. There seemed to be nothing to get up for.

Memory made it worse. Memory of the same feeling, which had gone on for weeks on end. Her son dead. Her arms empty. Her breasts sore and swollen with milk for a dead baby. No one to comfort her—not that anyone could have comforted her anyway. But no sympathetic voice. And apparently no purpose left to living.

How had she dragged herself out of it? She thought back, tried to remember exactly how it had come about. She had wandered up to the attic of her aunt's house one day, to an empty room that had once been inhabited by a servant. She had opened the window and looked out and down—down to the pavement below. It was a long drop. But she was not quite sure the fall would kill her. Perhaps it would only maim.

And then she had realized what she was doing. For the first and only time in her life the thought of ending it all had entered her consciousness. But she had known within a few moments that it was something she just could not do, that however far down she had sunk, life was still too precious a gift to be deliberately destroyed.

She had not wanted to live. But she could not end her life. And life could not be willed to an end. If she must live on, then—she had been only twenty—she must make something of her life. She must somehow make it worth living again without Bruce and without any of the people and things and surroundings with which she had been familiar all her life and with which she had identified herself.

She must start anew, become a new person, live a new life.

Yes, that was how it had begun. And somehow she had found the energy and the determination to bring it about. Less than three months later she had moved to this cottage.

She had been happy here. Contented. At peace. She had felt that her life was worth something again.

Well, then, she would do it all over again, she decided. She would put everything back together and carry on. Really she had no choice.

And so she dragged herself out of bed, let Toby out for a few minutes, washed and dressed and combed her hair, got the fire going, forced herself to eat some breakfast, and set about baking cakes to take with her on her afternoon visits to three elderly people. Life must continue. She would not stay home this afternoon. These people had come to expect her weekly visits and the cakes she always brought and the book from which she always read to them. She would not disappoint them.

Really nothing had changed.

She sighed when a knock came at the door. She wiped her floury hands on her apron and tried in vain to persuade Toby to stop barking—he had raced out into the hall and was expressing his displeasure to the front door.

If it was *him,* she thought, she would slam the door in his face and hope that his nose was in its direct path.

It was a footman from Bodley House, the one who usually announced a visit from Mrs. Adams. Catherine took off her apron, folded it, and prepared to step out to the gate. The last thing she felt like this morning was a state visit from the lady of the manor. Her sense of humor had temporarily deserted her.

But Mrs. Adams was taking the unprecedented step of getting down from the carriage with the assistance of her coachman. Catherine stayed where she was in the doorway.

"Hush, Toby," she said.

But Toby was guarding his territory.

Mrs. Adams did not pause in the doorway or even glance at Catherine. She sailed on by and into the parlor. Catherine raised her eyebrows and closed the door.

"Good morning," she said, following her visitor into the parlor. Though it must be close to noon or even past, she thought. "Oh, Toby, do hush."

"Get rid of that dog," Mrs. Adams commanded above the din.

Catherine resented the tone of voice when she was in her own home, and so was Toby, but it was a good idea nonetheless. She led the terrier to the back door, and he raced outside, his indignation immediately forgotten.

Mrs. Adams was standing in the middle of the parlor, facing the door.

"Slut!" she said coldly when Catherine reappeared.

Catherine did not pretend to misunderstand. Her heart began an uncomfortable hammering and there was a buzzing in her head that she hoped was not the harbinger of a fainting fit. She lifted her chin and clasped her hands in front of her.

"Ma'am?" she said calmly.

"Do you add deafness to your other vices?" her guest asked. "You heard me, Mrs. Winters. You are a slut and a whore and you will be out of this house by the end of next week. And out of this village. You have been tolerated here for too long. There is no further room for you among respectable people. I trust I have made myself clear."

They had been seen, then. Someonc had observed them leaving the house together. He had had his arm and his cloak about her. Her mind reached for an explanation to give. But her mind would not work as she willed it to do. Anger rescued her from abject muteness, however.

"No," she said at last, hearing with some surprise the calmness of her voice. "Of what exactly do I stand accused, ma'am?"

Her visitor's eyes narrowed. "I do not intend to stand here conversing with you," she said. "I shall get straight to the point by telling you that Lord Rawleigh was seen leaving this house—this *darkened* house—late last night. And that I myself have observed for the past two weeks your seductive wiles in his presence."

"I see," Catherine said. She felt almost like two persons. One of them was mindless with shock. The other was coldly thinking and speaking. "And have you banished Viscount Rawleigh from your home and this village too, ma'am?"

Mrs. Adams's bosom heaved and her nostrils flared.

"Mrs. Winters," she said, ice dripping from every word, "you are impertinent. You have a week during which to leave this house and neighborhood. Be thankful for such mercy. Do not try my patience to the limit. If you are still here at the end of next week, you may expect a visit from a constable and a meeting with a magistrate. Stand aside from the door. I would deplore having to brush against you as I leave."

Catherine turned and walked to the back door. Even though Toby was sitting there, waiting patiently to be let in, she did not give him a chance to come inside. She stepped out to the garden and closed the door behind her. He stood up, eagerly wagging his tail, and was rewarded when she strode down across the lawn to the river's edge. He frisked along happily beside her.

She tried not to think. She tried not to feel.

Impossible, of course.

He had been seen last night. Coming from her house. And whoever had done the seeing had jumped to what she supposed was the obvious conclusion. It had almost been the correct conclusion. She had been called a slut and a whore.

Not for the first time.

How could this be happening to her again? She had tried so hard.

She had convinced herself during the past five years that what had happened the other time had not been her fault, that someone else had been to blame. But it must have been her fault. This must be her fault. There must be something intrinsically evil in her.

She had been told to leave. This cottage and this village. She had to go. Within the week.

She went down on her knees beside the water suddenly and gripped the long grass on the bank with both hands.

Almost as if she would fall off the world if she did not hold tight.

She opened her mouth in order to breathe more easily. She was panting.

She could not leave. It had been the one condition. . . .

What would she do?

Where would she go?

She would be destitute.

Oh, God, oh, God. She bent her head and prayed desperately. But she could not get beyond the two pleading words.

Oh, God.

CATHERINE FORCED HERSELF somehow to go out during the afternoon to make her visits. If she stayed at home, she would surely go mad, she thought.

Mr. Clarkwell was unwell, his daughter-in-law reported, standing with the door half-opened, her face flushed, her eyes darting everywhere except to Catherine's own. He was too poorly for visitors.

There was no answer at the Symons's house, though the washing on the line and the curl of smoke coming from the chimney indicated that there was someone at home. Besides, elderly Mrs. Symons never went out.

Catherine did not try the third house. She went back home. She was too weary to take Toby for a walk, though he looked hopeful when she came through the door.

She was too weary even to set the kettle to boil. She slumped down in the rocker and shivered, her arms wrapped about herself.

They knew. Everybody knew. Or thought they knew. She had passed two people with whom she was acquainted on the walk home. Both had averted their faces.

There was a knock on the door.

She sat for a while with closed eyes. Perhaps whoever it was would go away. It could not be a friend. It seemed very likely that she had no friends left. If it was *him* . . . But she did not believe he would come here today, not now that everyone knew. Not that anyone would condemn him, of course. He would be seen merely as a gentleman appeasing very natural appetites. If it was . . .

The knock was repeated, louder, more imperiously. Toby, thank heaven, was outside and was not barking. She got to her feet. Why hide? Why care about anything any longer?

It was the Reverend Lovering. She almost sighed aloud with relief. Here surely was some small measure of comfort. He and Mrs. Lovering had always been her friends.

"Reverend." She tried to smile. "Do come in."

"I will not cross this threshold," he said with quiet solemnity. "It is my duty to inform you, Mrs. Winters, that fornicators and sinners are not welcome to worship with the righteous in the church of which I have been accorded the honor of being pastor. I deeply regret having to make this visit. But I never shirk what I consider my duty."

She found herself smiling. "No fornicators or sinners," she said. "Who is left to attend church, then, sir?"

He regarded her sternly. "Levity is not appropriate to the graveness of the circumstances, ma'am," he said.

"So you believe the story too?" she said. "You are here to cast your stone along with everyone else?"

"Ma'am," he said, his expression unchanged, "I believe the evidence of my own eyes. I *saw* his lordship leaving here last night. One cannot blame him, of course. Any man who is caught in the snare of a Jezebel is to be pitied rather than censured. His lordship has seen the error of his ways and has left Bodley House."

"Good day, Reverend," she said, and closed the door.

She stood with her back to it for many long minutes,

shaking, from her head to her feet. She found herself quite unable to move. At last she managed to crouch down on the floor. But she stayed where she was for many minutes longer. Toby was scratching on the back door. She ignored him. She had to. There was no getting to him.

DAPHNE HAD HEARD during a visit to the village and a call she had made on Mrs. Downes. She did not appear at luncheon. It was a gloomy affair, Claude found. Everyone seemed to be out of sorts, most noticeably Clarissa, who was doubtless punishing him for some of his unwise words of the morning.

But Daphne found him immediately after luncheon and told him. Told him about the stories that had been spreading like wildfire in the village during the morning. Told him about the Reverend Lovering's call at Bodley. Told him about Clarissa's visit to the village.

"Can it be true, Claude?" she asked, looking at him unhappily. "I know that Rex admired her. I encouraged him. I did not dream that his intentions might be dishonorable. Clayton often calls me a dangerous innocent. Is it possible that they were having an a-affair?"

He drew in a deep breath and released it slowly. "If they were," he said, "I cannot see that it is any of our business, Daph. But I know that is not the common view. And if they were and were indiscreet enough to allow themselves to be discovered, then it was Rex's fault. Entirely. It was his business to protect her reputation. And *he* was the one to be seen last night? Damn him! Pardon me, Daph." He clenched his hands. "And I had to be from home this morning!.

"Why would he leave if they were in the middle of an affair?" she asked.

"I don't know, Daph." He ran the fingers of one hand through his hair. "What a damnable mess. Well, one thing is clear. He is going to have to be sent for. She cannot be left to face this scandal alone. Clarissa called on her, you say? I had better find out from her what was said. Do you mind, Daph?"

"No," she said. "I will send her to you, Claude."

He sat down at the library desk while he waited and rested his head in his hands. Damn Rex. Damn him!

Clarissa came. She looked at his face and her own became triumphant.

"I see that you have found out," she said. "Now perhaps you will admit that I was right, Claude."

"Exactly what did the Reverend Lovering tell you this morning?" he asked.

"That he saw Rawleigh come from Mrs. Winters's darkened cottage late last night," she said. "It is obvious what was going on, Claude."

"To you, maybe," he said. "If it is any of your business."

"If—" She bristled immediately, but he held up a staying hand.

"You called upon Mrs. Winters?" he said. "For what reason, Clarissa?"

"Why, to order her to leave the cottage and the village by the end of next week," she said. "We cannot have a whore living so close, Claude. We have children to bring up."

He leaned across the desk with ashen face. "You *what*?" he said. But he held up his hand again before she could speak. "No, I heard. On what authority did you do this?"

She looked somewhat taken aback. "You were from home," she said. "It was something that had to be done without delay."

"It was something you have been itching to do for a long while," he said, not even trying to hide the anger from his voice. "And finally you saw your chance and took it while I was from home and could not stop you."

"It had to be done," she said. "The Reverend Lovering agreed with me."

"Did he indeed?" He strode around the desk to stand close to her. She looked at him with a mixture of defiance and uncertainty. "Clarissa, I am very displeased with you."

"You cannot believe ill of her, can you?" she cried. "Just because she is a beautiful woman."

"I am very displeased with you, madam," he said again, slowly and distinctly. "You are a spiteful, vicious meddler. Somehow I am going to have to smooth this thing over. I do not know quite how. You have made it extremely difficult. But you will certainly do no further harm. You will remain in this house until further notice from me. And yes, that is an order."

"Claude!" She was staring at him with wide shocked eyes. Her voice was shaking. "How dare you talk to your own wife like this?"

"I dare because you *are* my wife, madam," he said. "When you married me, you vowed to obey me. I have never called on you for obedience before. Now I insist upon it. I have a letter to write and then a visit to pay. You will leave me."

She opened her mouth to speak, shut it again with an audible click of teeth, and hurried from the room.

Twelve

THERE WERE TWO more knocks on Catherine's door that day. She was too deeply in shock, too stunned, too lethargic to keep from answering. Besides, humiliation, rejection could not be more complete than they already were.

Even so, she cringed when she saw Miss Downes outside the door. She had liked Miss Downes of all people in the village or neighborhood. But of course, the lady was the daughter of a former rector, a middle-aged spinster pillar of the community.

"You do not need to say it," Catherine said, holding up a hand. "I believe it has all been said by others. Good day, Miss Downes." She half closed the door again although Toby was outside, snuffling at their visitor's hem. He liked Miss Downes. She always fed him corners of her cakes and biscuits when she came to tea—with apologies to Catherine for wasting delicious food.

"No, please." Miss Downes in her turn held a staying hand. Her face looked pale and pinched. Her jaw looked rather like granite. "May I come in?"

"Why not?" Catherine opened the door wider and left it to walk back into the kitchen.

Miss Downes followed her and stood resolutely in the doorway while Catherine poked at the fire.

"I do not know the truth of the matter," Miss Downes said. "I do not want to know and do not need to know. It is none of my business. But the truth of my religion *is* my business. Papa always taught me that it was my personal business, that I should not let even a minister of religion, even Papa himself, speak for me when what he has to say is against the truth as I know it. The truth as I know it, the truth as Mother and Papa always taught it, is that the church is for sinners. Not for anyone else. Just for sinners. Being a sinner is one's membership certificate in the church—that was Papa's little joke. I am a member of the church, Mrs. Winters. I let that fact speak for itself."

Catherine set down the poker quietly and sat on the rocker, her hands clasped loosely in her lap. She stared into the fire.

"Mother and I do not condemn you, dear," Miss Downes said, her voice breathless now that her prepared speech had been delivered. "No matter what you have done—or not done. We do not need to know. It is your affair." She flushed scarlet. "That is, it is your *concern*."

"I am a member of the church too," Catherine said. "But I am not guilty of this particular sin, Miss Downes."

"As I said to Mother," Miss Downes said, "and as she said to me. We were in perfect agreement. Mrs. Winters is a *lady*, we said to each other. But you did not need to say it, dear. I did not need to know. I did not come to pry. I merely thought—and Mother thought—that you might like a little chat and a nice cup of tea. Oh, goodness me, it looks as if you have been baking for an army." Her eyes had alighted on the table and all the cakes that were to have been delivered to the elderly.

Catherine set her head back and closed her eyes. "I cannot

express the extent of my gratitude for your kindness, Miss Downes," she said. "But you must not stay. You were probably seen coming here. If you stay, and it is suspected that you are actually *visiting* me, you may find yourself without friends too."

Miss Downes crossed the room to the fire, lifted the lid of the kettle to check the water level inside, and set the kettle to boil. It was something she would normally have been far too well-bred to do in someone else's house even if she had been parched with thirst. She looked about her for the teapot and the tea caddy.

"We must always follow our own truth, Papa said." Miss Downes ladled a generous helping of tea into the teapot. "If others choose not to follow the same truth, then they are merely exercising the free will our Lord in his wisdom gave all of us. I can only do what is right in my eyes, Mrs. Winters. How others act is their concern. You made some currant cakes, I see. Yours are always more delicious than anyone else's I know. Even Mother's, though I would never say so in her hearing to hurt her. Shall I set some on a plate for us?"

Catherine opened her eyes at last and nodded. "For you," she said. "I am not hungry."

Miss Downes eyed her critically. "You have not eaten all day, have you?" she said. "I shall cut one up for you, Mrs. Winters, in bite-sized pieces. Like this, you see?" She had found a knife and proceeded to carve one small currant cake into smaller wedges. "This is what I do for Mother when she is off her food. There, dear." She handed the plate to Catherine.

Every bite tasted like straw. Every swallow was a major undertaking. But out of gratitude for kindness and unconditional love she persevered. By the time she had finished, there was a cup of strong, sweet tea at her elbow. It was a long time since she had been waited on in her own home.

Despite the breaches of etiquette that Miss Downes had deemed necessary, she stayed only the half hour that was polite for an afternoon call. Catherine followed her into the hall.

"I shall call again tomorrow after church," Miss Downes said. "Yes, I will go to church. I will not punish God because my truth does not coincide with the rector's. Oh, Mrs. Winters, Mother and I had great difficulty being properly civil to Mrs. Lovering when she called on us earlier. Great difficulty, indeed, though I believe we succeeded. There is no excuse for discourtesy to others, is there, especially when they are guests in one's own home."

"Miss Downes." Catherine had spoken scarcely more than a dozen words throughout the visit, though there had been not a moment of silence. "Thank you. I wish there were words more expressive of how I feel."

Miss Downes, thin, shapeless, ramrod straight in posture, severe of expression, was not the type of person one normally felt the urge to hug. But before she opened the door, Catherine did just that.

"Well, goodness me," Miss Downes said, flustered. "I just hope the tea was not too strong for you, dear. It is how Mother likes it, you know, though I prefer it a little weaker myself. And I remembered after putting two spoonfuls of sugar in your tea that you usually take just one."

Catherine stood at the open door for a short while, watching Miss Downes stride purposefully along the street. There were a few other people out at some distance from the cottage. There were probably others looking out of windows.

Miss Agatha Downes, fussy spinster daughter of a former

rector, had just performed what was perhaps the most courageous act of her life.

THE SECOND KNOCK came only fifteen minutes later. Her encounters with the outside world for today could not possibly end on a positive note, then, Catherine thought, making her weary way to the door.

And would this day never end?

Not for even one moment did she mistake him for his brother. Even so, her breath caught in her throat at the likeness. And more alike than ever. The customary good humor had left Mr. Adams's face. He looked pale and grim. So did Lady Baird, who was with him.

"I do not believe there is anything to add, is there?" Catherine said bitterly before either of them could speak. "Unless you have come to reduce the week's notice to a day."

"Oh, Toby, you darling dog." Lady Baird stooped down to cup his barking face in her hands. "You know me. We are friends, are we not?"

He agreed. He stopped barking, wagged his tail, and lifted his chin to be scratched.

"Mrs. Winters," Mr. Adams said, "I would like a moment of your time inside if I may. My sister has come with me to lend propriety to the visit."

Catherine heard herself laugh as she stood aside and ushered them into the parlor. Lady Baird went to stand facing the window. Mr. Adams took up his position before the empty fireplace, his back to it. Catherine stopped just inside the doorway and lifted her chin to look him directly in the eye.

She would not cringe. She would not despite the guilty memories she had of what she had done with his brother last night in the passageway just behind where she was now. Could that possibly have been just last night?

"Mrs. Winters," he said quietly, "it appears that my brother and my wife between them have done you a dreadful disservice during the past twenty-four hours. Not even so long."

His words were so unexpected that she said nothing.

"I do not know what happened between you and Rex last evening," he said. "I believe you are of age, ma'am, as is he. What you do in privacy together is your concern and his. Not mine. Or anyone else's. It is unfortunate, of course, that he was seen to leave your cottage. People will talk and gossip. And people will judge. And punish too. My wife acted hastily. She was given the facts and was upset by them. I was from home and so she did not have me to consult. She felt that she must act as she thought I would have acted. She is sorry for it now, sorry that she acted with what she perceived to be the harshness of a man instead of acting in accordance with her softer woman's instincts. Perhaps in time you will pardon her—and me. I hope you will disregard all that she said to you. Your cottage is leased until the end of this year. I will be quite happy to renew the lease at the end of that time."

"Mrs. Winters," Lady Baird said without turning away from the window, "forgive me. I deliberately threw you and Rex together on more than one occasion, knowing that he admired you. I did not realize the nature of that admiration. I suppose I should know my own brother better by now. Forgive me for my contribution to your distress."

They thought her guilty. But it did not matter to them. They thought that a physical affair between two adults was their business and no one else's. The realization was soothing, or would be when she had time to digest what was happening here. Mrs. Adams had *not* been acting on her husband's perceived behalf, of course. But it was understandable that he should wish to protect her from censure.

"Lord Rawleigh escorted me home last night," she said. "I was tired, yet the Reverend Lovering had already left. I was going to walk home alone but was afraid of the dark. Lord Rawleigh found me in the music room—I was supposed to be dancing with him at the time—and insisted on bringing me home himself. Toby was barking and it was very late. Lord Rawleigh stepped inside to quieten him. He left a few minutes later." She left them to imagine what had occupied those few minutes. "Nothing happened between us." Not what she stood accused of anyway.

Mr. Adams nodded. "Perhaps it is as well that my brother left Bodley early this morning," he said. "I do believe that the events of this day would have provoked me into separating him from some of his blood, Mrs. Winters."

"I might have helped," Lady Baird added.

"It would have been so simple—and so proper—for him to have called out my carriage for you," Mr. Adams said, "and even to have sent a maid with you. I apologize for him, ma'am. He was ever the impulsive one, and frequently the thoughtless one too, as witness his purchasing a commission when he was the elder son of the family."

"He always said you would make the better viscount, Claude," his sister said quietly.

"I feel for the distress you must have suffered today," Mr. Adams said. "But gossip dies and my wife will want to make her personal apologies to you. You are a valued member of this community." He smiled. "How are Julie and Will to become even competent pianists if you go away? You will stay?"

She could not go. That fact had been causing waves of panic all day. But she could not stay either. How could she stay?

"I am a pariah," she said. "How can I stay?"

"Oh, dear," Lady Baird said. She sounded angry. "People can be very vicious. With no proof whatsoever of what they believe. And even if there were proof . . ."

"We will call for you here tomorrow morning," Mr. Adams said. "You will come to church with us, ma'am, and sit in our pew. People will get the message."

Catherine closed her eyes briefly. "I have been told not to go to church," she said.

"By whom?" His brows shot up. He looked more than ever like his brother.

"By the Reverend Lovering," she said.

He stared at her in stunned silence for a few moments. "I see you did not exaggerate when you described yourself as a pariah," he said quietly. "I shall handle this, Mrs. Winters. This will not do at all."

"I will go away," she said. "If you will just give me a week or two."

"But do you have somewhere to go?" Lady Baird had turned away from the window now. There was concern in her face. "Do you have family to go to?"

"Yes." There was enough pity in their faces. She would not invite more. She would not be a helpless pawn in this drama that had developed today and was playing itself out about her. "Yes to both questions. I merely need to write a letter to warn them to expect me. I must leave. I would not be comfortable here any longer."

"I am sorry about that," Mr. Adams said. "But it will not be within the week?"

"No." She felt panic threaten again. A week. What would she do after that? Where would she go? There was nothing and nowhere and no one. She drew a deep and silent breath and held it for a few moments before releasing it slowly.

By that time they were leaving. But they did not do so

before Mr. Adams assured her that he would call on her again and that he would make all right for her.

Was he God? None of this could ever be put right. Some wounds could never be healed.

Lady Baird did what Catherine had done for Miss Downes earlier. She hesitated and then hugged Catherine in the open doorway.

"I could kill Rex," she said. "I could kill him."

They climbed into the carriage, which had waited for them, and drove away.

Catherine closed the door again and leaned back against it. Surely now, she thought, the events of the day were finally over. Surely now there would be peace.

If there could be peace in her life ever again.

LORD PELHAM AND Mr. Gascoigne had gone to Dunbarton in Cornwall to visit the Earl of Haverford. They had been feeling footloose and unwilling to go either to London or to Stratton. They had burdened Viscount Rawleigh with their presence there only a few weeks ago. They tried to persuade him to go with them, though neither was very insistent when he refused. He had not been good company on the journey south from Derbyshire.

They had sensed that his black mood was not something he might be teased out of. And so they had talked on neutral topics, laughed and conversed about people and events and issues that had no connection with Bodley or the couple of weeks they had just spent there.

Viscount Rawleigh was not quite sure why he did not go with them to visit Ken. It was probably just what he needed—a change of scenery, a chance to be with his three closest friends without other obligations and other affections intruding.

But he found that he wanted only to get home to Stratton,

where he might be alone to lick his wounds. Not that he would admit even to himself that there were wounds to lick. Women like Catherine Winters he could live without. The woman was a tease, whether she knew it or not. She had lured him into behaving shabbily, and he hated to be in the wrong over anything or anyone.

At Stratton he would forget about her. He would be in familiar surroundings, and there was always plenty of work to be done during the spring—when he was at home during spring, that was. He had a perfectly able steward, of course.

Life, since he had sold his commission, sometimes seemed almost frighteningly empty and purposeless.

A letter from Bodley had preceded his return. It was addressed in Claude's firm hand and lay accusingly on a silver salver where his eyes fell on it almost as soon as he had crossed his threshold. Doubtless it was a remonstrance on behalf of Clarissa for having jilted Ellen Hudson. But there had been no jilting, he thought irritably. There had been no courtship, except in his sister-in-law's determined imagination. He found the girl a bore and she found him a terror—hardly the basis for a courtship, not to mention marriage.

But Claude, of course, always gentle and fair, would be punctilious about putting forward Clarissa's views even if they did not coincide with his own.

Lord Rawleigh left the letter on the tray in the hall until he had retired to his own apartments, enjoying a hot and leisurely bath, dozed for half an hour on his bed, and dressed for dinner. He took the letter into the dining room with him and glanced at it irritably from time to time as he ate.

He would have expected Claude of all people to recognize his need to cut himself off from family and Bodley for a while. He did not need a letter to remind him. And good

Lord, Claude must have written it and sent it almost as soon as he and Nat and Eden had disappeared down the driveway.

He pulled it toward him eventually when there was only a glass of port left in front of him on the table. Just let Claude try to convince him that he was honor bound to offer for the girl. Just let him try!

A few minutes later he crumpled the opened letter in one hand and held on to it while he closed his eyes tightly. He did not move for a long while. When a footman tiptoed nervously toward the table to clear away a few more dishes, the butler motioned him with one thumb and they both left the dining room.

God!

He could not think straight.

There was really nothing to think about.

But he sat for many long minutes trying to convince himself that there was if only he could set his mind in motion.

When he left the dining room, his butler was hovering outside, trying to look busy.

"I'll be leaving for London at first light tomorrow morning, Horrocks," Lord Rawleigh said. "I'll be going from there straight to Derbyshire. See that everything is arranged, will you?"

"Yes, m'lord." The man made his bow. His impassive expression registered no surprise that his master was returning whence he had come only a few hours before.

"I will be taking the carriage," his lordship said as he strode in the direction of the staircase.

"Yes, m'lord."

MORE THAN A week had passed. She knew that she could not procrastinate for much longer. She had pretended that she was making plans, that she had written letters and was awaiting replies. She had pretended that there were alternatives to explore, a quite dizzying number of attractive options to choose among.

In reality there was nothing. During the long hours she was alone, she merely sat, staring ahead, knowing that in the end she must simply leave her cottage and leave Bodley-on-the-Water and go.

But go where?

She must just pick a place on a map and go there, she told herself. But that was impossible. What would she do when she reached the chosen place? She received a small quarterly allowance. There was very little of this quarter's money left. Not enough to take her very far by stage. And even if she spent it all to go as far as she could, there would be none left at the end of the journey. Nothing with which to start her new life.

She could get employment, she supposed. After all, thousands of other women must find themselves in similar case. She could teach, she could cook, she could be a companion. But how did one come by employment? Advertise? She would not know how to go about doing it. Visit an employment agency? She would have to go to a large center to find one. Go from door to door, knocking and asking?

She had no previous employment, no references. Mr. Adams would give her a reference, she thought. So would Lady Baird. But she could not bring herself to ask them. She had already invented for their ears the myth of the large and loving and welcoming family. She could not bring herself to admit that it was all a lie. She could not bring herself to apply to them for assistance.

She could stay, of course. Mr. Adams had told her so more than once since that Saturday visit. And if she stayed, the yearly lease on the cottage would continue to be paid and her allowance would continue to be sent regularly. Those were the conditions—she would be supported for as long as she stayed in the place she herself had chosen. Any move would have to be well justified.

She knew that a move under the circumstances would not be seen as justifiable. She was to live quietly and respectably. She was to draw no attention to herself. She was to be, to all intents and purposes, dead. If she remained dead she would be supported.

If she left, she would be destitute.

But she could not stay. Miss Downes, bless her heart, had called each day and had even invited her to visit Mrs. Downes. But she had declined the invitation. She would not make life harder for her only friends in the village than it must already be. And Mr. Adams and Lady Baird or Lady Baird and her husband had called each day too. Sir Clayton and Lady Baird even took her walking on two occasions, Sir Clayton between the two ladies, one on each arm. Once they walked south of the village for a mile or so, Toby running joyfully ahead of them—poor dog, he had been missing his exercise. Once, at Lady Baird's insistence, they had walked the length of the village and stood on the bridge for a while admiring the view before strolling back again. The street had miraculously cleared of people ahead of them.

But it was no good. She could not stay. How could she live in a village where she could not venture out alone? How would she shop for food? How could she live in a place where she was shunned just as if she had the plague?

The Reverend Lovering knocked on her door one day and made her a stiff and formal and pompous apology for the erroneous conclusion he had jumped to on that fateful night. But it was obvious to Catherine that he did so only because he was afraid of losing the patronage of Mr. Adams and therefore the living of Bodley. He did not call again. Mrs. Lovering did not call at all.

Catherine did not go to church on Sunday. She had missed two weeks in a row.

She had to leave.

But she did not know how it was physically to be done. She did not know how she was to walk out of her door, shut it behind her, and walk away to an unknown destination and an unknown future.

And so she procrastinated.

Lady Baird, with her maid in tow, had called on her during the morning. So had Miss Downes, bringing a book of sermons that her father had always enjoyed and recommended to his daughter's consolation. Perhaps Mrs. Winters would be comforted by them?

There seemed no one left to call, then. But someone knocked on the door late in the afternoon. Perhaps Mr. Adams? He was an extremely kind gentleman, though he had not been able to work the miracle in the village that he had promised. Catherine's feelings for him had grown during the week from respect to something resembling affection.

For just the merest fraction of a second after she had opened the door, she thought it really was Mr. Adams. But of course it was not. She hastily tried to shut the door. But his forearm shot up and held it open. They stared at each other for several silent moments.

"What are *you* doing here?" she demanded at last. It was only at that moment that she realized Lady Baird was standing behind him.

"Pitting my strength against yours to hold the door open," he said in his usual bored, rather haughty tone. "It is a battle you cannot win, Catherine. Let us in?"

She looked from him to Lady Baird, who was biting her lip and looking unhappy.

Toby was frisking about, panting but not barking, enjoying the company of three of his favorite people.

Catherine let go of the door and turned to lead the way to the parlor. But Lady Baird's voice, just behind her, stopped her.

"No," she said. "You are more comfortable in the kitchen, I know, Mrs. Winters. I shall make myself comfortable in here. You go into the kitchen with Rex."

Catherine turned without a word.

She was standing staring down into the fire when she heard the kitchen door close quietly behind her.

Thirteen

"WELL, CATHERINE," HE said.

In just over a week she had changed. She appeared to have lost weight. She had certainly lost color. She looked gaunt.

Of course, it was worse even than Claude's letter had indicated. It was not just the gossip and Clarissa's spiteful visit—not that Claude had called his wife spiteful. Apparently Catherine had been ostracized by almost all the community and she had been banished from the church by the Reverend Lovering and even publicly denounced by him on that first Sunday. It was true that Claude had insisted on an apology to Catherine, but the harm had been done. Besides, forced apologies were not worth a great deal.

She was standing now before the fire, her back to him, shapely and beautiful, and looking rather fragile. He hated being here. He hated this whole situation. He felt so damned guilty. Consequently, unfair as he knew he was being, he resented her. He almost hated her.

"What are you doing here?" she asked, as she had asked him at the outer door.

He could have said that he was standing in her kitchen, as

he had said earlier that he was holding her door open. But the time for facetiousness had passed.

"The answer should be rather obvious," he said. "I have come to do the honorable thing, Catherine. I have come to marry you."

He was surprised to hear her laugh, though it was true there was little amusement in the sound.

"What a wonderful, romantic proposal," she said. "Am I now supposed to rush into your arms and gaze at you with stars in my eyes?"

"Not unless you wish to," he said curtly. "We can hardly pretend that this situation is to the liking of either of us. But it is there and we must deal with it. We will marry."

She turned to face him then. She looked at him without saying anything for a few moments. There were faint blue circles under her eyes. The eyes themselves seemed darker, more brown than hazel. Her lips were almost as pale a color as her cheeks.

"You must put very little value on marriage," she said at last, "if you can be prepared to enter into it with so little feeling."

Good God! He could remember thinking only a couple of weeks or so ago that perhaps in a way he was even more romantic than Claude, who had married for love at the age of twenty. He himself had almost tumbled into marriage a few years ago, of course, but since then he had given up any thought of marrying. He could marry only if he found the perfect love, he had decided, but the older he got, the more he realized that there was no such thing as perfect love.

Yet now he must marry because animal appetite had made him indiscreet and he had compromised this woman.

"Feelings hardly matter," he said, "when one considers the circumstances, Catherine. I gather you have become the scarlet woman of Bodley-on-the-Water."

She did not look scarlet. She had grown paler if that were possible.

"That is my problem," she said. "And I have not given you leave to use my given name."

He clucked his tongue. "Do try not to be ridiculous," he said.

She swung back to face the fire and dipped her head. Despite annoyance and frustration and a reluctance to be where he was, doing what must be done, he found himself admiring the elegant arch of her neck. At least, he thought with unwilling resignation, he would have a beautiful wife.

Wife! The very word in his mind was enough to bring on a wave of panic. But he should be used to the word by now and the idea that he was to be a married man. He had known it for almost a week.

"Go away," she said. "I want nothing to do with you or your offer."

It would serve her right if he took her at her word and never came back, he thought grimly. And yet he could not order her to confront reality. Her face was evidence enough that she had already done that. He looked around the kitchen, which she had made so cozy. Only her dog was missing from the rocker—he was with Daphne in the parlor. He had destroyed all this for her.

"Claude and Daphne tell me that you are planning to go to relatives," he said.

"Yes," she said after a moment's silence.

"Who?" he asked. "Where? You husband's family or your own?"

"That is none of your concern," she said.

"As far as Claude knows," he said, "none of them have ever visited you here and you have visited none of them. In—five years, is it? You must be a very close family for the bonds to have held through such a long separation. Are you quite sure they will be willing to take in a scarlet woman?"

"I am not that," she said. "You know it. Besides, they love me."

She must have suffered quite badly during the past week and a half. If there were a family, loving or otherwise, would she not have gone to them before now?

"There is no family, is there?" he asked.

She hunched her shoulders but did not answer him.

"If you leave here," he said, "where will you go? What will you do?"

She would start all over again, he supposed, in another village, knowing no one. It would not be easy. He wondered why she had done it five years ago. Had there been some quarrel with her husband's family or her own? Or was she one of the unfortunates who really had no family at all? And yet, surely there must have been some friends, of her own or of her husband's.

Catherine Winters, his future wife, was certainly something of a mystery.

She did not answer his question.

"You have no choice," he said. "You will marry me, Catherine. As the Viscountess Rawleigh no one will dare ostracize you. If any do, they will have me to deal with."

She was hugging herself with her arms. "I do have a choice," she said.

He made a sound of impatience.

"You are right," she said. "There is no family to go to. And if I leave here, I will lose—I will have no means with which to support myself."

What the devil? He frowned.

"I will not marry you," she said. "But I was offered employment not so long ago. I might take that now if the position is still open."

"What position?" He should be glad that some solution seemed about to present itself, one that would leave him free. He should not be feeling this irritability.

"Mistress," she said. "You offered me the position more than once."

He stared at her back incredulously. "You will not marry me?" he said. "But you will be my mistress?"

"Yes." Her voice was quite firm.

"Why?" For some reason he felt furiously angry.

"It would be a business arrangement," she said. "It could be ended at any time by either of us. I would just ask, please, that there be some settlement agreed upon if you are the one to end it—provided I have given good service, of course."

Provided— Devil take it, she sounded as if she was applying for the position of housemaid or secretary. And he had offered to make her his *wife*!

She turned to face him again and looked him calmly in the eye. "I need employment," she said. "Is your offer still good?"

His *sister* was across the narrow passageway, a mere few feet away, waiting for the official confirmation of his betrothal. His brother was waiting at Bodley for the same news. All of them were preparing to go into action as soon as this formality of an offer was over with, letting it be known that his relationship with Catherine Winters during his stay at Bodley had been a courtship, that his short absence had been for the purpose of traveling to London for a special license so that his nuptials would not have to be delayed one day longer than was necessary.

They were to be depicted as a couple deeply, perhaps not too cautiously in love. Head over ears.

And she was calmly offering herself as his mistress.

"Yes." He strode toward her. "Yes, by God it is." He grabbed her none too gently by the waist—she surely had lost weight—and jerked her against him. He took her mouth rather savagely, thrusting his tongue deep inside, moving it in a deliberate simulation of copulation.

By God, if she was going to be his mistress, she would earn her keep. He was furious with her.

She was not impassive. She bent her body to his. Her arms came about him, one about his waist, the other about his shoulders. She held her mouth wide for him. Her eyes were closed. But her temperature did not soar with his own. She was already a mistress, performing her duty.

Damn her!

"I will return tonight," he said, looking down into her eyes without releasing his hold of her. "Be ready for me and get some rest before I come. You look as if you need it. We will discover how good you are and how quickly you learn."

She did not flinch. He did not even realize that he had spoken deliberately to make her do so until she did not.

"I will be ready, my lord," she said.

"*Rex,* damn you." He *never* swore in the hearing of women.

"Tomorrow we will leave," he said. "I will set you up in London with your own house and servants and carriage. You are going up in the world, Catherine Winters. You will like London."

Something flickered in her eyes. "No," she said. "Not London."

He raised his eyebrows. "Not London?" he said. "Where then, pray?"

"Not London," she said.

"I suppose," he said, "you expect me to take you to Stratton Park and set you up in a cozy apartment there. It would be wonderfully convenient, I must confess, but a trifle scandalous, perhaps. I might find that I had put myself beyond the pale. Or perhaps you think to stay here? You would expect me to travel to Derbyshire every time I wish to bed you?"

For the first time her face had flushed. "I know what is expected of a mistress," she said. "But not London, please."

Was that fear he saw in her eyes for a moment? She lowered them immediately and dropped her arms rather awkwardly to her sides. He released her and crossed the room to look out the kitchen window at her back garden and the river beyond. He had expected this all to be accomplished within a couple of minutes at the longest. Daphne must be wondering what was taking so long.

"This will just not do, Catherine," he said. "If I come here tonight, someone is bound to see me. I am sure your cottage has become a favorite focus for watchers. That is why I brought Daphne with me this afternoon. And the fact of my return will not have gone unnoticed. If you drive away with me tomorrow morning, many people will see. Your reputation will be gone without recall. That cannot be what you want."

She laughed but said nothing.

"I cannot allow it," he said. "I compromised you. I must make amends. No, I will not take you as my mistress. Only as my wife."

There was silence behind him.

"Well?" he prompted at last, half turning to look at her.

She was standing where he had left her, her hands clasped in front of her, her eyes closed.

"My choices have all been taken from me, have they not?" she said.

"Yes," he said quietly.

And his own too. But he had known that his had all gone as soon as he had read Claude's letter. He was almost accustomed to the fact by now. Almost, but not quite. He was to live the rest of his life in a loveless marriage. It was not a thought to be dwelled upon.

"That seems to have been settled at last, then," he said briskly. "We will be married tomorrow. Here. By the Reverend Lovering. It will be necessary for the restoring of your reputation."

Her eyes widened. "Tomorrow?" she said.

"I brought a special license with me," he said. "I realized the necessity of marriage before I came here. It will be here tomorrow in the presence of my brother and sister. There is no one you wish to invite?"

She had paled again. "Your special license will be invalid," she said.

What now? He frowned at her.

"You had to have my name on it?" she said.

"Of course," he said. "Catherine Winters, widow. Catherine with a *C*. Correct?"

She looked down at her spread hands for a moment and then directly at him again. "I am not a widow," she said. "I have never been married. And my last name is not Winters. It is Winsmore." Her eyes watched his warily.

Good Lord!

She was a lady, very obviously. What the devil was a *single* lady doing living alone among virtual strangers? And masquerading under a false name and a false status.

A lady he was about to marry.

"Perhaps," he said, his eyes narrowing, "you would care to tell me your story, *Miss Winsmore*."

"No," she said. "That is all you need to know. You may withdraw your marriage offer if you wish. I will not hold you to it. It was made, after all, to someone who does not exist."

He stared at her for a few moments before striding to the

door, jerking it open, and calling to his sister, who was talking to Toby—or herself.

She came immediately, the dog trotting happily at her heels, and looked questioningly from him to Catherine.

"Daphne," he said, "I would ask for your congratulations. This lady has just now done me the honor of betrothing herself to me. You will wish to make her acquaintance. Meet Miss Catherine Winsmore."

She gave him a look as if he had two heads and then turned to look at Catherine. "Winsmore?" she said. "Catherine *Winsmore*?"

Catherine was flushed again. And still wary. "Yes," she said.

Daphne darted him a strange look before returning her gaze to his betrothed. "Oh," she said. And then she appeared to give herself a mental shake and smiled brightly. "Well, it took the two of you long enough to come to that satisfactory conclusion. I am very pleased. Catherine—may I call you Catherine?—I am delighted. We are going to be sisters."

She crossed the room with light steps and hugged Catherine, who looked at him over his sister's shoulder and bit her lip.

"Thank you," she said.

"You must call me Daphne," his sister said, and then she turned to him and hugged him tightly too. "Rex, I am delighted for you. You are going to be happy, I know. The wedding will be tomorrow? We are going to have to be frantically busy for the rest of the day."

"Not tomorrow," he said dryly. "I have to return to London. The name I have on the license is the wrong one."

Daphne looked at him closely. "Oh, yes, of course," she said. "How awkward. How will we explain yet another journey to London?"

"My eager and tyrannical sister and brother and their

spouses insist on elaborate preparations," he said briskly, watching Catherine's face. "The impatient bridegroom cannot endure the unexpected wait for his wedding and his bride and has therefore been banished to the home of friends for a week."

"It will do," Daphne said thoughtfully. She smiled. "Catherine, we are going to have enormous fun for the coming week. We have a wedding to prepare. I have it, of course!" She clapped her hands. "You must move to Bodley House for the week. That is why poor Rex must leave. You can return here for the night before your wedding, after his return."

"Well, Catherine?" he said. She had been very quiet.

"It will be as you wish," she said.

The submissive bride. He hoped she was not going to play the part of submissive wife when they were married. He would be bored within a week.

"Well." He went toward her. "I shall leave early in the morning and see you on my return." With Daphne watching, he did not know quite how to take his leave of her. But she played her part. She smiled at him.

"Have a safe journey," she said.

He did not know if she lifted her face for his kiss or merely so that she could look into his face. But he kissed her, lightly and briefly on the lips before turning away.

"Come, Daphne," he said.

They had come in his carriage—so that no one in the village could possibly miss his visit or misunderstand its purpose. He handed his sister inside, climbed in after her, and closed the door. The door of the cottage, he noticed when he turned his head, was already shut.

"There," he said, putting his head back and closing his eyes. "That is done."

"Rex—" Daphne said.

"I would rather we did not talk, if you please, Daphne," he said.

They sat silently side by side as the carriage conveyed them back to Bodley House.

"HOW MANY CATHERINE Winsmores can there be?" Lady Baird asked her husband. She was curled into the crook of his arm on a small love seat in her bedchamber later the same night. "Of course it is she, Clay."

"Yes, I suppose you are right," he said with a sigh. "Poor lady."

"I always felt that way too," she said. "I do not know why it is always the women who bear the brunt of everyone's censure and the men who get off scot-free. Usually it is the men who are most to blame—this man in particular."

"It is the way of the world, love," he said.

"Yes." She rested her head on his shoulder. "You really think we should say nothing, then?"

"Her name meant nothing to Claude or Clarissa," he said. "They do not spend a great deal of their time in town, of course. And if it meant anything to Rex, he is keeping the knowledge to himself. One never knows with your elder brother, Daph. He is something of a cold fish, if you will pardon me for saying so."

"It was in his upbringing as the heir to keep things to himself and bear his burdens alone," she said sadly. "In a strange way I have always thought him even more sensitive than Claude."

"If the circumstances were different," Sir Clayton continued, "perhaps we would be honor bound to tell what we know. But she was badly compromised and almost without a doubt Rex was more to blame then she. He must marry her whether he knows the truth or not. Or rather, perhaps I should say that he *would* marry her whether he knew or not.

We must stay out of it, Daph. Let them work out their own destiny."

"I so wanted them to be happy, Clay," she said. "Rex and Claude, I mean. I love them so much. And now this forced marriage for Rex, and Claude being coldly civil to Clarissa."

"If she had been my wife," he said, "she would have had a good walloping, Daph."

"Oh, nonsense," she said fondly. "You could not beat a carpet, let alone a wife."

He chuckled. "Life goes on," he said. "Somehow they will all work things out."

"The eternal optimist," she said. "Talking of which, it has been *eight* days now. After two years of marriage. Are you holding your breath as much as I am?"

"That is rather a suicidal thing to do, love," he said, "especially if you are breathing for two. We agreed a year ago to let life take its course, did we not? And to be happy together even if we must remain a family of two for the rest of our lives?"

"Yes," she said.

"Well, then." He chuckled again after a few moments. "But I *am* holding my breath."

LIFE TOOK ON rather the aspect of a bizarre dream. Not quite a nightmare, perhaps, but close.

Viscount Rawleigh's carriage passed Catherine's cottage without stopping early on the morning following her betrothal. She was already up and saw it go. Two hours later Mr. Adams's carriage arrived to take her and Toby to Bodley House. She did not want to go there. But she did not argue. She went.

She had decided the day before that from now on—or for a while anyway—she would simply let life happen to her.

She was tired of trying to shape her own life only to make a mess of it.

She did not want to marry. She *could* not marry. It was one of the conditions. But she would not need support any longer once she was married to Viscount Rawleigh. She believed that he was very wealthy.

She did not want to marry *him*. Perhaps if she did not find him attractive, if she did not want him physically, she might feel better about marrying him. But she disliked him for his insensitivity and she despised him for his arrogance. He had made it so very clear to her that he wanted only her body for his enjoyment and that he did not want her at all in marriage—as she did not want him.

She would not think about it or about him. Her course had been set now. She had finally let it happen—though she had never actually said yes to his proposal—simply because there was no alternative. She had thought that perhaps he would change his mind once she told him the only part of the truth she was prepared to tell him. Then she would have had to find an alternative. But he had not withdrawn his offer.

She had thought perhaps he would recognize her name. *Then* he would have changed his mind. But he had not done so. And she felt no obligation to enlighten him. He was forcing her into this marriage. He knew there was more to her story than what she had told. He had decided to go ahead with the marriage anyway.

She went to Bodley House, where she was received with warm kindness by Mr. Adams, with cool courtesy—and a stiff, formal apology—by Mrs. Adams, with bright affection by Lady Baird, and with gentle amusement by Sir Clayton Baird. Everyone else who had made up the house party, including Ellen Hudson, had returned to their own homes. The children thought it great fun to have her at the house all the time, though William was wary at first that her presence was going to mean a music lesson every day.

Lady Baird's maid and Mrs. Adams's were set to work making a wedding dress out of the available materials and patterns. Mr. Adams's cook was given the task of preparing a wedding breakfast for as many guests as could be invited from the gentry within ten miles or so of Bodley—many of the same people who had attended the ball. Decorations were made for the dining room, the bridal carriage—Mr. Adams's, of course—and the church. The floral decorations for the church were to be entirely daffodils and other spring flowers growing wild in the park and woods. The few greenhouse flowers that had survived the ball were to be used in the house and in Catherine's bouquet.

Everyone who was anyone at all was visited by the three ladies and invited to visit. Flanked by a smiling and talkative Lady Baird on one side and a regal and dignified Mrs. Adams on the other, Catherine found that no one had the courage to cut her acquaintance. She had no wish to be accepted on such false terms, but she said nothing. She went through the motions of being sociable.

Everyone, of course, was charmed by the story of romance and impetuosity and impatience that Lady Baird told over and over with great enthusiasm and wit. Or pretended to be charmed. Catherine no longer knew what was genuine and what was feigned in people's behavior.

"Would you believe," Lady Baird—Daphne—always confided at the culmination of her story, her cheeks flushed, her eyes dancing with merriment, "that my brother actually thought that he could rush back to Bodley a mere week after hastening away in pursuit of a special license and whisk dear Catherine off to church the very next day? He has no idea, wretched man! Well, I can assure you, Clarissa and I had a thing or two to say to that, did we not, Clarissa?"

To which speech, Mrs. Adams always inclined her head in gracious agreement. "We did indeed, Daphne," she said.

"We came to dear Catherine's rescue," Daphne always said triumphantly, beaming at her future sister-in-law. "We sent Rex off to stay with friends and kick his heels for another week."

She was extremely kind, Catherine always thought, considering the fact that she *knew*. Catherine was not sure how she knew this herself, but she did. Both Daphne and Clayton knew. But neither had said a word to her.

The Reverend Lovering, echoed by Mrs. Lovering, had assured everyone who would listen that the honor of marrying Viscount Rawleigh to their own dear Miss Winsmore—no one had commented publicly on her mysterious change of name and marital status—might well be the pinnacle of his life's achievements. He was speechless with gratification, though he prayed on his knees daily to be saved from the sin of pride.

Miss Downes was the only person Catherine invited herself. Miss Downes hugged her, tears in her eyes, when Catherine made her visit with her two future sisters-in-law. Mrs. Downes took one of Catherine's hands in both hers and smiled at her.

He was away for one week. When the three ladies returned from visiting one afternoon, he was in the drawing room with Mr. Adams and Clayton. He stood and bowed to Catherine, as he did to the other ladies too, and told her she was looking well. He told her their wedding would take place the following morning. And he told her he would do himself the honor of escorting her back to her cottage.

At which Daphne threw up her hands and told him he had no idea at all how to go on, that *she* would ride in the carriage back to the cottage with Catherine and dear Toby, whom the children had tried to adopt only to find that he would not stay in the nursery but kept escaping to search for Catherine.

And then she was on her way back home, Toby curled on her lap, Daphne telling her that she would come in the morning to help her dress before Claude's carriage arrived to take them both to church. And Clayton, who had agreed to give Catherine away, would come with the carriage, of course.

Catherine let it all happen. All the plans had gone on about her all week without her active assistance. It did not matter. She was happy to be totally passive.

Finally she was home again and alone again with Toby.

Until tomorrow.

"Toby." She knelt down on the kitchen floor and set her arms about her dog, who was wagging his tail in an ecstasy of happiness at being back in familiar surroundings. "Toby. Oh, Toby."

She wept against his warm neck and felt his wet tongue licking her ear.

Fourteen

HE LOOKED AS if he was ready for a reception at Carlton House, Clarissa told him when she saw him. His blue coat was Weston's finest. He wore gray knee breeches, a silver waistcoat, white linen with lace at his cuffs. Claude's valet—he had left his own at Stratton—had made something admirably frothy of his neckcloth.

He looked like a bridegroom, Claude said, slapping him on the back and grinning at him. Any minute now they would be hearing about his cravat being too tight and the room being too warm.

He felt exhausted. It seemed that he had been on the road forever. And at the end of it there had been no relaxation but a wedding to prepare for and the necessity of looking cheerful.

She certainly had looked better—and worse. The shadows had gone from beneath her eyes. She had looked less gaunt, less haunted. And yet there had been something about her—something about her eyes. They had looked—empty. It was the only word he could find to describe what he had seen in her eyes.

There was a surprisingly large gathering at the church.

But then Daphne had told him how busy they had all been during the week of his absence, Claude and Clayton constantly calling on neighbors, she and Clarissa taking Catherine about with them to call on all the ladies and drink enough tea to sink a ship.

He waited at the front of the church with his brother. She was not late—he was early. He wished he could leave, just leap on a horse's back and ride until he could ride no farther. He would go down to Dunbarton to see Ken and the others. It would be like old times.

She wanted nothing to do with him. Although she had felt a physical attraction for him, she had never wanted him. She had refused to lie with him, to be his mistress, to be his wife—it seemed incredible to him now that he had actually offered her marriage at one time just because he wanted her so desperately in bed. She had said no.

And yet now, because he had been incautious enough in his anger and disappointment to leave her cottage without checking first to see that the road was clear, she was being forced to marry him after all.

Oh, yes, he wished himself a thousand miles away.

There was a sudden stirring at the back of the church and there she was with Clayton, Daphne behind her, smiling and doing something with the back of her dress. Then they were moving toward him.

God, but she was beautiful. He was struck by her beauty as he had been that first day, when she had been standing at her gate, nodding a greeting to Clarissa in one of the carriages, and then turning to curtsy and smile at him.

She was dressed in white satin. The gown was fashionably cut, high-waisted, modestly low at the bosom, the sleeves short and puffed. The two flounces at the hem and the smaller one on the sleeves were trimmed with embroidered golden rosebuds to match the posy of real rosebuds that she carried.

She looked like a bride, he thought foolishly.

She *was* a bride.

His bride.

Her cheeks were flushed with color, he could see when she came closer. Her eyes were bright—yesterday's emptiness had gone from them. They looked directly back into his.

Later, when he thought back on his wedding, he found that he could not remember who had sat in the congregation. He could not remember even Clayton giving Catherine away in the absence of any male relative of hers, or Claude handing him her wedding ring. He could not even remember the rector or the service.

He could remember only her, standing slim and lovely and quiet at his side; her eyes, sometimes lowered—he noticed the long lashes, several shades darker than her golden hair—but more often raised to his; her hand cool in his. She had long, slim fingers, a pianist's fingers, with short, well-manicured nails. He remembered wondering irrelevantly how she kept her hands so soft and beautiful when she had no servants to do the menial household tasks for her. His ring looked startlingly bright and golden on her finger.

He could remember only her, saying "I do" quietly but firmly when asked if she would take him as her husband, looking into his eyes as she said it. He remembered her promising in the same calm voice to love and honor and obey him.

And looking back, he could remember as an interesting fact that the wedding service and the words and vows they had exchanged had not at the time seemed to be either a farce or a sacrilege. They had promised before man and God to love each other.

Her lips were soft and cool when he kissed them.

She was his wife. This woman, whose beauty had drawn his eyes from the start, this woman whom he had desired from the start was his. For the rest of their lives.

Afterward he remembered that there had been no panic in the thought. Only a wondering sort of exultation. It had happened so fast. Could it really be so? But it was. She was his.

She was his wife.

SHE HAD ALWAYS thought him extraordinarily handsome, just as she had always thought it of Mr. Adams—Claude. She must think of him by that name now. He was her brother-in-law.

She had always thought her husband handsome. But today his beauty had made the breath catch in her throat. Like a love-struck girl she had been unable to take her eyes off him in church from the moment Daphne had straightened her hem and she had looked toward the altar and seen him. Yet it was not love she felt for him, but its antithesis.

He was dressed like a courtier or a bridegroom, she had thought foolishly. He had dressed carefully and splendidly for their wedding. She had half expected that the wedding itself would be unimportant to him, that he might even come to it dressed in his riding clothes.

The wedding was unexpectedly important to her. She remembered how as a girl she had longed for marriage with a handsome and loving husband—the dream of all young girls for a happily-ever-after. She remembered her severe disappointment when her come-out had been delayed until she was nineteen, practically on the shelf. And how so soon after the come-out, all her dreams, all her hopes, all her future came crashing about her ears. And the final cruel blow in the death of her baby just eight months later. For five years she had lived without dreams, without hope. For five years she had lived only for peace.

And now she was marrying after all. A handsome and wealthy man, a viscount. She knew that he desired her even though he neither wanted nor loved her. She was to have a husband after all, a man in her bed, at least until he tired of her or until she bore him a son.

Perhaps she would have a child again. A child who would wait the full nine months to be born. A child who would live.

She did not love this man she was marrying. She did not even like him. She did not want to be marrying him. But she *was* marrying him. And unexpectedly and rather painfully, hope was reborn in her. The hope of some sort of future that was not merely a dull peace.

Perhaps he would give her a child.

They stood outside on the church steps for a long time, shaking hands with guests, being kissed by some of them, smiling, laughing with everyone. She realized afterward that he had kept her there deliberately although they might have driven away immediately and greeted the guests at the house. He had kept her there so that they would be seen by the villagers, many of whom had gathered outside the church gates at the end of the path, and some of whom were standing out in the street at a greater distance, looking toward the church.

They traveled back to Bodley House in the decorated wedding carriage, alone together for the first time. But they rode in silence, her hand on his sleeve, held there by his free hand. She could think of nothing to say. He seemed uninterested in even trying to converse. He looked out through the window. For the first time she realized that it was a beautiful day with blue sky and sunshine. For the first time she realized that she was not cold even though she wore no cloak or even shawl.

And then at the breakfast again and afterward he kept her close to him, smiled, looked at her with warm and appreciative eyes, took her about so that they conversed with everyone who had come—and everyone who had been invited had come, of course, curious to see this couple whose marriage had only narrowly averted lasting scandal. A few times when they were talking with others, he addressed her as "my love."

It was a farce he played out with meticulous care so that her good name would be restored, so that scandal would be dead and so that gossip would not spread beyond the confines of Bodley and its neighborhood.

He was being the scrupulously honorable gentleman, she realized, protecting her name, taking the consequences of his own indiscretion. She understood all that and was grateful for it. And resentful of it. How helpless women were. The pawns of men. To be tripped up and pitched headlong into the dirt by men, and then to be picked up by them and dusted off and restored to uprightness.

But that was the way of the world.

Everyone stayed until evening. There was the garden outside to be strolled in on such a beautiful day, and there was the drawing room to sit in for conversation and tea. There was even some impromptu dancing in the ballroom to the music of the pianoforte, though the room had not been decorated for the occasion.

When darkness began to fall, it was time to leave. Time for bride and groom to leave. They were to spend their wedding night at her cottage and leave for Stratton tomorrow.

Claude's carriage, still decorated, waited outside the main doors to take them away.

Daphne was crying and laughing as she hugged them both very tightly. Claude hugged his brother wordlessly for long moments before turning to Catherine and smiling kindly and kissing both her cheeks.

"Take care of him, Catherine, my dear," he said quietly. "He is very precious to me and not entirely a blackguard, you know." His eyes were swimming with unshed tears.

She wished absurdly that it were possible to marry a family rather than an individual. She loved Claude and Daphne.

Clayton and Clarissa kissed her too, the former with a wink, the latter with smiling tenseness.

Other people smiled and nodded—there seemed to be dozens out on the terrace.

And then Lord Rawleigh was handing her into the carriage and jumping in beside her. Someone on the outside closed the door and suddenly they were enclosed in near darkness and in quietness. The carriage jerked into motion.

Lord Rawleigh! She could already think of her in-laws by their given names. She could think of this man only by his title. Rex. She was not sure she would ever be able to say his name aloud. Her husband. Despite the late-morning wedding and the afternoon and evening of celebrations, it suddenly seemed unreal again. Her husband. He was leaning back against the squabs, his eyes closed.

"Well, Catherine," he said after a while, "restitution has been made. You are respectable again."

She sat very still. If she had moved, she would have smacked him. Hard.

"Catherine Adams, Viscountess Rawleigh," he said. "Now the question of whether it was Winters or Winsmore is of no consequence."

And so the vestiges of her identity disappeared. She had none apart from him. She had his name and was his property. His possession. One he did not want. Except perhaps in his bed for his pleasure and for breeding. She breathed slowly and evenly, trying not to allow herself to be entirely engulfed by bitterness. In bitterness lay only self-destruction, as she knew from experience.

When the carriage turned at the bottom of the driveway to pass through the village, he spoke again. He still had his eyes closed.

"Tell me, Catherine," he said, "do I have a virgin bride?"

She had expected that he had drawn his own conclusion from the facts that she had been living alone and incognito. It was something she would have expected him to ask before marrying her if he was not sure. His sense of honor, it seemed, knew no bounds. But then for years he had been an officer in the cavalry. Of course honor would mean more than life to him.

"No," she said, so determined not to whisper and seem ashamed that the word blurted like a defiance into the closed confines of the carriage.

"As I thought," he said softly.

HER DOG HAD been inside alone for most of the day, though Miss Downes apparently had come to let him out for five minutes during the afternoon. He greeted them with barking enthusiasm, almost demented with joy, jumping up against Catherine and licking her face when she bent to hug him.

"He needs to go outside," she murmured, and the terrier raced ahead of her to the back door, woofing with excitement. She did not only let him out. She went outside with him and was gone for all of ten minutes.

He lit a couple of candles in the kitchen. He did not

bother to light the fire. It was really not a cold night and they would not be remaining downstairs.

He was feeling annoyed. Not so much over the fact that she was not virgin. He had suspected as much. He would have been surprised if she had answered his question in the affirmative. Indeed, there was some relief in knowing that he would not have pain and tightness and blood and skittishness to cope with tonight.

No, it was not her lack of virginity that annoyed him as much as the fact that she had steadfastly denied herself to him while she had opened herself to some other man—or men. It was a blow to his pride, perhaps, that with him she had remained unseducible.

What had happened to her was as clear as day now, of course. She had fornicated with a man who for some reason had not married her, and she had been banished by her family to live out her disgrace in a country backwater. The family must have been supporting her for as long as she remained where she had been placed.

He hated the fact that she had been happier with such a life than with what he had offered her. He hated the fact that he was taking her from this cozy home of hers almost by force and certainly against her wishes. He hated the thought of rape, even if it was legalized by the fact that he had just married her.

Devil take it! He had laughed at Nat's narrow escape earlier in the year and at Eden's. There had been no escape for him. He wondered if they would make merry over his fate. He had written to them at Dunbarton to announce his coming nuptials. He did not think they would laugh, though. They would understand his predicament and his feelings. They would sympathize.

Damn it, he wanted no man's pity.

The back door opened and Toby came trotting into the

kitchen. Catherine came more slowly behind him. Her satin gown shimmered in the candlelight and looked incongruous with her surroundings.

He blew out one candle and picked up the other. "Show me to the bedroom," he said. There was no point in delaying the inevitable, even though it was still only mid-evening. He thought back on the last time he had made that request of her, just over two weeks ago. He had burned for her then. Well, he burned now too. But then he had thought their hunger for each other to be mutual.

She turned without a word and led the way up the narrow wooden stairs to the bedroom. It was surprisingly spacious and noticeably feminine. The ceiling was high over the bed. It sloped with the roof downward to the wall opposite. It must seem strange to her, he thought, setting down the candlestick on the dressing table, where the mirror reflected and magnified the candle's light, after inhabiting the room alone for five years to have a man in it with her.

She turned and looked at him calmly enough. She was a woman of some courage, his wife. But then, of course, she was no virgin bride.

"Come," he said, beckoning with the fingers of one hand. She came. "Turn."

There must have been two dozen tiny pearl buttons down the back of her gown, each of them hooked into even tinier buttonholes. He undid them all with methodical care and removed all the pins from her hair before pushing the gown and her chemise from her shoulders and down her arms. She shivered as he turned her and the garments shimmered down to her feet. He knelt to pull down her stockings. She lifted her feet one at a time for him and stepped away from her garments. He straightened up to look at her.

She looked unblinkingly back at him, her features shadowed by her golden hair. It waved almost to her waist, as he had known it would.

"If there is one imperfection of form," he said, "I certainly cannot see it."

"Since you are bound to me for life," she said, "it is a good thing that you are pleased with your possession."

He raised his eyebrows. "Yes, indeed," he said, and lifted one hand to run the backs of his fingers lightly down one side of her jaw to her chin.

He closed the distance between their mouths and kissed her lightly with lips that were only just parted. He was in no hurry. There was all night. He touched her with his hands, setting them at the sides of her small and shapely waist, moving them up to cup her breasts. They were warm and silky. They were not large, but they were firm and uptilted. Enticing. Her nipples hardened instantly against the light pressure of his thumbs. He moved his hands behind her, sliding them lightly down her back to cup her buttocks. He kept a little distance between their bodies.

She shuddered violently and he drew her against him, the fingers of one hand spreading wide to hold her where she was, the other moving up to bring her breasts against him. He deepened the kiss.

There was something almost unbearably erotic about holding a naked woman to his fully clothed body. He savored the feeling, determined not to rush, though instinct would have had him tearing at his own clothes, bending her back onto the bed, and mounting her for release.

Despite her nakedness in a room without a fire, he felt her grow warmer over the next few minutes. He felt her arms come about him and her mouth relax and yield and open to his. Her body arched against his even when he eased the pressure of his hands.

At least he had the satisfaction of knowing that she

wanted what she was going to get. It was not rape, even if such a thing were possible within marriage.

"Onto the bed," he said against her mouth eventually. "We can better complete the consummation there."

She lay watching him as he undressed. He did so unhurriedly, feasting his eyes on her beauty and his mind on his own desire. She watched him without any pretense of modesty or timidity. He decided against blowing out the candle before joining her on the bed.

She had become passive. She did not resist him in any way. Neither did she display any eagerness to explore or experiment. There was warmth and compliance in her but no excitement. It had been five years for her. He set himself patiently to arousing her. There was no hurry. He was experienced at holding himself in check. He always enjoyed foreplay almost as much as the main feast. He liked his women hot and panting by the time he put them beneath him.

It took a great deal of time.

He raised himself on one forearm eventually and looked down at her with half-closed eyes. Desire was heavy in him. He ran the tip of one forefinger lightly across her moist and swollen lips.

"How many times?" he asked her.

She looked at him with uncomprehending eyes.

"Once?" he asked. "A dozen times? A hundred? More times than you can recall?"

She understood him then, though she did not answer immediately. She stared back at him. "Once," she whispered finally.

Ah. She was as nearly virgin as made no difference, then. And it had happened five years ago.

He slid his free hand down between her legs and probed there with light fingertips. She closed her eyes. She was unexcited, but her body was ready. He moved on top of her, keeping his weight on his forearms, and pushed her legs wide with his own. Her eyes shot open.

"Easy," he said. She was skittish after all. "Relax. Let it happen."

He watched her face as he pushed inside her, slowly, to his full length. Her teeth came down on her lower lip, but she gave no other sign of distress. Inner muscles contracted about him, causing exquisite pain, and she closed her eyes.

He moved in her slowly, rhythmically, giving her his full length with every stroke, forcing himself to take his time. Let her relearn the basics of intimacy. She could learn on future occasions what else he would expect and even demand of her as a bedfellow.

He stroked her for many minutes before she slid her feet up the bed on either side of his legs and lifted her knees to hug his hips. She whimpered once and then again. He stopped at her entrance, waited for the tension of anticipation in her body to reach its peak, waited for the moment that his body recognized by instinct, and then thrust hard and deep into her and held there.

She whimpered once more and shuddered against him.

He waited for the tension to go from her body, for relaxation to take its place. He waited until her feet rested on the bed again. And then finally, blessedly, he took his own swift fierce pleasure and released his seed deep in her body.

He was exhausted. That was his first conscious thought. He was also lying heavily on her. He must have dozed off—he hoped not for long. He was no featherweight. He disengaged himself carefully and rather regretfully and rolled to her side. He felt that he could sleep for a week. It was a comfortable bed and she was a warm and enticing woman. It was going to be a pleasure teaching her and enjoying her in the weeks and months to come. She did not know a great deal. He was curiously glad of it.

He reached for the bedclothes to pull them up, intending to slide his arm beneath her and turn her against him. But she moved faster, rolling over onto her side to face away from him.

He looked at her in the long shadows cast by the flickering candle—it had almost burned itself out. She was not sleeping or even relaxed. He could not see her face. He could not even hear her breathing.

"Did I hurt you?" he asked.

"No," she said.

"Did I offend you?"

"No."

He had the curious sensation after that that she was crying, though there was no telltale shaking of her shoulders and there were no sobs or sniffles. After a minute of hesitation he reached a hand around her and touched her face. She turned it sharply to hide it in the pillow but not before he had felt the wetness of tears.

He turned cold. And furiously angry. He clenched his hand. Too angry. He was too angry.

He got out of bed, scooped up his clothes, picked up the candle in passing, and went downstairs.

Toby, on the rocker in the kitchen, wagged his tail.

"Get down from there, sir," the viscount ordered sternly as he dressed again in his best wedding finery.

Toby got down.

Lord, he was angry. He could cheerfully break every cup and saucer and plate in the kitchen. He had taken care with her so that she might have some pleasure, so that there would be no semblance whatsoever of rape in what he did to her. Yet she had ended up in tears.

And they were stuck with each other for a lifetime.

But devil take it, he was ten times more exhausted than he was angry. He yawned until his jaws cracked. He looked about hopefully, but the only thing resembling a pillow in the room was the embroidered cushion on the seat of the rocker, and the only thing resembling a blanket was the tablecloth.

He tried to find a comfortable position on the rocker with the aid of both. He failed to find it, though he was at least slightly warmer once Toby had jumped onto his lap and curled up there. Somehow he dozed his way through the night.

Fifteen

SHE SLEPT BY fits and starts. She was surprised that she slept at all. She knew as soon as he left the room that he would stay downstairs, that he would not come back. She knew that she had made a terrible mistake.

It had been so very unexpectedly wonderful. Despite the shock of its beginning, when he had removed all her clothes and given her no chance to don the nightgown she had chosen for the occasion, and despite the fact that she had been as ignorant as a virgin and had not known quite what to do—despite everything, it had been the most wonderful experience of her life.

She had desired him from the start, of course, and felt a woman's need for the intimacy of his body ever since that first evening visit he had paid her. But she had not really expected that the act itself would be so achingly beautiful. Or that it would last for longer than a minute or two at the most.

She lay on her back, staring up into the darkness long after he had gone, taking the candle with him, and long after her tears had dried. Her thighs were aching from being spread wide. She was sore inside, though it was not exactly soreness. There was a slight throbbing there still. When he had come inside her, she had thought she would die of the shock of his size and hardness. And yet it had been the shock of wonder.

She had lost reality in the long minutes that followed. Not the reality of *him*. At every moment, perhaps more intensely as the moments passed, she had been aware that it was he who was loving her so expertly and so intimately. There had been no one in the world but him and her for those minutes and nothing but what they did together. Nothing at all. Everything else—all the series of events that had brought them to this moment—had fallen away from her consciousness.

He was her husband and she was his wife and they were in their marriage bed on their wedding night. It had been as simple and as profound and as wonderful as that.

Except that it had ended. There had been unbearable tension, the single, almost panicked moment when she had felt that she could bear no more. And then suddenly—she did not know how he did it—he had opened up some door to her and all the tension had gone flooding through, leaving her feeling so totally at peace that she thought it altogether possible that she would never want to move again. And then *he* had moved again, and relaxed and uninvolved, she had enjoyed the powerful thrusts of his body, and she had felt the hot gush of his seed.

Then his relaxed weight bearing her down into the mattress.

She had held him, feeling his weight and his heat, smelling the strangely enticing mixture of musky cologne and sweat, watching the dancing shadows cast by the candle on the familiar walls and sloped ceiling of her bedchamber.

And she had known reality again. He—Lord Rawleigh—had just finished consummating a marriage that neither of them had wanted. She did not like or respect him as a person. His only interest in her—he had never made a secret of it—was her body. He had tried several times to persuade her to give it or to sell it to him. He did not want to be married to her, but since he had had no choice in the matter, he would at least take advantage of the fact that her body was now his.

She could not argue with that. She would not argue. She had needs too and she had always found him attractive.

His breathing had told her that he was asleep. She had not moved. She had not particularly wanted to be free of his weight or of his body, still joined to hers. But she had realized the emptiness of what had just happened. It had been something purely physical, something done purely for enjoyment. There was nothing wrong with enjoyment, especially when a man was taking it with his wife.

But there had been nothing more than that.

She had told him once that there was a person inside her body. That person now felt bereft. Was it enough, what had happened? Would it ever be enough?

He had slept for no longer than a few minutes. Then he had moved out of her and off her. But the loss of him had left her feeling cold and empty and a little frightened. And very lonely. She had turned onto her side, facing away from him, afraid to look into his eyes and see a confirmation of all she knew she would see there. For the first time ever she had a man with her in her bed. For the first time, apart from brief social visits, she had company in her cottage. She was married and would be looked after for the rest of her life.

She had never felt lonelier.

Absurdly, unfairly, she had waited for him to say something, to touch her, to comfort her. She had longed for his arms quite as much as she had longed for his body minutes before. And yet when he *had* spoken to her, she had shut him out. She had not quite realized she was crying until his hand came around her to touch her face. Instead of turning as she might have done and burying her face against his chest, she had buried it in the pillow, shunning him.

How could she have ached for comfort and shunned it all at the same time? She did not understand herself.

Yes, she did. There was no comfort to be had from him. And she would not shame herself by letting him know that what she needed, what she dreamed of now that dreams had so painfully been aroused in her again, was a *relationship*. Not necessarily love, that nebulous something that no one could quite explain in words but most young girls dreamed of anyway. She could live without love if she could only have kindness and companionship and a little laughter.

All she could have was this—this that had just happened to her. Wonderful beyond imagining while it was happening. Only a powerful reminder of her essential aloneness once it was over.

And then he had got off the bed and taken the candle and gone downstairs. She had thought at first that he was going to leave the house, perhaps never to come back. But of course he would not do that. He had married her for honor's sake, for propriety's sake. Honor and propriety would dictate that he stay at the cottage.

She lay on her back through the rest of the night, dozing and waking, knowing that she had made a terrible mistake. A mistake in marrying him, and a mistake in not accepting that marriage for what it was once the deed was done.

Long and tedious as the night was, she dreaded the coming of morning even more, when she must face him again.

HE WOKE, DISORIENTED, when Toby jumped off his lap. Cramped muscles, a stiff neck, and general chilliness informed him that he was not in his own bed. And then his eyes opened.

Glory be, it was the morning after his wedding. And after his wedding night.

She was up. He caught the sound of the backdoor latch as she let the dog out. She did not come back immediately. She must have stepped outside with him as she had done the night before. Did she let one little—and poorly trained—terrier rule her life? he wondered irritably. It must be chilly, standing out there.

But it was far chillier in the kitchen. Especially with him there, he supposed. He remembered grimly the humiliation of having reduced her to tears with his lovemaking. *That* had never happened to him before. A shame it had had to happen for the first time with his wife.

He was making and lighting the fire with inexpert hands—even in the Peninsula he had always had servants, he reflected ruefully—when she came in. He was beginning to feel a certain respect for domestic servants.

"I could have done that," she said quietly.

He turned around to look at her. With her simple blue wool dress and her hair in a knot at her neck, she looked like Mrs. Catherine Winters, widow, again.

"I do not doubt it," he said. "But I have done it instead."

Impossible to believe that he had known that body last night. It looked as slim and as lovely and as untouchable as ever. And quite as enticing. He set his jaw.

"I shall make some tea," she said, moving past him with her eyes fixed on the kettle. "Would you like some toast?"

"Yes, please," he said, clasping his hands behind him. He felt awkward, damn it all, like an unwelcome visitor. "Get down from there, sir." It was a relief to be able to vent his spleen on some living creature.

Toby, on the rocker, cocked his ears, wagged his tail, and jumped down.

Lord Rawleigh became aware of his crumpled coat and breeches and of a general feeling of staleness about his person. He had brought a bag with him. It was time to wash and shave and dress for the arrival of his carriage and the beginning of the journey home.

With his wife. It was a strange, unreal thought.

His valet, had he been here, would have taken his clothes from the bag last night and set them out for him, making sure they were free of creases and lint. He had not thought of doing it for himself. Of course not. He had been too preoccupied with the desire to rush his bride upstairs and into bed as fast as possible.

Her movements were graceful and sure as she filled the kettle and set it over the fire to boil and as she sliced the bread ready to toast over the coals. She had not once looked into his eyes this morning. He was becoming more irritable by the minute.

"I shall go upstairs to wash and change," he said. Was that where she washed? Or was it here in the kitchen? He had not noticed a washstand in her bedchamber.

"In the room opposite the bedchamber," she said as if she had read his thoughts, busy spooning tea into the teapot. "If you would care to wait until the kettle has boiled, you may have some hot water."

Damn! Of course, there were no servants to have carried up warm water for his wash and shave. How could she bear living like this? How would she adjust to life at Stratton? It was the first time he had thought of it. Would she be able to adjust? Would she be a fit mistress for his house? Well, if she was not, to hell with it. The house had run smoothly without a mistress for years.

Strangely enough they maintained a conversation through

breakfast, which they ate while seated at the kitchen table. He told her about Lisbon, where he had spent a whole month at one time recovering from wounds. She told him about going to the stables at Bodley House to choose a puppy from a litter of five. She had chosen Toby because he was the only one who had stood on his stubby little legs and challenged her, squeaking ferociously at her for daring to invade his territory.

"Though he licked my hands and my face with equal enthusiasm when I picked him up," she said with a laugh. "What else could I do but bring him home with me? He had stolen my heart."

She was gazing into her teacup and obviously seeing the cheeky puppy Toby had been. She was smiling, her eyes dreamy and twinkling all at the same time. He would not mind at all, Lord Rawleigh thought, having one of those smiles directed his way one of these days instead of being wasted on a teacup. But the thought brought back his irritation. She had turned away from him last night and wept!

He pushed his chair back and got to his feet.

"The carriage will be here in little more than half an hour," he said, drawing his watch from a pocket. "We should be ready to leave so that we may have as much daylight as possible for travel. It is a long journey."

"Yes," she said, and he became suddenly aware of her cup rattling down onto her saucer and her hand whipping away from it—so that he would not see how much it shook?

What now? Was the thought of leaving with him so dreadful? Or was it the thought of leaving here? The cottage had been her home for five years. And she had made it a cozy haven, he had to admit, however inconvenient he found it with its lack of servants.

He looked down at her, trying to form words that would

show his sympathy for her feelings. Irritability vanished for a moment in shame that he was responsible for all this.

Would she really prefer to be staying here, alone again, living her life of dull and blameless routine and service to others? Single again? But there was no point to the preference or to his awareness of it and sympathy with her. They were married and she must come with him to Stratton. That was the simple reality.

She had got up too, without looking at him, and was pouring water from the kettle into a jug.

"I believe that will be enough," she said, handing it to him. "There is cold water upstairs to be mixed with it, my lord."

There was an awkward moment when she flushed and bit her lip and he felt a flashing of fury and perhaps too of pain. Then he turned and left the room, the jug of boiling water in his hand.

My lord.

She had married him yesterday. She had lain with him last night.

And she had wept afterward.

My lord.

MR. AND MRS. Adams—Claude and Clarissa—had come in the carriage. They were going to walk back home, they explained. Daphne had intended to come too, but she had felt bilious at breakfast and Clayton had had to assist her back to their rooms.

"The excitement of the past week or two has caught up to her," Claude said with a smile.

"I do hope it is no more than that," Catherine said, instantly concerned. Though truth to tell, she was glad of something on which to fix her mind and the conversation. There could be nothing more embarrassing than meeting the eyes of her brother- and sister-in law had been when they arrived unexpectedly and seeing the kindly laughter in Claude's eyes and the well-bred speculation in Clarissa's.

It must have been patently obvious from the blushes she had been quite unable to quell that the deed had been done last night.

"So do I," Clarissa said. "I do not want the children becoming ill. I have urged Claude to send for the physician to see Daphne and to look at them, but he insists we wait." She looked very unhappy.

Catherine touched her hand. She did not feel any deep affection for her new sister-in-law, but she had never doubted that Clarissa loved her children. And there were so many dangers to the survival of children, even if they successfully survived the birthing.

"I am sure it is just the excitement," she said. "Daphne hardly stopped for breath all the time I was staying at Bodley."

"Yes, I daresay you are right." Clarissa smiled rather bleakly.

But the arrival of the carriage, of course, heralded the departure. The leaving of everything she had known and held dear for five years. Everything with which she had identified herself for that time. She had grown up here from foolish girlhood to a somewhat wiser maturity. She had known a certain peace and a measure of contentment here.

"Well, Catherine." Her husband was standing in the open doorway. His coachman had carried out their bags already. All her furniture and most of her belongings were to be left behind for now. Claude and Clarissa had stepped outside and were standing on the path, ready to see them on their way.

She felt such a welling of panic suddenly that she thought for one moment she was going to crumple into a heap.

He was looking at her closely. “Five minutes,” he said, and he stepped outside and half closed the door behind him.

She went back into the kitchen and looked about her. Home. This had been the very center of her home. She had felt safe here. Almost happy. She crossed to the window and gazed out at her flowers and fruit trees, at the river beyond and the meadows and hills beyond that.

Her throat and her chest ached. The pain spread upward all the way behind her nose and pricked at her eyes. She blinked them firmly and turned away.

One last look around. The morning’s fire had been carefully put out. Toby was whining at her side and rubbing against her legs, begging to be petted. It was almost as if he knew that they were about to leave their home forever. She took up the embroidered cushion from the rocker and held it against her with both arms. She could not put it back. She had embroidered it herself in the early days, when her hands had needed occupation in order to distract her mind.

She left the kitchen and the house all in a rush, her chin up, a smile on her face. Her husband was waiting just outside the door. He took the cushion from her, drew her arm through his, and held it firmly to his side while walking her to the gate and the carriage.

“I am sorry to have kept you all waiting,” she said gaily. “I forgot something. Foolish of me. And it was only this old cushion, but—”

She was in Claude’s arms then, being hugged so tightly that there was no breath left for words.

“All will be well,” he was saying into her ear. “I promise you, my dear.”

Foolish words if she thought about them. What could he do to guarantee her happiness? But she felt enormously comforted and several stages closer to tears.

"Catherine." Clarissa was hugging her too, with slightly less enthusiasm. "I do want us to be friends. I do."

And then she was being handed into the carriage and Toby, nervous and excited, was leaping onto her lap and being invited sternly to get down—he jumped onto the seat opposite, ears cocked, tongue lolling, quite uncowed by the reprimand from his new master—and her husband was climbing in to take his seat beside her.

She kept her face averted, looking out of the far window as the carriage lurched into motion. It was ill-mannered not to wave to Claude and Clarissa, but she could not bear to look, to see her cottage disappear from her sight forever. She was gripping something tightly and realized that it was her husband's hand. Had she reached for it, or had he taken hers? She could not recall. But she drew her hand away as unobtrusively as possible.

And then she had a thought and leaned forward to look back after all. "I forgot to shut the door," she wailed.

Toby whined.

"It is safely shut and locked," he said quietly. "All will be kept safe, Catherine, until we send for it."

He spoke kindly enough. But he would not understand, of course, that it was not really thieves she was afraid of or the loss of her possessions. The possessions themselves were of little value. It was what they stood for that was lost forever. She had lost the only home she had made for herself. She had lost a little of herself.

Perhaps a great deal of herself.

She felt frightened and empty and diminished.

Her hand was in his again, she realized after a few minutes. She left it there. Somehow there was a measure of comfort in his touch.

CLAUDE TOOK HIS wife back home via the postern door and the woods beyond. They walked silently side by side.

He had offered his arm, but she dropped her own once they were through the door. He slowed his steps to match hers even though it would have suited him better to stride along in the direction of home.

She was the one to break the silence after several minutes. She stopped walking and gazed at him unhappily.

"Claude," she said, "I cannot bear this any longer."

"I am sorry." He glanced down at the slippers she had worn, suitable for the carriage, perhaps, but not for the walk home. "I should have taken you by the driveway. Take my arm again."

"I cannot bear it," she said, ignoring his offered arm.

He dropped it. Perhaps he had known as soon as she spoke that she was not protesting the uneven ground underfoot. He looked at her and clasped his hands behind his back.

"We have not spoken to each other in more than two weeks," she said, "except for meaningless civilities. You have not—you have kept to your own rooms for all that time. I cannot bear it."

"I am sorry, Clarissa," he said quietly.

She gazed at him uncertainly. "I would rather you ranted and raved at me," she said. "I would rather that you struck me."

"No, you would not," he said. "That would be unpardonable. I would never forgive myself or expect you to forgive me. It would put an insurmountable barrier between us."

"Is the barrier between us now surmountable, then?" she asked.

"I do not know," he said after a lengthy pause. "It will need time, I believe, Clarissa."

"How much time?" she asked.

He shook his head slowly.

"Claude, please." She was looking up through the spring

leaves on the branches above her. "I am sorry. I am so sorry."

"Because our marriage has been soured?" he asked her. "Or because you almost ruined an innocent woman? If Rex had not returned, Clarissa, and if Daphne had not gone into such determined action, Catherine would have been in a difficult situation indeed. Would you have been sorry then? If I had agreed with you and had not sent for Rex, would you have been sorry? Or would you be gloating with righteousness along with our rector and his wife?"

"I had hoped for a match between Rawleigh and Ellen," she said. "Mrs.—Catherine seemed to have ruined that hope. And it did seem that she had entertained him and been unpardonably indiscreet."

"So," he said quietly, "we are back where we started. Will you take my arm? The ground is rougher than I remember."

She took his arm and then rested her forehead against his shoulder. "I cannot bear this coldness between us," she said. "Can you understand how difficult it is to humble myself like this and plead for your forgiveness? It is not easy. Please forgive me."

He stopped again suddenly and drew her fiercely into his arms. "Clarissa," he said, spreading a hand over the back of her bonnet and pressing her forehead to his shoulder. "I cannot bear it either. And we are all—every living human—to blame for so many petty little cruelties to one another. I have been overrighteous. Forgive me too."

She shuddered against him.

"I have missed you," he said.

She lifted her face to him. It was white and set. He smiled at her and kissed her.

They walked on after a few minutes, her arm through his, their shoulders brushing. They had discovered something new about each other during the past few weeks. He had discovered that in addition to the selfishness and arrogance that he had been able to tolerate with some humor down the years, she could occasionally be vicious. She had discovered that despite his kindness and indulgent nature, he could sometimes be implacable and unforgiving.

It was not a happily-ever-after in which they lived. If they had suspected that earlier in their marriage, they knew it for sure now. But their marriage would survive more than in just name. They had both learned something. Perhaps too they had both changed.

But they were together at least. They had talked to each other. Both had asked and given forgiveness.

"Will they be happy?" she asked him as they emerged from the trees onto a lower lawn.

"If they wish to be." He looked down at her and smiled his kindly smile. "If they both wish to be, Clarissa, and if they work hard at happiness every day of their lives."

She looked ruefully back at him. "It is never easy, is it?" she said.

"Never," he said. "But the alternative is unthinkable."

"Yes," she agreed.

Sixteen

HE HAD FELT nothing but alternating moods of panic and gloom during the two weeks preceding his marriage. He had not wanted to be married, certainly not to a woman he did not love and a woman who had quite firmly and consistently rejected all his sexual advances. She had made it very obvious on his first return to Bodley, when he had gone to offer her marriage, that she would have taken almost any course that would have kept her from marrying him—even becoming his mistress would have been preferable because she would not have been trapped into a lifelong relationship with him.

Her attitude had been a severe blow to his self-esteem.

And of course their wedding night had been a total disaster. He could never remember without an inward shudder the fact that his lovemaking had reduced her to silent tears.

He was rather surprised to discover, then, that her presence with him on the return journey to Stratton somehow lifted his spirits. There were frustrations, of course, but there were things about her that intrigued him. And she was nothing if not a challenge. That was one thing that had been missing from his life since he had sold out of the cavalry—a challenge to take away the tedium of life. Certainly he did not find the journey home tedious.

She wore the same simple, neat, unfashionable clothes she had worn since his first acquaintance with her. Stupid of him to have imagined that as soon as they were married she would be transformed into a viscountess in every way. All her clothes were well-worn.

"I will have to take you to London," he said to her one day in the carriage, "to a modiste who will deck you out in all the necessary finery."

"I do not need new clothes," she said, flashing him an indignant look. "I am happy with the ones I have."

He had always been amused—and somewhat charmed—by her when she was on her dignity. "You do need them," he said, "and I am not happy with what you have." It was a lie really. The simplicity of her clothing had always emphasized her beauty. "It is my wishes that count. You promised to obey me, remember?"

Her jaw hardened immediately and her already straight back seemed to straighten further. "Yes, my lord," she said.

She learned fast. She knew that one sure way to irritate him was to "my lord" him in that meek and humble voice. She had never yet used his given name. He pursed his lips.

"We will go to London," he said. He had no real wish to go there. A modiste could just as easily be brought to Stratton. But he was watching her face. He wanted to know if she was as reluctant to go to London to shop for clothes as she had been to be set up there as his mistress.

"No." Her face had paled. "No, not London."

He should have insisted on knowing everything, he realized. As soon as she had told him that she was not a widow and that her name was Winsmore, not Winters, he should have insisted on hearing the rest of it. All of it. It was ridiculous to have married a woman who was harboring secrets. Not very savory secrets either, if his guess was correct. What was it about London? Was she merely afraid of it because she had never been there? Or had something happened to her there? He rather suspected the latter.

"Why not?" His eyes dropped to her lap, where that dratted dog was curled up having his ears scratched—with those slender, sensitive fingers.

"Because," she said.

Which was a marvelously eloquent and informative reply. He did not press the point. Why? he asked himself. Was it desirable to allow his wife to keep secrets from him? Was it wise to allow her to get away with such impertinent and evasive answers? Perhaps not wise, he decided. But amusing.

She was willing to converse. She was well informed for a woman, especially for one who had lived in the country for a number of years. She had opinions that she was not shy about defending even when they conflicted with his. She was well-read. They were able to exchange views on books both ancient and current. And she was willing to talk about herself—for the past five years. Any question or comment of his designed to trick her into revealing something about her life before then was always deftly turned. It was as if she had been born—and abandoned—fully grown at Bodley-on-the-Water just five years ago.

He thought about her name—Winsmore. It should mean something. There was a familiarity about it. But perhaps not. Perhaps it was just that the name had been turning over in his mind for so long that he had made it sound familiar. She had probably grown up somewhere far remote from both London and Kent.

He wondered how she would cope with life at Stratton. She showed no awkwardness of manner at any of the inns at which they stopped, but then she had never shown awkwardness at Bodley House either. She *was* a lady. But Stratton might be different. He talked about it quite often. He tried to frighten her with descriptions of the grand Palladian architecture of the house, of its large, square size, of the splendor of the state rooms, of the fine furnishings and works of art with which it was filled.

She appeared interested. She asked intelligent questions. There was no flicker of terror in her.

Whenever they stopped she would go striding off through village streets or along country lanes with Toby to give him exercise. She always insisted on going herself even when it was raining or the roads were muddy—and even though he told her that a groom could be assigned to the task. And so of course, he was compelled to go with her. He found that he did not mind—though his valet, if he had been in attendance, would have had an apoplexy at the murder he often did to his Hessians. He liked the color the exercise brought to his wife's cheeks and the brightness to her eyes.

She had infinite patience with the dog. If Toby decided to sniff about the trunk of a particular tree for all of ten minutes, she would stand and let him sniff. Even on the one occasion when a cutting wind was clipping through them without bothering to make a detour around them and a drizzling rain was raining on them for good measure.

If she was this patient and this indulgent with a mere dog, he once thought, what would she be like with a child? He did not put the question into words—she had ripped up at him once before when he had been incautious enough to say something similar. She would probably be one of those women who insisted on nursing her own babies at the breast instead of hiring a wet nurse as any decent lady would. The thought for some reason did strange things to his insides.

Not that there was any point in thinking about babies if

certain facts of their relationship did not change. He had not touched her in the way of marriage since their wedding night. He had no desire to emerge from the pleasurable exertion of a sexual encounter just to have cold water dashed in his face in the form of his wife's firmly turned back and the knowledge that her cheeks would be wet if he cared to touch them to find out.

Twice they were fortunate enough to be able to reserve a suite of rooms at the inns where they stayed so that he had a bed of his own in which to sleep. Once, when there was only one room and one bed, he stayed in the taproom all night listening to the stories of an old soldier, who never did realize that he was telling them to a veteran who had fought in all the same battles as the ones he described with such hair-raising—and such inaccurate—detail. For the price of a few jugs of ale, the viscount was provided with a night's entertainment, which was more than he would have got upstairs, he thought.

Another night he was less fortunate. There was only one room and one bed, and everyone who sat in the taproom during the evening either retired to bed or returned home before midnight. Lord Rawleigh spent the night on the floor beside the bed in which his wife slept. Though she was not sleeping either, he discovered after undressing quietly in the darkness and making a bed out of an old mat and his greatcoat. A couple of minutes after he lay down, a pillow landed with a thump on his face.

"Thank you," he growled. She might have given some indication of wakefulness when he came in so that he need not have felt around in the darkness for so long or stubbed his toe on the foot of the bed.

He heard her turning over and punching her own pillow.

And then he was sorry that she had thrown down the pillow, though it easily doubled his level of comfort.

Knowing that she was awake, he was suddenly aware of her. She was above him, a mere couple of feet away from him. Probably clad only in a flimsy nightgown. Probably warm. His wife.

One question he had asked himself some time ago had been effectively answered anyway, he thought grimly. He had wondered if he would be satisfied if he could have her just once. It usually worked that way with women he panted after. Not this time, though. He had had her once—and it was not a particularly good memory. But he burned for her still. He gritted his teeth and clenched his hands into fists. He was in a state of full arousal, just like a randy schoolboy.

She was his wife, devil take it. It was her duty and his right. All he had to do was get to his feet, take one step, and slide beneath the bedclothes with her. . . .

He counted sheep and soldiers and terrier dogs until his body accepted the decision of his will and subsided into inaction. Terrier dogs! He heard Toby heave a deep and contented sigh from above, from somewhere in the region of where her feet must be. Dratted dog.

He must have fallen asleep, uncomfortable as he was and sexually deprived as he was. He came awake to some noise. Someone was talking. No one was, of course, by the time he was fully awake. Someone must have been passing outside their door. He had never been able to reverse the habit of his years in the cavalry of being alert to even the slightest sound in his sleep. He sighed and wondered what the floor would feel like if he tried turning onto one side. Probably even less comfortable than it felt against his back.

"Bruce!" she said sharply, so that his eyes widened and fixed on the dark ceiling above him.

Toby woofed softly.

"Bruce." It was more of a wail this time. "Don't leave me.

Don't go. I am so lonely. My arms are so empty. Don't go. Bru-u-uce."

He was sitting bolt upright, his head turned toward the bed. Instinct would have had him on his feet and across the short distance to offer comfort. She was in such unbearable pain. He knew all about nightmares. He had had his fair share and had heard his fair share. Strangely, considering the fact that he had been an officer and one with a reputation for toughness, he had often got up during the night to comfort those who were wrestling with night demons, especially raw recruits, boys who should still have been at home with their mothers.

Instinct could not be obeyed this time. It was a man's name she had spoken. The man she had loved. The man who had left her. Bruce. He clamped his teeth together and clenched one of his hands into a fist again, as he had done earlier for an entirely different reason.

She stirred then enough to turn over on the bed. She lay facing him, the bedclothes pushed back to her waist, her hair disheveled and spread over her shoulder and along the arm that was draped over the side of the bed, almost touching him. She was not awake. She did not speak again.

God, he thought. God, what had he got into? What had unbridled lust and reckless incaution landed him in?

Bruce.

The floor got progressively harder as the night wore on.

But it was the last night on the road. They would be at Stratton by teatime on the following afternoon. Despite an almost sleepless and somewhat disturbing night, he was cheered by the thought. And eager to see her reaction to his home. And perversely exhilarated by the challenge of making a marriage of this mess he had got himself into entirely through his own fault.

• • •

THE TWO WEEKS prior to her marriage had been in the nature of a waking nightmare, which she had kept under control by deadening all emotions, by just allowing life to happen to her. Her wedding day, by contrast, had been unexpectedly meaningful. And her wedding night had been gloriously wonderful until she had spoiled it by remembering that there was no emotion to what had happened except lust—and until he had got up from her bed and left her room without a word. Leaving her cottage the next morning had been excruciating agony. Starting all over again on yet another new life had seemed an impossibility.

But life had the strange property of being able to renew itself and reassert itself over and over again. She had thought once before that it was impossible to go on. Very few things were impossible, she was discovering more and more as she grew older.

After the first dreadful day of travel, which took her farther and farther from the life she had made for herself five years ago, she found that she was—oh, not exactly enjoying her new life, she thought. But she was becoming interested in it, intrigued by it, a little excited by it. She had forgotten that new experiences and the unknown could be exhilarating. She felt somehow younger all of a sudden, almost as if the last five years had been suspended time and she was about to live again.

It was a strange feeling when she had not wanted to marry, when she did not like her husband, when nothing was really right with her marriage. He had scarcely touched her since their wedding night. That was at least partly her fault, of course. She felt embarrassed that she had allowed her terrible feeling of loneliness to spill out in self-pity when he had been with her and close enough to notice. She wanted no one's pity, not even her own. She was alive and healthy—there was nothing to be pitied.

She did not like him. He was far too arrogant and had been far too insistent in his attentions even knowing that she had not wanted them. But oh, she had to admit to herself during the journey that he was an interesting companion to talk with. He was knowledgeable and intelligent. But he was not so opinionated that he would not listen to her. And he paid her the compliment of arguing with her when they disagreed rather than merely dismissing her as a woman with an inferior mind. She had been starved for conversation for longer than five years, she realized.

And he was protective of her. It felt strange to be helped in and out of carriages, to be escorted from room to room at the inns where they stayed, to be accompanied on the walks she took with Toby. She had been alone for so long. It might have been irksome—almost like having a guard wherever she went and no privacy. But it was not irksome. Strangely, although she had come to value her independence and scorned to be treated like a weak and frail woman, it felt good to be protected. It felt almost like being cherished, though she put that thought firmly from her. Only pain could come of starting to think like that.

Of course she was not cherished. He slept alone when they had two rooms. She did not know where he slept the one night when there was only one room. He certainly did not spend it with her. The one night when he did come back to their single bed and she had lain in bed, faking sleep, her heart beating painfully with anticipation, he had slept on the floor. It had been a horrible humiliation. Had that once been enough to cool all the ardor with which he had pursued her before and during the night of the ball? Had her lack of knowledge and experience made her such an unenticing lover? Or was it the fact that she had not been virgin? Or the fact that she had turned from him in her loneliness afterward?

He was so very handsome and attractive. She wished she could like him. It did not seem right to desire him as much as she did, to be feeling as much excitement at the prospect of a married life with him when she did not like him. It seemed too—carnal. But there was no point in entering her new life in the deepest gloom, she consoled herself. Nothing would be served by it.

She was excited at the thought of arriving at Stratton Park. She had heard of it before. It was said to be one of the most stately houses and parks in England. And his descriptions of it only succeeded in whetting her appetite even more. She was excited by the thought of living there, of being mistress there. It seemed a little disloyal to her precious cottage to think so, but what was the point of trying to remain loyal to an inanimate object?

They arrived there in the middle of a sunny afternoon. She guessed that she was seeing it at its loveliest. She gazed from the window of the carriage, keeping her back straight and her hands relaxed in her lap, trying not to make a cake of herself by jumping up and down and showing the excitement she felt. Her husband reclined indolently across one corner of the carriage seat, gazing at her rather than at the view. He did a lot of that—gazing at her. She found it somewhat disconcerting. She had to school her hands not to stray to her hair to see that no strand had escaped its pins.

"Well?" he said.

Everything about it was square and solid and on a grand scale. The house, built of gray stone, was classical in design with a pillared portico at the front. The inner park was built in a great square about it, its lawns shaded by ancient oaks and elms and beeches and dotted with clumps of daffodils and other spring flowers. There were no formal parterre gardens. The relatively short, straight graveled drive took them over a Palladian bridge across a river. It was all breathtakingly magnificent.

"It is lovely," she said, feeling the inadequacy of her words even as she spoke them. Some things just could not be expressed in words. This was to be her home? She was to belong here?

He laughed softly.

Toby, sensing that they were nearing their journey's end, sat up on the seat opposite and looked alert.

"We are expected," her husband said. "By now my carriage will have been recognized. Mrs. Keach, my housekeeper, will doubtless be lining everyone up in the hall to receive their new mistress."

He sounded mildly amused.

"All you need to do," he said, "is nod graciously and smile if you wish and the ordeal will be over."

All— Men were quite impossible, she thought.

He was quite right, of course. After he had helped her alight from the carriage and had escorted her up the marble steps and through the great double doors, she had no chance to look about her at the pillared hall, though she had an impression of size and magnificence. There was a silent line of servants on either side of the hall, men on one side, women on the other. Two dignified middle-aged servants, one man and one woman, stood alone together in the center of the hall. The man was bowing, the woman was curtsying.

They were the butler and the housekeeper, Horrocks and Mrs. Keach. Her husband presented her to them and she nodded and smiled and greeted them. She looked to either side, smiling. And then her husband had his hand on her elbow, said something about tea to Mrs. Keach, and would have steered her in the direction of the great pillared doorway that must lead to the staircase.

"Mrs. Keach," she said, ignoring his hand, "I would be delighted to meet the women servants if you would introduce them to me."

Mrs. Keach looked at her with approval. "Yes, my lady," she said, and she led the way with great dignity to the end of the line and called each servant by name as they moved slowly along it. Her husband trailed after them, Catherine was aware. She concentrated on learning names and trying to associate them with their respective faces, though it would take her a while to remember them all, she supposed. She had a word with each of the servants. When they came to the end of the line and her husband reached for her elbow again, she turned toward the butler and asked him to perform the same duty for the menservants.

Finally she allowed herself to be steered toward the doorway and the grand staircase. Mrs. Keach went ahead of them.

"You will show her ladyship to her apartment, Mrs. Keach?" her husband said. "And make sure while she freshens up that someone waits outside to show her the way to the drawing room for tea when she is ready."

"Yes, my lord," the housekeeper murmured.

"I shall see you in a short while, then, my love," he said, bowing over her hand as he relinquished it. He was looking amused again.

Her apartments, consisting of a bedchamber, a dressing room, and a sitting room, would probably hold her cottage twice over, she thought over the next half hour. The thought somewhat amused her. And also the memory of Toby's trotting footsteps as he inspected the lines of servants with her. Her husband had scooped him up before he could follow her upstairs to her rooms. He was stretched out on the carpet before the fireplace when she entered the drawing room later but jumped up to meet her with wildly wagging tail.

"Toby." She stooped to pat him. "Is this all very strange to you? You will get used to it."

"As will you," a voice said from her right. He was standing by a window, though he came toward her and indicated the tea tray, which had been brought already.

She sat behind it to pour the tea. It was a beautiful room, she saw at a glance, with a coved and painted ceiling, a marble fireplace, and paintings in gilded frames on the walls. She guessed that most of them were family portraits. She was beginning to feel somewhat overwhelmed.

Her husband took his cup and saucer from her hands and sat down opposite her. "You really did not have to inspect the lines, you know," he said. "You certainly were not expected to speak to every servant. But they were all charmed beyond words. You now have a houseful of slaves rather than servants, Catherine."

"What is so funny?" she asked him, on her dignity. He was not looking just amused. He was actually grinning.

"You are," he said. "You look rather like a child's top, wound up and ready to start wildly spinning. You may relax. There has been no woman in this house since my mother died eight years ago. Everything runs perfectly, as you can see. Very little will be required of you. A mere token approval of the plans and menus Mrs. Keach will bring you."

Ah, she understood. He thought she was incapable of running a household larger than the one she had had—or not had—at her cottage.

"You are the one who may relax, *my lord,*" she said, emphasizing his title since it was one little way she could always be sure of annoying him. She was feeling mortally insulted. "The household will continue to run smoothly for your comfort. I will speak with Mrs. Keach in the morning and together we will come to an amicable agreement about how the house is to be managed now that it has a mistress again."

She enjoyed watching the smile being wiped clean from his face. But it was back soon enough, lurking behind his eyes as he regarded her in silence. He sipped on his tea.

"Catherine," he said, "one of these days you are going to tell me who you are, you know. You are not at all daunted by all this, are you?"

"Not at all," she said crisply. She had been wishing for a long time that she had told him everything that day she had given him her real name. There was really no reason why he should not have known. It was not as if she had been trying to prevent his crying off. She had hoped at the time that he *would* cry off. But now it was difficult to tell him.

"Catherine." He had finished his tea and set down the cup and saucer on the table at his elbow. He shook his head and held up a staying hand when she picked up the teapot again. He looked at her in silence for a few moments and she thought he had nothing more to say. But he did. "Who is Bruce?"

Everything inside her seemed to turn over. She seemed to have been robbed of air. "Bruce?" Even her voice seemed to come from a distance.

"Bruce," he repeated. "Who is he?"

How had he found out? How did he know that name?

"I have discovered," he said, "that at least occasionally you talk in your sleep."

She had started to dream about him again. About holding him and watching him just fade away into nothingness as she held him in her arms. She supposed it had been brought on by the fierce and unexpected desire for another child that had come with her marriage. Though there appeared to be no real chance of its happening anytime soon.

"I believe," he said, and the coldness and arrogance she had seen in him on their first acquaintance were there again, "he is someone you once loved?"

"Yes." The word was no more than a whisper. She should tell him now. Obviously he thought Bruce to be a man. But she could not tell him. How could she tell this cold stranger about the dearest love of her heart? She felt her vision blur and realized in some humiliation that her eyes had filled with tears.

"I cannot command your past affections," he said. "Only your present and future ones. Though I am not sure I can ever command your *affection*. Your loyalty, then. I do command it, Catherine. I suppose a past love cannot be forgotten at will, but you must understand that it is in the past, that I will not countenance any pining for what is gone."

She hated him then. With a cold, intense passion.

"You are an evil man," she hissed at him. Part of her knew she was being unfair to him, that he had misunderstood, that she should explain to him. But she was too deeply hurt to be fair. "I have married you because you left me with no choice. You will have my loyalty and my fidelity for the rest of my life, for what they are worth. Do not expect my heart too, my lord. My heart—every shadow and corner of it—belongs to Bruce and always will."

She got to her feet and hurried from the room. Oh, yes, she was being dreadfully unfair, she knew. She did not care. If he thought to play the heavy-handed lord and master with her, then she would fight him with every weapon at her disposal, even unfairness. She half expected that he would come after her, but he did not. Toby was woofing excitedly at her heels, though. She hoped, as she hurried toward the staircase, that she could remember the way to her apartments.

Seventeen

THERE WAS A pianoforte in the drawing room that had not been played much in ten years, though it had always been kept in tune. He asked her to play it after dinner and she did so without argument and stayed there for longer than an hour. Probably, he thought, she was as relieved as he to have something to do that took away the necessity of making conversation. Though they had done remarkably well at dinner. It seemed that they could be good companions when they steered clear of personal matters.

He sat and watched her as she played. She was wearing a pale blue evening gown, neither fussy nor fashionable nor new. Her hair was dressed in its usual knot at the nape of her neck, even though he had made sure that a maid had been assigned to her to assist in her dressing. She looked very typically Catherine. She played self-consciously, though correctly, at first. Soon she lost herself in her music as she had in Claude's music room that morning long ago—it seemed long ago. Beauty and passion came from the pianoforte and filled the room. It seemed almost impossible that one slim woman could be producing it. She could easily play professionally, he thought.

It felt strange to have her here at Stratton with him. She had obsessed him for those weeks at Bodley, the lovely and alluring—and elusive—Mrs. Winters. He had burned for her. He had schemed to win her. He had refused to take no for an answer. And now here she was with him in his house, his wife, his viscountess.

Even stranger was the fact that he felt a moment of triumph, almost of exultation. There was no triumph in what had happened. And no reason to exult. Their marriage was a mess, a nonevent. She loved and would always love a man named Bruce. He had even found himself racking his brains for any acquaintance of his with that name. But there was no one. Not even a corner or a shadow—how had she put it exactly? He frowned in thought. . . .

My heart—every shadow and corner of it—belongs to Bruce and always will.

And she had begun that impassioned speech by calling him an evil man. All because he had tried to establish a few ground rules with her, advising her that the past must be dismissed from her mind and the present take its place. What was evil about that?

She should have left him angry when she rushed from the room—and she did. She had also left him feeling shaken and bruised. Hurt. Though he was reluctant to concede that she had the power to hurt him.

Toby, who had been standing beside the pianoforte bench for a few minutes, slowly wagging his tail, had decided that there must be an easier way to attract his mistress's attention. He leapt onto the bench and nudged her elbow with his nose.

"Toby." She stopped playing and laughed. "Do you have no respect for Mozart? You are not accustomed to this sort of competition, are you? I suppose you need to go outside."

Viscount Rawleigh got to his feet and strolled across the

room toward them. She looked up at him, her eyes still laughing. He found himself changing plans abruptly. He had been about to inform her that there were footmen enough to take her dog outside whenever he needed to go, that it did not behoove the dignity of the Viscountess Rawleigh to be at the beck and call of a spoiled terrier.

"Maybe we could take a walk outside," he said. "I wonder if the evening is as pleasant as the day has been." What he was really wondering was how soon he was going to become the laughingstock among his servants. Belatedly he asserted his authority, his voice stern. "Get down from there, sir. The furniture in your new home is for viewing from floor level. Understood?"

But Toby was already prancing about his heels and yipping with excitement. And Catherine was laughing again. "You mentioned the W-word in his hearing," she said. "It was not wise."

He frowned down at the dog. "Sit!" he said curtly.

Toby sat and gazed at him with fixed, anticipatory stare.

"It must be your military background." She was still laughing. "He will never do that for me."

They were out on the terrace a few minutes later. She took his arm and they strolled all about the house while she examined it with interested eyes and looked about the park. It was a clear, moonlit night and not cold at all. Toby was dashing across the lawns, snuffling all around the trunks of the trees, acquainting himself with his new territory.

It would be bedtime by the time they went inside, he thought. Their first night home. The night that would set the pattern for all future nights, in all likelihood. Would he spend it in his own bed? By doing so he would be setting a precedent that would be hard to break. Was he willing to have such a marriage? A marriage in name alone?

It was ridiculous even to contemplate such a thing. She

was his wife. He had desired her from his first sight of her. He had needs even apart from his attraction to her. Why should he go elsewhere to satisfy those needs? Besides, he had what was perhaps a regrettable belief in fidelity within marriage. He certainly was not prepared to live a celibate existence. He was no monk.

And was he to be inconvenienced merely because she still loved a man from her past?

He stopped walking at one corner of the house, close to the rose arbor, which had been his mother's favorite part of the park.

"Catherine," he asked her, "why did you cry?"

It was a foolish question to ask. He had not intended to begin this way. He would be just as happy to forget that night and its humiliation.

She stood facing him, looking up at him in the moonlight. God, but she was beautiful with her smooth golden hair, which looked more silver in this light, and her plain gray cloak. He could see from her eyes that she knew just exactly what he was talking about.

"For no particular reason," she said. "I was— Everything was so new. I was a little overwhelmed. Sometimes emotion shows itself it strange ways."

He was not sure that she spoke the truth. "You turned away from me," he said.

"I—" She hunched her shoulders. "I did not mean to offend you. But I did."

"Did I hurt you?" he asked. "Offend you? Disgust you?"

"No." She frowned at him and opened her mouth as if to say more. But she closed it again. "No," she said once more.

"Perhaps," he said with unexpected and unwise bitterness, "you were comparing me—"

"No!" She closed her eyes and swallowed then looked

down at her hands. He saw her shudder. "No. There was no comparison whatsoever."

Which, in light of what she had said in the drawing room at tea, was a marvelous compliment indeed. He felt like a gauche, uncertain boy again and resented the feeling. He had become accustomed to thinking of himself as a tolerably skilled lover. Certainly the women with whom he had lain in the past several years had appeared well satisfied with his performance. But of course she *loved* the other man. Perhaps sexual skills were of little importance when one loved elsewhere.

"I am not prepared to conduct a celibate marriage," he said.

She looked up, startled. "Neither am I," she said, and bit her lip. He wondered if she was blushing. It was impossible to tell in the moonlight. But her words were encouraging.

"If I come to your bed tonight," he said, "will I be dismissed by tears again?"

"No," she said.

He lifted a hand to smooth the backs of his fingers down one side of her jaw to the chin. "You know," he said, "that I have always desired you."

"Yes." He felt her swallow.

"And I believe," he said, "that though finer feelings are out of the question, you have desired me."

"Yes." It was a mere murmur of sound.

"We are married," he said. "Neither of us wanted it but it happened. I will even take the blame upon myself. It was entirely my fault. But that is irrelevant now. We are married. Perhaps we can learn to rub along well enough together."

"Yes," she said.

"One thing." He cupped her chin in his palm, holding her face up to his. But he knew it was unnecessary. She met his eyes as unflinchingly as she almost always did. "I cede your right to 'my lord' me when you want to set my teeth on edge—it is an admirable weapon and it would be unfair to deprive you of it since we will undoubtedly do our share of quarreling down the years. But I have a hankering to hear my name on your lips. Say it, Catherine."

She gazed back into his eyes. "Rex," she said.

"Thank you." It was quite unclear to him why the sound of his own name spoken in her voice should cause a lurching of his insides. He had been too many nights without her, he supposed.

He closed the distance between their mouths and kissed her. Her lips were soft and warm and parted. They trembled against his, almost as if he had never kissed her before and they had never lain together. He felt the familiar soaring of his temperature. He had never known another woman who could ignite him so effectively with a mere kiss.

"I do believe," he said, lifting his head, still holding her chin, "we have given Toby sufficient time to stake out his claim to every tree in the park. Shall we go inside?"

She nodded. There was a look in her eyes that he recognized. She wanted it, he thought. She wanted him. He felt a rush of exultation, which for pride's sake he hid. He turned his head and whistled for Toby. The terrier came at a run.

She laughed, the sound a little shaky. "I am not sure I like the way he gives you instant obedience," she said.

"Perhaps," he said, looking at her sidelong as he offered his arm again and she took it, "unlike his mistress, he recognizes a master's voice."

She chuckled but did not reply.

It was a good moment, he thought in surprise. He had teased her and she had laughed. It was a small, seemingly insignificant incident. To him it seemed that perhaps it was momentous.

• • •

IT FELT STRANGE having a maid again. Marie was eager and anxious to please, though she must be somewhat surprised by the smallness and plainness of her mistress's wardrobe, Catherine thought. She had laid out the best of the nightgowns, the one Catherine had intended to wear on her wedding night.

She wore it now as she waited in her bedchamber for her husband to come. For Rex—she must begin using his name, even in her thoughts. He was right. They were married now, for better or worse. They could only try to make the best of it, try to rub along together, as he had put it.

It was a splendid room, with elegant furniture and a soft carpet underfoot. The bed was very grand, with finely carved bedposts and silk bed hangings and canopy. They would be lying there soon. . . .

She swallowed. She wanted it very badly. She was almost ashamed of her eagerness when she remembered how she had hated him just a few hours earlier for the autocratic commands with which he had tried to control her. But it was an eagerness she must cultivate. There was no point in trying to quell what might well be the only good aspect of their marriage. They desired each other—that had been established beyond doubt outside less than an hour ago.

Tonight she must take his lovemaking for what it was worth and her own response too. She must not allow her essential aloneness to wash over her once the ecstasy was at an end. Perhaps after all she was not so very alone. Despite herself and almost unwillingly, she had admitted during the course of the evening that there were certain things about him that she might come to like if she would allow herself to do so. She liked his intelligent conversation. Her mind had been unstimulated by anything except books for such a long time. She liked his direct, head-on approach to problems, though that had its drawbacks, like this afternoon when he had suddenly demanded out of nowhere to know who Bruce was.

Unexpectedly, she had liked laughing with him. She had not imagined that they would ever laugh together. But they had.

She liked his kindness to Toby, though she would never say so to him. She suspected that he considered it rather unmanly to be kind to a mere dog. She glanced fondly at Toby, who was stretched out before the fireplace, fast asleep. He had suggested when they first arrived that Toby might be more comfortable in the stables, but he had not argued when she had firmly refused.

How could she live without Toby? And how would Toby live without her?

She turned her head suddenly as a tap at her dressing-room door preceded its opening, and he came into her room. She had guessed earlier that the other door in her dressing room must connect with his. He was wearing a wine-colored dressing gown. He looked irresistibly attractive. She was glad suddenly that she was married to him and did not have to quell her desire for him. And she did not stop to remind herself that there ought to be more to marriage than this. For now this was enough.

He stopped and looked her over slowly from head to foot.

"How is it," he asked her, "that you can make simple cotton appear more alluring than the finest lace, Catherine? You look beautiful with your hair down. No, scratch that. You look beautiful with your hair up. With it down you look—is there a word more superlative than beautiful?"

How could she answer that? She felt herself blushing. The compliment felt good.

"If there is," he said, coming toward her, "I will think of it—some other time."

He kissed her, setting his hands at her waist. He did not this time strip her immediately of her one garment. She was glad of it, though she had not questioned his right to do so that other time.

"Come to bed," he said, his lips still against hers.

He blew out the candles this time before joining her there. She was glad of that too. Not that she had been particularly distressed the other time, but she had been self-conscious, aware that she was to a certain extent on display. She wanted to be able to lose herself in the experience tonight, rather as—yes, rather as she could lose herself in music when she played. She wanted to lose herself in beauty and harmony and passion. She liked the analogy.

He was naked when he joined her. She closed her eyes as he kissed her and as his hands began to fondle her through the cotton of her nightgown. She could remember how he looked, splendidly proportioned and beautiful, one old saber scar across his right shoulder and another over his right hip. But she did not need sight. She could feel his tall and powerfully muscled body. She could smell his cologne and his masculinity. Tonight she set herself consciously to enjoy what he did to her.

"Catherine," he said, "am I to have a passive lover again?"

Her eyes snapped open. Passive? Could he not tell how on fire she was for him already? It was as much as she could do not to move and squirm against him, not to touch him and let her hands roam over him.

"I could take my pleasure very quickly, you know," he said as one of his hands was working the buttons of her nightgown free of the buttonholes. "It could be over in no longer than a few seconds."

She knew that. She drew a slow breath through her nostrils and held it. Oh, she knew that.

"I would prefer to make love to you." His hand slid beneath the cotton of her gown and nudged it from her shoulder so that his mouth could feather across it. "I know that full pleasure comes more slowly for a woman."

Did all men know that? And act upon it? No, *all* men did not.

Her nightgown was moving lower. His hand was beneath her breast, lifting it, and his mouth was moving to her nipple and opening over it. His tongue touched it. She gasped.

"But what I would really like," he said, his breath warming the nipple his tongue had just wet, "is for you to make love to me too."

How? She could feel herself stiffen in his arms.

"How?" she whispered, and she was doubly glad of the absence of candlelight.

"Ah, Catherine," he said, his mouth against hers again. "How glad I am that you are an innocent after all. You allow me to touch you everywhere. Are my touches pleasing to you?"

"Yes," she said.

"Do you not think your touches would be pleasing to me, then?" he asked. "Do you feel no desire to touch me?"

"Yes." It was all right to touch him? It was not—improper? She almost laughed with nervousness when her mind latched onto that particular word.

"Then touch me," he said. "Make love to me."

He turned her onto her back briefly and stripped her nightgown down over her body and off her feet. He tossed it aside. Then one arm came about her and turned her against him again.

She spread her hands over his chest. It was broad, very strongly muscled, dusted with hairs. She could feel his own nipples as hard buds and moved her hands so that her forefingers could rub against them while she pressed her mouth to his chest. He was lying still, she noticed. Unfairly, he had become passive himself. But she was dizzy with the desire to explore him, to know him. For the moment she did not want him to move.

His back was as firm as his chest. And warm. She could feel the ridge of the old saber wound which must have almost slashed his leg off at the hip. It was not a thought her mind dwelled upon. Her hand slid lightly forward over the wound, over his hip—and would have shied away. But he would not allow it.

"Yes," he said almost fiercely. "Yes, Catherine. Touch me."

Hard and long. Ready for her. Her fingers moved lightly over him and then her hand closed about him when she knew from his sharp inward breath that she was pleasing him. How could there possibly be room? But she knew that there was. There was a throbbing deep inside her where she wanted him to be.

"God, woman," he said, and she was on her back again and he was rearing over her. "I should have tied your hands behind your back rather than invite you to make love to me. Do you have magic in your hands?"

"Yes," she whispered to him, lifting her arms to pull his face down to hers. She opened her mouth under his. "And magic in my body, Rex. Come and see."

He was in her in one deep, powerful thrust. She cried out into his mouth with the shock and the wonder of it.

"Now you have made me behave like a schoolboy," he said urgently. "Are you ready?"

"Yes." She was gasping and pleading, her hands moving hard down his sides and around to his buttocks. "Yes, I am ready. Give it to me, Rex. Give it to me."

What followed was fierce, panting agony and ecstasy. He pounded into her, but she was no passive vessel. She thrust her hips against him in a counter rhythm to his own. She heard his final cry mingle with her own. She felt the hot gush inside. And then she lost herself for seconds or minutes or hours—there was no knowing which.

She came back to herself only when a heavy weight was lifted from her and she realized he was moving to her side. She remembered then. She remembered the feeling she had had on her wedding night that what had happened had been only physical, that emotionally and in every way that mattered she was still alone and perhaps more alone than before because her body no longer belonged to herself. She waited for a return of that feeling.

"Well?" His hand smoothed over the shoulder nearer to him. Was that anxiety in his voice? No, probably not.

She turned her head and smiled sleepily. Her eyes had become accustomed to the darkness. He was gazing back at her.

"Mm," she said.

"Mm good?" he asked. "Mm bad? Or mm leave me alone?"

"Mm," she said.

"Eloquent." He reached down and drew the bedclothes up over them. At the same time he slid one arm beneath her head. She turned onto her side and nestled against him. For now she would pretend that the physical unity she had just felt with him was total unity. There was no harm in pretending. Not just for tonight. He was warm and sweaty. He felt wonderful.

He said something else. She was too sleepy to hear exactly what.

"Mm," she said one more time, and slid down the delicious slope toward sleep.

HE WAS RELAXED and satiated and very close to sleep himself. But he held oblivion off for a few minutes longer.

He rubbed his cheek against the silkiness of her hair. She was warm and soft and relaxed with sleep. She smelled of soap and woman and sex.

His mind, exhausted from so much traveling in the past three weeks, moved back over the past month and more, over all the events that had wrought such a change in his life. Such a catastrophic change, he had believed until—when? A few minutes ago?

He had wanted her from the start—as a mistress. As someone to bed and take pleasure with while he spent a few weeks in the country with his family and friends. He certainly had not wanted any long-term relationship with her, even though, incredibly, his desire had been so strong that he had offered her marriage even before he had been compelled to do so.

He was glad now that she was not his mistress. Catherine was not a woman just for a man's bed, even though ironically he was making the discovery just there. She was a woman for a man's life. He was not sure what he meant by that and he was far too sleepy to analyze the thought. But it seemed to him to be a profound thought and well worth returning to tomorrow when he had more energy.

He was glad that they were going to have a lifetime of nights together in which to perfect what happened between them in bed. Their wedding night had been a disaster. Tonight had been far from perfect, though it had seemed so to him just a few minutes ago. Certainly it was far below his usual standard as far as duration went. It had all been over within a very few minutes. And he had taken all the pleasure himself. He had done very little for her pleasure before mounting her in a frenzy of lust.

And yet she had seemed well pleased. She had shouted out his name at the very moment he released into her, and she had fallen asleep with flattering speed. In his arms. There had been no turning away tonight, no tears.

The next time, he decided, it would be all for her. He would hold himself back for an hour if need be in order to bring her all the pleasure he was capable of giving. Next time—perhaps later tonight. He would have to instruct her, though, to keep her magic hands to herself.

He smiled against her hair. He had had women with hands far more skilled and experienced than Catherine's. Why had hers caused him very nearly to disgrace himself?

He was very tired. He must sleep. But he knew he would not sleep all night. He knew he was going to want her again before morning came.

He was glad there was a lifetime. . . .

He could hear Toby shift position before the fireplace, yawn loudly, close his mouth with a snap of teeth, and fall silent again.

Lord Rawleigh almost chuckled aloud. But he was too sleepy to make the effort.

Eighteen

SHE HAD NOT expected to be happy or anything approaching happy. She had not wanted to marry Viscount Rawleigh. Being forced into marriage with him had seemed a nightmare, even though she had always felt an unwilling attraction to him. She had expected to mourn her cottage and the life of quiet contentment she had built for herself there.

In the event, she found herself unexpectedly happy during her first couple of weeks at her new home. It was lovely—oh, yes, she had to admit it—to be living in a large house again, surrounded by a spacious and beautiful park, with servants to see that it all ran smoothly. And it felt good to know that she was mistress of Stratton Park, that after all she was a respectably married lady, the Viscountess Rawleigh.

She spent the full morning with Mrs. Keach the day after her arrival—she suspected that the servants were amazed to see her up so early. The housekeeper showed her about the house and explained its running and showed her the housekeeping books and took her belowstairs to talk with the cook. The house was efficiently run and the cook's menus varied and nutritious and delicious. Perhaps many new brides would have been cowed into allowing everything to continue as before without her interference. Catherine did not interfere, but it was clear to everyone within a few days that she was indeed now mistress of Stratton.

It felt good to be mistress of a large home again.

Word was quick to spread, not only that Viscount Rawleigh was in residence again, but that he had brought home a bride with him. There was a steady stream of callers during the first week, almost all of whom issued invitations. During the second week Catherine was out almost every afternoon and evening, returning the calls, attending the dinners and entertainments to which they had been invited. It seemed that social life at Stratton would be brisk even when the novelty of her arrival in the neighborhood had died down.

Then there were the vicar of Stratton and his wife to be met during the first week and the villagers and farm tenants and laborers to nod and smile at on the street and at church while they gawked and smiled in return. During the second week she began calling on them all, fitting in the visits between those to the gentry.

She was busier during those two weeks than she had ever been before.

During the first week a dressmaker and two assistants arrived from London. Catherine had not known they were coming. But she was given orders to spend the whole of a morning with them and was quickly reminded of the mingled excitement and tedium of being measured for clothes and of choosing fabrics and trimmings and patterns for a dizzying number of garments of all kinds. She had no choice in the numbers—that had been preordained by her husband. It seemed she needed everything for all occasions.

She did not argue. She had sewn her own clothes for five years and had been satisfied with the simplicity of her garments and their sparsity. They had suited her needs. But she accepted the fact that she must now dress for her new role. And she discovered again how good it felt to be fitted for fashionable, well-made clothes. Some of them were ready very quickly. The three seamstresses were to remain at Stratton, it seemed, until all were finished.

As was to be expected, she did not see a great deal of her husband. She was busy all day with household duties and with visits. He was busy about estate business—Catherine discovered early that he took his duties as landowner seriously and that he was quite in command of the running of his estate despite the existence of a competent steward. In the evenings they visited or entertained together, but the demands of sociability kept them frequently apart.

And yet there was no sense of avoiding each other, Catherine felt. They usually took meals together. Occasionally they found time for walks and rides together.

She found that after all it might be possible to like him. Now that he was at home and busy he seemed less the idle, bored man of pleasure than he had appeared at Bodley. And now that they were married, he was no longer the dangerous, persistent rake. He seemed well liked at Stratton. He was certainly well respected. His father before him, one tenant's wife told her, had been an indolent man and something of a gambler. The estate had been in a sorry state when his lordship inherited. But he had succeeded in turning everything around within a few years despite the fact that he was fighting in the Peninsula.

When they were together, there were very few silences, and even when there were, they were not the bitter or sullen silences she might have expected from the inauspicious beginning of their marriage. They talked on a wide range of topics. She found him surprisingly easy to talk with.

It seemed that for now, anyway, they had both decided

that what could not be helped might as well be accepted as cheerfully as possible. It seemed that they were both trying to make something workable of their marriage.

He slept in her bed with her all night and every night. It was hardly surprising, Catherine thought, that that part of the marriage was good—very good. He had pursued her vigorously enough during those weeks at Bodley, and she had been unable to quell her desire for him. He had even been prepared to offer her marriage before he had been compelled to do so just so that he could bed her.

It was very good, what happened between them in bed. He was a wonderful lover and a good teacher too. He had insisted that she let go of all her inhibitions one at a time so that she could enjoy all the pleasures that could be had of the marriage bed. Even in her wildest imaginings she had not guessed that there were so many pleasures to be had—and every night brought new ones. He seemed insatiable—always once a night, often twice, sometimes more than twice. But then she was insatiable too. The thought could warm her cheeks.

Of course, she did not expect it to last. She had married a rake, she knew. A man of such devastating good looks—she saw how all the women of the neighborhood, young and old, looked at him—and of such vigor could not be expected to be satisfied with the charms of one woman indefinitely. The honeymoon would be over sooner or later. Perhaps when she conceived. She would know within the next few days if that had happened during the first month or not.

She would accept reality when it happened—when he finally turned his ardor elsewhere. She had become very good at accepting reality. Disloyal as the thought seemed to her precious little cottage and her life there, she was happier here. There was more of a sense of familiarity, of rightness about this life than she had ever known at Bodley-on-the-Water. She would continue happy here. It was not, after all, as if she loved him.

And yet the thought of his ardor cooling could bring a twinge of something—of some unidentified pain. Life was good as it was now. Sometimes, if she really thought about it—fortunately she did not have a great deal of time for private thought—she had to admit that it felt good to be with him in company, to see the deference with which he was treated by other men, to see the awareness of him as an unusually attractive man in the eyes of women, and to know that he was her husband, her lover. And it felt good to be alone with him, to have a companion, someone with whom to share her thoughts and opinions.

It felt good to have a lover, someone to make her feel alive and young and beautiful and feminine. She had lived a life of suspended animation for so long, it seemed. It felt good to know that she had a certain power over him there, in bed. She knew how to heighten his pleasure, how to have him gasping, how to make him lose control, how to make him moan and cry out. She liked to hear him complain about her magic hands and threaten to tie them behind her. She liked to hear him call her a witch.

It was a good thing she was not in love with him, she decided. It was going to feel bad enough when the change came, as it inevitably would, without her feelings being deeply involved. Yes, it was going to feel bad. . . .

But she was too busy to think such thoughts enough to destroy her basic happiness.

"IT IS BEAUTIFUL," she said with a little sigh of contentment. "Is it the loveliest estate in England, or am I just partial?"

"It is the loveliest estate in England." He grinned. "But then I am partial too, you know."

It was a perfect spring day, one that felt more like summer, but without summer's oppressive heat. The sky was a clear blue. There was the merest breath of a breeze.

They were standing at the middle of the Palladian bridge, looking down into the still waters of the river and at the overhanging boughs of weeping willow trees, and beyond to the park and the house. Every view from the bridge had an extra charm in that each was framed in some way by its pillars and arched roof. His great-grandfather had built the bridge almost a century before.

He had hurried home from estate business that might have kept him out until luncheon time or even later. He had hurried home because she had told him at breakfast that the seamstresses had demanded a final fitting with her during the morning. She would not be going out, then. She would be at home. And so he had hurried home. They were giving Toby his exercise—that pampered terrier had still not been turned over to the stables and the care of grooms or footmen. He was trotting along now beside the river, trying to catch flying insects.

"I have been wondering if the drawing room would be improved with lighter draperies," she said. "It is such a magnificent room, Rex. But there is something wrong with it. I have been puzzling over it for two weeks. And I thought yesterday that the heavy wine velvet perhaps takes some of the light and the—splendor from the room. What do you think?"

She was frowning slightly, obviously seeing the drawing room in her imagination and concentrating on her picture of it. One thing had surprised him and puzzled him and intrigued him. She was obviously quite at home in a place like Stratton. She had taken easy command of his household. Mrs. Keach deferred to her with as much respect as if she had been mistress here for a decade. And she had been received by his neighbors as if she were a princess. She moved easily in their company without any sense of awe or awkwardness—and without any arrogance.

"I think you probably have a surer eye for such things than I have," he said. "If the draperies must be changed, then they will be changed."

She was still frowning. "I do not intend to change the character of your home," she said. "It is too precious as it is. And I do not intend to spend all your fortune. But there are a few things. . . ."

He chuckled, and she turned her face, lost her frown, and chuckled with him.

"No more than half a dozen things," she said. "Well, perhaps a dozen."

He was becoming almost accustomed to the slight lurching of his insides whenever she looked at him and smiled at him. But then, so he should be. Whenever she looked at him, he was almost inevitably gazing back at her. It was something he had become aware of when they were out in company together—one of his neighbors had remarked upon it, and two other gentlemen who were within hearing had laughed and said something about bridegrooms and their new brides.

But it was not well-bred to be staring at one's wife all the time, mesmerized by her beauty and her charm, when one was supposed to be conversing with society. And so he tried *not* to look at her so often. It was not easy. He was constantly finding himself backsliding.

He waited for his obsession with her to pass. He had had her now every night—and usually several times each night—for two weeks, if he did not count his wedding night. It was time, and even past time, that his interest began to wane. It would be as well when it did. He was not sure it was quite the thing for him to be haunting his wife's bed as he was.

"A dozen things," he said. "Well, as long as one of those things does not include a complete rebuilding of the house and another a complete refurnishing of it, then I suppose I must consider myself fortunate."

She was still laughing. "And parterre gardens on all four sides of the house," she said, "and a bridge to match this one on each of the other three sides. Oh, and a marble fountain with a naked cherub. And—"

He set a finger over her lips to silence her. "We have no river on the other three sides," he said. "Do you suggest that I have a moat constructed all around the house?"

"Could I increase the number from a dozen to thirteen?" she asked.

That was another surprising thing about their marriage. They usually talked quite seriously with each other. But sometimes their conversation became absurd, as it had now. They could laugh together. He liked to see her laughing. It took away some of his guilt. He wondered sometimes if she was merely putting on a good act or a brave face. He wondered if deep down she would prefer to be in her idyllic little cottage by the river.

And he wondered consciously if she still pined for the man called Bruce. He tried to put the unknown man and his name from his mind, but the mind is not easy to control. Jealousy gnawed at him when he was not careful enough to guard his thoughts.

It was a good thing, at least, he thought, that he did not love her, even though he had never wanted a marriage without love. If he did, he might be feeling considerable pain along with the unexpected happiness these first few weeks of his marriage were bringing him. Of course there was something like pain. . . .

They both turned their heads at the same moment to look toward the great stone gateposts at the end of the drive, not far distant from the bridge. A strange carriage was turning in the direction of the house.

"Who is it?" she asked. "Is it someone I have not met yet?"

But he was smiling as he took her elbow and hurried her across the bridge so that they would not be bowled over by the approaching carriage. Toby came tearing toward them, barking with excited ferocity, as he did at all their visitors—it had not taken him long to lay claim to this new territory.

"No," Lord Rawleigh said. "One stranger to you, Catherine. And perhaps two old acquaintances. Yes, indeed."

The carriage had stopped as soon as it crossed the bridge, as its occupants had obviously spotted them. The viscount stepped forward to open the door. Lord Pelham jumped out without waiting for anything as unessential as steps to be set down, and proceeded to slap his friend on the shoulder and pump his hand.

"Rex, you old sinner," he said. "Married without even waiting for your friends to arrive in their wedding finery. Congratulations, old chap."

He turned to Catherine while Nathaniel Gascoigne took his place, laughing and slapping and assuring him that he was a lucky dog, luckier than he deserved. He demanded that Eden stand aside so that he could hug the bride and steal a kiss since he had not been at the wedding to do so.

And then the Earl of Haverford came jumping out of the carriage. The Fourth Horseman of the Apocalypse—tall, blond, and elegant.

"Rex," he said. "My dear boy. What is all this?"

They hugged each other. It had been several months since they had seen each other. Once upon a time they had lived and breathed together and fought side by side constantly—and almost died together on more occasions than they would care to remember.

"I read your letter with some amazement," the earl said. "And then Nat and Eden informed me that your marriage was no big surprise to them at all. I take it unkindly that you would not hold back the wedding for us. But then perhaps we would have fought over which of us was to be your best man. I take it Claude did the honors?"

Lord Rawleigh nodded and grinned. "Three best men—four with Claude—might have been considered a little eccentric," he said. "But you felt compelled to come, and three of you. All the way from Cornwall. I am honored."

The Earl of Haverford clapped a hand on his shoulder and turned to meet the bride, who was laughing and being laughed over by the other two. But they stood aside so that their other friend could be presented to her.

Lord Rawleigh looked at the earl, about to make the introductions. But he paused, seeing the arrested look on his friend's face.

"Why, Lady Catherine," he said.

A quick, sharp glance at his wife revealed to the viscount a face that had lost all color and eyes that stared with fear and recognition.

"My wife," he said, somehow keeping his voice on an even keel. "Kenneth Woodfall, Earl of Haverford, Catherine. I take it the two of you have a previous acquaintance."

His wife was curtsying. "My lord," she said through bloodless lips.

"Yes, indeed." Ken spoke loudly, heartily, quickly. "Pardon me, ma'am. It is Lady *Rawleigh,* is it not? Yes, I do believe we were in town at the same time a number of years ago. I was invalided home from the Peninsula for a few months. You persuaded Rex into matrimony, then, or the other way around. Nat and Eden have been telling me all the way here what a lucky dog he is. Now I can see for myself that they did not exaggerate." He was taking her hand and bowing over it. He raised it to his lips.

"I am perfectly well aware of my good fortune," the viscount said, taking her hand—it was icy cold—and drawing it through his arm as he smiled down at her. "It seems, my love, that we are to have houseguests."

"How very pleasant." She managed to smile. There was even color in her cheeks again. "I saw for myself at Bodley that Lord Pelham and Mr. Gascoigne were my husband's particular friends. I am delighted to meet another. It will be lovely for you all to be together again."

"We should have had that hound in Spain with us," the earl said. "He would have sent the French scurrying back across the Pyrenees for safety even before the first battle was fought. Yours, ma'am?"

Toby had pranced about in an ecstasy of ferocity and exuberance ever since the carriage had turned between the gateposts. It had not helped matters that Nat had wrestled with him.

They made their way to the house, all talking at once, it seemed, rather too loudly, rather too heartily. There was a great deal of laughter and excited yipping.

Lady Catherine.

The recognition and the fear in her eyes.

Ken's hasty cover-up. Too late.

Lady Catherine.

COOK MANAGED TO supply luncheon for three unexpected guests at very little notice at all. There was a great deal of talk and laughter at the table. Afterward Catherine had several visits to pay alone while the men remained behind to spend the afternoon together. Dinner was almost a repeat performance of luncheon. In the evening they all went to the Brixhams' for conversation and cards—her husband had sent notice of the arrival of three friends and the invitation had been extended to them too. The unattached ladies of the neighborhood were considerably charmed.

It was a day like most others—crowded with activity. There had been not a moment to themselves since the morning on the bridge.

Catherine undressed for bed, had Marie brush out her hair, and dismissed her for the night. She put on her dressing gown and went through to her sitting room rather than the bedroom to wait. She was shivering, she found, even though her husband's friends had been commenting on the fact that it was an unusually warm evening for spring.

They were such pleasant gentlemen. They had gone out of their way to make her feel comfortable, to make her laugh despite the fact that she was the one woman among four men. The Earl of Haverford had been especially charming. He had not shunned her or treated her as if she had the plague, as she had rather expected as soon as she had recognized him.

She had a vivid memory of him as he had been that spring, exceedingly handsome in his scarlet regimentals, romantically pale from the wounds that had almost killed him in Spain. All the young ladies of *ton* had sighed over him—herself included, though she had never done more than dance the occasional set with him at a ball.

"Toby." She allowed her dog to jump up onto a love seat beside her, even though he was learning not to dare make himself comfortable on furniture when her husband was present. She wrapped her arms about him and set her cheek against his warm neck. "Oh, Toby, this was bound to happen. Why did I not tell him at the start? Before we were married. Before I started to—care a little bit. Oh, I knew I should never allow myself to care for anyone. Not even a little bit."

Toby licked her cheek. But before he could participate further in the conversation, the door opened and he jumped hastily down.

"Ah, here you are," her husband said. "It was wise to come here rather than go to the bedroom, I suppose."

He did not look particularly angry. But then why should he? He had known that there was much of her story he had not heard. He had not tried to insist that she tell it. And she had never lied to him. Not really. She wondered what Lord Haverford had told him during the afternoon. But she knew the answer immediately. Nothing. He would have said nothing. She found herself on her feet.

"Well, *Lady* Catherine," her husband said, "at least now part of the puzzle has been explained. You have settled to life at Stratton as if to the manner born. It appears that you were to the manner born. Are you coming to bed? You look as if you are set for confrontation, but it does not have to be that way. I can hardly insist now that you spill all, can I, not having done so from the start. And you can rest assured that Ken will keep his lips buttoned."

"Lady Catherine Winsmore," she said quietly, "daughter of the Earl of Paxton."

He said nothing for a while, but stood close to the door, his hands clasped behind him, his lips pursed. "Ah," he said at last, "you are going to tell me more after all, are you? You had better sit down, Catherine, before you faint. Is it really such a dreadful story?"

She sat and clasped her hands loosely in her lap. She looked down at them. Yes, she was going to tell him more. She was going to tell him everything. But only one foolish thought lodged in her mind while she tried to compose herself and decide where to begin.

She was in love with him after all, she thought. What a time for such a discovery!

She was in love with him.

Nineteen

HE CROSSED SLOWLY to a brocaded chair close to the fireplace and sat down on it—not too close to her. Toby sniffed at his slipper and then lay down with his chin resting across it.

He looked at her—pale and composed, staring down at the hands in her lap. He was not sure he wanted to hear it. She had been his wife for three weeks. They had developed a working relationship during that time. They were almost friends. They were insatiable lovers. And yet they were strangers. He had not even known who she was until a few moments ago. Lady Catherine Winsmore—now Lady Catherine Adams, Viscountess Rawleigh—daughter of the Earl of Paxton.

For five years she had lived at Bodley-on-the-Water as Mrs. Catherine Winters, widow. Yet she had been the unmarried daughter of an earl. He was acquainted with the Earl of Paxton. He had just forgotten that his family name was Winsmore.

"I made my come-out when I was nineteen," she said. "A family bereavement had prevented it the year before. I felt old. I felt that I had been left behind." She laughed softly without amusement. "I was very ready for flirtation, love, marriage. Above all I wanted to enjoy my Season. A bereavement can be irksome when one is young, especially when it is for a relative one has not known well and can feel no great sorrow for."

This was the Catherine of five years ago. She would have been a beautiful and eager girl. He would have been in the Peninsula at the time. She had made her come-out the year Ken had been invalided home. He had come back to Spain and deliberately infuriated them with his descriptions of all the young ladies of *ton* with whom he had flirted and danced and walked. Perhaps Catherine had been one of them.

"I was fortunate enough to have several admirers," she said. "One in particular. He offered for me early. Papa was eager. It was a good match. I liked him. I was inclined to say yes. But—oh, but foolishly I found him a little dull. I would say yes eventually, I thought, but I did not want to be tied down by a betrothal before the end of the Season. I wanted other men to think I was free. I was not done with flirtation. I was such a foolish girl."

"It is not foolish to want to enjoy life when one is young," he said quietly. Toby, across his foot, heaved a deep sigh of contentment.

"There was someone else who excited me far more," she said. "He was handsome and gay and charming. And he was made quite irresistible by the fact that he had a reputation as a rake. It was rumored that he played deep at the gaming tables and that he was facing ruin and was in search of a rich wife. I was warned to stay well away from him."

"But you did not," he said.

She hunched her shoulders. "I had no illusions about the nature of his interest in me," she said. "I had no thought of marriage with him. I was not in love with him. But it was exhilarating to be admired by someone so notorious and so—forbidden. I would sometimes dance with him in defiance of my chaperon. I used to exchange glances with him at concerts and at the theater. Sometimes, if he suspected that I was being kept at a distance from him, he would contrive to send me notes. I even answered one of them—but only one. I was uneasy about doing anything so outrageously improper. I was just—very silly."

It must be very bad, he thought. She was taking a long while getting to it. She had not once looked up at him.

"Just very young," he said.

"But then I did something outrageously improper after all." She hunched her shoulders again and paused a long while before continuing. "We were both at Vauxhall—with separate parties. He asked me to dance with him, but my escort told him—very stiffly and firmly—that I was engaged for the evening. He smuggled a note to me with a wine waiter, asking me to meet him for a brief stroll along one of the paths. It was such a beautiful, enchanted place and it was the first time I had been there. But all my own party wanted to do was sit in the box that had been reserved, eating strawberries and drinking wine. No one was willing to dance or to walk. I was so very disappointed."

Her voice had quickened, become more agitated. He looked at her bowed head and knew one thing at least. It was a good thing she had not married the dull, respectable man who had sapped all the youthful exuberance from her first Season. Poor girl that she had been—he could feel the pull of the temptation she had felt. Surely a harmful temptation, which of course she had given in to. He supposed they had been seen alone together and she had been ruined. No, there must have been more to it than that. He remembered his wedding night.

"I said I was going to call upon a friend in another box," she said, "and rushed away before anyone could jump up to escort me. I went for the stroll I had so longed for." She laughed and spread her hands over her face briefly.

He had ravished her. God, he had ravished her.

"He had a carriage waiting," she said. "I did not want to get into it, of course, but he promised me it would be just a short drive so that he could show me the lights of Vauxhall from a little distance away. I was too embarrassed to make a loud fuss, which I would have had to make to free myself of his grip on my arm. He—he did something to me in the carriage—and he took me straight home afterward. He was quite bold about it. He told Papa we were in love and had been together and that he would have eloped with me but he had too great a regard for my reputation." She paused.

"He had ravished you?" It was hard to get the words past his lips.

Her eyes were closed and her hands tightly clasped in her lap. "Over the years," she said, "I have persuaded myself that it was not my fault. I said no—over and over again. But I went willingly to him, and I got into his carriage without any undue pressure. I suppose it cannot really be called ravishment. No one else ever called it that. It was all my fault."

"Catherine!" His voice was harsh and for the first time her head shot up and she looked at him. "You said no. It was ravishment. It was not your fault."

She closed her eyes again and tipped her head back.

"He wanted to be sure of your fortune?" he asked, though the answer was obvious, of course. "Why did you not marry him, Catherine? Did your father forbid it?"

She laughed harshly. "I would not," she said. "Oh, I would not. I would have preferred to die. He made no secret of what had happened, of course—or his version of what had happened. He wanted to make sure that I had no choice."

Ruin. Complete and total ruin. How had she found the courage to refuse to do what she had seemed compelled to do?

"And so," he said, "you were banished to Bodley-on-the-Water to live out your life under an assumed name and an assumed widowhood."

She did not answer for a few moments. "Yes," she said at last.

"Who was he?" His voice was almost a whisper. He felt such a murderous rage that he was almost paralyzed by it.

She shook her head slowly.

He would find out. She would tell him. He would find the scoundrel and kill him.

"Catherine?" he said.

And then he was struck by a thought. She had not loved either man—either the one to whom she had been almost betrothed or the one who had ravished her. She had gone to London eager for her first Season—so there could have been no one she had left behind. *Who the devil, then, was Bruce?*

She had not answered him. She sat with her head still thrown back and her eyes still closed.

"Catherine," he said, "who is Bruce?"

She looked at him then, her eyes at first blank and then filling with such torment that his breath caught in his throat. She opened her mouth to speak and closed it again. Then she tried once more.

"He was my son." There was despair in her voice. "The child of that ugliness. He was born a month early. He lived for three hours. It was a very good thing he died, everyone said. How fortunate for me and for him too. He was my baby. He was mine. And he was innocent of that ugliness. Bruce was my son. He died in my arms."

God! He sat rooted to his chair, frozen to it.

"There." He was not sure how much time had passed since either of them had spoken. The emotion had gone from her voice. "That is what I should have told you before we married. That is what you should have insisted I tell you. You have married a woman who was doubly ruined, my lord. I would not marry him even when the full truth of my predicament was known. I was sent to my aunt in Bristol. But she did not want me and I did not want to be there, being treated as if I were too depraved even for the gallows. So I suggested a future for myself that would rid my family of the embarrassment of my presence and would give me a chance for some sort of new life. I even chose Bodley-on-the-Water myself."

He found himself doing mental calculations. Yes, it was six years ago that Ken had been sent back to England, not five.

"Catherine," he said, "who was he?"

But she shook her head again. "Leave it," she said. "Let it go. I have. I have had to in order to stay sane."

"Who was he?" He recognized the voice as one he had used a great deal during his years as a cavalry officer. It was a voice that had invariably commanded instant obedience. She was looking at him again. "You will tell me who he is," he said.

"Yes," she said quietly. "I owe you that. Sir Howard Copley."

If it was possible to turn colder, he did it. There was a buzzing in his ears. He wondered with a detached sort of fascination if he was about to faint. Was such a ghastly coincidence possible? Yet he remembered the conversation he had had with Daphne not so long ago. Copley had been a known rake and fortune hunter for a number of years. He had been involved in a number of scandals and even in two duels. Somehow—but such things happened—he still moved on the fringes of Society and sometimes even closer than the fringes.

Lord Rawleigh had been told all about Copley at the time his betrothal had ended. The memories were all strangely mixed up with the events surrounding Waterloo. He had heard the names of a few other young ladies whose reputations had been sullied or even ruined by Copley. Could he remember any of those names now? Had Catherine's been among them? Was it possible to remember accurately? *Paxton's daughter.* Whom for some reason Copley had failed to marry even though *she had borne his bastard.*

Was he inventing the memory now? Or was it really there, lodged firmly in his subconscious? Angry as he had been at Horatia, hurt as he had been, he had thought at the time—at least she had been spared what that other foolish woman had endured. *Paxton's daughter.*

She had got to her feet, and Toby was scrambling to his. His tail was waving cheerfully back and forth, brushing Lord Rawleigh's leg as it did so.

"I am going to bed," she said quietly without looking at him. "I am exhausted. Good night."

Toby trotted out of the room at her heels. The viscount sat for a long time where he was before finally getting up and making his weary way to his own bedchamber, taking the candle with him.

SHE SLEPT DEEPLY and dreamlessly. She awoke early, surprised that she had slept at all. He had not come to her—for the first time since their return to Stratton. It was the end, of course. She accepted that quite calmly. She supposed she had always known that she would tell him one day or that he would find out. And if she had known that, then she had also known that it would be the end.

She would not burden herself with the guilt of having cheated him into marrying her under false pretenses. He had known there were secrets. He might have insisted on knowing them that day he had come with Daphne to her cottage. He had not insisted.

Well, now he knew that he had married a woman who could never again appear in decent society.

She would not allow her mind to move beyond the calm knowledge that this was the end. It was of no great moment. She had lived alone for five years and had even been happy. And it was not as if she loved him—she stubbornly refused to remember what she had admitted to herself just last night before she told him her story.

She would not go downstairs early. He had to be faced, of course, but not at breakfast. Not with the chance that his friends would be at the table too. She turned over onto her side and touched her pillow where his head usually lay. She willed herself back to sleep.

She woke up an hour later, surprised again that she had succeeded. It seemed that unburdening herself had released a great tension inside her and had left her totally exhausted.

His lordship was out riding with his guests, the butler informed her after she had entered the breakfast room and heaved a silent sigh of relief to find it empty. She hoped they would stay out all morning. She herself had three visits planned for the afternoon. There was luncheon to face, of course. But that would probably be like yesterday's meals. His friends liked to talk and laugh. She was not sure if they had all been covering up for Lord Haverford's revelation. She supposed they had been.

But she was not to be as fortunate as she had hoped. When she came up from her daily consultation with the cook belowstairs, it was to find all four gentlemen in the great hall, just returned from their ride. The Earl of

Haverford strode toward her and took both her hands in his before bowing over them.

"Good morning, ma'am," he said. "We took Rex away from you for a ride. Forgive us. It will not happen again. We will be leaving this afternoon for London. We merely called here to wish you both well, you see. But we will not impose upon your hospitality further."

She looked at him and at Lord Pelham and Mr. Gascoigne in some dismay. She did not want them to go away. And she was sure that they had planned to stay for a week or more.

"We will be disappointed to see you leave so soon," she said. "Will you not reconsider?"

They were all very complimentary. But they were all vocal in their eagerness to be in town now that the Season had begun. And none of them would dream of imposing for longer than a day on newly married friends.

And so a mere few hours later they were waving their guests on their way, she and her husband. They stood outside on the terrace, the silence loud after the turmoil of the farewells and the departure. He took her by the elbow and directed her along the driveway toward the bridge, where they had been standing yesterday—was it only yesterday?—when this had all begun. They did not talk. He dropped his hand from her elbow after a few moments.

It was not so lovely today. There were clouds and a chill breeze. The water of the river looked slate gray rather than blue and its surface was ruffled. Toby ambled along the bank as he had yesterday, looking for a foe to vanquish.

"My father will no longer support me now that I have left Bodley-on-the Water," she said, breaking the silence at last. "That was the condition. And I could not go back there anyway. But England is full of villages, and apart from the lease of a house, my needs and expenses are very few. Perhaps you will be willing to do what my father has done for the past five years. I can change my name again. I will never be any trouble to you."

"We are going to London," he said, his voice flat.

"No!" This was the last thing she had expected—the very last. "No, Rex, not London. I cannot go there. You know I cannot. And you would not wish to be seen with me there."

"Nevertheless we are going," he said. "There is a great deal of unfinished business awaiting us there."

"Rex." She grabbed his arm. It felt granite hard. "Perhaps you did not understand. Everyone *knew*. It was made very public. Even the fact that I was increasing. I was totally ruined. I could not possibly go back."

His eyes looked bleak when he turned them on her. "Were you guilty, then?" he asked her. "Did you consent?"

"No!" Had he not believed her? Would she have behaved afterward as she had if she had consented? "But what difference does it make? You know that a woman is always guilty once her virtue is gone. And I would not play by the rules and redeem my virtue and reputation in the only possible way."

"Then it is not finished," he said. "We are going back to finish it, Catherine."

She shook her head. She felt physically sick. "Please," she said. "Please, Rex. Let me go away. No one ever need know whom exactly you married. Your friends will say nothing."

"You forget something," he said. "You are my wife."

He must have been a good officer, she thought irrelevantly. His men must have known the impossibility of pitting their wills against his.

"You must be sorry for that now," she said bitterly. "You should have insisted on hearing all when I told you my name, Rex. You must have realized that—"

"Let us deal with realities," he said. "You are my wife. I want a life with you. I want children of you."

She felt a stabbing of longing. But she shook her head. "I should have told you," she said. "I have known for six years that marriage was an impossibility. I have known that dreams were forbidden. I tried to turn you away, Rex. I said no time and time again."

He had turned pale and his jaw had set hard. "Just as you did with Copley," he said. "An apt comparison, Catherine."

"Except," she said, dismayed, "that you left that night when I said no. You did not force me."

He laughed harshly.

"Let us stay here, then," she said, her voice pleading. "And hope that no one ever finds out."

"We are going to London, Catherine," he said.

She set her hands on the balustrade and gripped hard as she stared down into the water. "You are cruel," she whispered.

"And you are a coward," he said.

"A coward!" She whirled on him, her eyes flashing. "A coward, Rex? I am a realist. I know the rules. I have broken them—by refusing to marry *him,* by agreeing to marry you. But I know the rules and I know which ones can never be bent or broken. I cannot go back to London."

"But you will be going," he said. "Tomorrow morning." He turned to stride from the bridge in the direction of the house.

He did not wait for her, and she did not hurry after him. She stayed where she was, fighting faintness and nausea and panic. She should never have married him. She should have held firm even though there had been no alternative except total destitution. She should have held out as she had that first time. Why was it that courage came harder as one aged? Was it that one knew more of life as one grew older?

That one realized that courage was not something that applied just to the moment but something that set the course for the whole of one's life? If she had known when she refused to marry Sir Howard what was ahead for her—all the loss of identity, all the tedium—would she have refused?

She had not refused Rex—perhaps because this time she had realized what was ahead. She had lost her courage to do what she wanted to do regardless of the consequences.

He had just called her a coward. Because she did not want to go back to London. But she did not need the wisdom of advancing age to know what would be ahead of her there. Did he realize? He had spent so many of his adult years with England's armies overseas. Did he realize?

She could not go. She closed her eyes and lowered her forehead to the balustrade. She could not.

But choices had been taken away from her—again. All choices. She had married him three weeks ago. She had promised to obey him. He had just said they were going to London. She had no choice.

Ah, dear God, they were going to London.

HE WAS NOT at all sure that he was doing the right thing. He knew that he was quite possibly exposing his wife to a humiliation and a degradation from which she might never recover. And he knew quite well that he might be destroying his marriage. It was possible, even probable, that she would never stop hating him after this.

But he was sure of one thing. He was sure that he was doing the only possible thing. She was his wife. She would run and hide again now if he would allow it. But he would not allow it. Not ever. And there would be no cowering at home either. Sooner or later the truth would catch up to them there. And even if it did not, he would not allow her to be trapped there for a lifetime. Eventually there would be children to take out into the world, children who would have to deal with their mother's past.

He would prefer to deal with it himself.

He looked from the carriage windows at the distinctive sights of the outskirts of London. They would be at Rawleigh House soon—he had sent word ahead to have it opened and prepared. There was no going back now.

She sat beside him, as she had sat all the way from Kent, like a marble statue. They had not exchanged a dozen words. He wanted to offer her some comfort. But he had found himself quite incapable of doing so since the night before last. How did one comfort a woman who had been living quietly and respectably and usefully just a few weeks ago when one had brought her to this? And the comparisons had been quite obvious to him even before she had made them more so on the bridge yesterday afternoon.

Ken and Eden and Nat had tried to persuade him yesterday morning that they really had intended to stay just for a day en route to London. They had been very loud and jolly about it. It had felt as if there were a solid brick wall ten feet high between him and them. It was safe to go to town after all, Eden had said. His married lady and her husband had departed for their home in the North, and Nat figured that his single young lady—or rather her large family—must have got the message from his lengthy absence. It would be safe to go back. They had all tried to chatter together, the three of them.

"It is really quite all right, you know," the viscount had said finally and quite firmly, putting an abrupt end to both the chatter and the forced high spirits. "I have known Catherine's story since before our marriage. Did you believe I did not? How could I have married her if I had not known? The name on the license and register would have been false.

The marriage would have been invalid. I was merely taken aback yesterday to discover that Ken knew it. I have been foolishly trying to protect her by keeping her quietly here."

The looks on their faces had assured him that since the morning before Eden and Nat had been told the story. Ken would have known it was safe to do so. The story would go no farther through them.

"He is easily England's most despicable blackguard, you know, Rex," Ken had said. "You know that from your past experience. I never did believe Lady Catherine entirely or even mainly to blame. Many people felt as I did."

"You do not have to defend her to me," the viscount had said. "She is my wife and I love her. And she was not even partly to blame. She was ravished."

"Yet he would not marry her?" Nat had sounded appalled. "Why did Paxton not kill him?"

"She would not marry him," Lord Rawleigh had said.

"The devil!" Eden had said. "Even though—" He had cut himself off with a muffled oath.

"Even though she was with child," the viscount had completed quietly. "She is a courageous woman, my Catherine. I need advice."

Perhaps it was not quite the thing to ask advice of his friends for his marriage. But this was not a personal thing. And he would trust these three with his life—and had done so more times than he could count.

They had given advice, none of which he would have taken if it had contradicted what he had already known he must do. But they had all been agreed, all four of them. It had been quite unanimous.

He must take her back to London.

But his talk with his friends had revealed to him with appalling clarity the spreading and disastrous effects of his relentless pursuit of her at Bodley. He had brought fresh ruin on her because, like Copley, he had refused to take no for an answer. Oh, he had not raped her. He could console himself with that fact, perhaps. But he was not consoled nonetheless. She had chosen a way of life and she had been living it with cheerfulness and dignity. He had taken her from that and brought her to this.

How could he comfort her? He looked at her again across the carriage as they approached Mayfair and the more fashionable homes of the wealthy and titled. She was not even looking from the window. He had been unable to go to her either last night or the night before. He found himself unable to touch her except in purely impersonal ways, like assisting her in and out of his carriage. He found himself unable to talk to her.

He wondered if he would ever be able to forgive himself. He doubted it.

Twenty

CATHERINE HAD BEEN left much to her own devices for the four days since their arrival in town. She had seen little of her husband, either by day or by night. She did not question his long absences from home, though she knew those absences did not extend into the nights. He slept in his own room, the width of their two dressing rooms between them.

She was not with child. She had discovered that the day they left Stratton Park. Perhaps it was as well, she thought after the first twinge of disappointment. Although he had refused to send her away, he would surely agree to do so once he realized the disaster that would result from bringing her here. He had said he wanted children of her, but he would change his mind once he had realized the impossibility of a workable marriage with her. Finding herself with child now would only have complicated matters hopelessly. But there would be no further chance of its happening—he had stopped coming to her bed.

She did not go beyond the confines of the house and garden. She was sorry for Toby's sake. The garden was not very large and she knew he would love nothing better than a good run. She would have taken him to Hyde Park, but one never knew whom one might run into there even in the early morning.

She was letting life happen to her again, as she had done during the week before her marriage. Her life was beyond her control anyway—it was in her husband's hands. She did not try to fight him after that afternoon on the bridge when he had told her they were coming to London. She merely hoped that before she was forced to go out he would realize for himself that it was an impossible situation, that the only thing to do was to go back to Stratton.

But her hopes were dashed on the fifth day. He came back home late in the morning and found her in the morning room, seated at an escritoire writing a letter to Miss Downes.

"Here you are," he said, striding across the room toward her. He looked down briefly at her letter, though he did not try to read it. "I have brought a visitor for you, Catherine. He is in the library. Come and meet him."

"Who?" Her stomach lurched. "Another of your friends? I think not, Rex. You go along. I will stay here and finish my letter."

"Come." He set a hand on her shoulder. His voice was quiet, but she had learned something about her husband in a month of marriage—perhaps she had learned it even before then. He had a quite implacable will. He was not giving her a choice. "Toby, you stay here, sir, and guard the room against intruders."

Toby wagged his tail and stayed.

Her husband had a hand at the small of her back when a footman opened the door to the library for them. She stepped inside.

He was a very young man, and he had obviously been pacing before their arrival. He stopped halfway between the desk and the window and turned toward the door—a golden-haired, hazel-eyed young man who must have a good-humored face when it was not filled with anxiety as it was now. It paled on sight of her.

She almost did not recognize him. He had been only twelve the last time she had seen him. He had been away at school during the Season.

"Cathy?" he whispered.

"Harry." Her lips formed his name but no sound came. Oh, Harry. Such a very handsome, pleasing young man.

"Cathy?" He said her name again. "It really is you. I could scarce believe it even when Rawleigh insisted on it. I thought you were *dead.*" He turned paler, if that was possible.

"Harry." Sound came out this time. "Oh, Harry, you are all grown up." She walked toward him without quite realizing what she did and reached out a hand to touch the lapel of his coat. "And tall." Her eyes filled with sudden tears.

"You died in childbed at Aunt Phillips's," he said. "Or so Papa told me. But we did not wear mourning because . . ."

She smiled through her tears.

"Perhaps we should all sit down." It was her husband's voice, cool and very sane. "Come Catherine, Perry. This is a shock for both of you."

"Viscount Perry," she said, setting her free hand against her brother's other lapel. "The title sounds grander now that you are grown up. Harry, can you—"

But she had seen the sudden tears in his eyes too. And then his arms were about her, holding her fiercely against him. "Cathy," he said, "Rawleigh told me at White's that none of what happened was your fault. I believe him. But even if it was . . . oh, even if it was."

She had loved him and cared for him like a mother, even though she was only six years older than he. Their own mother had been sickly after his birth and had died before his third birthday. Catherine had poured all the love of her heart on her little brother and had spent all her free time with him. He in turn had worshiped her. She could remember his announcing when he was five years old that he was going to be an old bachelor when he grew up so that he could look after her forever and ever.

They sat down together on a sofa while her husband took a chair beside the fireplace. She held her brother's hand. It was slender, like the rest of him, but there was manly strength in it. In a few years' time, she thought with pride, he was going to set countless female hearts fluttering.

"Tell me about yourself." She gazed at him, ravenous suddenly for news of the missing years. He had thought her dead. She had lived as if he were dead, never making any attempt to communicate with him or learn anything about him. It had been another of the conditions. But she did not believe she would have tried anyway. It had been too painful even to think of him. "Tell me everything."

"Some other time," her husband said firmly, though not ungently. "There are other things to be talked about for now, Catherine. I think you must agree, though, that something good has come of your returning to London."

She was not so sure. Seeing Harry again, touching him, knowing that his long silence had not been caused by rejection, was all sweet agony. And he had said that he believed Rex, and that even if he had not, he would not condemn her. But he could not allow himself to be seen with her. He was a young man with his own way to make in Society. Even the taint of her memory might be a hindrance to him. Her return would be an impossibility.

"Rawleigh says you are going to call on Papa this afternoon," Harry said. "I think it is a good idea, Cathy, now that you are married."

"No," she said sharply, turning her head to look at her husband. He was gazing steadily back at her, his expression harsh, his eyes narrowed. "No, Rex."

"Everyone knows I have a wife," he said. "Everyone is avidly curious. You have probably seen the pile of invitations that have been arriving yesterday and today. I have chosen Lady Mindell's ball tomorrow evening for your first appearance. Eden and Nat and Ken will be there as well as your brother. And Daphne and Clayton too—I have been waiting for their arrival in town. They came last night. You will be surrounded by friends. And of course you will have me. The stage is set, one might say."

She was too paralyzed with terror to reply. She was unaware of the fact that she was gripping her brother's hand very tightly.

"But we do need to call on your father first," her husband said. "It is only fair that he know of your return, Catherine, before everyone else does. Does he know you have left Bodley-on-the-Water? Have you written to him?"

She shook her head. He had probably sent her quarterly allowance there. She had not thought of it.

"I sent my card in this morning," he said, "with notice of my intention to call this afternoon with my wife."

No. The word formed on her lips, but she did not speak it. What was the point? He would take her whether she wished it or not, whether she begged or not. And he would take her to Lady Mindell's ball. Harry's Season might be ruined. It was the only really coherent thought that would form in her mind. She looked at him.

"I know you are terrified, Cathy," he said. "But I believe Rawleigh is right. When I think of what you had to go through, and when I think that for five years you have been all alone because I was told you were dead . . . Well, when I think about it, it makes me just furious. I always have thought that the rules are not fair to women. They get the worst of everything even if they do not break the rules. Whereas men . . . He has been running loose here all this time, doing it again to other women, though I do not believe he has ever again done quite what he did to you."

Her husband's eyes, she saw when she glanced at him, were as hard as flint.

"Have courage, Cathy," Harry said, raising their clasped hands to his lips and kissing the backs of hers. "You were always so courageous. When Papa told me that you had ensured your own permanent ruin by refusing to marry Copley, I was so very proud of you. I do not know any other woman who would have had the courage to thumb her nose at Society."

She gazed at him for a few moments and then at her husband. Both looked silently back at her. There was a curious tension in the library, just as if she had a choice. Just as if they were waiting for her decision and would accept it, whatever it was.

Her father had not fought for her. Whether he had believed her or not she did not know. But he had done nothing to defend her. He had only done everything in his power to force her into marriage with the man who had ravished her and impregnated her. When she had finally gone away, both from him and from her Aunt Phillips's, he had told Harry she was dead. But he had refused to let Harry go into mourning for her because she had been a fallen woman.

Society had condemned her to perpetual exile. Because she had been ravished and had failed to marry her ravisher. He, on the other hand, had been free to continue in Society even if he was frowned upon by the highest sticklers as a rake. Society secretly loved rakes. They were seen as virile, high-spirited adventurers, and very masculine. He had done it again, Harry had just said. He had hurt, perhaps ruined, other ladies of *ton* who, like her, had been naive enough to be attracted by his charm and his reputation.

No one had ever stopped him.

And now she was married to a man of *ton*. It was a marriage that had begun in bitterness but had developed quickly and unexpectedly into something rather sweet and certainly valuable. The success, the very continued existence of her marriage, now hung in the balance. Because Society had rejected her. Because she had been ravished.

And she had accepted it all. Meekly. Sometimes abjectly. Recently she had been quite abject. She had begged and pleaded. She had allowed herself to be whipped into submission.

But she wanted to fight, she realized suddenly. She wanted to fight for Harry. Now that they had found each other again, she did not want to lose him. And she wanted to fight for Rex, for their marriage. It had never been perfection, but it had come curiously close during those two weeks at Stratton. It was worth fighting for. And he was worth fighting for. She could not bear the thought of losing him. She loved him—she stopped blocking the thought as she had been doing for the past week.

She loved him.

And she wanted to fight for herself. Perhaps most of all for herself. She had done nothing to be ashamed of—either with Sir Howard Copley or with Rex. She had done some foolish things, perhaps, some weak things, but nothing wrong enough to bring shame on her. She had been made a victim and recently at least she had behaved like a victim. She did not like the feeling and she did not like herself for cringing against it. And self-respect, when all was said and done, was a person's most precious attribute. If one could not respect and like oneself, then all was lost.

There had been a lengthy silence. When she glanced at her husband eventually, she found that he was looking intently back at her, a gleam of something in his eyes that seemed almost like amusement.

"Very well," she said, just as if she was making a decision that had not already been made for her. "I shall call on Papa this afternoon. Whether he receives me or not will be his choice. And I shall attend Lady Mindell's ball tomorrow evening. Whether I am received there or not will be her choice and that of her guests."

"Bravo, my love," her husband said softly.

Harry squeezed her hand. "Now I recognize you," he said. "Now you are Cathy again. I thought you had changed, but I see I was mistaken."

If she was to meet disaster, she thought, at least she would do it with her head high and defiance in her eyes.

THE EARL OF Paxton had been clearly mystified by the declared intention of Viscount Rawleigh to call on him with his wife during the afternoon. That much was obvious to the viscount when they were shown into the man's drawing room and he rose to his feet to greet them. His eyebrows were raised in polite inquiry.

"Rawleigh?" he said, inclining his head. "This is a pleasure. Ma'am?"

By that time, of course, he had looked at her and had frozen. A quick glance at his wife assured Lord Rawleigh that she had not crumbled. She was looking steadily back, her head high. He was enormously proud of her. And she looked more beautiful even than usual in one of the fashionable afternoon dresses that had been made for her at Stratton.

"Hello, Papa," she said.

There was a short silence.

"What is this?" the Earl of Paxton said, his voice strained.

"Your daughter did me the great honor of marrying me one month ago," the viscount said. "We have been at Stratton and have now moved to town for part of the Season. We have come to pay our respects to you, sir."

The earl had not taken his eyes off his daughter. "This is madness," he said. "I suppose she tricked you into it, Rawleigh?"

Sometimes it took almost a physical effort to contain fury. But fury would serve no one's purpose at the moment.

"If love is a trick, sir," he said. "I fell in love with her." But he did not want to talk about Catherine with this man or with anyone in the third person, just as if she were an inanimate object or else an imbecile who could neither understand what was being said nor speak for herself. He looked down at her and smiled. "Did I not, my love?"

It was a quite inappropriate moment, he thought, to realize that he was not lying. Or had he fallen in love with her since their marriage? The answer was not important at the moment.

She smiled back at him. What sort of pain was she feeling, he wondered, at this first reaction of her father to seeing her again?

"You are insane," the Earl of Paxton said. "And this is insane. You must leave London at once or we will all be ruined. My son—"

"—has believed his sister to be dead for five years." Lord Rawleigh could not quite keep the harshness out of his voice. "He knows she is alive. He met her this morning at Rawleigh House." He smiled at his wife again.

"It was cruel, Papa," she said. "I was not dead and I was not guilty of anything. I had agreed to go away and be no further embarrassment to you. Harry and I were always very dear to each other. You had no right to lie to him."

Bravo, my love, Viscount Rawleigh thought. Bravo.

The earl ran the fingers of one hand through his thinning hair. They had not been invited to sit down, the viscount noticed.

"We have no intention of being an embarrassment to you, sir," he said. "I will be escorting my wife to Lady Mindell's ball tomorrow evening. You have the choice of absenting yourself if you had intended to be there. Viscount Perry has a similar choice, though I believe he has already chosen to attend. He has declared his intention of dancing the second set with Catherine."

"He is just a puppy," the earl said. "He does not understand—" But he paused mid-sentence and sighed. "I might have known something like this would happen one day. You were always the stubbornest woman of my acquaintance, Catherine. If you had not been, you would have married that scoundrel and been miserable with him for the rest of your life. I cannot say now I am sorry you did not do it."

"Papa," Catherine said softly.

He looked from one to the other of them in obvious exasperation. "You are fools, the two of you," he said. "I thought you had more sense, Rawleigh. It is your brother, of course, who owns Bodley. Well, there is no point in your standing there for the rest of the afternoon. You had better come and sit down so that we can work out together how this thing is to be done. Not that it can be done. You must be well aware of that. Lady Mindell's ball, you say? A disastrous choice. It is always one of the greatest squeezes of the Season. But you will not change your mind, will you?"

"No sir," Lord Rawleigh said, guiding his wife to the sofa the earl had indicated and seating himself beside her.

"No." The earl nodded his head. "Well, we will have to

do the best we can. Ring for tea, Catherine. You are in good looks, I will say that."

"Thank you, Papa," she said, getting to her feet again and pulling the bell rope.

It was easy to see where she had got her training in running a household. It was she, a few moments later, who gave quiet instructions to the footman who answered the ring. Neither she nor her father seemed to think there was anything strange about her doing so.

"You had better come here for dinner tomorrow evening," the earl said, still sounding irritated. "We will go to the ball together from here. Unless the two of you come to your senses before then, of course."

"We will be going," Lord Rawleigh said. "And we thank you for the invitation, sir. We accept."

Catherine sat down beside him again, her face a shade paler, but her chin still up. He took her hand in his, laid it on his sleeve, and kept his hand over it to warm it.

SHE HAD BLOWN out the candles, but she had not lain down yet. She was standing at the window of her bedchamber looking down at the moonlit square outside. It was quiet and peaceful, even beautiful, despite its obvious urban look. She had loved London once, had longed to come here, had lapped up its pleasures and its excitement. She preferred the country now.

She wondered what she would be feeling this time tomorrow. The ball would be in progress. Would she still be there? Would everything be destroyed by then? But she felt curiously calm about the possibility. She had recognized during the day that this was the only thing to be done.

Her father was going to come with them. He had shown no deep affection for her during the afternoon visit—but then he never had—but he had agreed at least to stand by her. It had made her feel good to know that. And Harry was to be there. He was going to dance with her. She hoped she was not about to do him irreparable harm. But he was nineteen years old, a man even if he had not yet reached full majority. It had been his decision to attend the ball and to dance with her there.

Daphne and Clayton thought she was doing the right thing—not that she had any choice in the matter, of course. Rex had directed the coachman to drive to their home after they left her father's. Daphne had hugged her and Clayton had kissed her cheek. And of course they knew everything as they had since before her marriage. Catherine knew that even though nothing was said now. They had recognized her name and had remembered the old scandal. It made no difference to their kindness.

Daphne was increasing—after more than two years of marriage. She was almost delirious with happiness and did very little to hide it, as most women of breeding would have done. Catherine was happy for her. Very happy and—oh, yes, and envious too. She leaned her forehead against the glass of the window and closed her eyes. Oh, to hold a newborn child in her arms again. Her own child.

The door opened behind her and she straightened up in some surprise. Toby leapt up from his cozy perch in the middle of her bed and jumped down to the floor.

"Ah, you are not asleep," her husband said, coming toward her across the room. He had not brought a candle with him.

"No," she said. Had he come to stay? She had not realized how much she had yearned for his coming until now.

"Catherine." He stopped when he was close to her. "I have been nothing but a disaster in your life, have I?"

She opened her mouth but closed it again. How could she answer such a question?

"I called your life dull," he said. "I had no right. You were happy, were you not?"

"Contented," she said. "I had come to terms with what had happened to me and I had learned to like myself again. I was at peace with the world."

"And then I came riding through the village," he said, "bored and looking for something to alleviate my boredom, and you had the misfortune to mistake me for Claude."

"It was a shock," she said, half smiling, "to discover that there are two of you, even though I knew he had a twin."

"You have been at the mercy of ruthless men too often in your life," he said. "First Copley and then me. It hurts to couple my own name with his, but the truth must be spoken. I cannot even apologize to you. Apologies are just too inadequate to right some wrongs."

"You must not compare yourself to him, Rex," she said, closing her eyes. "I do not."

"But I must," he said. "I have brought you to this. First, marriage to a man you despise. And then the nightmare of a return to the scene of your first unjust humiliation. Do you understand why I have had to be so cruel during this past week?"

"Yes." She looked at him in the faint light from the window. "Yes, I do, Rex. And I do not despise you. You have come for comfort? Be comforted, then. I do understand. And now, tonight, I would not change our plans for tomorrow even if you were to give me the choice. This is something I must do. So be comforted. And I do not compare you to him."

He laughed softly. "I came to comfort *you* if I could," he said. "But you have deftly turned the tables. I thought you might be feeling lonely and frightened, Catherine. I thought perhaps you might need arms to hold you. Why you might want mine, I do not know, but I suppose they are the only ones available."

He was feeling guilty, she realized. He had been feeling guilty ever since last week when he had finally learned the truth about her. He was feeling that he had been no better than Sir Howard Copley. That was why he had been so remote, why he had not come to her bed at night. She had thought it was because he was disgusted with her.

She lifted her arms and framed his face with her hands. And looking into his eyes, she was surprised to see them brighten with tears. He cared, she thought suddenly. He cared just a little bit.

"I want your arms," she said. "I have been lonely without them, Rex. I thought you blamed me for not telling such a sordid story before you married me. I thought you were disgusted with me. It was not that, was it?"

He did not answer in words. He merely drew her into his arms and rocked her against him as she set her head on his shoulder and closed her eyes.

Love could sometimes be exquisitely sweet, she thought. She did not care about tomorrow. She would not even think about it. Or about the fact that guilt had made him tender. It did not matter what had caused it. She accepted his tenderness as a gift not to be questioned or examined and destroyed.

She accepted it as a gift.

"Stay with me," she said. "Make love to me."

"All night," he said, his voice low against her ear. "Every night, Catherine. For the rest of our lives."

Ah, it was a sweet and precious gift.

Twenty-one

FOR ALMOST A week Viscount Rawleigh had been very visible in the haunts of fashionable society. He had spent hours of each day at White's Club. He had walked and ridden in both St. James's Park and Hyde Park during the hours when half the *beau monde* was doing the same thing in the same place. He had made some afternoon calls, most notably on older matrons, those who had most influence over the opinions and behavior of the *ton*. He had even attended an evening concert in a private home, the type of event that was largely avoided by the young and foolish.

His lordship was more than usually sociable and charming. It was clear, the older matrons agreed with fond indulgence, that the unknown lady who had finally netted one of Society's most attractive matrimonial catches had also netted the boy's heart. They waited with some curiosity to meet his viscountess. He would be escorting her to Lady Mindell's ball, he had announced wherever he went.

Younger ladies were less inclined to be indulgent. Viscount Rawleigh had been a great favorite among them for several reasons, the most obvious of which were that he was titled, wealthy, and handsome. Also, of course, he had been a cavalry officer in the Duke of Wellington's armies, and was rumored to have the scars to prove it—none of which were visible, a fact that was vastly titillating to the female imagination. And there was the intriguing fact that he was a twin—most of them had seen Mr. Claude Adams and had sighed over the fact that he had been off the market for years and years. Perhaps most fascinating of all was the fact that Viscount Rawleigh had once been jilted almost at the altar—he had been in Belgium at the time involved in the events leading up to and including Waterloo, but the altar theory had more drama. There was something tragically romantic about a man who had had his heart broken—especially when he was a handsome man—and there was wonderful challenge in imagining oneself as the woman who could mend it.

No, the younger ladies were less than thrilled to hear of Lord Rawleigh's sudden marriage to an unknown woman. But they were no less curious than their elders to see her, to judge her worthiness for such a prize, to pick her to pieces in their minds and well-bred conversation if their judgment went against her.

The gentlemen, less interested in the viscount's marriage except perhaps silently to commiserate with him—a gentleman rarely married in a hurry, after all, unless he had been somehow forced into it—nevertheless considered him a good sort. He had talked and laughed and dined and drunk with them during the week, and he had lost moderate sums to the best of them at the tables. They wished him well and wondered, perhaps less avidly than their female counterparts, what manner of woman had succeeded in putting a leg shackle on him.

As Lord Rawleigh had assured his wife, then, the stage had indeed been set for the night of Lady Mindell's ball. Perhaps it would be an exaggeration to state that the *ton* flocked to Lord Mindell's mansion on Hanover Square for the sole purpose of seeing the Viscountess Rawleigh. Undoubtedly they would have gone anyway to the ball, since it was regularly one of the greatest squeezes of the Season. But certainly the knowledge that finally they would meet the elusive bride added a welcome interest to the event at a time, a few weeks into the Season, when collective ennui at the sameness of *ton* events was in danger of setting in.

IT SEEMED THAT every fashionable carriage in London must be lined up outside the Mindell mansion, waiting to disgorge its gorgeously clad passengers. And it seemed that every window in the house must be lit by a thousand candles. And that every servant in the house and every guest at the ball must be congregated either on the pavement and steps outside the house or in the hall or on the stairs beyond the doors.

There was nowhere—absolutely nowhere—to hide. Even the interior of the carriage was flooded with light as Lord Rawleigh's carriage took its turn drawing up before the doors.

The temptation for Catherine was to dip her head, to gaze at the ground, to put on a marble exterior, once again to become passive, to allow life to happen to her. But instinct told her that that would be the surest road to disaster. Disaster, if it was to come, was not going to be met meekly. She had decided that yesterday.

She looked at the two men sitting on the seat opposite. Her father was stiff and stony. But he was there at least. He had come. She smiled at him, though he did not return the look. Harry was silent and pale—and smiling with affectionate encouragement.

"You look beautiful, Cathy," he said when she met his

eyes. He had said the same thing before dinner and again before they left their father's house. He looked wonderful too, dressed all in pale blue and white. Surely even now, though he was still so young, there must be a few even younger ladies who were sighing over him. Rex's brother had married at the age of twenty, she thought—only one year older than Harry was now. She hoped tonight would not spoil his image with the *ton*.

The coachman was opening the carriage door and setting down the steps. One of Lord Mindell's footmen was hovering outside, ready to lend assistance if any were needed. The moment had come. Her father and her brother descended to the pavement.

"Catherine," her husband said quickly but quite distinctly before following them out and turning to hand her down, "you *are* beautiful. You are my pride and joy."

Surprise and gratification could not quite mask the sick dread that seemed to have lodged like a leaden weight in the soles of her slippers. But his words brought color to her cheeks, as perhaps he had intended. The smile on her lips would have been there anyway, and the sparkle in her eyes, and the lift to her chin.

The final temptation was to fix her eyes on some distant and inanimate object. Resisting temptation was incredibly difficult, but she did it. She looked around her, seeing people, not avoiding their eyes. But if she hoped to assure herself that after all no one was looking back at her, she was to be disappointed. There was the natural curiosity about any new arrival. There was in addition the heightened curiosity of seeing Viscount Rawleigh's new bride—he had told her that everyone knew he was married. Oh, yes, there were many eyes directed her way.

Harry and her father were on one side of her, her husband on the other. She had her arm on his sleeve. His free hand covered hers and he bent his head almost to hers as they climbed the shallow steps to the hall and entered it. He was smiling in a way that might under other circumstances have had her heart turning clear over in her chest.

"Courage, my love," he murmured to her. "We will bring this thing off. I promise you."

She let her true feelings for him shine through her eyes as she smiled back. Instinct told her that it was the right thing to do. She might have looked at him so even if it had been only an act.

Six years was both a long time and a short time. She read curiosity in many eyes but no recognition. She saw people—many of them—she had never seen before. But she saw both curiosity and dawning recognition in other eyes—in the eyes of people she herself recognized. And in some cases shock was clearly the third reaction to the sight of her.

Six years was a short time. An eternity was a short time with the *ton,* which never forgot the breach of its rules that had sent a former member into perpetual exile.

Her father was loudly and gruffly greeting acquaintances. Rex was doing the same thing in a quieter, more charming manner. Harry was smiling sweetly all about him, looking remarkably like an angel.

They were on the stairs, joining the line that would take them past their hosts into the ballroom. Would they get that far? Catherine wondered. Or would they be turned ignominiously away? Would anyone dare risk the public sort of scandal that would result from refusing admittance to the Earl of Paxton, Viscount Perry, and Viscount Rawleigh? Suddenly she felt like giggling and swallowed in some alarm. Her husband raised her hand to his smiling lips and replaced it on his sleeve.

By some stroke of good fortune Daphne and Clayton were just a few places ahead of them in the line. They left their place and came back to join the group. Clayton was quietly amiable, Daphne brightly voluble. She felt almost, Catherine thought, as if she was hedged about by a very comforting brick wall. Almost, but not quite.

And then finally the moment had come. It was almost anticlimactic. And of course—she might have known it—everyone was far too well-bred even to make a show of recognizing her. Lord Mindell probably did not do so at all, she decided. He looked at them all with vague boredom, as if to say that this had all been his wife's idea and he was there on sufferance, and murmured some polite platitudes. Lady Mindell raised her eyebrows in momentary shock, became noticeably haughtier and more regal, and greeted them with icy good manners.

"Even the plumes in her hair seemed to stand more stiffly to attention once she looked at me," Catherine found herself murmuring to her husband with the sort of humor that had taken her through numerous such meetings with Clarissa.

He chuckled and patted her hand.

But humor fled when she realized they were in the ballroom and facing much the ordeal they had encountered downstairs, but multiplied tenfold. It seemed to Catherine—and she did not believe she was mistaken—that the buzz of conversation faded for a moment and then launched itself into a newer, far more exciting topic.

She almost expected her guard to fall away from her to leave her exposed and isolated in the middle of a hostile mass. But of course, it was a foolish fear. Rex's hand was still holding hers on his sleeve. Daphne linked arms with her on the other side and chattered almost without pause for breath. Her father hovered, a massive and strangely comforting presence a few feet from her. Clayton was making use of his quizzing glass and was suddenly looking like a formidable champion.

"I love it when Clay uses his glass," Daphne said brightly. "It makes him look so delightfully toplofty. It was when I found it turned on me one evening that I first noticed him. I scolded him about it less than half an hour later. I was head over ears for him less than half an hour after that." She laughed gaily and Catherine joined her.

Harry had left their group for a few minutes only to return with another young gentleman, whose carrot-red hair and exaggeratedly high shirt points and scarlet blush made him appear even younger than his friend. He was presented to the group.

"H-how do you d-do, Lady C-Catherine," he said on being presented to Lady Rawleigh. "P-pleased to make your acquaintance. I was unaware that H-Harry had a sister, and such a lovely one, if I m-may make so b-bold."

Catherine smiled in genuine amusement. Sir Cuthbert Smalley began to discuss the weather in clinical and tedious detail while Harry grinned and winked at her from behind his friend's shoulder.

And then three other gentlemen made their appearance. Lord Pelham, Mr. Gascoigne, and the Earl of Haverford had just arrived together, it seemed. Each of them took her hand and bowed over it. Lord Haverford raised it to his lips. Each of them engaged her to dance a set later in the evening. Sir Cuthbert did likewise.

It was all contrived, of course. Rex had planned it and Harry had helped on his own account. But she felt deeply grateful. She was still not sure that when shock had worn off in the people about her there would not be some collective action to rid the company of her contaminating presence. But every moment that was becoming less likely. She was surrounded by a formidable bulwark of influential friends.

All of them were male with the exception of Daphne— until a pretty, plumpish, blond-haired lady dressed in a pale pink gown, which had the unfortunate effect of making her complexion look somewhat sallow, wormed her way between Clayton and Mr. Gascoigne, stared at Catherine, and then let out a sound resembling a shriek.

"Cathy!" she said. "It *is* you. Cathy! I thought you were *dead*!"

She launched herself at Catherine and they hugged and laughed together.

"I am not dead, Elsie," Catherine said. "I assure you I am very much alive. How lovely it is to see you again." And to know that at least the dearest bosom bow of her youth was not going to cut her.

"Good evening, Lady Withersford," her husband said gravely.

"Elsie," Catherine said, clasping her friend's hands and laughing at her. *"Lady Withersford?"*

"Yes, well," Elsie said, flushing a shade of red that clashed horribly with her gown, "I discovered that I did not hate Rudy quite as much as I thought I did, Cathy. In fact—but no matter. I married him five years ago. We have two sons."

And there, sure enough, was Lord Withersford, whom Catherine and Elsie had used to giggle over as girls and call—it had been Elsie's unkind description—the chinless wonder. He had always had a dignified sort of presence, though, to counter his lack of a chin. He bowed now, generally to the whole group. But he did not, as he might have done, take his wife's arm and propel her firmly away to another part of the ballroom. He struck up a conversation with Clayton and Lord Pelham that sounded to be on the topic of Tattersall's. It was impossible to hear clearly—Elsie and Daphne were vying with each other to see who could chatter most.

And finally the dancing began. The opening set was a

quadrille, which Catherine danced with her husband. Daphne and Clayton, Elsie and Lord Withersford were part of the same set. None of the other members of the set withdrew to another when Catherine joined it. No one silenced the orchestra in order to announce that she must leave the floor and the ballroom and the house.

It seemed that they had brought it off, as Rex had put it earlier. She fixed her eyes on his and smiled—and noticed consciously for the first time that the look in his was one of admiration, rather as he had always looked at her at Bodley, and something more than admiration. It looked like love. It was a look he had put there for their audience, of course, just as he often called her "my love" when other people could hear him. But it was a look that warmed her nonetheless.

And perhaps it was not entirely a false look. There had been no audience to last night's lovemaking, after all. And last night's lovemaking had taken on a new dimension. He had loved her not only with the usual expertise and consideration for her own pleasure as well as his own. He had loved her with tenderness. She was sure of it even though he had loved her in silence and she had fallen asleep so soon afterward that there had been no chance for words to be exchanged.

He was not entirely without feeling for her. He had married her reluctantly and had been carried forward, first by duty and then by guilt. But he had come, she believed, to like her a little more than he had at first. It was something. If only they could carry off this evening's daring and audacious business, perhaps their marriage could survive to be at least a working relationship. The thought was sweet.

He danced well. And she forgot the other members of the set and felt as if she danced only with him. There were memories of the ball at Bodley House, when she had waltzed with him twice, once in the ballroom and once in the music room. Aching memories of sweetness and the beginning of bitterness. He looked so wonderfully handsome tonight, dressed in shades of brown and dull gold to complement her gown of gold satin.

She deliberately relaxed and deliberately gave herself up to an enjoyment of the ball.

HE GRADUALLY FELT himself relaxing. For tonight at least, he believed, there would be no great unpleasantness. The moments at which it might have happened—when they entered the house, when they passed the receiving line, when they entered the ballroom—had passed. No one was going to make a scene now.

He wondered if Catherine had sensed his fear. It had been only partly a fear that she would crumble under the strain. If she had done so, then it would be something from which she might never recover. But he had not really expected it. He could remember her quiet dignity under even more trying circumstances at Bodley. His real fear had been of some very public unpleasantness, something from which he would have been unable to shield her. He would never have forgiven himself if that had happened. And again, it would have been something insurmountable, something that would have blighted the whole of her future, and his, and their children's.

All was not assured even yet, of course. Good breeding might prevent a public scene tonight, but tomorrow might plunge the two of them into a deep freeze. There might possibly be no further invitations. From tomorrow on they might be invisible or unrecognizable at the theater or in the park or in the fashionable shops of Bond Street or Oxford Street. Only tomorrow would bring the answers.

But her family and his, and his friends, and perhaps Lord

and Lady Withersford would continue to rally to the cause, he believed. Perhaps they would succeed in edging Catherine back into Society. He would keep her here for a few weeks, anyway, and see what could be done. Though if he had his way, he would take her back to Stratton tomorrow and proceed to live happily ever after with her there. He was going to try—he was going to try his damnedest—to make her fall in love with him. He thought there was a slim chance it might be done. Her tenderness last night had made him almost delirious with hope.

He felt an eagerness he had not found in himself since his engagement to Horatia to begin the rest of his life—to trust love and to make a lifelong commitment to that love. He wanted to start his children in her. He wanted to be family with her even if there were no children.

And so he danced the quadrille with his wife, seeing only her, relaxing past the tension that had held him together for a week, allowing himself at last to enjoy the ball.

He really had not looked about him a great deal since their arrival. But when the set was over and he had led his wife off the floor and her brother was preparing to dance the following set of country dances with her, Lord Rawleigh looked about him with some curiosity. He wanted to see if attention was as riveted on his group as it had been at the start. He wanted to assess the nature of what attention was still on them.

It was only then that he became aware of the presence of two people in particular—though one of those two was only then entering the ballroom and could not therefore have been noticed before.

Horatia Eckert was standing with her mother and her elder sister some distance away. She was fanning herself and not looking at him, though he was given the impression that she was very aware of both his presence and his glance.

Beautiful, dainty little Horatia with her bright auburn hair and her large dark eyes—he felt a pang of regret for all the ugly unpleasantness that had replaced love with hatred in his heart. He had called her a coldhearted coquette in his reply to her letter breaking off their engagement, and afterward, when he was back in England and when she was alone again, her flirtation at an end, he had spurned the tentative overtures she had somehow managed to make. He had felt nothing but rage for her presumption. Of course, there had been a year or so when she had not dared appear in town. The *beau monde* did not look kindly upon those who broke publicly announced betrothals. She was fortunate to have avoided total ostracism.

He did not look at her for longer than a few seconds. He knew that he was very much on public display tonight, and his connection with Horatia would not have been forgotten by the *ton*. But as his eyes swept in the opposite direction, to the doors, he saw the gentleman who had entered alone and looked about him with a cynical gaze.

Lord Rawleigh had known he was in town, though they had not run into each other during the week. It seemed that Sir Howard Copley moved very much on the fringes of Society these days. His debts were said to be astronomical, and he was not much welcomed at the clubs or even at the gaming halls. Over the years he had used his charm and his looks—now beginning to be marred by clear signs of dissipation—on so many heiresses, without success, that his reputation was too sullied to allow him any further chances. Young ladies of fortune, and even those without, were guarded from Sir Howard Copley as they would be guarded against ravening wolves.

Being a gentleman, however, he was not quite beyond the pale and still found entrée to some of the larger entertainments of the *ton*. And sometimes he put in an appearance, as much from the desire to show his contempt for Society's sticklers, it was thought, as from any thought of enjoying himself.

Lord Rawleigh, looking across the ballroom at the man who had destroyed his first betrothal and had debauched and impregnated and ruined his wife, felt a curious elation gather in his stomach like a lump of ice.

Yes. Oh, yes, indeed, he thought.

The music had not yet begun for the second set. There was another of those curious lulls in the general conversation, followed by a renewed rush of sound. The arrival of Sir Howard Copley and all its implications had been noted, then.

The viscount's eyes met Copley's across the ballroom and deliberately held them. Copley looked back for a moment, and his look of cynicism deepened as he raised one eyebrow. He would be remembering Horatia, the viscount thought, and the fact that the rejected fiancé had not called him to account.

And then Copley's glance moved to Catherine, whom he would be able to see in profile. It held there a moment and then moved back to Lord Rawleigh. There was something unreadable now in the cynical eyes—until he half smiled and turned unhurriedly to leave the ballroom he had entered only a few minutes before.

The ball of ice in Lord Rawleigh's stomach expanded to freeze his heart. And still there was the feeling of elation.

Catherine was laughing at something her brother had said and had taken his arm to be led into the next set. They looked golden and innocent, the two of them.

Twenty-two

SHE FELT STRANGELY exhilarated. She knew enough about life and Society, of course, to realize that all was not quite settled yet. It was true that no one had made a scene and that no one had even been subtly rude to her. But then very few people had been openly welcoming or friendly, either. Elsie and Lord Withersford had and Harry's friend Sir Cuthbert, and Lord Cox had solicited her hand for a set after supper—he had been one of her admirers six years before.

She knew that tomorrow she might find herself quite firmly locked out of Society again. There would be no nastiness, no vulgarity, merely a loud and frozen silence. It was certainly a possibility despite the presence with her tonight of so many titled and influential people of *ton*, her father included.

But tonight she refused to think of tomorrow. Tonight she was at a London ball again, wearing a new gown and a new coiffure, newly married to the most handsome gentleman in the ballroom, to the man with whom she had fallen in love. She had danced the opening set with him and was to dance the supper waltz with him. In the meanwhile she had had a partner for each set and was waltzing now with her father of all people. In the year of her come-out her father had never even ventured inside a ballroom.

"I did not know you could dance, Papa," she said, smiling at him.

He was frowning and merely grunted in reply.

"Where did you learn to waltz?" she asked him.

"A gentleman must do what a gentleman must do," he said.

"Including this?" she asked him. "Appearing with me here? Is it a terrible embarrassment to you, Papa?" She was not sorry if it was. It was time he was embarrassed for her sake. But though he had not given her the support she had needed six years ago, she could not hate him. He was her father and she loved him.

His eyes met hers as he continued to dance the steps of the waltz correctly but without flair.

"You have been fortunate, Catherine," he said. "Why he would be willing to marry you under the circumstances I do not know. Of course, you are in good looks and he is a young man with eyes in his head. But however it was, he did the right thing to bring you here, I must admit. Life would be insupportable to him with a disgraced wife, and it would be impossible for his children."

Nothing about her own feelings or about *her* children. She smiled.

"He knows, I suppose," he said, "that it was Copley?"

"Yes," she said, and realized suddenly another reason for the exhilaration she was feeling. She had feared that he might be at the ball. She did not believe she could bear to see him again—and to remember that he had been Bruce's father. She preferred to think of Bruce as her son, a son without a father and without the ugliness that had been his conception.

"Then you were doubtly fortunate," her father said, "or he

was doubly the fool, whichever way one cares to look at it."

She looked into his eyes, but he was looking off to the side somewhere. "Doubly?" she said.

"It was Copley who caused the ending of his betrothal a few years ago," he said. "Eckert's daughter. Copley did not marry her, but she broke off the betrothal all right. She is the fortunate one too. She disappeared for a while, but she came back and brazened it out. Of course, with her there was no bastard child."

Pain knifed at her. Bruce a bastard child. But there was other pain too. Rex has been betrothed to someone else? She had broken it off? Because of Sir Howard Copley? What a bizarre twist of fate. How must he have felt when she told him her story at Stratton? Had he loved the other woman? Did he still love her? The questions and the possible answers crowded at her even as she smiled and danced.

She came back. Catherine heard the echo of her father's words. "Is she here tonight?" she asked.

"Over there." He nodded his head to the sidelines. "Small. With auburn hair."

Miss Eckert. Vividly, exquisitely beautiful. She was looking back at Catherine and their eyes met for a moment until Miss Eckert looked away. But even in that moment and from some distance, the expression in her eyes had been readable. There was sorrow there, perhaps reproach. Not hatred. It was a look that told Catherine quite clearly that the other woman still loved Rex. Or perhaps the turmoil of the moment was making her read into a mere glance what she thought might very probably be there.

What had happened between Miss Eckert and Sir Howard? And why had Rex not defended her? Or forgiven her?

Perhaps Miss Eckert had not wanted forgiveness.

Rex, Catherine saw, was waltzing with Elsie and apparently giving her his full attention. How did he feel about being in the same room with his former fiancée? Had he loved her? Did he love her? The questions were beginning to repeat themselves.

She knew, of course, that he had never loved *her*. He had never made any pretense of any feeling stronger than lust. He had married her because he had compromised her. But it was one thing to know those facts and accept them; it was quite another to know that he had once been betrothed to someone else and that he might possibly still love her.

And then the waltz was over and she was with him again, her hand on his sleeve, while they conversed with the larger group and waited for the quadrille that the Earl of Haverford had reserved with her. The supper waltz came after that.

Her husband disappeared from the ballroom, she noticed, after Lord Haverford had led her into the set. Lord Pelham and Mr. Gascoigne went with Rex. She supposed he thought her safe enough with his friend. The earl was even taller and broader than Rex. Any man would think twice about tangling with him, she thought—and any woman too. Catherine had the impression that his smiling gray eyes could turn to steel in an instant. It was not difficult to believe that for many years he had been a cavalry officer.

And yet he was gorgeously handsome. She had wondered at Bodley why she had felt no attraction to either Lord Pelham or Mr. Gascoigne though they were as good-looking as Rex and certainly more charming than he. She wondered now if she would have felt attraction to Lord Haverford if he had been there with his friends. But she knew the answer. Six years ago she would have been happy enough to set her cap at the Earl of Haverford if he had given her any encouragement at all. Now she could see his good looks and his charm only dispassionately. No one attracted her but Rex.

"Perhaps," she said rather ruefully, "you would have preferred to go with your friends, my lord."

His smile deepened. "What?" he said. "When I can have the bride to myself for half an hour? Not a chance, ma'am."

She laughed. "It *did* sound as if I had thrown down the hook for a compliment," she said. "It was unintentional, but thank you anyway. You must have so many stories to tell, the four of you. We must have you all to dinner one evening and hear some of them."

"A few of them are even suitable for female ears," he said, laughing with her. "Doubtless, though, Rex would veto even some of those. But certainly there are enough to fill an evening if you would not be bored. I accept the invitation."

The music began then and there was no further opportunity for conversation. Rex and his friends did not return to the ballroom until the closing measures of the set.

Just in time for the supper waltz.

Oh, yes, Catherine thought again, she was feeling exhilarated. Let tomorrow look after itself.

HE WAS IN the card room. He had gone there straight from the ballroom and had remained there ever since. Mr. Gascoigne and Lord Pelham and the Earl of Haverford had checked there alternately every ten minutes or so and reported back.

It was likely he would remain there until the end of the ball. But there was no point in taking chances and even less point in delay. There was no great danger of public scandal in the middle of a ball. By some stroke of good fortune, cards were being played in two anterooms. All the lady players and a few older gentlemen were in one. There were only men in the other. Men could be relied upon to be closemouthed when necessity and good breeding dictated it.

The earl was the one elected to stay in the ballroom to

keep an eye on Catherine. Opportunely he had already reserved the set before the supper waltz with her. Not that much of a guard was needed. There would be no unpleasantness now at this stage of the evening. Anyway, her father and brother were with her as well as Sir Clayton Baird—and even Lady Baird could be formidable in a pinch. But they were all agreed that one of them should stay just in case. Lord Haverford could always be relied upon to freeze the blossoms off a spring branch with a single glance if the need arose.

The other three went to the card room together. There were not as many gentlemen in there as one might expect to see if it had been a club room on a normal evening. Most of them had doubtless been persuaded by their womenfolk to do their duty in the ballroom.

Sir Howard Copley was seated at one of the tables with three other players. From the pile of notes and papers at his elbow it appeared that luck was with him tonight. They ranged themselves around the table, the three of them, Mr. Gascoigne and Lord Pelham just far enough on either side of his shoulders that they were within his line of vision, Viscount Rawleigh directly opposite him. They stood in silence, staring at him. They took no notice of any of the other players or of the game in progress. They stared at his face, Mr. Gascoigne and Lord Pelham at his opposite profiles, the viscount at his full face.

He became aware of them only gradually. He darted a few sideways glances and a few straight ahead, each a little more uneasy than the one before. He said nothing and continued playing, but it became quickly apparent that he had lost his concentration. He lost the hand. He licked his lips and took a giant swallow from his glass. He lost the next hand too.

It was amazing how quickly a message could travel without

a single word having been spoken, Lord Rawleigh thought without shifting his fixed gaze from Copley's face. Even in this remote anteroom, of course, news would have arrived that Catherine was at the ball and that she was his wife. And memory would serve well enough to remind everyone that Copley had been the one who had ruined her. The significance of this spectacle would not be lost on anyone.

A curious silence descended on the room. Curious because the room had been silent even when the three of them had first entered. A card room was not usually characterized by noise. But this silence was tense and expectant. With his peripheral vision Lord Rawleigh could see that play at the next table had been suspended.

Sir Howard Copley tossed down his cards when he lost the second hand and glared up at the viscount.

"What do you want?" he snapped.

Lord Rawleigh did not answer. He let the silence stretch.

"What the hell are you staring at me for?" Copley's hand reached out for his glass and knocked it over. A brown stain spread and soaked into the tablecloth. No one made a move to mop up.

Copley jerked to his feet, pushing back his chair with the backs of his knees. "Stop it this instant," he said. "And you two." He half glanced at Lord Pelham and Mr. Gascoigne. "Get out of here if you know what is good for you."

Lord Rawleigh stared. His friends stood. Sir Howard Copley dragged a handkerchief out of his pocket and mopped his brow with it.

"I suppose," he said, putting the handkerchief away, pulling himself together with a visible effort, and sneering, "you discovered that you had a less than pure bride on your wedding night, Rawleigh. And I suppose she forgot to mention the fact in advance. Don't blame me. I was not plump enough in the pockets for her taste. She had her pleasure of me and then poked her nose in the air as if she were a duchess instead of a whore."

There was a sigh of something in the room. It was not sound as much as a collective expelling of air, an awareness that some crisis point had been reached and that there was only one possible outcome.

Viscount Rawleigh felt again the cold elation he had felt earlier in the ballroom. He strolled slowly around the table. Nat stepped back to let him pass.

"I did not bring gloves with me, Copley," the viscount said, breaking the silence at last. "My bare hand will have to suffice." He whipped the back of it across Copley's face, snapping his head to one side. "Name your weapons and the time and place. Your second can call on Lord Pelham tomorrow morning to discuss the details."

He turned to leave the room, his friends behind him. Everyone else stood aside to let them pass. No one voiced any objection to the breaking of a law that was about to happen. No one would. No one would spread the word except perhaps to other gentlemen. It was doubtful that any woman would hear of it. This was gentlemen's business after all.

"Rawleigh." Sir Howard's voice stopped the viscount for a mere moment, though he did not turn to look back. "It will be pistols, with which I have a certain skill and have had some success. It will be as much a pleasure to kill you as it was to deflower your wife—and your betrothed."

"Shame!" several voices said at last.

Viscount Rawleigh and his two friends returned to the ballroom, where by chance the quadrille was coming to an end. They had timed their business well.

IT TOOK A while after he had loved her to recover breath and energy enough to speak. She could easily have slipped into sleep as she usually did, but she did not want to sleep just yet. She suspected that such moments could be precious to the marriage they must somehow build into something meaningful. At such moments there was a tenderness between them that had been aroused by their physical union but which was not entirely physical in itself.

"Rex?" She cuddled her head more comfortably against his shoulder and spread her hand over his chest. It was warm and still damp from their lovemaking.

"Mm?" He rubbed his face against the top of her head. "Am I slipping? Have I not put you to sleep tonight?"

"I have realized," she said, "that sleeping immediately after robs me of some pleasure."

He chuckled. "You learn fast," he said. "Incidentally, I have noticed that before."

She liked it when they talked teasingly to each other. There were all sorts of possibilities for healing and for the growth of friendship and affection when two people could tease each other.

"You did not mind my inviting your friends to dinner tomorrow?" she asked. "I should have consulted you first, but I made the suggestion to Lord Haverford when I was dancing with him, and somehow the idea blossomed."

"I would have done so myself," he said, "but I would have felt obliged to invite an equal number of ladies—it seems that I have something in common with Clarissa, perish the thought. I would not have wanted to bore you with all male guests and all male conversation."

"But I want to know about your friends," she said, "and your experiences with them. Not that I want to pry into any secrets or worm my way into a friendship that is precious among the four of you. I just want to know you better, Rex. I want to know about your childhood too and your life with

Claude and Daphne. I want to know more of what it is like to be a twin."

"Claude is not happy," he said.

"He always seemed contented enough," she said.

"I mean recently," he said. "I have not heard from him since we left Bodley, yet I know that about him, you see. It is part of being a twin."

She thought about it for a moment. "And what does he know about you recently?" she asked. She was sorry, then, because he hesitated in his answer. She did not want him to lie to make her feel better. But she did not want the truth—not now, at this moment.

"He saw me sullen and rather bitter," he said quietly. "I believe he will know that my mood has changed. That I am content."

Content. He might have used a far worse word. She consoled herself with that fact.

"Catherine." He lifted her chin and kissed her softly before lifting his head away again. "I must learn to know you too. For so long you were a total stranger to me, a mystery. I want to know about Harry—he is a fine young man. And about Lady Withersford. About all the people who were important to you. I want to know who Lady Catherine Winsmore was. But not tonight. Can it wait until tomorrow? You have worn me out, I am afraid. You are an energetic lover."

The description pleased her. And she was tired too—within a hairbreadth of sleep. But she could not leave it at that. There was warmth between them because they had loved and because they had taken steps to reach out to each other in ways other than merely the physical. But she could not leave it at that.

"Tell me about Miss Eckert," she said, her face pressed to his shoulder.

He sighed after a short silence, during which she braced herself for his anger. "Yes," he said. "Someone was bound to tell you. I should have done so myself before now. I am sorry, Catherine. We met during the year between the Peninsula and Waterloo, and were betrothed within a month of meeting. Then I went off to Belgium with the armies and she wrote me there breaking off the engagement. She did not marry the—the man who came between us, but we did not revive our relationship. It was destroyed."

"Sir Howard Copley," she said.

"Yes." The muscles of the arm holding her bunched before relaxing again.

"Did he— What happened exactly?" she asked.

"I am not sure," he said. "My guess is that he thought her fortune larger than it actually was and discovered the truth before it was too late. At the time I thought that she had merely been dazzled by good looks and charm during my absence."

"And now you are not so sure?" she asked him.

"I knew of him as a wastrel and a rake," he said. "I had heard of his sullying the reputations of other women. I believe your name was even mentioned. But even so I never—until very recently—suspected that perhaps there was more to it than what Horatia said in her letter to me. She said she was in love with him."

"You think she was not?" she asked him. "You think perhaps she felt obliged to break off the betrothal and gave a reason you would be most likely to accept without question?" She could feel Horatia Eckert's pain as if it were her own.

He swallowed. "I pray I am wrong," he said. "I would have nothing to do with her when I returned to England."

"As she had planned," she said.

"Yes, but— Ah, it does not matter," he said.

She felt deep sorrow for Miss Eckert and pain for herself. She asked the question she ought not to ask.

"Do you still love her?" she whispered.

"No," he said quite firmly. "No, Catherine. I feel sorry for her, but pity is not love. And I feel guilty that I was not as perceptive as I might have been in seeing through what was very possibly a lie. I was too caught up in my own pain and humiliation. But I do not love her. She was there tonight, as I suppose you were aware. I could see her only with pity."

She could not help the elation she felt, though she remembered Miss Eckert's eyes.

"She still loves you," she said.

She felt him draw breath to answer, though he said nothing.

"Forgive my questioning you," she said. "I had to know."

"Yes." He kissed the top of her head. "I feel sorry for her, Catherine, but she must make her own future. My future is in my arms here and I have the feeling that it is going to consume all my energy. Not just physical energy, you understand."

Yes, she did. They were precious words. Words of hope and commitment. Just a month ago, when she had married him, she had not expected any more than the protection of his name. She had not expected commitment.

"I am just glad of one thing," she said. "I am glad he is not in town this year—Sir Howard Copley, I mean. I feared he might be. I hope he never comes back. I hope I never have to see him again."

His arm tightened again. "You have nothing to fear from him, Catherine," he said. "You have me to protect you now. I will protect what is my own with my life if necessary."

That was part of what she was afraid of. Coming face-to-face with Sir Howard would be dreadful indeed for her. But what would happen if Rex ever met him, knowing what he now did, both about her and about Miss Eckert? There would quite possibly be a challenge and a duel.

And perhaps Rex would not be the one to walk away from it.

She shivered.

"I really must be slipping," her husband said. "Are you cold? Or is it just the mention of his name? Either way, I had better think of a way of warming you up, had I not?"

He turned her and came on top of her and thrust inside her without foreplay, something he had not done before. He was learning her needs, she thought. His weight and the hard fullness of him inside her were wonderfully comforting. And the knowledge that he would bring her to passion again made her put aside dark thoughts.

She sighed as his mouth found hers.

"Relax," he said against it. "No participation is required. This is purely from me to you."

Ah, he knew that too. That she needed the gift of his body and his strength.

Twenty-three

HE HAD ALWAYS hated the day before a battle—though no battles had been fought by appointment, it was usually obvious to a seasoned soldier when one was imminent. He had always hated it because, busy with preparations as one had always been, there had been too much time for thought, too much time for fear. He had always scorned those soldiers who professed to feel no fear—on the assumption that it was unmanly to be afraid. On the day before a battle he had always been dry-mouthed and weak-kneed with fear. His stomach had always been queasy.

He felt fear on the day following the Mindell ball—the day before the duel with Copley that he himself had deliberately provoked. He had, of course, rejected Nat's offer to do it for him.

"After all, Rex," Nat had said with a careless shrug, "I have no one dependent upon me. And I always did enjoy a good scrap, especially against a bastard like Copley."

No, he was not sorry he had done it. He would do it all over again if necessary. And it was certainly not something he would allow someone else to do for him, even one of his dearest friends.

But he was afraid. Afraid, of course, of dying—only a fool would pretend not to fear death. But afraid too of failing to avenge the terrible wrong that had been done to Catherine and the anguish she had suffered over the conception and death of a child. But fear, as on the day before a battle, gave him energy and clarity of thought. It made him attentive to duty and to detail.

A morning call on Eden confirmed the fact that the challenge had been taken up. Copley's second had already called and all the details had been worked out. Nat and Ken were there too. Lord Rawleigh discussed his new will with them, talking quite openly and calmly about the possibility of his death. His will provided more than adequately for Catherine's future. Her father and her brother would probably give her the emotional support she would need. His friends undertook to provide any further protection that might be necessary.

They went with him to take his will to his man of business. Then they spent an hour with him at pistol practice—he had not fired a pistol since selling out of the cavalry.

During the afternoon he paid calls with Catherine on the ladies with whom he had left his card in the days before the ball and on a few others who were known to be at home to visitors. And at the fashionable hour they drove in Hyde Park in his curricle. If he was to die tomorrow, he would do all in his power today to ensure her acceptance back into the *ton*. They were rejected nowhere. And a few invitations had arrived this morning.

All the men *knew*, of course. There was a certain look in their eyes that assured Lord Rawleigh of that fact, though nothing was said in the presence of the ladies. None of the ladies knew.

In the evening his friends came to dinner and the four of them talked unabashedly about their friendship, about some of their experiences together in the Peninsula and Waterloo. They talked because Catherine insisted upon it and because she was very obviously interested. She did not retire alone to the drawing room at the end of the meal in order to leave them to their port. They all sat on together and then adjourned together to the drawing room for another hour or so.

If he could have chosen how to spend what might well be his final evening, the viscount thought, he could not have done better than this—to spend it in company with his closest friends and his wife. He felt a pang of longing for Claude. Could his brother feel his uneasiness? Would he sense . . . But he would not indulge in such thoughts now any more than he had ever done during the war.

His friends did not stay late. They all planned to be up very early in the morning, they explained, having dared each other to watch the sunrise from horseback. They made a great show of persuading him to rise with the lark and ride out with them, begging Catherine's pardon, assuring her that they would not drag him out so early ever again. All three of them were shamelessly charming. She, of course, realized it and laughed at them all. But she did not understand what was really going on.

He made love to her when they went to bed. Holding her afterward—he was thankful that she was not inclined to talk, as she had been the night before—he wanted to say the words to her that would complete what he had just said with his body. But he would not burden her with them. Not when tomorrow she might have great enough burdens to bear without that.

He held her close until she was asleep and then set himself to endure the hours of dozing and dreaming and waking that always preceded battle.

• • •

"TOBY," SHE SAID, cupping his head with her hands, "I am a neglected wife. He took himself off even before dawn to ride with his friends and has doubtless gone somewhere to breakfast with them and will just as doubtlessly go on to White's with them afterward. We will be fortunate if he sees fit to return for luncheon."

Toby cocked his ears, puffed eagerly into her face, and wagged his tail.

"But I am not offended," she said. "You must not think that. It is right that he lead his own life and that I lead mine—provided we also spend time together, of course. But the trouble is, Toby, that I have had no life of my own to lead since I married him. That fact is irksome, is it not, after all those years of independence?"

Toby whined eagerly.

"Yes," she said, "you are quite right, of course. It is time you and I ventured out together for a walk."

Standing still with his head being held was too restricting for Toby. He pulled away and began a circular tear about the morning room, pausing hopefully at the door with each revolution.

Catherine laughed at him. "If you do not wish to accompany me, Toby," she said, "all you have to do is say so, you know."

They walked out together a short while later, Catherine's maid with them. Toby, on a leash, was indignantly trying to pull Catherine's arm from its socket. When he was finally released in Hyde Park, he raced about so exuberantly that the maid laughed and Catherine joined her.

They met very few people and none that Catherine knew. It felt so wonderful to be out walking again. Hyde Park at this time of day was like a piece of the country. One could forget that it was surrounded by the largest, busiest city in the world. It was a beautiful, sunny day. Catherine was sorry that she had not suggested getting up to ride with the men. But perhaps not, she thought. She must respect her husband's male friendships as she would expect him to respect her female ones—with Elsie, for example. She must not always be hanging on his sleeve.

She did not want to go home immediately. But where else could she go? Elsie's? Elsie lived too far away. She would have to go home and have the carriage called out. Daphne lived within walking distance of the park. Catherine brightened. She would go and call on Daphne.

When she and her maid and Toby arrived at the house, though, it seemed for a while that they had come in vain. Sir Clayton Baird's butler was not at all sure that Lady Baird was at home. But he came back with the invitation to go up to her ladyship's private sitting room. Toby, looking indignant again, was led off to the kitchen by the maid.

Daphne, red-eyed and distraught, threw herself into Catherine's arms before the door could even close behind the latter.

"Have you heard anything?" she cried. "What has happened? Is he dead?"

"Daphne?" Catherine looked at her in amazement. "What is the matter?"

Daphne looked wildly at her. "Rex?" she said. "Is he dead? Clay went out ages and ages ago to find out for me, but he has not come back."

Catherine could feel a buzzing in her head. The air of the room felt icy in her nostrils. "Rex?" she asked faintly.

And then Daphne's look became one of horror as she helped Catherine to the nearest chair and lowered her into it. "You did not know?" she said. "Oh, what have I done? He is fighting a duel with Sir Howard Copley, Catherine. Early this morning. With p-pistols," she wailed.

• • •

CATHERINE WAS ALONE at the cold, dark end of a long tunnel. Someone was coaxing her to the other end, chafing her hands, calling to her—leaving her. And then there were voices and something was being pressed against her teeth and fire was coming down the tunnel and forcing her, coughing and sputtering, up to the warm, bright end.

"She is coming around, ma'am," a male voice said.

"Yes," Daphne said. "Thank you. The brandy was just the thing. Leave the glass in case she needs more."

Sir Clayton Baird's butler left the room after assuring his mistress that he would be just outside the door should she have further need of him.

"But Sir Howard is not even in town," Catherine said foolishly as if the conversation had not just been interrupted by her fainting dead away. "And why would he want to challenge Rex?"

"He was at the ball," Daphne said. "Did you not see him? And of course it was *Rex* who challenged *him*. I found out only this morning. Clay went out for news but he has not returned yet. Oh, where are you going?"

Catherine was on her feet, swaying, light-headed. She did not know where she was going. She had to find him. She had to stop him. She had to . . . "I have to tell him that I love him," she heard herself say. What foolish words! She set a shaking fist to her mouth.

"Oh, Catherine." They were in each other's arms then, sobbing on each other's shoulder.

It was too late to go looking for him. It was too late to stop him. It might forever be too late to tell him that she loved him. Duels were always fought at dawn, were they not? He had left home well before dawn.

"I have to go home," she said. And suddenly there was a dreadful panic on her to be home. "I have to go."

"I will come with you," Daphne said.

It did not occur to either of them to wait for a carriage. Waiting was something neither could do. They hurried along the streets together, heads down. Catherine did not even remember that she had left a maid and a dog in Sir Clayton's kitchen.

NOW THAT THE time had come, fear had given place to an icy calm. He had known it would. It had always been thus. He had not been afraid of unsteady legs or shaking hand.

Copley had brought one second with him. Nat and Eden and Ken were all there, all grim and white-faced. This must be worse for them, Lord Rawleigh thought with a flash of insight, than it was for him. They were not accustomed to inaction on the morning of battle. They were not accustomed to watching one of their friends fight alone. There was also a surgeon in attendance.

Viscount Rawleigh did not look at Copley as he removed his cloak and stripped off his coat and waistcoat. He looked him in the eye as Eden and Copley's second made the token gesture of attempting a peaceful reconciliation. He refused and Copley sneered. They were to stand back-to-back, take twelve paces each, turn, and fire after the signal.

"Tell Catherine," he said to Eden at the last possible moment—she should know after all, he decided, exactly why he fought for her. He drew a deep breath. "Tell her that I love her."

"You can tell her yourself later," his friend said crisply. But he nodded.

A few moments later Lord Rawleigh was walking off his twelve paces, his pistol at the ready, steadying his mind on his decision to take careful and sure aim and not to follow the impulse to fire quickly and wildly before he could be fired at. He would have the chance for only one shot.

Copley, though, had made quite a different decision. As they turned, he leveled his pistol, and well before the signal to fire could be given, he fired.

It was amazing what a valuable thing experience could be, Lord Rawleigh thought. Experience enabled him to know that the pain was too severe for the wound to be serious. If it had been, he would have felt no pain for at least a few seconds. Shock would have cushioned him for that long. His right arm hurt like the devil. He was aware of redness on his white shirt sleeve, though he did not look down. It was only a flesh wound. He doubted that the bullet had even lodged in his arm.

He was aware too, though he did not look, of Nat with a gun in his hand.

"You are a dead man, Copley," he called in a voice Viscount Rawleigh had only ever heard on the battlefield. But he held his fire.

Lord Rawleigh was taking careful aim, ignoring the pain. He had a lengthy acquaintance with it and knew that pain alone did not kill. Copley had no choice but to stand and wait. He stood sideways to make as small a target as possible.

Time moved at one fraction of its normal speed. Space became a tunnel, almost a telescope. He was aware as he leveled his pistol of Copley's white and contemptuous face. In a matter of seconds a whole world of thoughts had found their way into his mind for consideration. He was tired of killing. He had always found himself vomiting for hours on end after a battle, knowing that he had killed men who had deserved death no more than he would have if they had killed him. He had killed to avoid being killed and to protect his friends and his men from death. He was not now in danger of death. Neither were his friends.

But Copley was a rapist. He had raped Catherine and very

probably Horatia too. Possibly other women as well. If he lived, even if the events of this morning could persuade him to take himself into perpetual exile from Britain, he would be alive to do it again. To make other women suffer as Catherine and Horatia had suffered.

Up to the very moment he fired, Lord Rawleigh was not sure whether he would raise his arm into the air at the last moment and show his contempt for the worm that was Sir Howard Copley by wasting his bullet on the air, or whether he would hold his arm steady and kill him.

He kept his arm steady.

And then he strode toward his friends and his clothes and dressed himself with unshaking hands, not even looking at what the surgeon and Copley's second were doing over the dead body of Sir Howard Copley. But he did have to take several hasty steps away after a few moments in order to vomit onto the grass. He was dizzy with the knowledge that he had killed. But for perhaps the first time he felt no remorse.

Catherine had been avenged. And all other women were safe from the bastard who had caused her suffering.

"Breakfast," he said resolutely to his friends, turning back to them. He felt as much like eating as he felt like jumping into a fire. "At White's?"

"At White's." Nat clapped a comforting hand on his left shoulder. "He would not have lived anyway, Rex. I would have done it if you had not."

"Perhaps my house instead of White's," Eden suggested. "A little more privacy and all that."

"I will have to leave immediately," Ken said. "I have to return to Dunbarton."

The other three looked at him in some surprise. Lord Rawleigh noticed that the look of tension and the ashen color had not left his face as they had Nat's and Eden's.

"To Dunbarton?" he said. "Now, Ken? This morning? Even before breakfast? I thought you were here for the rest of the Season."

His friend's face looked ghastly. "There was a letter waiting for me when I arrived home last evening," he said. He tried to smile and failed. "It appears that I am to be a father in six months time."

The duel was forgotten for the moment. His three friends stared at him.

"Who?" Eden asked at last. "Anyone we met when we were there, Ken? A *lady*?"

"No one you met," Ken said grimly. "A lady, yes. I have to go home to marry her."

"Dare I comment on the fact that you do not appear thrilled?" Nat said, frowning.

"Her family and mine have been enemies for as long as I can remember," Ken said. "I do not believe I have ever disliked a woman more than I dislike her. And she is with child by me. I must marry her. Wish me joy."

He did smile then, and Lord Rawleigh found himself feeling pity for the unknown bride-to-be.

"Ken," he said, frowning, "what are we missing?"

"Nothing that I care to divulge," his friend said. "I have to be going. I am glad things turned out as they did this morning, Rex. Have that arm seen to before you leave here. I am glad you did not reprieve him. I feared you would. Rapists do not deserve to live."

And without another word he strode away in the direction of his horse. He did not look back. None of them called after him.

"Poor Ken," Nat murmured.

"Poor lady," Lord Rawleigh said.

"We had better have that arm looked at, Rex, before you

bleed to death," Eden said, turning from their departing friend, his voice brisk. "The surgeon is free again, I see."

Yes, Lord Rawleigh thought, looking down at his arm. His sleeve was soaked with blood from shoulder to elbow.

Catherine, he thought then. He had lived to see her again. To tell her himself that he loved her.

THEY BOTH HEARD the outer door being opened and the sound of voices from the hall, even though they sat upstairs in the drawing room. But there was no hearing whose voices they were.

She sat stiff and upright on her chair. She could not get to her feet as she wished to do to run onto the landing and peer down the stairs or call down. Her legs felt alternately like lead and jelly. She guessed that Daphne was feeling the same way. They did not exchange any words—they were both listening too hard.

Who would come? she wondered. Who would be elected to break the news to her? Papa? Harry? Lord Pelham or one of his other friends? A stranger?

And then the door opened quite quietly and he stepped inside. For a moment her brain would not even accept the knowledge of who it was standing there. He was looking quite pale. The right sleeve of his coat was empty. His arm was in a very white sling. He was wearing what looked like someone else's shirt.

There was a curious silence. Daphne was on her feet, clinging to the back of a chair.

"Ah," he said quietly. "I see there is no point in telling my story about being tossed from my horse's back, is there?"

"Rex," Daphne said, her hand spread over her womb.

"I am all right, Daphne," he said. "A mere flesh wound in the arm. Nothing but a graze. But the fool of a physician insisted on the sling. I think it looks rather impressive." He grinned.

"If you only knew," she said, "what we have been through. Waiting is the most abominable activity in this world, Rex. And women are called upon to do so much of it."

Catherine felt rather like a disembodied spirit observing the scene but not really present in it. She could neither move nor speak. But he turned to her then and came across the room to her. He went down on one knee in front of her chair and took her hands in his despite the sling. His right hand was colder than the left.

"He will not trouble you or any other woman ever again, my love," he said gently.

"You killed him?" It was Daphne's voice.

"Yes," he said.

But the door had opened again and someone else came striding in. A moment later Daphne was crying noisily.

"Oh, Clay," she was saying. "Oh, Clay, you promised me after that dreadful Battle of Waterloo that I would never have to suffer this again."

"Yes, love," he said. "I just heard. You were not at home. I guessed where you were especially after discovering that Catherine had been at the house. This excitement will do you no good, you know. It is to be home and to bed with you without further delay. Rex and Catherine need to be alone, anyway."

Catherine had not looked at them. Neither had Rex. They gazed only at each other, their hands clasped. After a minute or so there was silence in the room. Neither looked to be sure they were alone.

She found her voice at last. "I could have endured having him in the world far more cheerfully than having you out of it," she said.

"Could you?" With his left hand he raised her right to his lips. "It had to be done, my love. I did it."

"There is no one to hear it," she said. "It does not need to be said." Her mind could seem to latch only onto trivialities.

"To hear what?" He looked mystified.

"'My love,'" she said.

"You are my love." He was smiling at her. "Perhaps it is something you do not wish to hear, Catherine, but I plan to spend the next eternity or two earning the right to say it again and again. My love." He kissed her hand again. "What? Tears? Is it quite that bad?"

She bit her upper lip hard, but it was no good. Her face crumpled ignominiously and she hid it against his right shoulder. She jerked upright again when he noticeably winced

"If you love me," she cried, "how could you have done something so stupid, stupid, *stupid*? I hate you. Do you think I wanted you dead just because of your foolish sense of honor? How could I have loved you if you were dead? How could I have told you when it was too late?"

He was still smiling. She could see that with her clearing vision. "Catherine," he said softly. "My love."

"All I could think of," she said, "was that I had not *told* you."

"Told me what?" he asked her.

"That I *love* you," she said, and remembered to use his left shoulder this time.

She looked up again when she could feel that there were unmistakably two arms about her. He had slipped the right one free of the sling.

"To hell with it," he said, grinning at her. "It was merely for theatrical effect anyway. So we find ourselves in a love match after all, do we?"

She nodded, gazing into his eyes, realizing anew how

close she had come this morning to losing him. A bullet had been fired at him and had hit him. She knew that the reality of that fact would haunt her for a long time to come.

"And alone." He drew her closer and set his lips to hers. "No one would dare enter unbidden, even though the door is unlocked. I am suddenly feeling decidedly amorous, my love. It comes after danger has passed, you know. Life reasserting itself, I suppose."

But even as he spoke the door was opened a crack from the outside by an unseen hand and a mere second or two later an ecstatic little bundle hurled itself at them, barking loudly.

"Down, sir," Viscount Rawleigh said sternly.

"Oh, Toby," Catherine said, "you came home."

Toby sat down beside his new master, panting and thumping his tail on the carpet.

"We are going to have to teach that terrier something about good manners," Lord Rawleigh said.

"No, we are not," Catherine said. "I love him just as he is."

"Well," he said, "perhaps I will try exerting my authority to more effect when it is a child we are discussing. And talking of discussions, shall we continue this one in your bedchamber?"

"Your arm?" she said.

"Is still attached to my shoulder and can still hold you," he said. "Shall we go?"

She nodded.

But before either of them got to their feet, he kissed her very thoroughly. For both of them it was a kiss of uninhibited, unconditional love. A kiss full of awareness of the fact that the moment must be seized, that life is too short and unpredictable in its course for love to be delayed.

"I am *so glad,*" she said during a momentary lull, caused

by the necessity of breathing, "that for the merest moment once upon a time I mistook you for Claude."

"Mm," he said. "For which error you are forgiven, my love—provided it does not happen again."

Toby rested his head on his outstretched paws, his eyes on them, and yawned loudly and contentedly.